Praise for
THE SHAMSHINE BLIND

"[An] appealingly strange novel. Pardo pulls off a difficult feat, delivering a novel that's both topical and entertaining."

—*San Francisco Chronicle*

"A rollicking romp without sacrificing emotional depth. Sharp, clever, and bitingly original, it left me feeling like I'd injected a double dose of Sunshine Yellow Happiness."

—*Strange Horizons*

"A heady mix of high-concept speculative fiction, alternative history, and hard-boiled detective fiction. Pardo's novel is full of wit and wild invention and is sure to leave readers wanting more."

—*CrimeReads*

"The blend of mystery, sci-fi, and alternative history works well to create a completely new and fascinating read. Telling the tale in the mode of noir with naturally subtle world building pulls the reader right into the setting of the story."

—*Booklist*

"High, high concept meets classic detective fiction . . . A heady, deep-dyed debut that suggests more thought-provoking work to come."

—*Kirkus Reviews*

THE
SHAMSHINE
BLIND

A Novel

Paz Pardo

ATRIA PAPERBACK

New York   London   Toronto   Sydney   New Delhi

ATRIA
PAPERBACK

An Imprint of Simon & Schuster, Inc.
1230 Avenue of the Americas
New York, NY 10020

First Atria Paperback edition November 2023

For information about special discounts for bulk purchases, please contact Simon & Schuster Special Sales at 1-866-506-1949 or business@simonandschuster.com.

The Simon & Schuster Speakers Bureau can bring authors to your live event. For more information or to book an event, contact the Simon & Schuster Speakers Bureau at 1-866-248-3049 or visit our website at www.simonspeakers.com.

Interior design by *Yvonne Taylor*

Manufactured in the United States of America

1 3 5 7 9 10 8 6 4 2

Library of Congress Cataloging-in-Publication Data
Names: Pardo, Paz, author.
Title: The shamshine blind : a novel / Paz Pardo.
Description: First Atria Books hardcover edition. |
New York : Atria Books, [2023]
Identifiers: LCCN 2022036963 (print) | LCCN 2022036964 (ebook) |
ISBN 9781982185329 (hardcover) | ISBN 9781982185343 (ebook)
Subjects: LCGFT: Noir fiction. | Science fiction. |
Alternative histories (Fiction) | Novels.
Classification: LCC PS3616.A738 S53 2023 (print) | LCC PS3616.A738 (ebook)
DDC 813/.6—dc23/eng/20220805
LC record available at https://lccn.loc.gov/2022036963
LC ebook record available at https://lccn.loc.gov/2022036964

ISBN 978-1-9821-8532-9
ISBN 978-1-9821-8533-6 (pbk)
ISBN 978-1-9821-8534-3 (ebook)

for Quique,
without whom I never would have
braved the Daly City fog

CHAPTER 1

Shamshine and Sunshine are not the same thing. Anybody with training can tell the difference. Just like anybody with training could tell that Winfred Pimsley was a crook. But he was my kind of crook.

His antique shop perched on a hilltop just south of the ruins of San Francisco. On the Daly City side, little houses made of ticky-tacky sat back from the street, guarded by picket fences. Cars smuggled up from Mexico were parked across lawns, rusting steadily in the Pacific fog as they waited to get their plates changed. Kids playing hooky raced bikes held together with duct tape and resignation. A block away in San Francisco, moldy Victorians crumbled onto shattered sidewalks. Wild anise poked through the cracks in the deserted streets. Even daredevil teens knew to stay out of the old city.

The area had seen plenty of illicit psychopigment spills over the last thirty years, permeating the landscape with a thick emotional haze at odds with its appearance. As Tommy and I drove past yards overgrown with mile-high dandelions, the aging pigment's mix of ennui and affection made me feel like I'd just walked into my dad's old hardware store. Most antique dealers would've chosen a nicer neighborhood, but Pimsley had weighed the weeds against the ambient nostalgia and moved his operation from downtown faster than you could say "Falklands." That was the inveterate salesman for you: everything calculated to pull customers' heartstrings before they passed the fence.

We left my red Renault 4 on the curb outside the shop. I made sure it was locked before heading to the cornflower-blue garden gate. Not that anyone would bother breaking into a clown car with a lousy paint job, but it was the principle of the thing. Tommy jerked open the shop's stained-glass door and shouted, "Psychopigment Enforcement! Hands up!"

A low-throated chuckle greeted us from the back. Pimsley's gray pompadour peeked over the top of an overstuffed recliner. A lever thumped, lowering the footrest, and he stood slowly. His impeccably tailored pewter suit needed no smoothing, but he plucked at his pant legs to make sure they fell straight.

I'd known him since his mane had been a lush chestnut, but he'd embraced the first strands of white as a sign it was time to go full silver fox. He'd always played a man of another era. With his shift in hair color his persona had become even more outlandish. Sometimes I felt like I was talking to a parody of a 1920s matinee idol. But the sharp mind underneath cut through the gingerbread often enough to keep me on my toes.

"Agent Kay Curtida herself!" He spread his manicured hands at me in welcome. "With her delightful cadet! I was just thinking of putting on another pot of tea."

We weren't there for a social visit, and he knew it. Getting information out of Pimsley always happened on his terms, but the beverage was negotiable. "Don't suppose you've still got that coffee maker lying around," I said, producing a packet of old-school grounds from my navy fanny pack.

Pimsley's smile cut lines in his pale cheeks. He looked like an albino lizard hiding its teeth. "I'm still waiting for the buyer on that one. Perhaps it will be you?"

"Guys, do you have to go through the whole thing about the coffeepot every time?" Tommy asked, sauntering over to the vintage records lining the back wall. "Couldn't you just drink the instant stuff like everyone else?"

"Youth! That lack of patience, that burning urgency—what a thrill!" Pimsley sighed. "I will make the java. I have a new disc for you, Tommy, darling. Let me get the key to the turntable." He took the grounds and moved to a Victorian rolltop desk. Reaching for a hidden lever, he shooed me away. "This is not for the prying eyes of the law, Agent."

I already knew plenty about his fondness for clandestine compartments, but I dutifully wandered off to look over his wares. Even with a dead-end case on my hands, the shop was soothing. Something about the abundance of *stuff*, the sumptuous piles of costume jewelry, the stacks of elegant chairs from another age. A cluster of Tiffany lamps shed wholesome, comforting light on a dish overflowing with currency from back before we had a thousand-dollar coin; a ten-gallon jar of marbles gleamed in the corner. Everything came in oodles and gobs.

In the cozy confines of the space, it was easy enough to forget that the antique bounty was a front for Pimsley's real business. It was a poorly kept secret that he was involved in off-label psychopigment collection, plying a network of wealthy collectors hungry for the rarest of pigments: batches of vintage experiments from the 1980s or recent breakthroughs that had yet to reach even the black market. More than once, I'd waited across the street while a bodyguard escorted a bespoke suit out to his Lamborghini. After spending a good part of an hour watching one particularly geriatric patron make her way across the lawn, I'd asked Pimsley why he hadn't set up shop in one of the big cities. "They all think I'm their special discovery. That's catnip to collectors," he'd said.

I figured there were other reasons but I'd immediately regretted my question. The less I knew, the better. Our deal was that I didn't peer too closely into the darkened corners of the store, and he kept me in the loop about the goings-on in the rinky-dink underworld of Daly City. If he ever needed out of a tight spot, he had my number. Our arrangement worked just fine for me—it was his tip that had led me to the cache of unstable Cobalt pigment that had been turning folks maudlin in San Carlos. That job had almost gotten me a mention in the union quarterly. Almost. Would've been the highlight of a career spent chasing hoodlums too dumb to tie their own shoes.

Pimsley put on the coffee and started up the record player. With those two appliances running, we could have been back in my childhood, before boom boxes, microwaves, or the war. Tommy settled into the recliner. The first time I'd brought him here, he'd jittered all over the place, anxious to get the scoop and get out. Over time, he'd gotten the hang of the gentleman's rhythm. Now I wondered whether he would notice if I left without him. The strains of the vinyl 45 drifted across the room, a girlish voice soaring over a drum machine and the twanging beat of an electric bass. "What is it?" Tommy asked.

"Bootsie Poots's first single," Pimsley said, producing three porcelain cups with rose-pink detailing. "She was an R & B singer before Hollywood got ahold of her."

"R & B?" Tommy asked.

"Rhythm and blues, dear. Back before electronic tango took over the airwaves, there were whole radio stations devoted to it."

We all listened to Bootsie croon. *I thought I'd found happiness, but all I've got is something like hope . . .*

Tommy let out an appreciative "mmmmm." Pimsley's eyelids drooped with pleasure. I tried to figure out what was so great. It was just another lady trying to convince me she was having feelings. I found a pile of laminated paper clippings next to the Tiffany lamps. On top was a *WHAT IS PSYCHOPIGMENT?* pamphlet I'd seen in my high school nurse's office. A cartoon dog said *So it's like paintball, but with feelings?* A cat in a lab coat responded *Sure. But any way it gets inside you—sinking through your skin, breathed in through your mouth, or eaten—it's going to give you some gnarly emotions.* I'd never understood why anyone thought talking animals were the best way to communicate with teenagers.

Underneath the pamphlet was a stack of front pages from the *San Francisco Chronicle*, one of the local rags from before my time in the Bay. The first was almost twenty-seven years old, from April 23, 1982. "NATO Enters Falklands Conflict, Declares War on Argentina." Then followed a litany of lost battles and blitzed cities: New York, DC, Los Angeles, Chicago. I flipped through, reliving Uncle Sam's topple from the bully pulpit to the third world.

"Military Confirms Deep Blue 'Psychopigment' Involved in Mysterious Incapacitation of Leaders." I'd watched that press conference with my mother. Everybody had already known the blue stuff causing mass amnesia in our urban centers had to be a weapon. Newly anointed President Fletcher Rigby made the announcement, looking surprisingly unfazed for someone who'd been ninth in the line of succession mere days before. The final head-line was from 1984: "Surrender in Mumbai Ends Malvinas War: NATO, China and Russia Capitulate; Argentina to Annex Great Britain." First time the *Chronicle* referred to the sheep-covered islands that had kicked off the war by their Argentine name of "Malvinas" instead of "Falklands."

Pimsley hummed along to Bootsie Poots, carefully arranging bullet-sized macaroons on saucers. I hoped his information would be more satisfying than the cookies.

"Shamshine," the Chief had said as she handed over the file on the case. The fake version of Sunshine Yellow, the prescription psychopigment De-pressives relied on to stay functional. Any agent could tell it wasn't the real thing, but if you were one of the thirty million laypeople filling your monthly prescription, you probably wouldn't notice if the counterfeit had been slipped into your gelcaps. At least, you wouldn't until the rip-off had permanently seared the capacity for joy from your brain.

The legitimate happiness pills were big enough business that criminals salivated over breaking into the market. The Yellowjacket Cartel up in Idaho had been the first to develop a cheap imitation. At the height of their power, they'd had infiltrators at every step of the supply chain. All of us knew some-one who'd been burnt. Tommy'd told me he had three relatives bedridden after getting bad pills. Since the crime ring had been busted, smaller players were moving into the vacuum, copycats popping up from sea to shining sea.

The Chief said our local cult, known as the Pinkos, had gotten their hands on a recipe for the dangerous Sunshine knockoff. We were to sniff around, find out what there was to know. It was the kind of case that we never got out here in Daly City. The kind of case that could get me noticed. Get me out of this backwater, up to the big time in Boise or Iowa City. But we'd had it on our docket for almost a week now, and every trail we'd traced had been cold.

Bootsie sang out a final *"something like hope"* and Tommy nudged the needle back to the edge of the record. "I like it," he said. "How much are you asking?"

"For you, my dear?" Pimsley's voice went snake-oil smooth, pulling out one of Tommy's nasal guffaws. If the salesman didn't have anything for us, we'd have spent the week going to Pinko Temple meet and greets for nothing. I skipped ahead in the pile of papers, flipping through the past as they haggled. The scent of fresh coffee slipped through ebony chair legs and over piles of wheat pennies.

The two men agreed to disagree about the price of the record, leaving it for another visit. Tommy sank back in the recliner and mouthed Bootsie's lyrics. Great. Another earworm for my songbird cadet to torment me with. An ornately carved chair with flaking gilt and a high, upholstered back balanced with prim pride on top of a stack of furniture. Didn't look like it had a match. Pimsley brought over my cup. "If you'd told me, when this came out, that in the year of our lord 2009 the youngsters wouldn't have even *heard* of R & B . . ."

"Seems like he likes it," I said.

"Well, he's a pearl." I looked over at my cadet and tried to see where Pimsley got that impression. Tommy Ho was square jawed, tall and lanky, all elbows; his black crew cut looked particularly bland today. I was not in the pearl-detection business. Pimsley followed my gaze, lips puckered fondly, then turned back to the seat I'd been ogling. "So. Has my Louis XIV chair piqued your interest?"

"Maybe."

"Or is it something else you came for?"

I took a mouthful of coffee, calculating how many beans to spill. Pimsley was a cog in the rumor mill, and it would take a favor to keep anything I said on the premises. I chose to go with half the details. "You heard anything about new players in the Shamshine racket?"

"Shamshine?" He bit one of his tiny macaroons in half. Chewed slowly and swallowed. "I haven't seen any that made a splash out here since the Yellowjacket Cartel took their tumble. Heard whispers of a group out in Boulder, but nothing ever showed up. Same with the stuff from Sedona, New Memphis, Bend . . . Is somebody local moving in? That would be big news. Big news indeed . . ."

I'd been playing this game with Pimsley for two decades. Long enough to know that he clammed up when he was holding out and let his tongue run when he was fishing for more. A sentence naming three different cities was definitely him baiting the hook. I looked back at the chair, trapped high up on the pile of its distant cousins. "Just rumors. Nothing definitive. Yet."

There went our last possible source of information. I curated my ignorance of his off-color doings, but I knew enough to know that if Pimsley'd heard nothing, there was nothing to hear. We'd be heading back to the Agency empty-handed. Bootsie warbled *"I thought I'd found happiness, but all I've got is something like hope"* for the hundredth time. I blew a curl off my forehead and readjusted the bobby pin in charge of keeping it out of my face. Losing battles are my forte. "How much for the Louis whatever?"

Pimsley paused, macaroon halfway to his mouth. "You want the . . . piece of furniture?"

"I could use an extra seat in my apartment."

He called Tommy over to extricate the chair from its precarious perch. I bargained the price down to a hundred and thirty thou. At the register, Pimsley smiled as he straightened his gray cuffs. "All these years, I never thought of you as a Louis XIV kind of a girl."

"You learn something new every day."

"Keeps one young, doesn't it?" The lines around his eyes crinkled.

"Sure does. You know, I've been feeling kind of old, lately."

He looked up from handwriting my receipt. "My dear, the minute I hear anything about Shamshine, I will make your buzzer go bananas. I wouldn't forgive myself if I let you get any more frost in those curls. Tommy, let me help you with that chair—"

● ● ●

My Renault 4 was almost vintage enough to be featured in Pimsley's shop, but the chair fit fine in the back. "Why are we driving around with a beat-up seat?" Tommy asked, riding shotgun.

A forlorn eucalyptus shivered in the morning breeze. I turned down the hill toward the devil's trident intersection at Hillcrest and Vendome. Telephone wires bunched and splayed overhead like a grid drawn by a drunk. "Gotta sit on something," I said.

"You already have a chair."

"Sure. One."

I could feel him squinting at me. "You expecting company? I haven't known you to have anyone over the whole time we've worked together."

"You came over when we were tracking the San Carlos cache."

"Yeah, and you had me sit on the floor. This isn't about that R & D guy from Boise, is it?"

The R & D guy was Doug Nambi, an old buddy from the Psychopigment Enforcement Training Academy. Research and development sounds pretty boring when you're a teenager, but as I'd learned since, *what* your title is in this line of work matters less than *where* it is. Your assignments can only be as challenging as the criminals you're up against. Where I'd wound up giving glorified parking tickets to a bunch of would-be crooks, Doug had gone straight to the heart of the action in Boise, Idaho.

He'd been integral in getting the Yellowjacket Cartel's dangerous imitation of Sunshine Yellow off the street and had brought us this current Shamshine case as a follow-up. We'd lost touch since our fifteen-year reunion. When he walked into the Psychopigment Enforcement Agency office on Tuesday morning, it'd felt to me like finding a years-overdue library book under the front seat of the car. "I took a shine to the chair, that's all," I told Tommy. I don't like to be interrogated, especially about my reasons for doing things. If I don't care what they are, I don't see why anyone else should.

We pulled up to the stoplight in front of the old elevated train tracks. Shrubs had pushed through the cracks in the parking lot that had once served the station. My mind ground down a familiar rut. Showing up with nothing on the biggest case the Daly City department had seen in decades would put the final nail in the coffin of my dream of extending my time as an agent. Normal retirement age was forty. Some stellar field agents held out another ten years. At the ripe end of thirty-nine, with my track record of rapping small-timers across the knuckles, I was staring down the barrel of a warm handshake and polite dismissal. I blew the damn curl off my forehead again. The light turned green. It took two tries to get the shifter into first.

On the radio, KFOG was running a report on the economic fallout from the national scourge of Yellowjacket Shamshine Doug had put the kibosh on. Just what I needed to brighten my mood. There was an interview with a daughter who'd quit her job to care for her incapacitated mother. Tommy sighed. I knew he had an aunt with a similar story. Most of his offers coming out of the academy had been in R & D. But Tommy had been dead set on fieldwork because of the damage he'd seen Shamshine causing around the turn of the millennium. Back when folks thought it was just batches of their daily pills getting accidentally "contaminated." Back when no one could believe a shadowy criminal network was adulterating their meds, profiting off fried brains.

The radio moved on to the Hope Count and weather report. Dreary days ahead. We rattled toward downtown, passing La Parrilla, the local Argentine grill. The sign featured a horseback-mounted Gaucho, a figure more melancholy than a cowboy and shorter. It was a national symbol of Argentina, extolled in their literature and films, a callback to an idealized, simpler past. The cartoon version's droopy mustache matched how I was feeling, thinking about the big fat nothing we'd be taking into our department meeting this afternoon. If only Pimsley'd had dirt to share. If only the Pinkos'd had a "Shamshine this way" sign at their temples. If only I had any idea where else to go.

I was saved from dropping down the Depressive rabbit hole by a squawk from the radio. "Agent Curtida, I need you to head over to the Icarus campus," the Chief said. "The cops have been called in to check out a suicide, and they think it's pigment related."

Suicides were a bushel a Benjamin in the Pigment Enforcement caseload. Wasn't exactly an uplifting assignment, but it beat filling out paperwork about the case we'd failed to solve. I turned the wheel, taking us south to see who'd had a worse morning than us.

CHAPTER 2

Icarus Corporation was headquartered in one of Daly City's most architecturally forward offices. Brutalist pillars supported an angry bunker, pierced by long windows. It looked like a cross between a hostile UFO and a tulip.

The corpse was around the back of the building, surrounded by broken glass. The stink of urine and feces and rancid sweat rolled off it. Looking up, I could see a dark hole near the top of one of the glass slivers that passed for windows. The site of the jumper's self-defenestration.

The body had landed nose down, arms splayed across a parking line. One hand clutched a battered chair leg. A pool of blood, dry at the edges, spread outward from the spot where a receding blond hairline met the asphalt. The guy wore a striped polo, a style that had gone out of fashion when I was in high school. I squatted, holding my breath. I could never get used to the smell of death. A looping scar ran from the stiff's left ear toward the pavement, accompanied on either side by suture marks.

We'd crossed paths more than a few times. Tucker Cutts, better known as Blufftown Tuck. He was a petty crook who got into the pigment business trying to find a cure for his mother after the Magenta Attack in 1989. He'd always been unfortunate. Didn't mean I'd expected him to end up like this. I identified him out loud as I stood, brushing off my jeans.

The neurotypical officer who'd been first on the scene let out a huff of air. "I knew this case was one of yours." The way he said *yours* made clear his disdain for the mess. Our two arms of the law never got along too well. All us Pigment Enforcement agents were Depressives—had to be, to make it through the work. Like the psychosoldiers in the war, we'd been selected because of our neuroprofile. Depressives tend to deny our own emotions, which translates nicely into being able to function through the psychological effects of bad pigment hits. The old-school cops claimed their force was "free of any anomalous psychiatric profiles" and looked down on us as a bunch of gloomy loons. I'd seen enough to suspect there were plenty of undiagnosed psychopaths among them. The fact that their budget was big enough for things like patrol cars and overtime pay didn't endear them to me, either.

I'd had plenty of experience with their tendency to shove anything connected to mental health our way, pigment related or not. I told the cop we might recognize Blufftown Tuck, but that didn't make his sticky end our business. That was when the man bothered to mention that there were two more "nutcases" upstairs. He led us back into the building. "One of the scientists found them. Real nice little Asian lady. Pamela something or other—Wang or Wong or whatever. Wanted to be helpful but couldn't get her story out for the shock. I mean, imagine, you come into work and there are crooks tripping out in your office."

Tommy was bristling at the "Wang or Wong" comment, so I sent him off to call the coroner and track down witnesses. As the officer escorted me to the mirrored elevator, a short man came hurrying across the lobby's polished floor. He had a box of pastries under one arm. His navy suit sported the shiny elbows of the overworked and underpaid corporate PR flack. He kept a steady patter of inanities going as we rode up to the twelfth floor and walked toward the crime scene. Icarus shared our deep desire to get to the bottom of things, anything they could do to help, so utterly bewildered at this mysterious tragedy, and would I like a warm *medialuna*? He'd run out to get them as soon as the cops called in Pigment Enforcement.

I could read between the lines on the sudden hospitality: a suicide on campus was no big deal, but Icarus's product was pigment. So if there was a chance something colorful was involved, they'd do their best to keep the situation on lockdown.

The corporation was the brainchild of the military doctors who had first come up with the idea of using psychopigment for mental health treatments. Argentines had won the war with their first color, Deepest Blue. While they continued developing pigments after achieving world domination, they'd never considered their secondhand emotions to be anything but weapons. It took the American psychiatric mindset to see swords that could be beaten to profitable ploughshares. Less than a decade after the war, we'd appropriated our enemy's emotional artillery to treat our country's psychic woes.

Military shrinks had started out using Slate Gray Ennui to attempt to prevent veterans' PTSD-spawned violent outbursts. That first attempt went about as badly as could be expected. Sunshine Yellow Happiness was the game changer. After demonstrating its effectiveness at increasing the productivity of depressed veterans, the docs had a smooth path to legalization and lucre. With a couple pharma executives to draw up the Icarus Corporation and lobby Congress, they soon had all thirty million Depressives in the States clamoring for prescriptions.

The Argentines found American pharmaceutical applications of psychopigment downright batty, but they allowed Icarus to operate as long as they conducted their research within arm's reach of the Gaucho base down in Palo Alto. Rumor had it the general who ran the base had said, "If the gringos want to put our weapons into pills and take them every morning, who am I to stop them?" Personally, I figured popping a gelcap was preferable to lying on a couch talking about my feelings multiple times a week, the de rigueur method of mental health treatment in Buenos Aires.

The jet-black tiles of the twelfth-floor hallway bounced the flack's nasal voice back toward us. Cold sunlight cut through the window slits at either end. The telltale lime green of a hazpig suit hung in a case across from the elevator. *IN CASE OF PIGMENT SPILL, BREAK GLASS. Minimize exposed skin. Avoid inhaling vaporized pigment. Examine your emotions. After exposure, your feelings are not your own.* We passed potted ficus and unmarked doors on both sides, heading for the room where Blufftown Tuck decided to end it all.

When we entered, the "real nice little Asian lady" was sitting by the door, looking just as put out as I felt. She wore a coral skirt suit with shoulder pads that meant business. A spray of lace that had to have cost twice my paycheck billowed from her collar. Her dark hair was pulled back into a perfect bun. But the boardroom-ready look was marred by a pair of cream-colored stilettos that were five centimeters too high and a layer of makeup that could've stood up on its own. The overall effect reminded me of a high school valedictorian trying too hard to match the age on her fake ID.

She stood and came toward us, her disconsolate look morphing into a vacant, pleasant expression. She was surrounded by a cloud of vanilla-scented perfume. Shiny Elbows introduced her as Priscilla Li. The woman's expression stayed placid but her voice was stiff as she said, "Priscilla Kim. Dr. Kim." At least it'd been closer than the fuzz's Pamela Wang or Wong. Great start to her day, I could tell.

In the middle of the space, a brunette in a maroon leopard-print cardigan and salmon slacks slumped in her business casual. The medical restraints around her torso and wrists were the only things keeping her upright. In the corner, a man with shoulder-length black curls was trying to wiggle his chair into the wall. He was wearing a teal T-shirt from the Dead Sentiments' 2007 reunion tour.

The far end of the room featured two floor-to-ceiling windows. One had a large hole in it, presumably courtesy of the dearly departed. The remains of another waiting-room chair were scattered nearby. A rickety desk lay on its side, surrounded by plastic cups and an upended ashtray. A two-liter bottle of bright orange Fanta had rolled across the gray carpet. There was a faint smell of stale cigarette smoke. The walls were padded. The whole thing seemed like an office party gone horribly wrong.

I walked to the broken window, the flack droning at my heels about how none of these people had *ever* been seen by *anyone* at Icarus before. Down on the pavement, someone had thrown a sheet over the body. Four floors below me, a crow darted from one streetlamp to another. Glass shards glinted on the carpet. I checked the broken chair. The wooden back had split into spikes. Padding material poked out of the collapsed seat. As expected, I could find only three of the legs. It hadn't been a flimsy piece of furniture. The glass was reinforced at this high level. Tucker had wanted out at whatever cost.

I turned back to the living and chose my target. I approached the slumped woman slowly, giving her ample opportunity to respond to my presence, but there was no sign of consciousness. I reached out and pulled back an eyelid. Her skin was slippery with sweat. If she'd been wearing makeup, it would've smeared. Most women whose tastes ran to colored leopard print wore matching kohl these days. I wondered if this meant she'd had some sense of what was coming when she showed up for whatever this was. Her eyeball stayed rolled back in her head. Sure enough, flashes of dark pigment wriggled through the veins around the edges. It looked like a pretty harsh dose of Blackberry Purple, the phobia fabricator. I wiped my hand on my jeans. The case was ours.

Purple's eyes flashed open and she snarled at me. Seemed the restraints were there for a reason. My Renault 4 was not going to cut it as safe transport for these folks. I went back to the flack and told him I'd need to call an ambulance unless Icarus could provide better transport. He was off to rustle up a van in a split second. It would be easier to work without him hanging around like a bad case of tinnitus.

The scientist's features had settled back into the harried lines they'd been in when we arrived. This investigation had already eaten up a chunk of her morning. I sent her with the cop to find Tommy and get him going on her interview. Wasn't like we needed much from her beyond the time she'd found the group, and my cadet was good at setting folks at ease. She gathered a tan handbag and rumpled overcoat and followed the officer out into the hall.

I went to ID the remaining two. The rock fan thundered a song at me that I vaguely remembered metalheads playing in high school. Satan with eyes of flame, dark figure in the road, so on and so forth. When I told him who I was, he shouted, "The power of Christ compels you!" Seemed they'd watched *The Exorcist* before painting themselves. Most people who took Blackberry did it because they thought they liked feeling scared. Most of them were wrong.

I managed to get both their prints and found their licenses. The man passed out when I asked what had happened, which made it easier. He was Leonard Gobble of apartment 3B at 1911 Hickey Boulevard. Purple was Jenny Crotty. Same address. Looked like they were a couple. A business card marked her as a massage therapist. From the calluses on his fingers, I guessed he did some sort of manual labor. I looked for pigment smeared on their skin—the usual method for recreational users of the harder colors. No sign. They must have had it in pills. Could explain the long duration of the trip. Blackberry Purple usually wore off after a couple hours.

In the search for pigment, I found bruises on both their upper torsos. Seemed someone had held them down to restrain them. That detail stuck out like a sore thumb. Tucker's dramatic exit was an outlier, too. The suicides we dealt with were usually deaths of opportunity. A reinforced window would've been plenty to deter most folks with panic frying their brain.

There were six sets of fingerprints in total. Two were from Jenny and Leonard. I lifted Blufftown Tuck's from the chair. The other three I only picked up on the crumpled plastic cups, still sticky with Fanta. I figured the mystery prints would include the people who'd tied Jenny and Leonard down. It was a nice working theory. Did nothing to answer the big fat *why?* at the heart of the situation.

The overturned ashtray's spent trail of cigarettes stretched from the table halfway to the broken window. They were all the pale blue butts of Caravanas, imported from Argentina. Fancy stuff. Didn't see many of those outside of the movies. Each sported a ring of lipstick. I counted a couple dozen, thinking of Priscilla Kim's pancaked makeup.

The cop reappeared with the news that Tommy was interviewing the scientist in her office. I was about to ask where that was when Shiny Elbows announced from the doorway that the van had arrived. We lugged the wigged-out seathuggers to the elevator. It was turning out to be a day full of chairs.

Once they were packed off, I asked the flack to take me to Priscilla. That stopped his stream of platitudes for a second, but he recovered enough to buzz like a midge all the way to our destination. I focused on the decor to keep from swatting at him. Hung in the hallways were old ads for Icarus's rainbow of products, and photo ops from the FDA approvals of the various pigments. Big shots shaking hands with representatives of Congress over vials of Cerulean Guilt or Cobalt Sadness.

Ever since Sunshine Yellow, whatever colors Icarus found useful rapidly moved to prescription status. Most of them came from labs in Argentina, but some were legalized through a "compassionate use" clause for criminally developed pigments. What was defined as "useful" had more to do with its utility for the corporation's bottom line than its value to the fabric of society. Some of the ads were vaguely funny, at least. A woman, shouting in anger, aimed a hair dryer like a gun at the camera lens. *Need a reset? Icarus's Rage Purge™ is here to help.* Wondered whether Shiny Elbows had dreamed of writing copy like that.

He led me to a back elevator and then down to level minus seven of the building's deep basements. As I shut the grate of the lift behind me, I could hear Tommy's guffaw bouncing down the hall. A giggle rang out over it. Seemed he was managing to build rapport with the subject. "And then," the woman's voice said, "he wanted to mix it in the *shaker*!"

"An *old-fashioned*?" Tommy's voice went high in disbelief.

Well. That rapport might not be yielding the results I'd wish for. I stuck my head into the windowless cube. Priscilla's ears were pink with laughter. She sat behind a desk bare except for a pair of fashionably tiny espresso cups of instant coffee. The bright overhead light brought out her under-eye concealer. Her lip liner was perfectly applied. Her jacket and purse hung from a hook on the back wall. The PR flack set to rubbing his elbows when he realized my cadet had been interviewing her without his supervision. Tommy grinned up at me from where he sat on a tiny stool. There was almost enough room for him and his clipboard in the corner behind the door. "Curtida," he said, "I see you've met my cousin."

"His favorite cousin!" Dr. Kim said. "I had no idea he was working in Pigment Enforcement—you're lucky to have him." I told her we were and that they should feel free to continue with the interview. Tommy's back straightened when I said that and he launched into another question, but Priscilla interrupted to ask for a little break to freshen up.

The flack wedged his way into the door, saying, "Of course they'll let you, sweetie, after the morning you've had—" By then she'd grabbed her purse and popped past me. Shiny Elbows took her arm and walked her down the hall. I watched her coat sway on its hook as her stilettos clicked away, a staccato beat. My cadet wasn't smiling anymore. Seemed he knew I wasn't going to be thrilled with a notepad full of bartending techniques. "Having a nice family reunion?" I asked.

"Sure," he said, "except that she's lying through her teeth." He rubbed the back of his neck as our escort came back into the room.

I walked around to the other side of the desk. The petite coffee cup had a perfect imprint of the woman's rose lipstick. Opened the drawer, ignoring the flack's incensed squawk. Inside was a pack of Caravanas. I told Tommy to search the office and went to find the ladies' room. I wasn't surprised it was empty. Wasn't surprised it was by the back stairwell. Booked it up to the lobby. The receptionist confirmed what I was expecting: the scientist had walked out the door just minutes before. There was no sign of her in the parking lot.

Sure as fog under the midday sun, Dr. Kim had vanished.

CHAPTER 3

Normally, misery loves company, but a roomful of Depressives in a Monday afternoon meeting could sour a pack of caramels. My colleague Meekins, the department's other full agent, was already hunching his thin shoulders by the window when we got in. He'd been perfecting his scowl since he arrived as my cadet a decade back, and today's edition looked to be his full-body special. Couldn't tell if it was his standard sourness or if there was something particular making his lips curl.

Tommy and I had done what we could to gather leads on the Icarus case once our truant scientist waltzed out of the building. Her prints in her office matched one of the sets from the crumpled plastic cups upstairs, so we knew she'd been at the crime scene longer than she'd let on. Otherwise, the room yielded little that could count as evidence. A box under the desk held a mostly empty vodka bottle and a collection of the Processing Journey™ and Purge™ samples that companies like Icarus gave away to pharmacists and doctors to help familiarize them with their wares. The Purges had been Icarus's breakthrough products after Sunshine had been normalized. At their success, they'd launched the more complex Journeys. The curated combinations of positive and negative pigments with a guidance tape were meant to "eliminate ineffective emotions and keep a clear mind."

Priscilla had put some time into building her collection: some of the packages in the box were over a decade old. They ran the gamut, from Grief to Anger to Persistent Anxiety. Several were open, with the tiny squeeze packets of certain psychopigments missing: Cool Teal, Golden Peace. I got the sense that she hadn't been in a good place even before getting mixed up in whatever had sent Tucker plunging to his death. Didn't clarify what she'd been doing upstairs. Or why she'd run out on us.

We'd had no better luck in the wood-paneled personnel office. Tommy glanced at the address on file for her and shook his head. She'd put down her father's place. No way she lived there. She was on the books as a part-time contractor, not a full employee. She'd been in that precarious position for almost three years. I thought about the pricey imported smokes, the cramped basement office. The two things didn't go together.

There'd been a moment in the car when I'd thought Tommy might have actionable background information on her. As we bumped along the pothole-scarred streets back to the department, I'd asked about his cousin. "You two are close?"

"Close? I don't know." He ran a hand through his hair, leaving black spikes sticking up in every direction. A motorcycle puttered past, a bunch of brightly colored balloons tied to the back: green, cherry, azure. "I haven't heard from her since she went down to do her PhD in Argentina in 2001, but we spent a lot of time together before she left." He told me how she'd introduced him to the practice of Purging his emotions after his first breakup. How she'd taught him to mix a mean Manhattan. The specific details of generic adolescent bonding. Seemed the relationship hadn't continued into adulthood. Didn't sound like I had to worry that Tommy would cover for her. None of it would keep me from eating humble pie at this afternoon's meeting, though.

I tuned back in when Tommy started talking about Priscilla's dream of joining the People's Pigment Movement. "This was back when they were spiking politicians' confetti with Bull's Blood Rage, so it felt like a big deal that she told me," he said.

The PPM were a guerrilla group who'd emerged from the peculiar crossbreeding of scientists and left-wing radicals in 1980s Berkeley. They'd formed around the same time as the right-wing paramilitary Knights of Liberty. Both groups spouted rhetoric about kicking the Argentines back to Buenos Aires, but mostly they just squabbled with each other and made domestic messes. Their plans for achieving their goals were direct opposites. The Knights argued we could regain full sovereignty only by rejecting pigment and taking the US back to its "traditional values." The PPM were all about appropriating the Gaucho weapons to create some sort of transnational socialist utopia.

The leftists had gone legit in the early 2000s, ending their terrorist activities and forming a political party. But they were still on the fringe. Could Priscilla be involved with some radical group, dedicated to Blackberry Purple Phobia overdoses? People's Purple Party. The idea was so absurd that it unraveled before I'd finished coming up with it. "She wanted to join the PPM but took the spot to study in Argentina?"

Tommy looked out the window. "She always had those contradictions. She joined the Catholic Church in Mountain View so she could lift the designer clothes the Argentine military wives would donate 'for the poor.' Wore the outfits to parties, let the folks who complimented her think she'd been down to Buenos Aires. All while complaining about imperialism. I figure it's all the same thing—she wants to be *somebody*. She's ambitious. But maybe doesn't know for what. And if someone's offering her an opportunity, well . . . deep down I don't think she cares who they are."

The Gauchos were famously tight-fisted with visas, so winning a spot to study down south would certainly stroke one's ego. "How does she go from shipping out to Argentina as one of our most promising brains to languishing as a part-time contractor at Icarus?" I asked.

"You've got me there. Like I said, she never wrote." His voice was almost steady enough to cover its bitterness. "My grandmother always said, 'Priscilla may look like a poodle, but the blood of wolves runs through her veins.' And this morning . . . I think she thought it was her lucky break that I was interviewing her. When she's lying—she has this—'we were definitely home by curfew' voice. Bright and harsh. And she was using it on me. Like I wouldn't notice."

Or because she knew he wouldn't call her on it. He was playing tough but I could tell Tommy had idolized her. Her taking him for a chump today couldn't feel good. He didn't have any better idea than I did about what it was she'd been doing.

My thoughts bumped along the fissured pavement. I had a hunch that she'd been the one painting Tucker, Jenny, and Leonard Purple, but what Tommy had told me just opened up more questions. Not only would we be going into the afternoon meeting with nothing on the Shamshine case, we'd be announcing that we'd let the primary suspect in the Icarus mess slip through our fingers. As usual, today wasn't my day.

The afternoon didn't look any cheerier from the cramped conference room where we had our weekly meetings. The small window in back didn't get much light. It made up for it by letting in the smoggy breeze from the freeway. Obsolete psychopigment equipment sagged against the wall: the psychospectrometer we'd upgraded three years ago, a pile of old *Psychopigment Guide*s, burnt-out pigment detectors, and a box of expired hazpig.

The top of a grimy filing cabinet served as the coffee station. Tommy flicked on the electric kettle and opened the jar of Nescafé, then stood waiting for the ancient appliance to boil. I glanced at Meekins's frown. Maybe we'd both brought in bubkes on Shamshine. Maybe Tommy and I would get another week to dig something up. Maybe. The table's wooden veneer peeled, the fluorescents flickered, the tiny espresso cups gathered dust.

Doug Nambi's entrance broke the flow of my funk. I'd hardly seen my old friend in the week since he'd popped up with the Shamshine case. I was struck again by how the peppering of gray across his tight black curls framed his dark face, accenting the widow's peak that had deepened over the years. The placement of his hands in his pockets held the same attempted nonchalance I'd seen after countless schoolyard pranks. "Hey there, Ninja," he said as I walked over.

"Hello, Plato," I said. Funny to hear my academy nickname all the way out here in California. We'd christened each other within days of meeting: I knocked him flat in judo class and became Ninja; he tumbled into my dorm room with a thesis about free will in the era of psychopigments and became Plato.

"Where were you this week? Every time I stopped by your office you were out."

"Chasing after this Shamshine case you brought us," I said.

"Oh." He took his hands out of his pockets, put them back in. "I've been meaning to talk to you about that. Not here. We should grab a drink."

"Sure," I said. Wondered why he didn't want to talk about the case at the office. "How's Boise been treating you?"

"You know. We're blinded by the big-city lights and glamour whenever we emerge from the sordid underbelly." He had laugh lines around his eyes now. "They don't actually let me out of the lab much."

"How's the girlfriend?" I didn't even try to remember a name. Doug went through women like donuts. He'd date a baker's dozen in a year, and it was going on half a decade since we'd caught up.

"Nonexistent, currently."

"What? Are you okay?"

One side of his mouth twisted up, the old tell that he was trying to play it cool. "I'm taking a break."

The arrival of our Agency boss ended the conversation. The Chief was a bristly little boar of a woman, unstinting with praise and merciless with criticism. She was the Twenty-Fiver among us, the draw to our little Agency outpost. The ill-fated Twenty-Fifth Special Tactics Squadron had been the first and last unit of Depressives in the Malvinas War with Argentina. Their tendency toward denial had allowed them to keep functioning longer than neurotypicals during hits from the Argentine's first psychoweapon, Deepest Blue. The only pigment developed before the war, it caused symptoms ranging from amnesia to suffocation as the autonomic nervous system forgot to do its job. The Twenty-Fivers trucked through plenty of Blued-over territory, winning some tardy victories in a war that was already lost. President Rigby was convinced of the need for psychosoldiers only when it was already too little too late.

After surrender, they became the backbone of the new Pigment Enforcement Agency, heading up offices in the hubs in Iowa City, Boise, Miami. Nobody knew why the Chief had ended up in this backwater; word on the street ran from a treacherous falling-out with the other veterans to the more mundane explanation that her mother had had some sort of debilitating accident and needed care. Whatever the reason she was here, the Chief was the crown jewel—well, the only jewel—of our little outpost, and we were all loyal to her above country, kith, or kin.

She rapped on the table, calling the meeting to order. The sign-in sheet went around, gathering our five Hancocks and thumbprints as we discussed the first order of business: the Shamshine case. There was a gratifying moment when Meekins admitted that he'd uncovered just as much diddly-squat as us. It didn't last. Tommy and I had picked up flyers during our various outings to Pinko Temples. It was the same bunk the cult always peddled—phrases berating the country's *weakened moral FIBER* and invocations for each of us to strengthen our *HOPE receptors*, a made-up neurological system.

Meekins, on the other hand, had snagged a new leaflet. The stiff card stock announced the Pinko guru's upcoming book launch. *4.6.09, hear from Ananda Ashaji herself!* A month away, and they were already handing out flyers. Our boss read it over, looking at the long list of overflow locations, and then told Meekins to keep pursuing the Pinko beat. "Curtida, you focus on Blufftown Tuck and whatever was going on at Icarus."

There it was. I'd been taken off the Shamshine case. Tommy was doing his best impression of a brick. We'd both suspected it was coming. But still. I could've used a whole lot more than the thimbleful of caffeine in my hands to pick me up. The Chief asked for a summary of what we'd found at the pharma giant. I launched into a rundown of our morning, staring at the yellowing poster curling away from the wall across the room.

KNOW YOUR PIGMENTS. What do they cause?
Slate Gray: Ennui
Cerulean: Guilt
Deepest Blue: Memory wipe
Envy Green: Jealousy, covetousness
Sunshine Yellow: Happiness
Magenta: Obsession

All the synthesizable colors when the thing had been printed twenty years ago. We'd started out scrawling other pigment names in their approximate locations on the rainbow as the recipes developed. *Apricot Awe, Rose Affection, Ginger Curiosity, Bull's Blood Rage.* Over time the space got so full we gave up. I picked out *Blackberry Purple Phobic Fear,* written in the Chief's spiky all caps. The poster was easier to look at than Meekins's rapidly climbing eyebrows as I described Priscilla Kim prancing away down the hall.

At least chasing her would make this case less dull. I'd plug away at the mystery behind my single corpse while my colleague prevented another nationwide scourge of burnt joy receptors. There'd be thousands of suicides if a new wave of the fake Sunshine got to the market. But I'd keep myself entertained hunting down the scientist while Meekins rode the Shamshine ticket up to the big time.

After that we droned through the usual topics, supply questions and budget updates. The Chief reminded us that the annual Magenta Cares charity auction was on Friday at Hotel La Estancia. Our attendance was required. Meekins picked up the sign-in sheet to drop on the notary's desk. Doug was coming toward me. He looked ready to commiserate. I left fast. Paperwork was preferable to well-intentioned sympathy from my illustrious buddy.

I rowed my way through the afternoon doldrums, trapped in my two-meter cube of an office. I'd managed to fit a desk, chair, filing cabinet, and a small bookcase into the space. The wastebasket had been a squeeze. A few sentimental newspaper clippings hung on the wall. A high strip of window kept me up to date on the spider population under the eaves of the building.

I faxed the unidentified fingerprints off to the database. Got together the warrant for CCTV footage from Icarus. Called Tucker Cutts's mom and arranged her ride to the morgue. The first time I had to inform a next of kin on a suicide it felt real important. By the tenth I knew it was just going to be a hassle of paperwork and a sour stomach. It wasn't that it brought up bad memories. I could wrangle my own baggage. But sometimes it was all I could do to keep from shaking the bereaved, who always acted like nobody'd ever lost somebody.

Coming up on dinnertime I threw in the towel, took two aspirin, and headed down the hallway to the parking lot. As I passed the lab, Doug opened the door. A stale blast of old colors rushed out: first Envy, then Rage, then Ennui. I swallowed down the nausea that accompanied the shock of emotion. One of the many reasons I preferred fieldwork. Most crooks focused on a single pigment. The hodgepodge of test materials that lingered in the places R & D occupied did funny things to my stomach. Didn't help that the stuff that jumped out of the jumble was always a little too close to feelings I preferred not to think about.

"You've been stomping back and forth from the photocopier like you don't know what to kick. What's going on?" Doug asked.

I didn't feel like hashing out my sentiments with him. I would've liked to know what it was he'd meant to tell me about the Shamshine case. But for whatever reason, he wanted to talk about that somewhere else. Might not even want to at all, now that I was stuck poking around Icarus instead.

He'd left a large backpack leaning against his workstation. I asked where he was off to. Boise, of course. Taking the sleeper bus up for a few days of meetings. He'd gotten permission to come down for only a week, but with the lack of progress we'd made he'd be coming back for a longer stint. He picked up his knapsack, walked out with me into the parking lot. As we stepped into the twilight, he asked if I was sore about getting taken off the Shamshine case. Added "It's not worth stewing on."

The horizon was turning peach behind streaks of gray clouds. The headache I'd taken the aspirin to ward off was sending exploratory tendrils across my temples and down my neck. "I'm sure you see things like it all the time, but I've gone a whole career without touching something of national importance."

He said he just didn't think there was that much to it. I pointed out that there was enough to bring him down here. He jangled his keys in his pocket. Lowered his voice. "Not really. It was a good excuse, but I'm actually here to look into—"

The end of his sentence was cut off by Meekins stomping through the doorway. "Off to Boise to bad-mouth our work? Why don't you just stay up there?"

"I need to tie up some loose ends, that's all."

"Keep all the glory for headquarters, you mean."

Doug laughed a little, turning the gibe into a joke. "Any glory'll be all yours. I'm on full loan. Everything I do down here is under the orders of Chief Louise Knorr, since you don't have an R & D op."

That was true. With the cretins we were up against, we never, ever needed one. They went back and forth like that, Meekins making nasty comments and Doug doing his best to defuse the situation.

Back when we were at the academy, Plato wouldn't have been able to resist meeting Meekins's territoriality with chest puffing of his own. He'd reached out to me on a couple of occasions in the past few years but I'd been focused on work and had blown him off. I wondered what else he'd learned in that time. Wondered if it would be enough to defang my rabid colleague. The headache had attached itself definitively to my scalp. Nice little capstone dropping with a thud into the ruins of a useless Monday.

It was Meekins's cadet who ended the standoff. Cynthia Nguyen pulled up in her Volkswagen and asked if Doug still needed that ride to the bus station. Her platinum-bleached hair was pulled back into a ponytail. Her Bettie Page bangs cut straight across her forehead. The style emphasized the finger's width of jet-black roots that she always sported. When she'd shown up at the department I'd figured she needed her first paycheck to get to a salon. Turned out it was some sort of fashion statement. As usual, the honky-tonk punk sounds of psychobilly blared from her stereo. I'd never figured out how she managed to get along with her mentor Meekins, whose life philosophy of clipboards and to-do lists seemed antithetical to the distorted screams of her favorite music.

I wondered when Doug had asked her for a lift. She'd been out most of the day on a ration bar run with the department notary. I wasn't surprised my old friend had zeroed in on her. She may have been edgier than the girls

I'd seen him with before, but he didn't really have a type. More a proximity detector. Well, I liked her. She had a sarcastic streak that made me think she was smart enough not to take him seriously. Keep herself from getting hurt.

Doug gave my arm a squeeze. "Aunt Amy never looked good in yellow," he said. "Always wore purple to church. Let's grab a beer when I'm back on Thursday." And with that, he stepped into Cynthia's car and was gone.

Meekins glowered his way back into the office to finish organizing his checklists. I stood, watching indigo drain from the dome of the sky down toward the horizon. Aunt Amy. Hadn't thought about that name for decades. Doug and I had invented a nonexistent relative for him that we'd bring up to tip each other off when something funny was going on. Just one of the cloak-and-dagger games we'd come up with to keep ourselves entertained at the academy. We wanted to be just like the heroes in our comic books. They didn't have to do their own laundry or take history tests, but we could match their birdcalls, codes, and secret handshakes. With teenage certainty, we'd known that our adult adventures would surpass theirs. Twenty-odd years later, here we were, using the same tactics to talk office politics.

My old friend thought the Blackberry Purple Icarus jumble was more interesting than the Shamshine Yellow investigation he'd brought down from Idaho. Or he was trying to buck up his small-town pal, who'd gone from top of the class at the academy to an also-ran in her tiny department.

Scattered lights came on across the hills of Daly City. The windows of the ticky-tacky bungalows flickering to life. Trying to ward off the dark. Somewhere out there, Pimsley would be making a call, sending out feelers about the Shamshine rumor I'd put him onto. Tucker Cutts's mom would be crying into her microwaved cream-of-mushroom soup. Priscilla Kim would be paying cash for a bottle of vodka to drink alone in a beige-carpeted motel room. Nothing I could do about any of it tonight. I got in my car and pulled out onto the narrow street, heading home to my empty apartment.

CHAPTER 4

Tuesday morning, a box of videocassettes arrived from Icarus. I set myself up in the meeting room to scan through the footage of the twelfth floor. The first tape showed nothing of interest. The second through fifth were all blank. Either someone had erased the contents or the camera room operator hadn't hit record in the first place. Checked the rest and found the same thing. Whoever'd sent them over hadn't bothered popping them into a VCR. No way the PR flack would've let something this incriminating out of the building.

I had the names, numbers, and addresses of the security team from Sunday night. If the operator were in on Priscilla Kim's scheme, she'd probably be out of town by now. If she wasn't, she'd be getting home from her overnight shift. Tommy was tracking down info on our two seathuggers, and the paperwork I had left could wait. The operator lived ten minutes away, just over the border of Pacifica. I got in my car and headed out to see if I could find her.

The woman lived in a brown mammoth of an apartment building. When I rang the buzzer for her ground-floor condo, she came out to get me without asking who I was. She was large and white and blond, with the core of an athlete sheathed in the doughy husk of middle age. She wore taupe sweatpants and a green T-shirt advertising the 2005 Russian River triathlon. Showed her my badge, said I was doing some follow-up on the death of Tucker Cutts. She let me right in.

Her living room was oppressively cozy. The iron bars over the window were twisted into fanciful curlicues, and a flower box sported scarlet petunias. Needlepoint samplers hung framed on the walls over a sofa with well-maintained prewar upholstery. They were all quotes from Ananda Ashaji, the leader of the Pinkos. *Open Yourself to HOPE. Take your daily fiber—MORAL fiber. Gratitude = Positivity = Hope!*

The cult held that the effects of the Global Hope Depletion Events on the US population were due to a weakening of our country's morality, which had led to an atrophying of our "Hope receptors." Only through deep personal work—aided, of course, by pricey "integrity" courses and private counseling sessions with the cult's "Hopetrollers"—could citizens return the United States to its former superpower status.

I'd never understood the appeal. The rah-rah America thing wasn't really to my taste. But telling folks it was their personal responsibility to be un-affected by Hope Depletion Events was what really turned me off. Living through the Depletions had been nasty for everybody. When the first one hit, I'd been taking a sixth-grade math test. I was working out the decimal version of seven-eighths when my stomach dropped three floors. I remember being confused because I knew the answer. The class bully started crying. The teacher stood up, took off her wedding ring, and left the classroom. The cult's demand that I wallow in guilt because I'd felt bad just seemed backward.

Then again, I was a Depressive who knew that there was no such organ as a "Hope receptor." Essentially the antithesis of the cult's ideal mark. Plenty of other folks thought the Pinko ideology was the snake's ankles. Here in Daly City, one in three people attended services at the Pinko Temple regularly. Including, apparently, the camera room operator on the security team at Icarus. Too bad I wasn't following a lead on the Shamshine case. Would've made me feel like I was onto something.

The room smelled like dust and old onions. What looked like a fuzzy throw pillow revealed itself to be a quivering bunny when the woman lifted it up. "She was having her playtime but I'll take her back to the hutch," she said. I told her there was no need. Asked her how long she'd had her, if she'd always liked rabbits. Small talk to put her at ease. "I got Barb after Mama passed. You know. Something to occupy my days off."

There'd been a fad a few years back of psychiatrists prescribing "companion leporidae" to folks with severe anxiety. I was pretty sure the shrinks had some other justification, but as far as I could tell the theory was that caring for something more high-strung than the patient would make them feel better. Had a feeling that was the case here. The fact that the woman had named her rabbit Barb was the loneliest tidbit I could imagine.

Asked if "Mama" had been responsible for the needlepoint. The operator nodded, smiled. "They're all quotes from Her Holiness. Mama was one of the original members, can you believe that? Back when they were based up in San Francisco, right after the war. Volunteered with them on the first ration bar distribution efforts back in '85, helped organize everything. It was a really ragtag group back then. Some of those folks were a little hippie for my taste, you know? A lot of marijuana, a lot of deviants . . . but after I started going to Temple, I began to see how Her Holiness was helping folks straighten out." She waved a hand, clearing the air. "You're not here to hear me reminisce. How can I help you?"

I told her I was glad to have her time, figuring she'd want to go to bed soon after her all-night shift. "I called in—I was sick last night," she said. Then leaned forward, nervously eager. "You're following up on yesterday's suicide?"

I'd seen the attitude in plenty of witnesses. Folks for whom an investigation was the highlight of their week. Or month. Either she hadn't covered for Priscilla Kim, or she thought she could get away with it. I hedged my bets and said yes without asking anything specific. Wanting more time to get a sense of who she was before asking about the blank tapes.

She launched into a detailed retelling of the events from Sunday. Told me who on the security team had looked tired and who'd looked perky, who was still recovering from a sprained ankle and who'd been wearing a new shirt. "Nano—Filipino, fifty-four years old, one seventy centimeters, sixty-five kilos, black crew cut—he reads the whole *Reader's Digest* every month, always brings things in from books to 'think about during the dark night.' He recited a poem about sand, and eternity . . ."

Her delivery alternated between the clipped tones of a soldier reporting for duty in an old movie and something more natural, as she went from data about those around her to her own memories of the evening. The whole time her hands were running through the rabbit's fur, soft as prayer. Seemed she saw this as her big moment to shine. Easy to imagine that she'd failed a screening for the neurotypical police force at some point. The more she talked, the less I suspected her of being in league with Priscilla.

But when she got to the part where she was sitting in the chair, surveying the screens from all thirty floors, things got fuzzier. "It was the usual—the usual folk." She rattled off a list of names but couldn't give me time references for any entrances or exits. When I asked for details, she took back some of the names and added others. Her fingers were moving faster through Barb's fur. I asked why she'd called in sick the night before. The rabbit started making a grinding noise and suddenly needed a lot of attention. I watched her fuss over it. She excused herself to take it to the hutch. She was dodging my question.

"Listen," I said when she came back. "I'm here about the tapes."

Her hands went tight in her lap and her chest buckled a little bit. Like someone waiting for bad news and wishing it could've been a surprise. "The tapes?"

"Why are they blank?"

"Blank," she said.

"Why did you erase them?"

"It's not like that!" She closed her eyes for a second. Inhaled, opened them, looked out the window. The cold morning light picked out the wine-dark veins at her temples. She moved her shoulders back like she'd remembered someone telling her to mind her posture. "They changed my meds. And I—the new ones—I keep falling asleep. You probably don't know about these things—" I assured her that I did know about psychiatric drugs and the adjustment period. Everybody on the force had been on traditional psych meds in addition to their daily Sunshine at some point. "Well. On Friday morning at the end of my shift, there was a message in my mailbox that they'd identified something wrong with the prescription I had. I went in and they switched me up, told me to wait to start the new pills until Sunday night. So I got in and took the pills at nine, just like the doctor said, and pretty soon after that I just . . . I was so tired, so tired, and I couldn't focus, and I might—I might have fallen asleep a couple times." I didn't like to look at the blotches of heat rising in her cheeks. "I thought that I'd put the tapes in—I really did. Set the alarm on my watch and everything. But I couldn't go in last night, knowing it could happen again, so I used a sick day to see if it would go better . . ." She trailed off. Didn't seem like that had worked out.

I thought about how excited she'd been to help, how easily she'd let me in. Would've had to be a real fine actress to fake that ugly blush. I asked her to show me the pill bottle. She went to the bathroom to get it and brought it back to me.

The first red flag was the lack of a label on the orange plastic. I asked if that were standard practice at the Icarus psychiatry department. She ran her thumb across the end table, pushing around nonexistent dust. Said no. I opened it and ultramarine capsules tumbled out into my hand. Amytal. Sleeping pills. Standard dose would've been a single one, and someone had told her to take multiple. "Who's your doctor?"

"It was a new girl—I didn't catch her name—Asian, one hundred fifty-five centimeters, forty-five kilos, wore her hair in a bun. Dressed really nice . . . normally doctors wear sneakers. This woman had on stilettos, ten centimeters high."

And there it was. The click of Priscilla Kim's heels, walking away down a trail of trashed minds.

CHAPTER 5

Monterey pines lined the highway back to the department, letting glimpses of the stony ocean through their branches. Out over the Pacific, a fogbank was forming. Promise of a gray afternoon. On the radio, KFOG reported on the plummeting Hope Count. I could feel it ebbing, a dull throb in my chest and a buzzing behind my temples. Indigo Joe's gruff voice announced that future Counts would be more accurate, since the Hyderabad Hope Measurement Station was getting its Etchegoyen capture filters replaced. *Chiozza condenser, Bion rectifier.*

The jargon took me back to long nights studying history at the academy, tracing the path of a young Argentine psychoanalyst on an odyssey to the country's northern tropics. Etchegoyen had been researching a case of amnesiac mass hysteria when he proposed his theory of *miasma emocional*, the invisible fog of feelings that humans emit with every sentiment. The mass hysteria, he suggested, had been caused by an overwhelming concentration of that same miasma—a concentration strong enough to become contagious, pushing the emotions of one village member into another, gaining strength from every carrier. Perhaps, he even suggested, this stuff could be distilled and artificially synthesized.

He'd been ridiculed by his fellow psychoanalysts and psychiatrists, but the military took notice. A decade later, the armed forces had debuted the first synthesized psychopigment, Deepest Blue.

Doug had already known everything in our textbooks, having spent high school in the library reading up on the history of the colors we'd spend our careers chasing. "Of course, they don't mention the massacre that kicked off the amnesia," he said. A group of natives had fled from slavelike conditions on a sugar plantation in search of humanitarian aid. Instead, suspicious landowners called in the Argentine border security force. The *gendarmería* gunned down hundreds of fleeing men, women, and children. It was the survivors who had suddenly forgotten everything, a sort of mass trauma response.

To identify, capture, and synthesize that first psychoweapon, the military would've had to repeat the atrocity. More than once. I'd heard stories of the dictatorship's campaign to disappear "subversives," but this was on a different scale. None of that, of course, made it into the history books.

The annals of pigment development were dark and bloody. Priscilla Kim's tactics would fit right in with them. Prescribing near-overdose levels of sleeping pills, driving Blufftown Tuck to suicide—that kind of recklessness would've been par for the course in the wild early days. Now, though, the breakthroughs kept at least a veneer of corporate responsibility. New colors came out of regulated labs at the Argentine universities, not from corpse-strewn fields of sugarcane.

And Priscilla had been painting people with a known substance, not honing an experimental pigment. I thought about the bottles of vodka under her desk. The fall from rising star to part-time contractor. Tommy's descriptions of her grandiose ambitions. He'd checked with his uncle to see if he could help track her down. Spent the visit listening to the man bellyaching about his wayward daughter. She occasionally showed up at the house to pick up her mail but not much else. He'd had no idea she was working for Icarus; the paychecks he knew about came from work for the women's magazine *Minas*.

My cadet had produced a glossy folded page. Priscilla pouted out from under her impeccably coiffed bun. Printed next to the headshot in bright purple was *Pretty Prissy, PhD: Our resident pigment expert.* Underneath were several chatty answers to questions about the difference between normal colors and psychopigment ("Wearing hot pink eyeshadow won't make your man go gaga—unless you hit him with a dose of active Magenta!") and DIY pimple cures. So much for her dream of being the People's Pigment Movement's Girl Friday.

Apparently her father had a whole shelf devoted to old issues of *Minas*. I could imagine it. Bet he'd been planning to line that space with his daughter's accolades. Instead, he was filling it with copies of fluff pieces. It was almost as sad as the rabbit named Barb. Maybe this whole thing was a case of a woman staring at the winding downward road of her future and deciding to bust through the guardrails.

● ● ●

Wednesday I headed to the hospital to see if a couple days of heel-cooling had made the Icarus seathuggers more articulate. In the waiting room, Dr. Trumbull's presence was a nice antidote to the midweek slump. A short woman with a sensible haircut and the build of an armchair, she marched me straight to Jenny Crotty's room. All business, no small talk. Just a rapid-fire update on the patient's status ("As good as she's going to get") as her oxfords tapped down the hallway.

The patient was squatting on a chair when we came in, eyes bloodshot and open wide. She trembled violently, her wrists abraded where she'd wriggled out of the restraints on the overturned bed. An IV stand lay tangled in its cords, its pigment packs dripping slowly onto the floor. Sunshine Yellow steamed up from its little puddle, evanescing cheerfully into a flaxen fog. The pool of Golden Peace also sent translucent tendrils into the air.

"'As good as she's going to get'?" I said. Trumbull just sighed.

There was blood on Crotty's teddy-bear-print hospital gown. Her bare toes clutched at opposite edges of the seat. Her hands clasped and unclasped, unclasped and clasped. That sort of self-soothing tic was typical of damage from one of the pigments in the fear-inductor class. She drew back her lips, showing her teeth. A breath hissed out. A sharp inhale. Her knees bent deeper and she launched herself at me.

I ducked out of the way. She slammed into the wall behind me and slid to the floor, leaving a smear of gore on the CPR instruction poster. The Purple was supposed to scare the daylights out of neurotypicals, not turn them into walking nightmares. I spun to face her. She crouched again, palms flat against the linoleum. Trumbull stepped between us and asked the patient if she could explain what she was feeling. The question refocused her on the doctor's presence. "The devil," she started, then stopped, eyes going wet. "The devil's in the details . . ."

The doctor knelt next to her, rubbing her back. Told her that was right. Started talking her through a breathing exercise, taking her hand. The muscles in the woman's neck relaxed. Trumbull got her up. I realized she'd somehow positioned her into a loose armlock. If she lunged again, the doctor would have no problem stopping her. Trumbull's no-nonsense guidance was enough to keep her calm all the way back to the bed. She tucked Crotty in, telling her to count her breaths, then turned to me and asked for a full description of how I'd found them.

I gave her the rundown. It went fine until I said Priscilla Kim's name. Suddenly Jenny was moving again. The snarl was back, and she was coming at me. Before I had time to dodge, Trumbull's arms were around her, spinning her into a hold on the floor. The doctor waved the patient's wrist through the fog evanescing from the puddle of Golden Peace. The tension faded from the prone woman's body. "These feelings come from the pigment. They aren't you," Trumbull reminded her. "Breathe." Jenny'd gotten blood all over the doctor's white coat. Back at Icarus, I'd figured she'd taken a pretty severe hit. But to be acting like this three days later was atypical.

A curly-haired head poked into the room from the hallway. Trumbull didn't even look up. "I assume this mess is yours, Howie?"

The wiry nurse quailed before acknowledging that he'd loosened the patient's restraints. The doctor let him know exactly what she thought of that decision. Her tone was calm, but her words made clear that she would have been much more cutting if not for the patient she was holding on the floor. By the time she stopped talking the man looked like he wished he could melt through the linoleum.

Trumbull led me to her office, leaving young Howie to do penance for his poor choices while bandaging Crotty's wounded wrists. The usual stale-coffee scent welcomed me to her workspace. A poster of a Texan highway running through bluebonnet-covered hills hung on the wall. The doctor had been allowed back to her home state only once since the Gauchos had annexed it. The fact that she'd hated growing up there didn't mean she didn't miss it. Mounds of papers, books, dirty cups, and medical pamphlets overflowed from her desk onto the sofa, end table, and floor. The arm of the sofa was the only place free of papers, so I sat there.

"Priscilla Kim was the scientist you mentioned?" The doctor stood at her bookcase. It looked like an earthquake disaster zone, but she knew exactly where to find what she was looking for. Pulling out an academic publication, she ran her finger down the table of contents and passed me the journal.

The list was in Spanish, the lingua franca of the pigment research world. Sure enough, one "P. Kim" was listed as first author on *"Anhelo melancólico lila de plata: entre el ennui y la esperanza."* Silver Lilac Wistfulness: Between Ennui and Hope. "I had no idea somebody'd identified a pigment for Wistfulness. Much less come up with a recipe," I said.

"That's because this article is a sham. It's all about how little Miss Priscilla Kim found a revolutionary method for developing new pigments. Something about modeling the relations between them in three dimensions instead of two, focusing on an axis she called the 'grayscale'—the distance from Slate Gray, in either a positive or negative direction. But it came out pretty quickly that the trials she'd run were a shoddy mess. A whole group of Americans lost their positions at the Universidad Nacional de Comahue down in Argentina. Including the guy who's now the head of R & D over at Icarus."

So chances were R & D had gotten Kim the job at the corporation. But only as a contractor, and with a contract for—what exactly? Didn't seem like poisoning civilians with Blackberry would be part of it. And she would have managed to parlay that into a full-time position by now if they'd believed her research were on the up-and-up. I slid a bobby pin back over a wayward curl. So . . . what? She was a pity hire someone had forgotten to knock off the payroll for three years? The gig as Pretty Prissy with *Minas* fit with that possibility. But Icarus's ruthless layoffs were the stuff of legend in Daly City. The new information was just one more puzzle piece that didn't fit with any of the others.

A timid knock on the door ended our conversation. The nurse had gotten Jenny back to bed with no more damage to himself than a shiner and a bite mark on his right forearm. We made our way back to her room, where it was clear that he'd used every restraint he could find. She'd been reattached to her IV drips of Sunshine Yellow and Golden Peace. The spots where the pigments had spilled had been taped over with green hazpig. A monitor beeped frenetically, announcing the patient's sky-high blood pressure. She stared out from under her straps. Her black hair fell lank across her face as she tracked us with her gaze.

I started in gently, trying to convince the woman I wasn't there to hurt her. She clearly had a strong conviction that I was a demon, but at least she was willing to talk to me with Trumbull by my side. My questions took us down a surprising path: she couldn't recall her address.

Amnesia was not one of Blackberry Purple's effects. I wondered briefly if she was stonewalling me, but the scabs on her wrists suggested otherwise. This was a neurotypical who had been thoroughly fried. Lying was next to impossible in her state. "What's the last thing you remember, Jenny?"

"I was at work—no, that's not . . . Lenny and I were going to—I can't—" She jerked, and her face folded in a grimace of pain. The monitor went crazy. She began rhythmically muttering the Lord's Prayer, fingers twitching in time to the beeping. Trumbull cocked her head at me.

Seemed like Jenny's short-term memories were inaccessible. Like it hurt when she tried to retrieve them. Textbook symptoms of psychopigment damage—from Deepest Blue, not Blackberry Purple. Which would mean that Priscilla Kim had given her victims a mix of pigments.

The Blue would mask most other colors. Eyeballing the way I had, it would have been easy to mistake a blend with just about any of the pigments on the red-to-violet part of the spectrum as Purple. Hell, if Priscilla gave her victims the Blue when she knew the police were on their way—

the most likely option—she may very well have added some Blackberry to muddy the waters even further.

Things were snapping into focus. Tucker wouldn't have been able to plan out his suicide several steps in advance with his brain cooking in panic. The rock fan passing out when I'd asked what had happened had seemed like a generic sign of pigment overdose at the time, but now looked like an effect of the Deepest Blue. On the other hand, Crotty's long-term aggressive personality shift didn't line up with anything that either Deepest Blue or the Phobia Fabricator were known to do.

Priscilla Kim's actions had been inscrutable because I'd been peering through the wrong lens. Running out of an interview when that would immediately make her suspicious made no sense—unless she was hiding something huge. Impersonating a psychiatrist to dope the guard made no sense—unless what she was doing was verboten on Icarus's corporate grounds. Even the choice to have enough Deepest Blue on hand to paint over these three pointed toward her having some secret to cover up.

It wasn't quite a theory. Still. It was more than a hunch. I met Trumbull's gaze. Her lips were pursed, mirroring the expression I could feel on my face.

Priscilla Kim was developing a new pigment.

CHAPTER 6

The interview with Leonard Gobble was a wash. He still talked like he was trapped in a nightmare mass led by a heavy metal band. Couldn't remember where he lived, either. We left the beeping monitors and IV drips behind and headed back into the hallway. The midday light outlined the windowpanes on the greige tiled floor. I sketched out my thoughts to Trumbull. Hadn't even finished before she started spitballing possibilities. "Priscilla Kim could be back on her old game, trying to make Silver Lilac Wistfulness. Or something totally new—Chili Pepper Spite?" That would fetch a nice price on the street. The doctor tugged at the lapel on her lab coat. "I wish we had a better psychospectrometer. The damn thing we've got is a prototype from the Dark Ages. It can ID a single pigment, but anything more complicated it just beeps, shakes, and shuts down."

I offered to have Doug take a look when he got back from Boise. The possibility of an actual R & D op taking over pushed her cheeks up to her eyes. When she smiled like that, I caught a glimpse of who she could've been in some other, easier life. Less business and beef jerky, more gardening gloves and fresh dumplings. She told me she'd fill out the paperwork and send the samples over as soon as possible.

● ● ●

The samples were waiting in the office fridge when I got into the Agency Thursday morning. Tommy and I had already put in an extra hour of work, heading to Icarus early to catch the security guard from the twelfth floor before he finished his night shift. Nano Panganiban was the literary fellow the camera room operator had been so impressed by. Given her description, I'd been expecting a little professor, but the man looked more like a soccer star who'd aged off the field but could still make free kicks better than anyone.

He had a grand total of no information to give us on Pretty Prissy. "I patrol three floors and the rooms on the twelfth are soundproofed," he'd said, spreading his palms wide in a shrug that encompassed a world's worth of powerlessness. We'd thanked him and he'd run off with the rest of the team to Sharlene's, a local dive, for a nine a.m. happy hour. A standing appointment for the man, it seemed.

The car ride back to the department had been nice and dreary. Tommy's one attempt at conversation was informing me that Sharlene's had been the bar that scandalized Priscilla with their shaken old-fashioneds. KFOG ran a special on the Lausanne Laboratory for Official Emotions in Switzerland, the internationally recognized psychopigment research body. *It is here that the world's sole vial of Lavender Hope resides*, said the narrator. *Captured during a massive operation before the Fourth Global Hope Depletion Event in 1993, it is believed that it will remain the only example of this rare pigment—forever.*

I could remember when we'd thought that the solution to the regular drops in the Hope Count would be synthesizing Lavender Hope, like we had with Sunshine Yellow. Unfortunately, the process for coming up with a recipe always began with capturing wild emotion. Scientists would get together enough folks feeling the sentiment they were trying to make and siphon the neurosteroids out of the charged atmosphere. Analyze their unique structures, find some other similar molecule in yams or mushrooms or cicadas. Run it through a bunch of processes involving Bunsen burners and the suffix *-ation* and voilà: the birth of a pigment. But the whole exercise required a group of humans who felt hopeful. Hard to find any of those anymore. Especially in weeks like this one, with the Hope Count dropping daily.

So it was a nice pick-me-up to find that Trumbull'd already gotten the samples to the office. The hospital had done the work of isolating the pigment markers from the patients' bloodstream, so all Doug had to do was run them through the psychospectrometer. He looked dopey after his overnight bus ride down from Idaho, but he was wide-awake by the time the words *unidentifiable cocktail* were out of my mouth. He grabbed the package and shut the lab's pigment-blocking door on me before I'd finished explaining the situation.

It was how he'd always been. At the academy, a tricky mix could keep him in the lab for eighteen hours straight. Then he'd spend nearly as long explaining everything he'd found to me. Never mattered what else I had planned. One time he followed me around the track for fifteen kilometers, breathlessly narrating the signs of Slate Gray contamination in Sunshine Yellow batches. Before heading to the bus station on Monday, he'd suggested we get a beer tonight. Maybe I'd get the same kind of rundown. This time I was looking forward to it.

Tommy's report on the victims at the hospital had included the fact that Jenny Crotty's unemployed sister, Penelope, lived with them. I figured if the women were close enough to share a bathroom, Penelope might know something useful. I grabbed my cadet to go check out their place at 1911 Hickey.

The news on the drive was that the Knights of Liberty, the right-wing "resistance" to the Gauchos, had started in on a fresh spate of school bombings. Happened every March, timed to keep US history classes from addressing Uncle Sam's doddering decline. This week some kook out in Bakersfield had got ahold of Deepest Blue and painted *GOD BLESS AMERICA* across the blackboard of the eleventh-grade social studies classroom. Two teachers and sixty students had been wiped before someone remembered Pigment Enforcement's number. I stopped us for a cup of coffee to wash away the bad taste that story left.

Fifteen minutes later, we were walking up a mildewed staircase to the Crotty-Gobble residence. The first floor stunk of cabbage and cat piss. On the second floor, a remodel in progress had coated everything with a layer of sawdust. The banister wobbled under my grip, in time to the hammering. Sunlight streamed weakly through a small, dirty window at the end of the hall. The ochre paint peeled. A crack was developing along the ceiling. "Pleasant," muttered Tommy.

Number six was at the far end of the third-floor landing. A grimy ribbon wreath hung around a hand-shaped knocker. I rapped sharply. A distant voice called back, "It's unlocked!"

The door was heavy. Reinforced with something. Walking in, we were immediately overwhelmed by a complex olfactory symphony. A bass line of old shoes played counterpoint to brighter notes of fermented orange rinds, underscored by the funk of rancid bologna. My mother liked to complain about the state of my apartment, but I was several notches above these guys when it came to taking out the trash.

"I'm back here," the same voice called from the end of the narrow hallway. We passed the living room on the right, furnished with a ratty couch and rickety bookshelves. A poster for the radio soap *Painted Love* hung next to a framed record sleeve of the Dead Sentiments' album *Medusa Complex: Your Feelings Are Not Your Own*. Could've been the decorations for any couple in their late thirties. But the bookcase was filled with the spiritual writings of Ananda Ashaji, the Pinko guru. A signed glamour shot of Her Holiness sat on top. Make that any Pinko couple in their late thirties.

A bedroom with an unmade queen came up next. All the windows had sets of iron bars. The neighborhood wasn't great, but it wasn't that bad, and this was the third floor. We passed a closed door. The bottom panel had been cut out, leaving a ten-centimeter gap. A thick metal chain snaked through, wiggling across the hall's wooden floorboards toward the kitchen in the back. The tinny sound of music from a blown-out boom box drifted toward us. I stopped. The song was "Sensual Rain," off the Saigon Sallies' debut—a band played exclusively by the hardest-hit victims of the Magenta Attack.

The 1989 spray-bomb explosion had marked the end of the postwar boom in San Francisco. The metropolis was one of the few to come through the conflict relatively unscathed. In most cases it was Argentine interests that protected the cities—the oligarchy's real estate investments in Miami;

Dallas's early overtures to the Gauchos about seceding from the US to become a protectorate of the Southerners. On the Western Seaboard, bigger targets like Los Angeles and San Diego took the heat. San Francisco just wasn't as important as it thought it was.

The reprieve lasted until a bunch of anachronistic hippies decided to turn it into the real City of Love. The perpetrators didn't realize that Magenta doesn't cause true devotion, just something akin to high-intensity teenage fandom. When the detonation went off at Twentieth and Church Street at five p.m. on a rare sunny Saturday, an open-air concert had been kicking off at the other end of Dolores Park. The poor Saigon Sallies had formed only three months before, taking their moniker from a club manager's mishearing of "José Gonzalez," the lead singer's name. They were utterly unprepared to face a crowd whose adoration was of the take-no-prisoners variety.

The bassist and drummer were dismembered. Within half an hour, there was no sign of the singer and guitarist. It took two months for the national guard to pacify the city. Folks who'd been as far away as Sausalito that day were still dotting their "i"s with hearts twenty-five years later.

The smell of festering garbage thickened the closer we got to the kitchen. Tommy came to a halt next to me. I pointed at my ear. His Adam's apple bobbed as recognition set in. We'd be dealing with a hard-core victim of the Magenta Attack. The cadet shifted his case folder from one hand to the other. I gave him a nod, and we stepped out of the hallway.

What the kitchen lacked in space it made up for in light. Windows ran along the back of the room above the stove, sink, and beige counter, wrapping around the corner of the apartment. The panes that could be opened were propped up. The dishrack was empty. A fruit bowl held two shriveled oranges and a bruised apple. To the left, a wall of cabinets ended in a freestanding fridge-freezer covered in photographs.

In the sunny corner on the right, a round table and three wooden chairs made up the breakfast nook. The gingham tablecloth was clean and crisp, a surprising contrast to the stink. A blue teapot and a chipped porcelain cup and saucer sat in front of a prettier version of Jenny Crotty.

She looked mournfully out toward San Francisco. A rose-colored bathrobe draped around her shoulders. Her sable hair fell gracefully down her back. The chain we'd been following zigzagged across the yellowing linoleum, ending in a manacle around her ankle.

"Penelope, I presume?" I said.

A sad smile spread across her mouth, and she turned toward me. I did my best not to react to the immense scar that spread from her right cheek up to her scalp. Her eye was a bubble of white jelly in the mass of shiny red tissue. Tommy coughed.

"Oh, did I surprise you?" she asked, fingers tracing her hairline. "I meet so few people, I forget that not everyone . . ." She flashed a melancholy half-moon. It disappeared as she took us in, Brown lady and skinny Asian kid standing in her kitchen. I wished, once again, that we had uniforms. I pulled my badge out of my fanny pack and introduced Tommy. She took the enameled metal oval and ran her fingers over it. Her movements were slow, like she was pushing through water. I played my usual game: lithium or clozapine? Lots of pigment victims with a neurotypical profile ended up on some sort of antipsychotic. "Oh my," she said. "Pigment Enforcement."

I told her we were there about her sister and Leonard. At the news that they were in the psych ward, she reached for her tea, and the cup rattled on the saucer. I was leaning toward lithium. "I've been here all alone—waiting for them—all week—when they didn't come back, I didn't want to think . . ." A tremor ran through her torso. She pulled a dirty tissue out of her bathrobe pocket and blew her nose, still facing away from me. A breeze highlighted the reek of cumin-laced Argentine-style chorizo from the garbage. "And here I was, mad at them for not coming home to take out the trash." A tear dripped onto her robe.

I stepped away to give her some space. "*Sensual raaaaaaaaaain,*" sang the Saigon Sallies. On the neighbor's roof, a cat decapitated a pigeon and settled down to its meal. A pile of feathers built up as it plucked the unfortunate bird. Penelope's crying got worse. Tommy shifted his weight from foot to foot. We didn't have all day.

"Is there any alcohol in the house?" I asked. It wasn't textbook, but sometimes you need a little lubrication to get out of a tight spot.

The girl pulled another tissue from her pocket. "Leonard has some vodka."

I started going through the cabinets. The first was packed with the foil-wrapped ration bars that became a household standard during the war. There were ten hundred-unit packs. In addition, there were two shelves full of freeze-dried meals, putting the total at over one thousand two hundred. A surprisingly high number out here in Daly City. Unlike the Midwest and the Eastern Seaboard, we didn't have regular food shortages. The second cabinet had more common staples—powdered milk, instant coffee, eggs—and jars of dried legumes and brown rice. The bottle of Russian River Vodka ("Central California's Finest") was hidden in the back of the final cabinet by the window, surrounded by mismatched plates and cups. Didn't look like the inhabitants were big drinkers.

Tommy found an ice tray packed among frozen meat and beans in the freezer. As he juiced one of the shriveled oranges, I looked at the photos stuck to the fridge. There was one of Leonard, twenty years younger, playing bass behind a top-hatted, two-meter-tall drag queen. I recognized the singer as Pinky, the onetime second-in-command of the Pinkos. I asked Penelope about the picture. Maybe better memories would help her deal with her present predicament.

"Oh gosh, they were friends since forever, since before Pinky was Pinky," she said. "That's how Leonard and Jenny started going to Temple—the memorial service, you know, this whole part of their friend's life they hadn't really paid attention to, and Ananda Ashaji herself crying over the casket."

So much for better memories. Back when the local cult had been known as the Church of the Divine Spirit, Pinky and Ananda had been inseparable. Folks said that Ananda was the soul of the church, but Pinky was the heart—organizing food relief programs during the famine of '85, setting up memorials for veterans who died homeless and alone. Pinky's sudden and mysterious demise rocked the Church in the early nineties while I was still a cadet. Ashaji gave an impassioned eulogy, single tears running perfect mascara tracks down her pale cheeks. Announced the group would officially take on the name "Pinko" in memory of her sidekick.

Penelope was watching Tommy mix her screwdriver, garnished with a twist of orange peel. He placed the drink in front of her with a flourish. Priscilla Kim had taught him well. The girl's lips worked like she couldn't decide whether to smile. "I can take out the trash, too," Tommy suggested.

"Oh, that would be—I've wanted to, but . . ." She looked down at the chain around her ankle. Tommy tied up the pungent bag and whisked it out the door while she drank up. She put down the glass and inhaled. The stink hadn't fully dissipated, but it at least it was weaker.

The song on the boom box came to an end, and she stood slowly to flip the cassette. The chain rattled as she moved. Without the music playing, the whine of a buzz saw came clearly through the floorboards. She tenderly turned over the tape and slid it back into the deck. The shaking in her hands made it difficult. She pushed play and clasped her fingers together, observing the tremors. After a while she came back to the table. Lined the empty highball glass up with her teacup. "Of all the people to get caught in another attack . . ."

"So you didn't know they were involved with psychopigment?"

"Involved?" Penelope drew back like a stunned sloth. "They weren't involved. They can't have been . . . Jenny and Leonard are the straightest pair you'll ever find. There's no way they would mess with that . . . *stuff*. Not after what happened to me," she said. "Do you know how crazy it makes people?"

"I've had a little experience," I said.

"You know, I was at Dolores Park the day of the Magenta Attack." I tried to look surprised as the Saigon Sallies launched into another maudlin ballad. The girl wanted to talk. Whatever kept her from crying was fine by me. "It was the best and worst day of my life. I met the man I'll always love"—her good eye strayed toward the boom box—"and lost him. People really went wild. I was one of the true fans, you know. I'd been to all four of their shows. But this . . . this was something else. The mob just swept me along. I couldn't escape it. And then—there he was. José, just standing on the sidewalk. It was love, pure and simple. I took a step toward him. He took a step toward me. We touched." I nodded, hoping it didn't show that I'd heard this same story dozens of times from other Magenta victims. "And then someone threw gasoline on my face and torched me with a lighter."

"Jesus," I said. She looked to be about five years younger than me. In '89, she would've been in eighth grade. Tommy came back in and started washing his hands.

"The last I saw of him he was running toward Mission," she continued. "He's still out there, somewhere. I know he is. That's why I have this," she said, gesturing toward the chain around her ankle. "Some nights, when the Hope Count is high, the longing gets too strong. I know that if I were free, I would run back to that cursed place. I'd risk anything to get to him. He still loves me. I can feel it in my heart. I lost my eye that day, but I gained something infinitely more precious. Someday we'll be together." That explained the bars on the windows and the reinforced front door. I hoped for her sake they never found his body. "You can see why Jenny and Leonard wouldn't touch pigment after that."

"Sure," I said. There were holes the size of the Argentine Navy in her logic, but there was no evidence these people were crooks. The legumes and brown rice suggested they might be health nuts, but the only crime I could've pinned on them was not tossing the garbage in a timely manner.

Tommy decided it was time to put his oar in. "You know your sister has been seen around town a lot with a man known as Blufftown Tuck . . . was there something going on there?"

I hadn't realized that Tommy had been imagining some sort of lurid love triangle among the unfortunate seathuggers. Luckily Penelope's reaction was just a tremoloed giggle. "Tucker Cutts? That—that's not . . . Tucker doesn't swing that way. Jenny met him at a support group for relatives of people . . . like me," she said, suddenly serious again. "They'd go together, get a drink after, and Tucker would give her a ride back here."

Priscilla had recruited her guinea pigs at a support group for caretakers of Magenta victims? Would've been nice to know what to make of that. I asked

THE SHAMSHINE BLIND 49

Penelope when the next meeting would be, and she sent Tommy for Jenny's calendar in the bedroom. He returned with a battered agenda, bound in colorful paisley. It had the requisite single Spanish word (*amor*) printed in gold on the front in curly calligraphy. He handed over the book, and it fell open at the beginning of March. The pages were covered in crabbed handwriting. Every entry had a name, a place, and very specific times—*12:25–1:05 p.m., 8:30–10:10 a.m.* Jenny Crotty's schedule was full up. "Must be a good massage therapist," I said, remembering the woman's business card.

"She's one of the best. She's even done Ananda Ashaji."

Masseuse to the leader of the Pinkos. There were whispers that Pinky's sticky end may not have been a surprise to Her Holiness. Even ones suggesting she may have been involved in some way, preemptively knocking out a challenger for her growing power. Apparently those rumors hadn't reached Jenny. Or maybe she'd been flattered enough by the requested session to ignore them. The guru spent so much time traveling around the nationwide circuit of temples that it was rare to catch a glimpse of her in the cult's hometown.

I paged forward, looking for the details of the group where Jenny and Tucker had met. Sure enough, the last entry penciled into the woman's packed schedule for the coming Monday was *Support group (Fred B. hosts)—7 p.m.—92 Bepler St. #12.* I turned back to Penelope. "When did you last see your sister and Leonard?"

"Sunday." Saigon Sallies' "Lovesick" had just come on the boom box. It was clearly more interesting than we were. "Night—I think."

I flipped back a week. Every appointment on Sunday evening and all of Monday had been erased, leaving the only clear centimeters in the entire calendar. Better yet, at 4:30 p.m. on Sunday afternoon, Jenny had been planning to meet with one "Priscilla K." at Sharlene's. The dive near Icarus.

"Penelope," I asked, "do you know a woman named Priscilla Kim?"

Tommy pulled the headshot he'd gotten from her column in *Minas* from his folder and passed it across the table. Penelope wrenched her attention from her true love's voice long enough to inspect the photo. "No idea."

It would have been too easy if she had. We got her okay to enter the calendar as evidence, and I handed it over to Tommy. The song came to an end, and Penelope's face dropped as she returned to the world of the living. It was a bum deal, living manacled in a fetid apartment with barred windows. I asked if we could take her someplace she wouldn't be alone. "I don't have friends," she said. "What with all this . . ." She kicked her leg back and forth, tugging the chain across the floor.

Poor woman. "Do you want us to move you to the hospital? You could be with Jenny there . . ."

The word *hospital* made her go still. She shook her head, silent. As an agent of the law, I knew I should take her in anyway, but once she was there they wouldn't let her go. I wasn't sure it was worse than wearing a manacle around your ankle, but she was an adult with her own preferences. I gave her my number and told her we'd pick her up some groceries. Those ration bars wouldn't hold off scurvy indefinitely. A corpse would mean a lot more paperwork.

"I hate to ask," she said, "but my meds are also about to run out . . ."

"Lithium?" I asked.

"How did you know?"

● ● ●

As we passed the remodel on the second landing, Tommy started up humming the song Pimsley had played us. He seemed quite pleased with himself. As we crossed the dirt patch that counted as a yard, I asked him what was up. He smiled a prim little smile. "Oh, I was just thinking that it looks like we're back on the Shamshine case."

The car was parked on the curb, wheels turned in against the slope of the hill. I would've loved to indulge in the kind of wishful thinking behind Tommy's statement. I just asked, "How do you figure?"

"Jenny and Leonard are the connection between the Pinkos and Icarus. Their bedroom just screams it. Pictures and pictures of the two of them at Pinko events. They even had framed certificates from their Hopetroller classes."

"Seems more like a coincidence than a connection."

"I've just got a feeling," he said. "Bet you a bottle of Valentina there's something there."

He had to be serious about this hunch to offer up real hot sauce like that. The Argentines had banned international trade in anything higher than 1,000 on the Scoville scale, just because they could. These days, you had to have a hookup with the Mexican car runners to get a bottle. The eagerness of youth. Well, chili peppers had long been the only reliable source of spice in my life. "I can't resist a bet," I said, sliding the key into the lock. "Especially when someone's playing to lose."

CHAPTER 7

Doug had his feet up on my desk when I got back to the office. If I hadn't known he'd been on a bus all night, I never would've guessed. Seemed his enthusiasm from when I'd dropped off Trumbull's exotic samples in the morning had lasted all day. "Glad to see you've admitted your dream of being a field agent," I said.

"Nice try. The chairs in the lab are much more comfortable. No way I'm giving up on that perk. Even if R & D comes with headaches like this damn mix your doctor friend sent over." He unfolded a pile of dot-matrix-printed paper. He hadn't bothered separating the pale blue pages, and they still had their punched-hole edges. He ran his finger down the results. "Look. Here it came back as Blackberry Purple, then here it was just 'unrecognizable.' The next time it came back as Deepest Blue. Then here it's a mix, but the next run it was unrecognizable again—whatever's in there is something I've never seen. I did the Ungar test—tried breaking it down into its Etchegoyen components—"

"You going to run through every chapter in the academy textbooks to explain what's going on?" I asked. Doug's sweater vest was the exact color of Salmon Satisfaction. I wondered if he had one to match every pigment on the synthesizable spectrum. Would be just like him.

"Point is, I'd like to send the sample to a friend of mine in Boise. He's . . ." Doug took off his specs and leaned toward me. His eyes looked even closer together without his horn-rimmed frames. "He's PSI."

Psychopigment Service Investigators. "You've got a 'friend' in PSI?" Everybody on the force knew PSI were officially in charge of policing us.

Watching the watchers. Unofficially, there were rumors that they had their own agenda. There was always some dolt at the Psychopigment Convention who bragged about having seen them in action. The rest of us figured ignorance was bliss.

"You meet a lot of people, living in Boise." Big-city big-time. The dust bunny in the corner swayed in a draft. Doug shrugged. "He owes me a favor. I've been banging my head against this all day, and it shows no sign of cracking. I think he's our best bet. I'd have to get it off today, since the receptionist on Mondays is the Argentine spy."

Every large department had an informant sending regular reports down south, an outgrowth of the massive Gaucho espionage apparatus that had been decisive in winning the war. Down here we were too small to have one. Didn't stop Tommy from entertaining himself spinning far-fetched theories about who it might be.

I wasn't a fan of the idea of sending the sample off our turf, but Doug was one of the top R & D agents in the country. If he couldn't break it, nobody in Daly City could. I told him to send it to Boise and shooed him out of my chair. "I was thinking that instead of a drink we could do dinner tonight. I've got nothing in the fridge."

Doug's hands went into his pockets, then came back out again. "Oh jeez, Ninja. I'd forgotten all about that. My boss needs me on a call with Iowa City, and I'm not sure when it'll be done."

"Another time, then." I watched him skitter out the door. The years may have put gray in his hair, but the way he walked hadn't changed since he was seventeen. When I met Doug, he was a skinny lab rat with an outdated Afro, obsessed with comic books, pigment science, and armchair philosophy. He sat next to me on our first day of Pigment Analysis. The rampant sympathy for the Knights of Liberty at the academy meant that a lot of our classmates were equally suspicious of the dark-skinned Black guy and the Hispanic mutt. When I blew his dandruff off my notebook without comment, our friendship was cemented.

That first year, Doug was constantly barging into my dorm with philosophical quandaries for us to argue over. Free will and psychopigment—the value of true feelings versus induced ones—the definition of "self" if our feelings were not our own. I'd try to put him off, pleading upcoming tests or sparring matches, but he always sucked me in. One time he held forth for hours on something he called "mental sovereignty in the age of psychoweapons." It sounded fancy, but was mostly about how terrified he was of someone wiping his brain with pigment. I asked plenty of questions but never figured out how he squared that with training where we were regularly exposed to the stuff.

In the fall, I beat him in all our self-defense classes, and he beat me at pigment identification. As the year went on, he grew ten centimeters and I hunkered down in the library. By the time spring came, I'd stopped avoiding his pontification sessions and he'd started trouncing me at track. We were tied in the first-year ranking. Over the summer, Doug went to work on his aunt's farm in Alabama. He took the bus down to Tampa for a visit during August's soupiest days. Farm work and farm food had filled him out after his growth spurt, and it was the first time I'd seen him in pants that covered his ankles.

My mom cooed over him and made us *arepa*s. He played tennis with her and laughed raucously at all her jokes. We spent the week reading through my comic-book collection and bumming around town. We ate Cuban sandwiches and ice cream in every strip mall we could find, watching the war widows go about their daily business. Four years after the surrender, the slump of defeat had settled permanently into everyone's posture. Occasionally a veteran would trudge past, the peculiar glaze left by Deepest Blue in their eyes. We tried to calculate the number of male soldiers Tampa had lost based on the gender imbalance on the streets.

The night of the full moon, we filched a six-pack from the fridge and snuck into the abandoned Busch Gardens. We climbed up the rails of the old Python roller coaster and sat looking out into the treetops, arguing about pigment regulation. I didn't care either way, but I enjoyed the debate. Doug was in favor of loosening up the laws, adding a "recreational" classification to the existing categories of "medicinal" and "harmful." I gathered this had to do with a cousin of his handing out Magenta gelcaps at a party on the farm. Two of our white classmates had gotten caught with the stuff back in April. Their only punishment had been an assignment to bathroom cleaning through the end of the year.

It was the first time I'd encountered the gap between the theory and practice of the "enforcement" in our Agency name, but not the last. We were only human. I was surprised that Doug had tried it, but not shocked. He waxed lyric about the pink pigment. "It's like you can fall in love with anybody," he said. "At least for the hour or two it lasts."

"And then what? Take more Magenta? It's not real love, anyway." My T-shirt stuck to my damp torso. "Not that we would know."

A heavy breeze brought the smell of sargassum weed from the Gulf. I could've done with a storm to break the muggy heat. Doug stretched a long arm behind him. "Haven't you ever been in love?"

"We're teenagers."

"We've got four years on Romeo and Juliet. We're legal adults."

I blew air through my lips and took a pull of my warm beer.

"Don't you want to know what it's like?" he asked.

I thought back before the war—Dad coming home late from the store with lists of inventory to organize. Mom doing the accounts at the table with him while he ate his dinner in silence. Love hadn't done much for them. "Not really."

That same cousin bought Doug a hair clipper, and when we got back to the academy he had to fight the ladies off with a stick. Not that he really tried. By mid-October, my friend was officially girl crazy. Maybe he'd been all along, but I'd been the only one who would put up with him. In any case, I settled into the role of wingwoman, teasing him as he fell hard and helping him strategize exits when he inevitably tired of his flings. We'd kept it up until our assignments came down, him to Boise and me to Daly City.

Nothing happened between us at the academy, but a few years later I went up to Idaho for his birthday. The drinks at his local dive were strong and cheap, and I'd wound up spending the night in his bed instead of on the couch. The next morning, I'd taken one look at the Magenta flashes in his eyes and bought a ticket for the first bus back to Daly City. Fog was preferable to a paramour with a pigment problem. On the ride home I'd bought a tuna salad sandwich. The taste stayed forever tied to that hungover feeling of skin-crawling nausea, broken-in boots tight around swollen feet, mind skipping like a scratched record over and over the image of Magenta lines around Doug's hazel irises. I hadn't eaten tuna since. We always said we'd visit but never did.

I listened to Plato's leather soles, squeaking toward the lab. My office felt small. I called the fingerprint people. Tomorrow morning, they promised. First thing. I asked Tommy to be at the database when the doors opened. Traffic grumbled outside. The notary's seal thumped rhythmically. I sat alone with my typewriter and a blank F-27 report form. The long afternoon stretched out in front of me. I'd been planning on introducing Doug to the best burger in town after work. I thought about my empty fridge. The dishes in the sink. I made a note to pick up a can of chili and paper plates on the way home.

● ● ●

Friday, I woke up marooned in the vast emptiness of my bed. The ashen light of morning skulked around the curtain. My upstairs neighbor already had the TV on full blast. It was the anniversary of the great Blue Out, the beginning of the Argentines' psychopigment blitzkrieg that painted over so many of our country's metropolitan areas. Through the ceiling, I could hear the murmur of the list of lost cities over a choral rendition of "America the Beautiful." *Chicago. DC. Denver. Detroit.* I'd heard the reading so many times at school assemblies and swim meets that I could still recite along. Back in high school, classmates' relatives came back from the front and succumbed to the damages of war and psychoweapons. *San Diego. Santa Fe. Seattle.* We lost our football coach, the social studies teacher, and the best swimmer on the team to a doomsday cult. Seemed everybody was looking for an authority figure, and with the hubs of the interstate all knocked out, the president felt too far away to be real.

In those discombobulated postwar years, our losses had felt like the only thread tying us together. Day by day, we learned to navigate our new existence on a continent moth-eaten by lacunas of Deepest Blue. The faint strains of "United We Stand" came through the floorboards, the only hit by the Breakfast Club. We'd picked ourselves up and put ourselves back together enough to raise lighters as some girl named Madonna Louise Ciccone sang *From Fresno to Cape Cod / One nation under God.* Grim days, grim years. Thinking about what the country had been and what it had become still left me feeling bleak, decades later.

Even my daily Sunshine pill couldn't beat back my funk. Depressive denial works like Vaseline over the lens of life. The daily gelcaps of Happiness normally brought little things into focus: the heat of the shower cutting through the seven a.m. chill, the smell of the rain, the toddler yelling "Good *morning*, Agent Curtida!" out her grandmother's window as the door to the building slammed behind me. Normally. Today, the kid's garbled speech sounded a lot more like *aging Curtida.* The fog crept down my collar and the odometer in my Renault 4 pointedly turned over another hundred-thousand-kilometer mark. When I bought the car, I'd figured it would have good trade-in value when I upgraded once my promotion came through.

After the weather forecast, Indigo Joe ran through the Hope Count numbers on KFOG. There'd been a dip in the night. That explained my mood. I'd been starting to think it had something to do with Doug standing me up. But that had been a regular fixture of our friendship ever since he updated his haircut at the age of eighteen. We'd make plans and he'd bail for some girl he'd forget two weeks later. A call with his boss and Iowa City, the biggest department in the country, was a much better reason to scuttle our beer. So I was glad to hear my gloom came from the low Hope Count.

The file on my desk was the only thing that could have broken my blahs. Tommy'd managed to wrangle the results from the fingerprint database and get back to the office before I'd even made it in. For that, I forgave his unbearably peppy attitude. Didn't even tell him to stop singing the damn Bootsie Poots song while I opened the folder. The first set of unidentified prints I'd submitted from the crime scene had no match.

The second belonged to one Nano Panganiban, security guard at Icarus Corporation. The man stationed on the top floors, who'd told me he'd seen nothing.

It was now nine fifteen. He'd gotten off his night shift forty-five minutes earlier. Driving to Icarus at this point would be a wild-goose chase. We had his home address, but I somehow doubted he'd be there. There was one bar that kept popping up in this investigation. I figured it was time to call Sharlene's.

The phone rang only once before the bartender picked up. Probably didn't see too much business at this time of day. He had a voice smooth enough to ease anyone's doubts about the wisdom of drinking this early. I asked if Nano Panganiban was there. He said yes immediately and went to get him. Clearly my hunch that the man was one of the regulars had been spot-on.

Nano was laughing as he got on the line, but he got quiet real fast when I started talking. "You told me you had no idea what Priscilla Kim was up to," I said. "That you saw nothing untoward on Sunday night. But your prints were all over the crime scene. I'm going to need your cooperation, Nano. Because this is a murder investigation, now, and if you're an accessory to the crime, well . . . that's going to be serious."

Glasses clinked down the line. Someone laughed. It sounded very far away. The phone rustled. Nano sighed. "I just wanted to help the lady. Priscilla, you said? That's her name? I don't even know her name. She was so overwhelmed, with those nuts running around, and the guy with her was no help—just left us there—" One of his coworkers yelled for Nano across the bar. Someone made a joke and hooted. The security guard's voice got tight. "Listen. I can explain everything. But I can't talk here. She's got friends in high places. I could lose my job."

I pushed for specifics then and there. He refused to say more, repeating that he could lose his job. If I let him off the phone, he could skip out on me. The bad taste from Priscilla's exit was still in my mouth. But I could hear fear in his tone. Finally I told him that we'd meet him at the bar in twenty minutes. That there was a lot more at stake than just his employment. Asked to be passed back to the bartender.

Told the smooth-voiced man that Nano was wanted in a murder case, and that if the security guard left he should call the cops immediately. If we showed up and he was gone, I'd consider him an accomplice. He assured me he'd keep Panginaban close. Fingers crossed that he'd stick to it. I'd seen loyalty between bar staff and their regulars mess up enough investigations. Usually if the barkeep felt they had skin in the game, they'd keep their word. Usually. It was a chance I'd have to take. I told Tommy we had to make tracks.

● ● ●

The bar was ten kilometers south of the Agency, a winding drive through Daly City's urban decay. Every stoplight gave the morning's gloom another chance to needle back up, bringing with it the worry that I'd let yet another lead slip through our fingers. That this was the kind of sloppy work that had gotten me taken off the Shamshine case. I turned on the radio. The news program on KFOG was running a segment on self-styled "conscientious objectors," teenagers who were refusing to take the Neuroprofile Standardized Examination everyone went through in their junior year of high school.

President Rigby had instituted the testing for all draft-aged adults in the late '80s. The guidance counselor hadn't known how to break my results to me, and I hadn't known how to feel about the diagnosis. It meant I was eligible for a career in Pigment Enforcement, something I'd been dreaming of ever since pigments started showing up in my comic books. But I'd imagined Depressives as the kind of people who'd spend hours staring stony-eyed out windows or keel over in fits of melancholy. I'd always just kept plodding through. Making myself useful. When I noticed I was having feelings, keeping myself busy made it easy to ignore them. I'd thought I was just normal. Funny to discover that was wrong.

"There's not a war on. There's no draft. So what exactly are you objecting to?" asked the radio show host.

"Getting who I am put in a box. Getting told I have to take Sunshine every morning for the rest of my life," a young woman responded. Tommy laughed at that line. As if Sunshine was a punishment. Ignoring the benefits of pigments was the kind of choice I expected of aging hippies like my mother, not outspoken teenagers. "We want to experience the feelings the world causes us, not overwrite them with preprogrammed 'Journeys' or emotional purges," the girl continued.

"Would be nice to go through life without ever needing a purge," I said.

"Sure would," Tommy said. "Although sometimes I think they're overused."

A government warning sign loomed by the empty vastness of the abandoned Serramonte Center's parking lot: SLATE GRAY SPILL AT THIS SITE — YOUR FEELINGS MAY NOT BE YOUR OWN. "It's not like she's going to be able to avoid every spill in the country, either. At some point you gotta accept that you live in a world where most of our feelings come from outside."

Tommy said "yeah" in a way that made me think he didn't really want to have this conversation with me. At Southgate and St. Francis, the old Methodist church had been taken over by the Pinkos. The door was flanked by two mean-looking white guys with shaved heads. Bodyguards? Or general security, I wondered. Tommy started humming the Bootsie Poots song from Pimsley's. The tension in my neck whispered that something was about to go wrong. That we'd never get Nano's information. My bobby pins tugged at my scalp.

The scene when we arrived did nothing to calm my nerves. Nano was in the parking lot of Sharlene's, wrestling himself out of the grasp of a pony-tailed man in a faded black apron. Apparently the velvet-voiced bartender was holding up his side of the bargain. The Icarus security guard wasn't. I killed the motor and jumped out as Nano broke away. He sprinted to his peeling Ford pickup. I caught up with him as he opened the door.

"It's my mother—she's at the emergency room—" He was out of breath, pale under his tan. The patina of cool that had defined him in our last encounter had rubbed right off. "We can talk at the hospital—"

"We can talk right here," I said, grabbing his arm. Might've been true, what he was saying. Might've just been an excuse to dodge my questions. The nylon of his ultramarine windbreaker crinkled under my fingers as he twisted away. I tightened my grip, but he threw his full weight toward the driver's seat. I held on, snatching for the hand that held his keys. Too slow. He turned the ignition.

There was a rumble, then a bang. The throttle choked down. He turned it again, and again. Nothing but clicks. Gray smoke oozed around the headlights. "No, no, no," he said, banging his fist on the dashboard. I let go of him, stepped back. It was real fortunate for me, his engine bursting into flames when I needed him to stay. Tommy was coming toward us. I gestured at him to wait. Nothing I trusted less than a lucky break.

Nano moved to the hood, extinguisher in his hand. I got a whiff of the smoke. Smelled like gunpowder, not burning oil. It was some kind of a bomb up there. That would multiply today's paperwork fivefold. Had the thought I could just choose not to bother. I'd been checking boxes, plodding through procedure on this case since day one. Wasn't yet noon and my legs were already tired.

Nano's gaze had dropped, his shoulders gone slack. I took a breath, focusing on nothing. Sure enough, I caught the telltale flickers of Slate Gray at the edge of my vision. The smog was spiked with psychopigment.

The extinguisher slipped out of the security guard's hand, hit the pavement with a clatter. Clever. A smoke bomb wired to the ignition. Wouldn't need much punch, just enough to spit out a cloud big enough to envelope a neurotypical's head and fry his brain.

Tommy was pulling hazpig out of my trunk. He must have reached the same conclusion. The thick haze boiled around Nano. Every second he stood there, the worse the damage would get. If he wasn't already gone. What did I think I could do about it? I was just as useless in this mess as on the Shamshine case. What was I trying to prove, anyway? I was well on my way to washed-up. A friendless Florida transplant destined for early retirement in the fog headquarters of the country. I might as well start adopting stray cats now.

The listlessness of the Ennui draped me like damp wool. Tommy was marching in my direction. No need for him to be exposed as well. "Stay there!" Took all I had to call out to him. I forced myself forward. *Useless. Useless.* "Sing that song—the one from Pimsley's—"

"What?" The lime-green hazpig swayed in his hands, but he kept in place.

"*Now*, Tommy!"

"*I thought I found happiness,*" he sang. His jittery vibrato made the melody extra grating. I wanted to get away. "*But all I've got is something like hope.*" My nerves screamed. I got my legs moving to get me away from him. He started oohing the verse line. It sounded stupider without words. I hated the song. Gray lines buzzed at the edge of my vision, turning the world into a tunnel. *Useless.* Hated the song, hated it. Fight Ennui with loathing. I made it to Nano and dragged him away from the open hood. My cadet kept singing. I let my irritation yank us to my car. *Give up*, whispered the pigment. I clung to the bright spot of my annoyance. Tommy finally figured out how to be useful and took Nano's other arm. Together we wrangled him into the back seat of the Renault.

I handed Tommy the keys, leaning on the roof for support. *Not even capable of standing up straight.* I ignored that thought. "You drive. We've got to get this man to the hospital."

CHAPTER 8

The first time I encountered Slate Gray was at the academy. As part of our training, we were exposed to plenty of colors, learning to distinguish our own feelings from pigment-induced ones and to identify the symptoms in others. Most of this happened in the "Practical Identification" lab class, a free-for-all created by Bob Tadlock.

A skinny, pasty-faced vet with a constant runny nose, Tadlock had found a line between cowboy and mad scientist that he liked to walk. He was the kind of guy who would pass around a deactivated pigment grenade and laugh about how, with an explosion weaker than a roundhouse punch, the weapon could spray enough paint to permanently fry a roomful of neurotypicals. Back in those early days of the academy, it was the Wild West. Professors were inventing the curriculum as they went, and sometimes things got out of hand. I avoided telling Tommy stories about those days. Didn't want him trying to replicate something stupid by himself.

I'd spent months going cross-eyed staring at formulas and psychospectrometer printouts, wondering if we'd ever see the stuff we were all here for. And then, one cloudy Thursday in November of our first year, we walked into the converted cattle barn that housed the lab to find four inhalers lined up on Professor Tadlock's desk. There was tape over the level indicators on the beige tubes. No way to see what was inside. I started getting excited. "We're going to do this three times. Each round, the volunteers will take a hit of their pigment. Then I'll get them talking—we'll have a nice civil debate. Pay attention to anything that seems out of character: movements, gestures, vocal patterns. The doses are mild, but by the third one even you numbskulls in the back should be able to guess." Laughter rippled through the class. Tadlock didn't respond, just turned back to the chalkboard. His bald spot gleamed the same color as his pale suede jacket. The man's hard-assed schtick got him a lot of respect, but I was on the fence about him. He was real chummy with the popular kids. Sometimes I wondered if he had any friends his own age. "If you fail at that, the final confirmation will be inspecting their eyes. If you have ideas, write them down. Otherwise, don't waste my time. Wait until you're sure you've figured it out." He passed around four forms, with space to guess during each round.

The volunteers were Tracy, a blond cheerleader who'd escaped the suburbs of DC with her parents during the war; Jonathan, a skinny white boy born in Chicago who'd made it to Boise in time to finish high school; Craig, a "rah-rah America" kind of a jock who didn't see the irony in modeling his mullet on tangopop sensation Maxi del Mundo's; and Doug.

Tadlock handed out the inhalers, and each volunteer took a short puff and sat at the front of the classroom. Doug moved slowly, like he was watching something happening deep in his core and wouldn't trust his body until he'd figured out what it was. Craig's legs sprawled even wider apart than usual. Tracy's attention flitted from the inhaler to her best friend to the professor, and then back again. Jonathan stared at his pencil. "How do they get the lead into the wood?" His curls bounced as he shook his head. I penciled *Ginger Curiosity?* onto my sheet.

"All right," said Tadlock. "What are everyone's thoughts about the second constitutional convention?"

The afternoon light came through the barn doors but gave up a meter or two into the room. The fluorescents did their best to beat back the autumnal gloom. We sat in silence as the group played the inevitable game of chicken about who would be lame enough to speak first. As usual, it was Doug. "The idea of combining all of New England into a single state is a blatant power grab by President Rigby's Dixiecrats."

"Who cares? It's not like the Fed has any real power anymore," Craig said, then shook his mullet and winked at Tracy. *Cool Teal*, I wrote down.

Tracy quailed at Craig's coquetry. Normally she was a big flirt. Strange, but not enough to tell what was in her inhaler. Doug took off, throwing out population statistics—more people resettled in Barnerville, New York, than lived in South Carolina before the war, but no one was suggesting we merge the Carolinas—and Craig baited him with apathy.

Was Scarlet Passion the pigment in my friend's inhaler? No, Plato was always passionate. Give him a topic to debate, no matter how inane, and he could work himself into a froth over it. And the topic Tadlock had chosen was tailored to bring out his fervor. Neither of us was a fan of anything President Rigby did, with his good-old-boy smile and lifelong love affair with Jim Crow. The proposed reforms would solidify the president's grip on power. At one point Tracy interrupted the boys, announcing "I'm not racist!" We all waited for her to go on. She shifted in her seat. *Cerulean Guilt*, I wrote down next to her name.

"Can you believe the atoms in our hands come from outer space?" asked Jonathan, wiggling his fingers. I updated my guess from Ginger Curiosity to Apricot Awe. Curiosity was an active feeling, an itch you had to do something to satisfy. Awe you just sit there and feel. Like Jonathan was doing.

The volunteers took their second hits. Jonathan got more new-agey. Craig's responses got more asinine. As he lectured Doug on how the Blued-out highways and devastated infrastructure in the Northeast made communication with the capital in Miami too difficult, my friend began running his thumb over his knuckles. I watched it slide back and forth, listening to the measured tone of his voice. There was a tightness underneath. I wondered why he didn't change the subject. That took me back to the possibility of Scarlet Passion. But Passion would have had Doug interrupting, gibing, making fun of Craig. Instead, he was just getting quieter.

Bull's Blood Rage. That was what was in his inhaler. Had to be. He knew how to hide his anger well. But the false confidence of Cool Teal was pushing Craig to see how outrageous he could get, and at some point Doug would snap. Tracy kept dropping anxious non sequiturs, finally looking at Tadlock through tears and admitting that she'd cheated on the last test.

After the third dose, Craig suggested that maybe the federal government should go the way of the dinosaurs, "Like it should've instead of fighting the dumb civil war."

Doug launched himself out of his chair and tackled the jock. Tracy's mascara started running faster as she apologized to Doug about the time she hadn't wanted to sit next to a Black lady on a bus. Jonathan broke into a hymn about the glory of humanity. I jumped up to pull Doug off Craig before he did something that would really get him into trouble.

Tadlock was laughing as I dragged my friend across the room. "I knew you had some scuffle in you, boy," he said. "Good thing you've got Mercedes Sosa there to keep you in check."

Nicknaming me after the only Argentine who'd ever admitted they weren't white was classic Tadlock humor. Doug's pecs tightened under my arms. I squeezed tighter. "It's just the pigment," I said to Doug, even though I knew it wasn't. Just like I knew Tadlock had given him the inhaler with the Rage on purpose.

After that, I started consciously focusing on controlling my feelings. I was one of the best at guessing which pigments Tadlock had given to my classmates, but neither Doug nor I were pale enough to make it into the group of his favorites. When it was my turn to volunteer, I could expect a doozy.

Sure enough, the first round was Cobalt Sadness. The months holding myself together after Dad passed paid off in spades there. Nobody except Doug was able to diagnose me until they got up close after the third round and checked my eyes. Half the class had assumed I hadn't been given anything at all. After a silent sob session in the bathroom, I felt pretty good about how I'd done.

I managed well enough until our third year, when Tadlock gave me Slate Gray. The first puff almost knocked me out. The second hit left me staring blank-eyed at the wall. Jonathan accused the professor of frying me with Deepest Blue. But there was nothing special about the dose, and the pigment was run-of-the-mill. It was my own damn weakness. That Gray voice in my head, telling me everything I did was useless, flattened me with painful efficiency. Nobody else reacted that way. I just had no defenses against Ennui.

The effect of the hit didn't end when the pigment wore off. Tadlock thought my reaction was hilarious, and soon enough his pet students were joking about my mental state every chance they got. I had a few scuffles with the ones dim-witted enough to think they could take me, but the fist-fights didn't change anything.

It all came to a head when Doug got involved with Tracy at a party where Magenta gelcaps were going around. I watched my friend making puppy eyes at the blond bangs we'd previously laughed at, and said *no thanks* to the kid with the medicine bottle. Apparently that marked me as pretty damn square.

There were muttered comments all through lab the next Monday, in between lessons about the emergency uses of chloroform to subdue lab personnel exposed to unstable pigment mixes. As I packed up after class, Tracy pulled out an old rumor about my dad. "He cracked after too much pigment exposure. That's probably why Curtida won't even try fun stuff like Magenta. The *trauma of her loss* has made her *risk averse*." Her psych jargon looked bad with her scrunchie, but I just told her I had no problem with taking risks. Somehow that escalated into her dipping a cloth in the chloroform Tadlock had been using to demonstrate and daring me to inhale. I soaked the damn rag and slapped it on my face.

I came to with a tongue depressor in my mouth. Doug hovered over me, haloed by the lab lights. The barn's timber ceiling swam above him. I'd been convulsing. It had been more chloroform than I'd bargained for. I batted at his hand with a shaky arm. He got me on my feet. My nose burned where the sticky cloth had touched it. The room started spinning like a merry-go-round. On the path outside the barn, I lost my cafeteria mac 'n' cheese into the snow. I made some joke about it looking the same coming back up as it did on the tray. He didn't laugh, just said "You could have gotten yourself killed."

It wasn't anything that bad, really. The nurse made me come back every day for a week, but I didn't have any long-term damage. Apparently it scared Tadlock's pets enough that they stopped talking about me and went straight to avoiding me. Suited me fine. The dizziness passed in a couple hours, and the sores on my face closed up fast. Doug looked at me funny for months, though, and sometimes I wondered if he thought I'd been trying to off myself. Of all the fallout from my Slate Gray hit, that hurt the most.

● ● ●

Even twenty-one years later, exposure to Ennui took me right back to that Indiana winter. Sitting in the hospital parking lot in Daly City, I watched Tommy drag Nano through the emergency entrance. I'd sent my cadet to check the security guard into the psych ward. It was better if I stayed out of Trumbull's sight. Last thing I needed was her deciding I had to be kept under observation on a Sunshine drip.

Some still lucid corner of my mind was overflowing with questions. The attack must have been meant to keep Nano from talking. The bomb had been homemade, sure, but not in the half hour between me getting on the phone with him and him starting up the truck. I hadn't seen anything like it in Daly City. The local scum usually shot at each other if they wanted to play paintball. But how had they known he was going to talk?

I knew the questions should feel urgent. But wrapped in the effects of the Slate Gray, they buzzed futilely like wasps caught in a window screen. I stared at the empty construction site where the planned Magenta wing had stalled due to budget problems. Told myself my mind was silent.

My cadet returned with a hazpig mask and gloves that Trumbull had sent out "just in case." Nano was stable, but the outlook was grim. Tommy hadn't told the doctor much about the circumstances but she clearly figured I must be up to something dumb. He'd asked around about Nano's mother, but no elderly women had come in that morning. The security guard had been baited to his car.

We made our way back to Sharlene's to clean up the mess the pigment bomb had left and get a full statement from the bartender. When we pulled up, he was smoking a cigarette at a plastic table outside the dive. The sign on the door said Closed. I let Tommy handle him while I dealt with the lingering Slate Gray. Most of the pigment had evanesced in the initial explosion, so there wouldn't be much lingering effect. But best practice was to get the remains of the incendiary device away from neurotypicals.

The hospital's hazpig did come in handy as I gently tugged at the fifteen-centimeter cardboard tube. It had charred where it was attached to the car's ignition. Even with the gloves and mask on, the nasty voices in my head got louder when one of the Ennui-soaked cotton balls from the jury-rigged fuse chamber fell out. *Useless. Dead weight.* I got the improvised explosive into the boxy pigment containment cooler in my trunk.

Over by the door, Tommy had moved from the man's statement to asking him about Priscilla and her guinea pigs. I could see him waving around his cousin's headshot. "Yeah, sure. She tried to tell me I was making her drink wrong," the bartender said. He sounded tired, but his voice was as velvety as before. Probably an actor. With that ponytail, an aspiring Shakespearean. "There were five of them, so I couldn't slap the automatic twenty percent tip on the bill. It was her, Blufftown Tuck, a couple, and a skinny dude in a suit. Some serious creepy-crawlies come through here, but this one was special. Had a real lean and hungry look about him. Slick dark hair, slicker dark glasses. Stuck around for a drink after the others left—double rye, neat. I got the sense he was there to make sure nobody followed them." Nano had said *the guy that was with her was no help*. I tried to get fired up about it. I still felt like a beige-carpeted waiting room.

From there it was a silent twenty-minute ride to the office, where I sent Tommy to put on the department's full hazpig suit. Once he was out of sight, I slumped against the Renault 4. I used to eat lunch out here in the parking lot under an old elm with Walter Lopez, the agent who'd mentored me through my cadet years. His wife had taken to packing him sandwiches for both of us, in a campaign to get me to eat food that didn't come from a can. We'd sat in that elm's shade when he got promoted to deputy and after I got the news that Mom had sold Dad's store.

I'd come out here alone a few times in the weeks after I found Walter's body. His absence just brought back the memory of his corpse, slumped behind his desk. The empty bottle of sleeping pills and the handle of vodka. He'd choked on his own vomit.

Like plenty of other Malvinas vets, it had been the aftereffects of all the Deepest Blue hits that had gotten him. Too many holes in your memory can do screwy things to a person. Later the tree got infested with beetles and lost all its leaves. I stared at the stump, gone ashy with a decade of rain. I wished I still smoked.

Meekins pulled in two spots away, cadet Cynthia Nguyen's bleached bangs riding shotgun. He'd recently detailed his prewar Buick station wagon, and the faux-wood panels gleamed. Relief washed over me. A surprising feeling upon seeing my coworker. He and the girl sat in the car, going over one of their endless checklists. I couldn't figure out how he thought she would function in the field if every task had to be a box to be ticked.

Tommy'd told me she'd been the only student at the academy who made it through all the tactical paintball exercises without her car ever getting tagged. "She'd hit an ambush, rev the engine, and just zigzag her way through. Like she knew where every pellet was going to fall." I'd never seen Meekins give her the wheel. Then again, wasn't like there was much call for evasive driving in Daly City.

Tommy emerged from the department, suited up in lime green. The baggy hazpig coverall was two sizes too small, showing inches of skin between the gathered ankles and the cadet's cerulean socks. He hadn't bothered with the booties. I went ahead and popped the seal on the pigment containment box—a tough one to manage with the gloves my cadet was wearing. The wave of Slate Gray that had built up during the ride rolled over me like a one-night stand with an actuary. I told him to get the bomb to the lab's clean room and wrap it up tight. I clung to the car door until he got the offending package inside.

With a deep breath, I started the journey to my office. Felt like the parking lot was kilometers across. Took a break at the glass double doors that led into the building. The dreary fluorescents of the hallway weren't a pick-me-up. I counted the steps to my door. In my desk I had a cache of Sunshine Yellow. Five more steps. Now four—three—two—

The Ennui raised an eyebrow and dropped me to the floor. My fanny pack pressed into my bladder. I hadn't noticed how grimy the baseboards were. The gray-green linoleum cracked where it met the wall. Rat droppings, dust bunnies, an abandoned pen cap. What had happened to the pen? Probably dried out, unused, in the back of a drawer somewhere. Utterly forgotten. I rested my shoulders on the ground. Just for a second.

Tommy's feet came into my line of sight. "You okay?" His sneakers were dirty. "You need help getting up?"

"Sunshine. Second drawer in my desk."

His shoes trudged away and then came back. Hands appeared in my vision: one with a Yellow pill, the other holding a small cup of instant coffee gone cold. I didn't think about where the coffee came from or how old it was. I bit down gently on the gelcap. Not exactly approved procedure, but desperate times. Tommy lifted my head and I took a swallow of the tepid liquid, shuddering as the pigment returned color to the world. "Christ Almighty." Muscles I didn't recognize were relaxing. "That was awful."

"Is Slate Gray supposed to be this strong?"

"I'm particularly sensitive. Have been since training." No need to go into that with Tommy. His forehead was already knitted up in worry. I tried to stand by myself, and then thought better of it. He helped me to my feet and then into my office. He pulled out my desk chair and lowered me down like a rack of test tubes. I try to keep up the old hard-boiled demeanor, but sometimes it's nice to be cared for.

● ● ●

I'd made it through only six of the twenty-four forms required to report the morning's events when Berdie, the department notary, appeared in the doorway. His bow tie was bedazzled and his spats matched his marigold-and-cyan houndstooth tailcoat. He gave a little twirl. "Aren't you just thrilled for the gala?"

The glow from the Yellow faded abruptly. "That's tonight?" Christ. I'd have to wear heels.

His spectacles gleamed. "You agents! Can't even remember *the* social event of the year! And with all the buzz around this one—the Pinko's co-sponsorship is a coup, just a *coup* for the foundation—they're expected to break fundraising records by *kilometers*. Gruber-Shaw and the rest of the board must be thrilled." After that enlightening lecture, the notary and his houndstooth tailcoat bounded into the hall to remind the rest of the staff about the evening do. The man's three passions were couture, Daly City's small-town gossip, and amateur mycology. I'd never figured out how tromping through the woods in search of wild mushrooms fit in with the first two.

Usually I found all three topics equally grating, but the reminder that Dr. Gruber-Shaw would be at the auction gave me something to look forward to. He was the head of R & D over at Icarus. The one who'd likely brought Priscilla Kim on. I'd met the man at the mayor's Christmas party when he first got hired at the pharma giant, and the coldness behind his eyes made me want to skip the figgy pudding and deck the hallway out of there. A chance to ask him about Dr. Kim might make up for the blistered toes I'd be sporting tomorrow.

That line of thought was interrupted by the Chief calling me into her office. Her chestnut-brown head bent forward over her work. I could see the thin spot on her crown. Her workspace was four times the size of mine, making it small instead of tiny. The room was immaculate, as always. Not a speck of dust on the frames of the fading photographs of the Twenty-Fivers. There was a picture of President Rigby pinning a medal on the Chief at the Reagan Memorial. One of the whole squadron from the signing of the Mumbai accord. It showed a grim-looking group of thirty-four men and seven women, the remains of the original five-hundred-strong squadron. Some had pulled off feats that would go into the history books. Some had just survived. All of them carried the marks of the war they'd inherited too late, with morale and manpower down and the nation's strongest military strategists already packed off to a Deep Blue oblivion.

When the Agency was founded, a Twenty-Fiver got attached to every hub. Iowa City, Boise, Miami—each had its own war hero. But one by one, the old soldiers had opted against fading away and swallowed their guns, their pill bottles, or a handle of their liquor of choice. The Chief was one of the few who'd stuck around. If her dusting seemed compulsive, her pencil sharpening some sort of ritual, I figured that was between her and her demons.

She pushed aside her paperwork and asked about the Slate Gray hit. I told her it was just a bomb someone left in one of my witness's cars. "And you rushed into the pigment-filled haze without protective equipment?" I said yes and braced for the lecture. This time around, though, she skipped the scolding and asked what I'd found. When I'd finished describing the cardboard tube, she looked thoughtful. "Maybe there's finally a crook worth your time out here." She flashed her wry grin. I hadn't seen it in months. Then it slid off her face like water down the drain. "Unfortunately, we'll never know. Someone higher up wants the Icarus case."

Someone higher up. That could only be PSI. I knew I shouldn't have let Doug send that sample up to Boise. "This mess is our jurisdiction," I said.

"Sure, but with the Psychopigment Service investigators sniffing around, my hands are tied."

I hadn't wanted this case, but now that I'd taken the Slate Gray hit trying to save Nano, I didn't want to let it go. I pointed out that the Shamshine matter was a collaboration with Boise. Asked how this was different. Why they were taking it away instead of working with us locals.

She lined up three pencils with weapons-grade tips in a row next to her typewriter. "You don't want to piss these people off, Curtida."

My curls itched. "You tell me to drop it, I drop it."

"On the upside, word came down today they're looking at you for Iowa City. Said they've been keeping tabs on you for years."

"Sure hasn't felt like it."

"You may be hearing from them." The Chief's mouth pulled back. "You should get some rest." The same smile as in the photo with the president. Same flat eyes. She had a lot more wrinkles now.

My desk looked even more cluttered after her pristine office. Up on my wall hung a profile of Walter Lopez from the *Daly Daily*, the frame askew as usual. I straightened the portrait. It tilted slowly back. Straightened it again. When we cleared out his belongings after he passed, Walter's wife said I should keep the write-up. She was the grieving widow, but she acted like I was the one who needed comfort.

I watched the damn thing slant back to its typical cant. Pushed the mess of forms roughly into a pile. Nothing helped. I took out a pencil. I'd just been offered a ticket out of here—but in exchange for what? Searching for my sharpener, I found a dried-out pen with no cap. I slammed the drawer shut and walked out the door.

CHAPTER 9

Nothing good on the radio and no place to be. Maxi del Mundo sang an ode to his shrink. Some said heading down the psychoweapon path was the logical outcome of the Argentine temperament—the navel-gazing melancholy of tango combined with the adolescent arrogance of a nation inventing itself. Others said the cause was Argentina's absurd concentration of psychoanalysts. Where Americans flush with the post-WWII boom put their cash into dishwashers, Argentines put their money on the couch. They flocked to Freudians, Lacanians, Kleinians, and Jungians. Appointments five times a week for years. Within a couple generations, everybody and their mother had been analyzed. Newspaper articles described politics through the lens of the Oedipal complex. Elementary schools advertised their psychopedagogical approaches.

Of course, it wasn't a straight line from psychoanalysis to psychopigment. Analysis, terminable or interminable, wasn't exactly known for instigating action. Etchegoyen had originally proposed Deepest Blue as a cure for the nostalgia that psychologically crippled large parts of the Buenos Aires population. Aside from the fact that it wouldn't have worked, it certainly wouldn't have moved the Argentines toward world domination. It took the military to see the potential for the Blue.

Had our home appliances had the same latent power, missed because of our laser focus on atomic weapons? We'd been so sure of our arsenal's supremacy. We'd never imagined someone could make Swiss cheese out of our chain of command's minds, leaving our mighty warheads to molder in their silos. But it really didn't feel like our KitchenAids and Whirlpools held the missed opportunity that would've kept us on top of the world. Seemed more like the Gauchos' psychodominance was inevitable.

Heavy clouds coiled over the hilltops. Worse weather to come. Blufftown

Tuck's body on the pavement. Jenny Crotty's fearful gaze. Nano, fire extinguisher slipping from his limp fingers. Penelope Crotty left without caretakers. Could I just wash my hands of it all? Walter would've said the Chief didn't have a choice if PSI wanted in. But that admission would've come after a long silence that meant he'd run through just about every worst-case scenario.

Walter had held to his principles but knew not to cling too tight. Life had thrown him enough curveballs that he knew sometimes ideals had to remain platonic to keep from cracking. By his last year of high school, he'd been working two jobs to support his widowed mother. His old man had been a pharmacist who'd moved the family up from Mexico for a position in a relative's drugstore. The breadwinner's death in a car accident meant my mentor was clocking in at a food processing plant before school and burning the midnight oil as a pinboy in a bowling alley. When the arrival of the automatic pinsetter quashed that gig, one of the regular bowlers suggested the paid training of the police academy. "It was just a stroke of luck. I've booked more than a couple former classmates," Walter told me. Then he chuckled. "Of course, one of the other pinboys got recommended for a construction outfit. Married the owner's daughter and became the top developer in Daly City. So I could've been luckier."

Times like these I sure missed Walter's perspective. His advice was always offered with a laugh, no matter how grim the situation. I would've told him it felt like the Chief had handed over the case without a fight. She hadn't answered my question about how PSI could take this from us. He'd probably assume I was overreacting but tell me to keep my eyes peeled. What did I know. Maybe in Iowa City, PSI swooped in and took over cases all the time.

The little houses made of ticky-tacky slid by, doors like speechless mouths offering no answers. I switched the station. Electronic tango whined, matching the drizzle dribbling across the windshield. My hands on the wheel had steered me to Edie's, the greasy spoon I'd been daydreaming about introducing Doug to. Before he'd gotten back and stood me up for his call with Iowa City. A hole-in-the-wall across the street from the hospital's psych wing, Edie's had tattered bunting and the best hot sauce this side of the Bay. If I ever found God, it was going to be in one of their spicy Spitfire burgers.

It was long past the lunch hour, but Edie herself unlocked the door for me. Without the clatter of customers, the joint felt spacious. Her husband, Pablo, was singing along to Mercedes Sosa's *"Gracias a la vida"* in the kitchen. "You look like you need something a little stiffer than coffee. You sure you came to the right place?" she asked.

"Your hot sauce will be plenty strong for me," I said. The grill's warmth burned off the clammy cold caught in my jacket. I asked after her son and sat down at one of the small tables near the register. I had a soft spot for the kid. I'd helped him clear his name when a neurotypical cop decided that "Black guy in Daly City" was enough of a description to book him for a crime that was committed across town while he was on shift at Edie's with twenty witnesses. The morning charges were dropped, he told me he'd decided to follow in my footsteps. Today's update was that Jason had made black belt in tae kwon do but was still waiting to hear from the Pigment Enforcement Academy.

While we talked, Pablo whipped up a Spitfire burger. Edie brought the plate and a warm mug to go with it. "Now you've got to tell me why you're looking like something the cat didn't bother dragging in. Anything to do with the Pinkos? I've heard Meekins has been making the rounds, asking about them and Shamshine."

Jesus, Mary, and Joseph. If Edie knew, everybody knew. My colleague's subtle manner had struck again. The Slate Gray had killed my appetite, but I took a bite of burger to cover my grimace. "No, I've been on another case."

"Damn. I was hoping you'd find some dirt. Tie up all their money in legal fees. You know they put in an offer with our landlord for this place? As if buying up every church in town wasn't enough!"

I was off the Icarus beat. Maybe I should dig around, see what I could find. Of course, I was off the Shamshine case, too. "You know I'd like nothing better." Two days ago, I would've been thrilled to hand off Blufftown Tuck's unseemly end. Helping out Edie could be the silver lining to the lump in my gut. You'd think the possibility of a promotion would lift my mood. But I knew what got folks noticed in Iowa City, and it wasn't setting snares for the birdbrained wannabes we had around town. "You ever felt caught between the devil and the deep blue sea?"

"Sounds like my love life."

"Hey!" Pablo yelled from the kitchen.

"Until you showed up, honey," she called back. I'd run background checks on two dozen suitors before he'd come onto the scene. She had a point. She pulled out the maroon vinyl-upholstered chair and sat across from me. "I wouldn't mind knowing what's going on. For once."

It was a line I'd heard from her before over our fifteen years of friendship. Edie'd been a Daly City fixture since she'd arrived in the mideighties, driven out of her native Atlanta by the racial strife that had erupted in the postwar chaos. She and her first husband had taken one look at the advancing tide of burning crosses, thrown what they could fit into their Pinto station wagon, and started the treacherous journey across the smoldering remains of the country.

Every once in a while she'd tell stories of the drive—the empty roads and abandoned gas stations, the emotional toll of traveling downwind of pigment-soaked cities strafed by the Argentines. "I'm just glad we weren't trying to make it from New York," she'd told me, late one night after the diner closed. "The Deepest Blue haze around Memphis was bad enough." In the years since, it had grown safer to take the old highways, but folks still disappeared in the memory-sucking barrens between the remaining population centers.

We'd grown close in the midnineties. Her husband had been one of the victims of the San Jose Bull's Blood Rage Massacre around the time Walter passed. We'd nursed our grief and countless beers with a dash of hot sauce. Edie was one of the few people I could be straight with, and we both knew it. I forced myself to take another bite. I needed the food, whether I wanted it or not. I could feel her brown eyes on me. Part of the story wouldn't hurt. "I got caught in a Slate Gray bomb this morning."

"Holy hell."

"It's part of the job."

"And when was the last time you ran across a bomb laced with pigment?" she asked. She had a point there. That cardboard tube would have been worrisome in Boise City. Even the Chief had been impressed. This was a step above the lame tricks our local scumbags usually pulled. Edie worried at her bright red manicure. "We both know that some of the line cooks aren't always on the up-and-up. I could ask them to check around, see if any of the usual suspects have been studying up on homegrown explosives. Quietly."

It was quite an offer. Especially if I was off the Icarus case. "I can't ask you to. But . . . if you hear anything—"

She nodded. "I'll let you deal with the devil. You let me deal with the deep blue sea." I was at the door when she said, "By the way, tends to be that when the devil offers you a bargain, he catches you in the fine print. Just a word from the wise."

"I'll keep my reading glasses close," I said.

●●●

Pulling into the parking lot of my apartment building, I caught a glimpse of Mrs. Fernandez's white perm going into the lobby. I waited in the car long enough to give my Pinko neighbor time to get well up the stairs. I'd asked her about the cult when I was on the Shamshine case, and she'd been more than happy to spread the good word. And would be more than happy to keep spreading it on me until I converted or she gave up the ghost. I had no patience for a lecture on Ashaji's "Hope receptor exercises" this afternoon. Saying positive phrases on repeat into the mirror seemed like a good way to strengthen my capacity for denial, but not much else.

My apartment was even dimmer than when I'd left in the morning. The storm had come into its own, darkening into one of our rare spring downpours. The bare bulb in the living room was losing the battle against the dun carpet and the watery light trickling through the window. I'd thought about buying a lampshade when I moved in, but the place was supposed to be temporary. I'd just made agent, figured it wouldn't be too long before I nabbed that transfer to someplace with more action. Better not to have too much stuff to move when it came through. Going on two decades of staring at the light bulb, now.

I tossed my clothes onto Pimsley's fancy chair and started the bath. While it ran, I went through the mail. Bills, coupons, a flyer from Pan Am Airlines urging me to *Visit the Argentine Pampa! Only $5,599,000.00 or fifteen easy payments of $550,000.00!* The only thing of interest was a care package from my mother. It contained a jar of Mom's homemade rosemary–coconut oil conditioner, a bottle of stinging-nettle pills, and a photo from her last outing with the Tampa chapter of the Military Widows Association.

I put the conditioner in the bath and slid the new pills into the medicine cabinet with their encapsulated vegetal brethren. Seemed like its contents should have been some sort of coded message, but this was my mother. She'd once sent me actual snake oil. I stuck the picture up on the fridge with the dozens of others she'd sent. Mom playing tennis, Mom at the Christmas parade, Mom at the beach. It was like she was trying to use Polaroids to make up for the years we hadn't talked. Maybe she was hoping I'd find someone to take my picture.

When I was a kid, it had been our neighbor Monica who'd overseen the documentation of my quotidian existence. An exiled Argentine psychoanalyst, necessity had forced her to trade the couch for a series of odd jobs, among them babysitting the latchkey child next door. I loved the smell of her house, cigarettes and soap and the roses she always had on the kitchen table. She never questioned my obsession with comic books or told me to stop fiddling with my curls.

Instead, as the screen door banged shut, she'd mix me up a measure of coffee-milk to match her espresso and demand a full account of the escapades of my favorite superheroes. I don't know if it was the forbidden beverage, but I was fascinated by her cups. The tin enamel was speckled with blue, light as a feather, nothing like our hefty ceramic mugs at home. A couple times a week, out would come her camera, and she'd have me pose as Superman or Invisible Girl. Her big wooden bangles would clatter as she framed the picture, her cat-eye frames and white bun poking up above her Instamatic.

The best of my portraits joined a series of photos sitting on her mantel: people in wood-paneled rooms with dark windows, laughing and smoking over giant platters of meat and sausages; family members lined up at weddings; a few studio portraits. There were two girls who showed up in posed photographs at ages two, five, ten.

In the last picture of them, they were in their late teens. The older one had short hair and was wearing jeans and a T-shirt. She wasn't smiling. The younger was in a shapeless camelhair dress, black curls spilling down to her waist. She had an arm slung around her sister and was laughing at something off camera. The picture was old enough that the colors were starting to bleed.

I asked Monica about the girls one day. At eleven, the idea that they were her daughters but not living with her was strange. Her explanation was circuitous. We backtracked past my understanding of communism (the bad guys in my comic books) to ideas like injustice and distribution of resources. By the time Dad arrived to pick me up, I'd learned about political dissidents, mass graves, and the reason Monica was in Florida. The first daughter was probably dead "for thinking women should be able to work," she said in a voice that stayed strangely level. The second one had gone underground with her child. "If they make it out, I'm here for them." We didn't talk about her kids again. After she moved away, no one took pictures of me.

The only person I knew in California who used a camera for people instead of evidence was Jenna Lila Fifi, the *Daly Daily*'s crime, fashion, and society reporter. The occasional snapshot of me that ran in the paper (handing out pamphlets at a Just Say No event, or at the joint Post Office/Pigment Enforcement December food drive—"Services Summon Sustenance for Strapped Subjects") had been enough to make Mom search down a way to get the rag delivered all the way across the country in Tampa.

Across the collection of snapshots, Mom's hair shaded from bright red to platinum blond. Going gray had only widened the range of dyes she used. She'd never been a fan of our natural dark brown. I wondered how anybody could spend so much time on their hair. Wrestling my curls into a ponytail was plenty of effort for me. I inspected the latest addition. She was raising a large glass of merlot over a white linen tablecloth. Her ringlets were piled on top of her head, and her burnt orange blouse exposed plenty of cleavage. The bosom genes had definitely skipped me over.

I had something to do tonight. Might as well call when she couldn't rag me for being a homebody. I pulled the telephone off the counter, base and all, and grabbed a beer from the fridge. I took them both into the bathroom. The five-meter-long cord connecting the phone to the wall skittered behind me. I put the base on the toilet seat and settled into the water. Leaned over the tub's edge to reach the handset and dial. The answering machine picked up. Parents are always out when you ring, and always call back at the worst possible time.

I put the phone back and cracked open the beer. The warm water worked on the knots under my shoulder blades. Iowa would mean bigger cases, better crooks, a shot at the big time. But Edie's words wouldn't get out of my head. What would the fine print be? How would it look when Nobody Curtida from Daly City showed up to the big city, ready to ring in her fortieth birthday? I'd have to work ten times as hard to prove myself, and they could easily retire me after a year or two.

I imagined a farewell party with a bunch of jerks I'd been competing with for eighteen months. Was that better than ending my career in the Chief's office? Daly City was a backwater, but the Chief appreciated me. Tommy did as well. Whoop-de-do. I was two coworkers away from being a cat lady. At least Daly City's worst weather was fog. Winter at the academy in Evansville, Indiana, had been no fun at all.

I was counting my chickens before they'd hatched. The offer might never come down. But what other chance would I have to get out? I thought about the pigment victims in the padded room, the gobbledygook mix Doug couldn't make heads or tails of, the last mystery set of fingerprints. The Icarus case had been shaping up into something I wanted to solve.

In the faucet, a pinheaded fun house version of my body shifted. *Insubordination* was a word I'd always found ugly. I wouldn't go against the Chief telling me to let it go. I thought about the wrinkles around her smile. She thought she was protecting me—and if the Chief thought I needed protection, maybe I did. Maybe this was over my head. Maybe PSI was right to come in and take over.

The water had gone cold, my beer had gone warm, and my dark speculations had to be an aftereffect of the Gray. I got out of the tub and popped another Sunshine gelcap. Taking three pills in twenty-four hours was only recommended in extraordinary circumstances, but I damn well figured today was extraordinary. I wrapped myself in a bathrobe, drew the blinds in the bedroom, and fell into a dreamless sleep.

● ● ●

I woke up groggy two hours later. It was dark, I had to pee, and there was a charity gala to get to. Just the thought made my temples ache. I could use the Slate Gray hit as an excuse to stay home. But I'd already been out for half a day. Well, at least it had stopped raining. I pulled on my only dress. It was black and somebody complimented me on it once. It would do.

I wondered what Doug would wear. We'd gone shopping together for the farewell cookout at the end of our final year at the academy. He'd swiped listlessly through the mothball-scented blazers at the thrift shop. The one he picked looked fine to me, but I could tell he'd been hoping for something else. Until then I hadn't realized that style was important to him. Now, with his Boise salary and fancy Peugeot, I could bet he'd be all dolled up.

I didn't know how I was going to tell him about losing the Icarus case.

Sending the unidentifiable cocktail to PSI was the only reason I could come up with for why they'd notice Priscilla Kim's antics. What would my old friend think about me getting yanked from both active cases in the department in less than a week? In that light, the transfer to Iowa City seemed like a pipe dream.

I mostly brushed my hair, splashed water on my face. Broke out new bobby pins. I glanced at my dusty pumps but didn't have the willpower to force my feet into them. Wasn't like anyone would care. I was stiff after my nap, my calves tight. Worn out from running circles through my gloomy thoughts.

I found a tube of lipstick under the sink, left by Mom after her last visit. Put that on instead of my fancy footwear. Told myself my nerves were a left-over effect of the Gray. The good news was that I was starving, suggesting that it would finish wearing off soon. I counted back: approximately seven hours since my brush with the cardboard tube. Right on time. My stomach rumbled. I headed out in search of canapés and distraction.

CHAPTER 10

The Magenta Cares Foundation was a nonprofit set up to help the victims of the '89 Magenta Attack. The charity did what they could. They supported the cases that lived permanently in the psych ward at the hospital. Continually tried to get construction on the Magenta wing restarted to house more of the victims abandoned on the streets of San Francisco. Did weekly food drop-offs in Magenta territory. The organization was nominally run by a bunch of ladies-who-lunch, but the board members included Icarus's president and the head of R & D.

The gala was the foundation's annual fundraiser. Every year, everybody who was anybody showed up at the event. Folks with money bid on backstage passes to the upcoming Maxi del Mundo tour, autographed Daly City Fog soccer balls, and antique vases donated by Pimsley. Folks like those of us in Pigment Enforcement were required to attend in order to get our pictures in the social pages as evidence we cared about our community.

Fortunately, a waiter was depositing a tray of shrimp just inside the entrance to the ballroom at the Hotel La Estancia. Unfortunately, Jenna Lila Fifi and her camera stood guard at the door. The journalist's bleached blond perm was gelled into a weltering mass, the closeness of her dark eyes emphasized by thick lines of aubergine kohl. Her off-the-shoulder goldenrod shirt sported a letter-to-the-editor's worth of crocheted trim. It matched the color of her pedal pushers perfectly. Her feet were girded in ebony gladiator sandals with twelve-centimeter platforms.

"Agent Curtida! Fabulous boots! Love the fanny pack! Super retro, super *divina*!" Fifi visited Buenos Aires every few years and wasn't about to let anyone forget it. I calculated the distance to the shrimp platter. She stepped deftly between me and the crustaceans and stretched her thin lips chummily. "Tell me about this big Shamshine case Pigment Enforcement is about to break."

Even the press knew about Shamshine now? Thanks, Meekins. "I am unable to comment on any investigation that may be underway."

"You always say that. Couldn't you give me something? Sister to sister?"

"I'm sure the *Daly Daily* will be fine without my input. You've managed so far." She wasn't looking at me. I turned around to find Doug rushing up from my left. If it hadn't been for the spare test tube peeking out of his breast pocket, the forest-green suit he had on would have completely disguised his lab rat nature. Jenna Lila's lashes started going like fans. Doug pulled me away from her questions, but she got a photo of us before we made it to the door. "Prepare to be immortalized in the *Daly Daily* weekend edition," I said.

"*Daly Daily*. Has a kind of a ring," he said. In the seconds it had taken us to extricate ourselves from the journalist, the shrimp had been decimated. He served me one of the last four on a cocktail napkin. "What's this I hear about you getting painted with Slate Gray?"

I began reeling out the story. A few sentences in, I suggested we move on in search of other appetizers. He clearly didn't want me to stop my recount of the morning's events. I was too hungry to keep going. At least I figured that was it. The tale led inevitably to the Chief informing me I was off the case. I wasn't sure yet how I wanted to tell Doug that. A few extra minutes would give me time to figure it out.

We headed farther into the Olympic-pool-sized reception hall. The room was decked in hot pink balloons and bunting. Showy chandeliers shed too much light on the guests. The ratio of hors d'oeuvres to attendees was depressingly low. New this year were the life-sized cardboard cutouts of Ananda Ashaji scattered throughout the space. Ananda in a fuchsia sari with gold detailing, Ananda in a white sari with cerise detailing. Hand over her heart, hands pressed together as if in prayer. I CARE—YOU CARE—WE

CARE printed across her skirt and chest. Berdie, our resident gossipmonger, had said that the cult was cosponsoring the event. I hadn't realized the decor would be quite so emphatic about it.

At the far end of the room, a large banner emblazoned with MAGENTA CARES drooped above a stage. An aging band played mediocre tango. We moved past the blue-rinse brigade, swaying on the rented wooden floor. Shook hands with the mayor. Nodded at the captain of Dr. Trumbull's amateur softball team.

I'd just spotted sausage rolls emerging from the kitchen when the department's notary tangoed up with a woman dressed in a chintz sofa. "Curtida! The antique dealer—Pimsley—called this afternoon. I couldn't find you so he asked to be passed to Meekins—well, it was about the Shamshine case, which I know you're not on anymore, but I promised him I'd let you know as soon as I could," the notary said.

Pimsley ringing up the department's main line instead of my extension? Pimsley talking about Shamshine to Meekins? Pimsley telling *Berdie* he was calling about Shamshine? It was all out of character. The man didn't talk to anyone else in the department. He would've known I'd be at the auction, and he schmoozed his way through the event every year. Why couldn't he have waited to tell me here? The notary introduced us to his date, "One of the top scoop providers for gossip columns statewide," and she handed me a business card that read *Afflatus*. I was deciding whether to double back to my questions about the call or ask what the hell the *Afflatus* was scooping in Daly City when somebody knocked me into one of the cardboard cutouts of Ananda Ashaji.

I caught myself on Doug's shoulder before trampling the guru's effigy. Turned around to find the person who'd bumped me was none other than Dr. Gruber-Shaw, head of Icarus's R & D department. His baby blues swept the room and he marched off toward the stage. Seemed he had more important things on his mind than apologizing. Berdie's lady friend beetled after him, the notary on her tail. Well. I guessed that interaction answered my question about her interest in Daly City. Left me to swallow all my doubts about Pimsley's call. Along with the thought that if I'd been faster, I could've asked Gruber-Shaw about Priscilla Kim's sinister experimentation. Except, of course, I was off that case, too. There was a nasty lump of feelings sitting heavy on my sternum.

Doug asked if I was okay, helped me set Her Holiness back in place. "You know," he said, "with a name like Ananda Ashaji, I would've thought she'd be . . ."

"Less Swedish?" I'd gotten so used to associating the guru's name with her blond hair and blue eyes that I'd forgotten folks could be nonplussed by it. Strange that Doug hadn't looked up a picture of the woman leading the cult behind the Shamshine case he'd brought us. I was glad he didn't go back to asking about the Slate Gray bomb. A waiter with hot crab dip appeared near the bar. We made tracks and got in before the rest of the crowd had noticed its arrival, but the slimy mixture on the rock-hard melba toasts didn't do much to settle my stomach.

The Chief, decked out in her formal Twenty-Fivers uniform, was speaking with the bartender. She caught my eye and waved us over. Her gleaming patent-leather shoes made me regret my choice not to bother with my pumps. "Didn't think you'd make it tonight after handling that bomb without hazpig," she said.

"You went in bare-skinned?" Doug asked, then turned to the Chief. "She wasn't wearing protection?"

My boss raised her martini. "You're surprised?"

Lord. Just what I needed. Another reason for Doug to look at me funny. "I didn't expect there to be Slate Gray under the hood when I chased the victim to the car," I said.

A swarm of Argentines was elbowing its way up to the other end of the bar. "Louise!" A tall man, looming above the pale blue throng of dress regimentals, called out to the Chief. General Antonio Moretti, head of the base down in Palo Alto. He wore a crimson star on his lapel, insignia of his time as an embedded spy in the American army during the war. After our surrender, the Gauchos had traded the secrecy surrounding much of their espionage program for a chance to rub our noses in how far the wool had been pulled over our eyes. The janitor in charge of smuggling Deepest Blue–infused irises into President Reagan's bedchamber had gotten rich off a tell-all bestseller about the operation. Just two years ago, in 2007, he'd been appointed the Argentine ambassador in Miami.

The general was pushing through his underlings toward us. We'd have to make small talk. I didn't know where I'd find the energy. Our relationship with the force stationed down in Palo Alto was uncomfortable at best. Since our department dealt with psychopigment, the Argentines thought our business was their business. We generally disagreed with that assessment, but a backwater office like us causing a diplomatic headache with the superpower's military would get no sympathy from the feds. "Be polite," the Chief would always say when I complained. "Someday we might need their help." That statement was enough to make me reach for a phantom rosary.

The lump of feelings pulled on something in my back, stiffening up a muscle tired from dragging Nano's dead weight all those hours ago. I hadn't been looking forward to this event, but it was turning out to be one damp squib after another. The Chief finished off her martini, gave me a look, and cocked her head. *Get going*, clear as if she'd said it out loud. She was letting me off the hook. Didn't know if it was out of pity for the day I'd had or because my boots didn't pass muster.

I should've stayed. Proven my mettle, been diplomatic. Tonight, I just couldn't find the will. Told myself it was the empty stomach, the roller coaster of a day. Not just the tension of wondering what expression Doug would make when I told him I'd lost my second case in a week. *Aunt Amy always wore purple*, he'd said before he headed up to Boise. I'd figured he was just being nice to me. But PSI swooping in made me think the case would've been plenty interesting for my old friend's imaginary aunt. Now that it wasn't mine to solve. I spared a sad glance for the ravaged crab dip as we moved on.

"What did the Chief mean, 'are you surprised?'" Doug asked. "You do this regularly, running into pigment without proper protection?"

Jesus, Mary, and Joseph. "I did it *once*," I said. I'd gone into a Slate Gray manufactory without proper gear or backup ten days into my tenure as Meekins's mentor. I'd had to be carried straight to the psych ward. After a week under Trumbull's care, the Chief had given me an earful about the line between bravery and suicidal recklessness. "I learned my lesson after that lecture. It was more than a decade ago, but she still jokes about it sometimes."

"I feel like 'learning your lesson' would mean you'd stop throwing yourself into clouds of active pigment."

The thin cream of Daly City was still dribbling through the door, posing for Jenna Lila's camera with the self-importance of the small-town big time. "I'm still here, aren't I?"

"Sure," he said, "but someday you might not be."

I spotted Tommy cornering a waiter, effectively monopolizing an entire platter of miniquiches. I pointed it out to Doug and headed toward the cadet. Plato could follow or not. I figured what I did with my own brain was my concern. There was no reason to be talking about it at a charity gala. Berdie and his date were back on the dance floor, the woman's multihued kitten heels tracing number eights on the parquet. When he'd been hired, I'd assumed the notary was gay. Instead, he had a conveyor belt of girlfriends who rarely lasted a month. The bandleader reminded everyone that the silent auction would be open until ten. "Don't miss out on the Fresno spa getaway package!"

Doug politely took a single quiche from Tommy's new friend. I swiped four before the server extricated himself. I'd just ditched the Chief with General Moretti. No point pretending I was standing on ceremony after that. The appetizers tasted like salty chalk and were too small.

Her Holiness, in the flesh, sat on a nearby divan. Her entourage billowed around her. The waiter approached the troupe. Ashaji passed on the sustenance, but the crowd of faithful set to it like pigeons attacking a dropped donut. Even the turtlenecked bodyguard standing over her dove into the melee.

Ananda's blond hair fell in gentle curls around her surprisingly youthful face. Carefully calculated makeup de-emphasized her strong nose and made her blue eyes seem bigger. It must have been her first moment alone the whole night, but she showed no sign that the glad-handing had worn her down. She motioned to someone I couldn't see in the mass of hungry partiers. Trumbull, wearing a brown jacket cut exactly like her lab coat, emerged from the tumult. Why on earth would Ashaji be summoning the doctor? And why would Trumbull be at her beck and call?

I headed after the waiter, trying to look interested in the food. With my stomach rumbling, it wasn't a tough act. Doug and Tommy trailed behind me. We made it to the edge of the scrum surrounding the miniquiches. "How's Aunt Amy doing?" I asked my old friend, tilting my head at the two women sitting on the couch. I couldn't tell if he caught my drift, but Doug launched into a complicated description of the relationship between farming economics and the dollar's weakness against the peso. His voice was pitched low enough to let me eavesdrop, and his story gave me exactly the cover I needed.

"They're doing better now that they're not tied to chairs," Trumbull was saying. "They need rest and real psychological care, not calisthenics for made-up 'Hope receptors.'" Her Rs had gone hard, her frustration showing in a reversion to her Texas twang.

"I just wish you'd take a chance on us. Our team is doing cutting-edge work—they trained in Argentina." The guru clasped her fingers under her chin, gaze fixed on the psychiatrist.

Better now that they're not tied to chairs. Tommy elbowed me as Doug continued his pecuniary patter. They had to be talking about Jenny and Leonard, the seathuggers we'd found at Icarus. Why would Ananda Ashaji be worried about Priscilla Kim's victims? It couldn't just be because they were Pinkos. The woman's flock numbered in the hundreds of thousands, spread across the entire country. There must be a more substantial reason she'd be interested in their fate.

Tommy was doing a subtle shimmy, the world's smallest victory dance. Looked like I owed him a bottle of hot sauce for that bet that the Icarus and Shamshine cases were connected. Announcing we were off both of them would sure take the air out of him. I put the last of my four quiches into my mouth. It disintegrated rapidly into sandy crumbs. Would've been nice if we'd managed to get drinks at the bar before Moretti descended. The band had finished their first set, making way for the event's endless lineup of platitude-filled speeches.

The bodyguard reached down and squeezed Ashaji's shoulder, bicep straining against his pin-striped suit coat. She looked up and he nodded across the room to Gruber-Shaw, who was mounting the steps of the stage. Maybe he was something more than a hired hand, given that familiar gesture. The move didn't have the chemistry it would with a date. The Pinko leader stood, following her turtlenecked escort toward the stage. As they moved he turned his head, watching the Argentines at the bar. Same nose as Ashaji, just without the makeup. A relative, then. Not that it mattered to me, as Berdie had pointed out. Ashaji was Meekins's concern, not mine.

Over by the entrance, a drunk veteran yelled "Blowfish—go home!" at a bunch of Argentines as he was escorted out the door. Didn't hear that ugly wartime epithet very often anymore. The idea that our enemies had puffed themselves up to take on NATO and would deflate just as fast hadn't aged well.

Go home. I could take his advice. Go heat up a can of beans, crack open a beer. One of the soldiers launched a rude gesture after the Yankee. El Gordo Muñoz, Moretti's second-in-command, rounded up the aggrieved parties. A phone rang behind the bar. I could just go now. I'd greeted the Chief, shaken hands with the mayor. Jenna Lila had my photo with Doug. She could run it if she wanted in tomorrow's spread on the event. More than Meekins could say. I hadn't seen him anywhere. The phone rang again. If I left now, I'd have time to eat and take another bath before bed. Stop worrying about what to tell Doug and Tommy about the Icarus case until Monday.

I caught a flash of cyan houndstooth as Berdie took the phone from the bartender. Dr. Gruber-Shaw was at the podium, thanking everyone for coming out in support of Magenta Cares. "The foundation particularly wants to thank our partners, the Pinkos, for joining us at this pivotal moment. They've given us the opportunity to really make a change. We've got a big announcement coming up—something we've been working on for quite some time. We want to bring back hope for the victims of this awful attack—for their families—for all of us, really."

Bring back hope? That kind of rhetoric had fallen out of fashion decades ago. Berdie was picking his way through the cheering crowd as Ananda took the stage. Her Holiness said a bunch of empty phrases, stuff about "being ambitious enough to be compassionate," "daring enough to really hope." Nothing particularly elucidating about Gruber-Shaw's vague promise. The only specific Ashaji offered was that the full announcement would come at her book launch event. Weird choice to combine the two things.

Were they restarting the plan to build a secure facility for the fifty thousand victims still roaming the streets of San Francisco? That would fit the bill for "ambitious." If the Pinkos were going to bankroll that, Trumbull would have to play nice. But why wouldn't they just come out and say that was what they were doing? I couldn't help wondering about the timing of the cult's Magenta Cares involvement. It was clearly a PR stunt. Were they trying to preempt bad publicity in case their Shamshine activity came to light? In any case, the attendees were lapping the teaser up.

Berdie was suddenly next to me. "I hate to do this before the party really starts, but that was Meekins on the line. He and his cadet are holed up near the Magenta border. Pimsley's tip-off led them to the Shamshiners, and they need backup—right now."

CHAPTER 11

We sprinted to my car. Tommy, pulling the detachable siren from the trunk, ducked a puff of decaying Slate Gray that slipped out. The dark haze rose toward the sulfurous parking lot lights. In this final gaseous stage before it faded, it would be especially potent. I was glad I wasn't the one dodging it. I'd dealt with enough pigment for one day. Doug slid into the passenger seat and Tommy jumped into the back, bobbing excitedly. "I'm ready for the chase."

"In this piece of . . . engineering?" Doug asked.

"My car is an old hand at this sort of thing." The burger stains on the front seat were the only trophies I'd ever see from nights spent casing Daly City's underbelly.

"The stick shift comes out of the dashboard," Doug said, as if that proved something.

I told them they could get out and walk if they didn't like it. They were quiet after that. I wasn't really in the mood for lighthearted banter. KFOG advertised the late-night replay of *Painted Love*, its seven p.m. soap. Over the department two-way, Cynthia gave us a summary of the situation. They'd taken cover in a little pink house at Shakespeare and Rhine with a briefcase of Shamshine. The three pigment dealers were peppering the house with lead whenever they saw movement, and Meekins had taken a shot to the side. We could hear him grousing in the background, telling her it was a scratch that wasn't worth mentioning.

"Have you checked on Pimsley?" Tommy asked from the back seat. On the corner, a metallic shutter was grinding down the front of a Filipino video club. "If he's the one who set you on these guys—"

"We told him to lie low, and he said he'd be going underground," Cynthia said.

I wrapped up the conversation and stepped on the gas. The freeway loomed ahead. *GAUCHO GO HOME LONG LIVE RIGBY GOD BLESS AMERICA* was blazoned in spray paint across the overpass. A Knight of Liberty had been by and wanted us all to know it. I turned the siren volume up. We wove around the few cars still driving home from Friday-night outings. Tommy fidgeted in the back seat, staring out at the darkened storefronts.

"Pimsley's fine," I said.

"He left me a message this afternoon." Tommy's voice was flat. "On my home phone."

"Pimsley has your home number?" I passed a slow-going Cadillac driven by a blue-haired old lady on the right and zipped around a Lada on the left. Thought about how comfortable my cadet seemed at the antique shop. Pimsley's pursed lips as he described him as *a pearl*. Well. It wouldn't be the first time somebody with a cadet's salary had accepted the attention of a sugar daddy.

Tommy ignored my question and its implications. "At first I thought he'd misdialed, because he was talking about some chair that had just come in. But he never gets straight to the point, so I was waiting for . . . I don't know. An invitation to tea. He sounded on edge. At the top of the message, somebody came into the shop. Then he started talking fast." A cloud slipped over the moon. "I wonder if he was trying to tell me something."

"I wish Berdie had put him through to you when he called the office, instead of sending him on to Meekins." Meekins getting the scoop on me was the sour milk in the weak coffee that was today. The radio nattered quietly on. No point putting off the inevitable any longer. "We're off the Icarus case, by the way."

That stopped Tommy's fidgeting. "What?"

"PSI's taken it over."

Doug let out a sharp breath, nostrils flaring. I kept my eyes on the road. Didn't want to see what expression his face settled into. This far north, the grocery stores gave way to pawnshops and auto mechanics. Nobody who could avoid it took their chances this close to the Magenta border. The news wrapped up; the Hope Count and weather forecast came on. I turned left onto De Long and cut an immediate right onto Los Olivos. A dark car refused to get over. After nearly bumping its tail several times, it finally got the message and pulled up onto the sidewalk. As we passed, the driver—a sallow man with a face like a squeezed-out tube of toothpaste—gave us a nod. He was wearing sunglasses.

"You know," Doug said, looking out the window, "I'll support you. Whatever you do about the Icarus case." The dumb lump of feelings unknit a little bit, hearing him say that.

We turned onto Shakespeare. I killed the engine, coasting toward our target house, its pink paint gone gray in the moonlight. It was the last in a row of cookie-cutter cottages that some starry-eyed architect had imagined would bring about the American dream. Like all their siblings in Daly City, after the war the bungalows had been asked to hold too many orphaned cousins and widowed aunts, leading to sagging couches on brown front lawns and bunk beds pushed up against windows.

Our destination would have matched its neighbors perfectly if it hadn't been for the flash of gunfire and shattered glass. In front of us, pointing the wrong way down the street, a beat-up Fiat Topolino was idling with its windows down. Inside, three crooks peeked up at us over the wheel.

"Well," said Doug. "You're in luck. The Topolino's the only car that this baby *might* be able to catch."

I ignored him and yelled "Go!," turning the key and wailing down on the car. Tommy and Doug jumped out, pigment guns drawn. Over the PA system, I yelled "Psychopigment Enforcement! Surrender yourselves!"

The first Shamshiner leapt from the car. Ran like a bat out of hell. The second came out guns blazing and shot himself in the foot. He went down with a scream, clutching at his toes. Dropped his weapon—looked like a prewar pocket pistol, from back before the Gauchos torched the Second Amendment as part of our surrender. The third put the Fiat in reverse and burned rubber up toward Mission Street.

Doug hurtled after the runner at a speed that belied his thirty-nine years. Tommy disarmed and cuffed the lowlife clutching his foot in pain. Didn't even need to let off a shot. Probably a good thing for the department's budget. Our specialized guns were the only place we didn't cut corners. The bullets, coated in Cloud Gray Listlessness, didn't come cheap. The effect was worth every Benjamin. Even a scratch from one of them would sap the motivation of the most hardened hustler.

I tore off down the street after the driver of the Topolino. He backed onto Mission and then shot forward. We went on a nice joyride through the neighborhood. I got to see the light-rail station, the freeway, and a lovely pocket-sized park before he turned north, heading toward the San Francisco border. I pushed the Renault up onto my quarry's tail as we flashed past the pigment warning sign: NOW ENTERING MAGENTA TERRITORY. YOUR FEELINGS MAY NOT BE YOUR OWN.

It's impossible to anticipate the impact of driving into a ruined city. I'd never known San Francisco in its heyday, but I could see how far it had fallen. Once-grand Victorians gutted by fire, earthquakes, and mold watched like fallen angels over the pitted streets. The few left intact stood shamefaced for their sagging roofs and pitted facades. Garbage moldered in sweaty piles or crawled along the sidewalks baring its obscene entrails. I'd braced myself for the effect of the lingering pigment, but the wave of obsession hit me with surprising force. *Get him. Get him. Get him.* The speedometer needled up to sixty.

We raced through the rubble, jouncing across potholes and pigment spills going stale under the full moon. The Magenta bomb hadn't been the only pigment disaster in the city, just the biggest. My emotions went haywire. By the rubble of City College, the mix of the pink with an old Cerulean

Guilt spill had me dwelling on the memory of my father's face when he caught me using dirty words with a friend. His tone of voice, making my eight-year-old self think he'd never see me the same again. As we turned east onto the remains of Alemany, a Cobalt patch brought back the feeling of packing up Walter's office after his suicide.

Gaunt figures flickered in the night, lit by burning trash cans. Two people fought under a guttering streetlamp, the only sign of electricity for miles. Under everything, my focus throbbed, burned, oozed. *Get him. Get him. Get him.* A rusted cable car sagged in the crossroads at Mission and Dolores. I was overcome with a crying jag. The Fiat slowed—my mark was feeling the storm of sentiment, too. "Good," I sobbed at the steering wheel, stomping on the gas.

The gangster heard my motor roar. The mousy little car jumped forward, scurrying up Dolores. I wiped my eyes and shifted into a higher gear. We veered across the broken street, dodging the debris of dying palm trees. Our engines screamed with the effort of climbing the steep hill. We were headed straight toward Dolores Park—the epicenter of the Magenta Attack.

The longing in my stomach grew with every block. I imagined it as something unconnected to me. It was an old Agency technique Walter had taught me to separate myself from the effect of pigments. The yearning was a tiny creature with big teeth that just happened to be chewing on my rib cage.

The squawk of the radio broke my focus. It was Doug, checking in on me. "Getting close," I muttered. When I got the crook, I'd hold him so tight he'd have no idea what hit him. I'd fold him up into a little ball. Squish him so hard he'd fit into a can. I'd carry him around in my pocket, a demented jack-in-the-box.

"You doing okay there?"

I pushed the Magenta creature to one side of my mind. "Still on the Topolino's tail." I unclenched my teeth. "Twenty-Fifth and Dolores."

Through a crackle of static, I could hear Tommy and Meekins talking over each other as I crested the hill. "You're in *San Francisco*?" Doug said.

"Curtida, are you crazy? You suffered a pigment attack this morning! You're going to be much more susceptible—"

The Topolino slowed, pulling up to the corner of the park. "I've got him," I said, zooming toward the Fiat. "You're mine now, you little—*holy*—!"

Out of nowhere on the sidewalk, a pair of headlights appeared, floating in darkness. They pulled out into the street, the automobile they were attached to nothing but a stain on the night. The moon glinted off the cracked windows of the town house in the background. The door of the Topolino opened and the driver disappeared into the getaway car. The black vehicle came racing toward me.

"What's happening?" Doug asked. I yanked the wheel to the left, crashing over the center divider. "Ninja?"

A pale hand appeared out of the driver's-side window, holding a pigment dart gun. My breath caught. A finger settled on the trigger. As the barrel of the gun turned my way, my lizard brain took over. Pedal to the metal, I steered the car over the sidewalk. A fléchette whined behind my bumper and thudded into the crumbling Victorian town houses on the corner.

The dark pit of the park spread beneath me, littered with rubble and human refuse. The panorama of the wasted city opened in the distance, fires burning on the tops of abandoned skyscrapers in the festering remains of the Financial District. My poor Renault skidded down the park's dusty dunes, narrowly missing an overturned porta-potty and a small playground. She settled with a groan in a pile of dry palm fronds at the bottom of the hill.

I killed the engine, unbuckling my seat belt. "He's gone. Some sort of freakish getaway setup. They had a pigment gun, but they missed me. I'm going to check out the Topolino." *Get it*. The animal was gnawing on my insides.

Doug's voice cracked across the radio. "Why would you—the Magenta saturation in that area is strong enough to bend brains for another fifty years! You're not thinking straight!" I opened the door. A Topolino could be crushed into a can, too. "What did the pigment gun have in it? If they missed you, it'll be splattered all over—" Doug's voice faded behind me.

I began the steep hike up the hill toward the car. My feet beat the dusty ground, pounding out *get it, get it, get it*. My skirt swished around my thighs. A Topolino could be a jack-in-the-box. To my right, something rustled on the light-rail tracks at the edge of the park. The broken metal railings gleamed azure under the night sky. *Get it.* I kept moving. I'd make that Topolino mine. *Get it.* Make it mine and never let go. My steps seemed to thunder out my longing.

Screams yanked my attention from the car to the town house where the pigment had hit. A group of moaning people stumbled out, clutching their heads. Several fell to the ground. One howled at the moon. A balding man with a bushy beard broke away from the herd and ran down the hill. A sweatshirt girded his loins. Otherwise he was naked. I ducked behind a trash can. The creature in my abdomen shrank at this new threat.

The man passed me, sobbing "It's all gone—" He was far too close for comfort, heading straight toward my car. His back was streaked with Deepest Blue. Wisps of heavily colored fog stretched out in his wake, leaving an extended shadow in the moonlight. The gun must have been equipped with exploding darts: hollow ammunition filled with liquid pigment that injected some into the target and spewed the rest into the air. Exposed to atmosphere, the stuff would turn to gas within minutes. A drop on the skin could fry a neurotypical pretty bad. I had no idea what a full paint job would do to a Magenta victim.

Some remaining practical fragment of myself wrested control from the Magenta. I peered through the darkness at the man's uneven steps, praying that Doug didn't choose that moment to resume his lecture. I could just see myself stranded in Dolores Park with a Saigon Sally Screamer tweaking out in my car.

The bearded man abruptly swerved toward the light-rail track. I checked the group at the top of the hill—they hadn't noticed me. I booked it back to the Renault and locked the doors. With shaky hands, I turned the key in the ignition. I didn't realize I was holding my breath until the car started.

"Anybody there?" I said unsteadily to the radio. "The dart was laced with Deepest Blue."

"Are you okay?" Doug asked. A cat bolted across the park.

"It didn't touch me." A mess of feelings rolled over me like a bulldozer. My too-big bed. The paperwork on my desk. The taste of cold coffee. A dried-out pen in the back of a drawer. I grabbed the seat. A giant mug. Warm beer. The delicate flare of Doug's nostrils. The screech of feedback over a PA system.

"What's going on?"

I'd been alone a long, long time.

"Ninja. Talk to me."

Doug. I can talk to Doug. *Doug*, sighed the pigment congealing in my rib cage. "The Magenta . . ."

"I'm here." His voice wavered. "You say whatever you need to say. I just want you to get out of there."

So I poured my heart out to him as I drove back toward the Magenta border.

CHAPTER 12

I found myself talking about the spring of '84, around the time of Dad's death. If there was one thing those months taught me, it was that it's best to do your remembering alone. But with a brain painted pink, that lesson faded into the background.

The news about the loss of the USS *Teddy Roosevelt* had filtered down the halls at school. I was far from the only kid with family on the brand-new aircraft carrier. The ship had sunk off the coast of Cartagena. First they said everyone aboard was lost. Then they said several lifeboats had made it off, but those troops had been captured by the Argentines. No, the boats had been firebombed. No, they'd been seen headed toward Guantanamo. Nobody had a strong grasp of the geography of the thing. Everybody knew it was a disaster.

Mom, true to her pagan Hindu Catholicism, lit candles to Ganesh and San Gregorio Hernandez and said we didn't need to worry. Positive thinking was the core tenet of her patchwork belief system. She put it to good use with her friends: someone would call in tears, and she'd have them laughing and looking at the bright side in no time. People who weren't her daughter were continually telling me it must be great to have such a warm, understanding mother. I always thought her silver linings were more like polyester lamé than something you'd want on the dining room table. But this time I did try to take her advice to heart.

The days of waiting for word from the navy plodded by. Little things suddenly felt significant. I was growing out of last summer's swimsuits, the straps leaving angry red marks on my shoulders after practice. Somehow I decided that if I switched to my new suit it would mean Dad was dead. Same thing with sharpening pencils. Or replacing the worn-out rubber bands I used to pull my curls into my daily ponytail. I knew it was pretend, but I did it anyway. Wasn't any sillier than Mom's made-up religion.

Still, it didn't feel like a surprise when I saw the car pull up with two uniformed sailors. One of them had salt-and-pepper at his temples and walked with a hitch. The other was a skinny kid with thick glasses. We sat in the kitchen as they told me what they knew about Dad's death: last seen sprinting toward the admiral's bridge, which had been taken by enemy infiltrators with pigment. There was a tear in the screen at the top of the kitchen window. In a house he'd always kept shipshape, it seemed like the saddest thing. They stayed with me until Mom arrived from the store. "Missing in action," she said.

"Presumed dead, ma'am."

I didn't need to listen to the story again, so I went back to my room. I could hear Mom asking questions, the rise and fall of the soothing voice of the older soldier. A letter from Dad sat on my bedside table, under the bulletin board where I hung my swim medals. His last one, I figured now. I unfolded the thin sheet of paper. Read it over, yet again. *Tony was impressed with your freestyle speed (he made me write that, wouldn't stop pestering me). He's twenty, but you're more reliable. First thing he did when we got into* ▓▓▓▓▓▓ *was find the nearest bar. Guess his ribbing keeps the other men entertained, at least. Keep swimming. Stay useful.*

Dad had been one of the team's official timers, so he'd gone with me to every meet. He'd make me toast and a whole mess of eggs for breakfast. Load me and my gear into the truck and get me to wherever the race was with forty minutes to spare. On the way home we'd talk—my technique, how we'd all done. The wooden rosary would swing gently as he'd merge onto the freeway. Sometimes he'd accidentally let me in on the drama among officials. When that happened, his cheeks would go dark above his beard and he'd crank up his bootleg cassette of Hank Williams Jr. live in concert and sing along. When I was twelve and heartbroken about not getting onto the medley relay, he calmed me down. "You've got to look at the big picture. Understand how you're useful to the team." He pointed out that I was on the freestyle relay. My times meant I should've been on both. He said Coach must have a reason.

"Sure," I said. "It's because Sandra's mom brings the snacks to practice."

"Well, that sounds useful to the team." I asked why he never brought snacks. He rubbed his mustache and said, "Do your friends like sardines and pickles?" I rolled my eyes but he just smiled and kept driving.

If Mom called a handyman because Dad had been too busy at the store to swap out an O-ring or rehang a door, he would be redoing the job the following weekend, muttering *want something done right, gotta do it yourself.* I didn't ask him then how he aligned that sentiment with a philosophy of putting the team first. Now I'd never get the chance. I wondered if he'd known this would be the last time he'd write.

I'd started my letter back, but couldn't figure out what to say. I knew next to no one at Chamberlain High. One of the juniors on the team had gone to the same middle school as I had, but she always had a perfect manicure. There was no chance of a friendship there. The rest of my teammates looked at me like I was a spy because of my Spanish last name. Didn't seem right to complain about dumb things like that when Dad was at war. I put his letter and my half-finished response into the table drawer. Pulled down my medals and shoved them in there, too. Then I sat with the latest issue of my favorite comic open for a long while.

I was pretty sure I was feeling something. Whatever it was came through an ocean of static. It got dark. I sat in the rectangle of light cast by the streetlamp as the colors bled out of the comic book. Eventually the soldiers left. Mom moved around the kitchen. I heard the hiss of the pressure cooker, smelled beans. She knocked on my door and asked if I was coming out for dinner. I didn't say anything. When the house was still, I padded out to the kitchen and served myself some cold food from the pan. I ate and put myself to bed.

I couldn't sleep that night. Kept imagining Dad running toward enemy fire, clouds of Blue steaming out of the bridge as the giant ship listed and then slid under the water. I didn't know what the inside of an aircraft carrier looked like, and I could only picture the Blue as a cartoony cloud straight out of my comic books. Sometimes I saw him covering for his men, diverting fire so they could get on the lifeboat. Sometimes he was just running alone. Was that being useful? Or was the choice he'd made something else?

The candle to San Gregorio Hernandez was already burning when I got up. Coffee was burbling into the pot, eggs frying. The herbal supplement of the month was on its little saucer next to my plate. Mom seemed totally normal, even though Dad's name was in the list of casualties in the newspaper, *MIA Presumed Dead*. I couldn't understand how she was managing the brave face.

I figured it out a week later, when the real final letters from Dad arrived. I was the first one home. I sat with the envelopes at the kitchen table. There was one for Mom and one for me. Dad's cursive turned the "t" in the middle of our last name from spiky and angular to something gently rounded. I couldn't believe I got to see it one more time. I couldn't believe I'd never see it again.

The tear in the screen had gotten bigger. The static blocking my feelings was fading. It was a miserably muggy afternoon. My shorts were stuck to my thighs. I figured I ought to turn on the air conditioner, but I didn't move. I kept telling myself that I'd already known he was dead. But there was knowing and there was knowing.

Mom found me there when she got home from the store. It had rained some and then cleared up. My eyes hurt after crying so long, but I'd managed to keep my snot in a paper towel. She hung her keys from the hook and put her purse on the counter. Flipped on the overhead lamp. "What's the matter, sweetie?" I pointed at the letters. She picked up the aerogram addressed to her, opened it. Read it. Smiled when she got to the end. Sat down in the other chair, grabbed my hand. "Listen. He's not gone. I can feel it."

Seemed like the light dimmed. "He ran into enemy fire, Mom. On a Blued-over bridge. On a sinking ship."

"He's missing. But he'll find his way home." She moved a curl out of my face. "If there's one thing I know, it's that we've gotta have hope."

Anytime she saw me looking down after that, she'd remind me that she knew he was okay. It would've been annoying if it hadn't hurt so much. I discovered that pressing my tongue against my top molars held off tears pretty well, so I could usually make it to the bathroom before I started crying.

Walking to the bus stop after practice one afternoon, I found myself whistling one of the riffs off Dad's bootleg Hank Williams Jr. cassette and realized I'd forgotten some of the lyrics. *Now he's gone but the songs still linger* something something *played . . .* The country star had sung a bunch of his father's hits at the concert, so I didn't even know who'd written the song. I would've gone into Dad's pickup to get the album, but Mom kept the key on her ring. I didn't want to deal with her reaction if I asked for it. Eventually we'd have to use the truck for something and I'd get the cassette. Meanwhile, the words faded.

News from the fronts just got worse and worse. The Gauchos and their Chinese allies had captured Subic Bay in the Philippines. The bases in Bahrain got blitzed with the Blue. There were rumors of an impending invasion. Throughout it all, Mom lit her candles to Ganesh and San Gregorio Hernandez every morning. A parade of her friends traipsed through the living room. It was like a Pan-American conference in there most nights, immigrant neighbors from Bolivia and Chile and Uruguay drinking Mom's preferred Colombian coffee. They came in groups, supposedly to do patriotic activities like sorting used cans and packing up old newspapers. If their productivity was indicative of the home front's morale, the country was in a bad place. Plenty of them had lost someone. There were a lot of unfinished sentences, lots of staring off into space.

Mom moved among them, calmly upbeat. She always seemed to know what to say or when somebody needed a hand to hold. The women tended to leave looking happier than when they came. We didn't have a name for what the Global Hope Depletion Events had done yet, but even so Mom's hopefulness was conspicuous. I could've used a little of her soothing magic. The whole situation felt like too-tight jeans.

As a friendless fourteen-year-old in a city built for cars, though, there wasn't really anywhere else I could go. The days were an endless succession of things I just had to get through. At swim practice I wanted to be dry and in class. At school I wanted to be home. At home waiting for Mom, I wanted her to get back from the store. Once she arrived with her troupe of grieving widows, I wanted to be asleep in bed. Sleepless at night, I wanted it to be time to go to practice. The cycle repeated every morning.

Casseroles would come in and Mom would redistribute them to other families who'd lost somebody. "We don't need this," she'd say, rewrapping stroganoff in plastic wrap as chicken stew simmered on the stove. The only gift that survived the purge was a pot of Bolognese from our exiled Argentine neighbor, Monica. She came by while Mom was at the store and when I told her all the food was getting passed on she put her sauce straight into the freezer. Then she asked for an explanation about Mom's behavior. I didn't want to get into it but she was giving me her psychoanalyst stare. After I told her Mom thought Dad was coming back, she asked what I believed.

"He's dead." I hadn't said it out loud to anyone like that. My scalp itched. She said *mmm* and waited. With anybody else I would've heard *poor girl* in the silence. I figured Monica had seen too much to pity me. But she wasn't saying anything else. Finally I said, "It's tough but I'm fine."

"Sometimes," she said, "friends like to hear what's going on, instead of just 'I'm fine.'"

Cold comfort, given that I was living with Pollyanna. Monica gave me a tobacco-and-rose-scented hug on her way out the door. She left me the pot and the speckled mug I'd always had my coffee-milk in at her place. I was fourteen, so it didn't occur to me to ask why she was giving away her kitchen supplies. It felt different to have named Dad's death. For the first time in a while I was glad to have the house to myself. That afternoon, I went out to the garage for some of Dad's tools and tacked the torn screen in the kitchen window back up.

The Bolognese saved me a month later when the penny finally dropped for Mom. We were watching Rigby's Siege of Guantanamo address in our living room, with the windows open and the lights off. The crickets sang loud in the backyard. We were alone, for once. All patriotic packing events had been canceled at the news that the military was surrendering the Cuban stronghold.

The president detailed the "strategic thinking" that had led to the decision, the retreat effort that was finishing up. As he ran through the list of battles we'd lost, Mom got quiet. I was thinking that if they had Guantanamo they'd probably want Tampa, and wondering if this meant we were next on the list for a strafing. I figured she was worried about the same thing. But at the mention of Cartagena, she let out a noise like a strangled hiccup and put her hand over her mouth. I knew she was crying but didn't know what to do about it. I kept looking at the TV.

"He's not coming back. Is he." She said it like a statement, not a question. I just nodded. She got up and went straight to her bedroom. I was surprised that she'd really believed he was still alive. Out of all her talk about positivity I'd mined the hope that maybe she was faking.

Swim team kept practicing even through the bomb drills at school. Some of the other girls started carrying "recall envelopes" with them, with cues to jog their memories in case we got Blued over and forgot everything. I figured if I couldn't remember that Dad smelled like Old Spice and iron filings, I wouldn't want to know what I'd lost.

We all had dog tags printed out with our names and addresses and out-of-town emergency contacts. It was a real pain trying to figure out how to wear them in the pool, but state championships were coming up and we were all trying to act like everything was normal.

At home, things were dicey. Mom stayed in bed for days. When the ladies showed up for their patriotic meetings, I'd send them away saying she wasn't feeling well. The biggest busybody, Sylvia, wouldn't let me off the hook until I told her Mom'd figured out Dad was dead and needed some space. She did everything but pat me on the head. Booked it back to her car, itching to spread the news. Sure enough, they all left us alone for a while after that.

When Mom finally started coming out of her room, I never knew what to expect. She'd have crying fits at the store. I'd find her moaning in the backyard at three in the morning. I learned pretty quick which bottle had detergent and which had bleach in the laundry room, but groceries were a mystery. I wandered the aisles of the Kash n' Karry, aimless enough that one time the store manager checked me over for shoplifting. I knew Mom normally bought vegetables and meat and then somehow they became food. In my hands potatoes turned into charcoal coating the bottom of the pan. Chicken was always the wrong color. One time a teammate was talking about pasta night with her family and I made her explain how they cooked spaghetti. I got weird looks but it helped to know you needed to use water. The pity casseroles sure would've come in handy. I ate a lot of cereal and canned beans. Mom didn't eat much of anything.

I remembered Monica's Bolognese in the freezer the week before championships. It was a lucky break. My times had been off, and I figured it had to do with a diet based in cans or boxes. I cooked a big batch of macaroni and mixed it in with the sauce, then portioned it out in Tupperware to make sure it would last until the meet. It tasted real good.

Mom even had some. She asked about the team and managed to suggest that my slipping times were a good thing—something about the nerves making me swim twice as hard at the actual race. We were at the kitchen table. The outline of the rosebushes through the window was fading with the twilight, our reflections gradually taking over the glass. "Do you want me to come watch?" she asked.

She was wearing one of her embroidered muumuus. Before the news about Dad clicked, I'd never seen her in one after seven a.m. I imagined her in the bleachers, fuchsia cloth billowing around her. Cheering me on had always been Dad's domain. Seemed she'd really accepted that he was gone. Somehow that made it hurt more.

A piece of pasta fell from her fork onto her napkin. She went to the sink, put on her floral rubber gloves, scrubbed out the stain. It might be nice to have family there. Even in a muumuu. "Sure," I said.

On Tuesday, I woke up to the smell of *arepas* toasting on the stovetop. On Wednesday, there were peaches on the kitchen counter. Then, early Friday morning, the news came in about the fall of Port Arthur in Texas. It was the first time the Argentines occupied territory on the mainland. We already had plenty of abandoned cities and places that ate the faculties of any who set foot on them. They'd been lost, though, not taken. It felt different to know there were households of Americans under alien curfew. Foreign soldiers patrolling US streets.

Coach canceled afternoon practice, told us to get extra rest before Saturday's meet. I doubt anybody slept that night. The sound of traffic became approaching aircraft. Any misremembered date became a sign of Blue wafting down from the sky. Voices in the street became an invasion creeping on foot from the bay.

The next morning, Mom wouldn't get out of bed. I knocked, I yelled. Finally I ate five bowls of cereal and grabbed my bag. I'd finished the Bolognese the night before. The only food I had to take for lunch was a pack of Oreos. Told myself I must've been expecting this or I wouldn't have gotten up early enough to catch the bus. There weren't many people heading out at six thirty on a Saturday morning. I got the back row of seats to myself.

I did swim twice as hard. Helped the team win the 400-yard freestyle relay. Didn't realize that I'd been thinking Mom might have come late until I got out of the pool and didn't see her. I managed to smile in the team picture with the trophy. I caught a ride home with one of my teammate's families. Her mom got out to give me a hug in front of the house. "You swam really well today," she said. "Ricky would've been so proud." I couldn't get up the front walk fast enough. In the hallway, passing the wedding portrait, I had a moment where Dad's face over his rental tux looked like a stranger's.

Mom was at the stove. As I headed to the laundry room I saw she'd managed to put on jeans. I was the jittery kind of tired. I threw my towel in the dryer, changed out of my team sweats. The smell of toasting corn reminded me that five hours had passed since my all-sugar lunch, but I didn't feel like going to the kitchen. Then I heard the sizzle of hot dogs hitting the pan and my stomach let me know I didn't have a choice.

I stood in the doorway, watching her slide the sliced links around with a spatula. She beat a bowlful of eggs and threw them in. She must've gone grocery shopping, too. There hadn't been hot dogs in the house when I left in the morning. I could still feel the goggle imprints around my eyes. Mom piled the scramble on an *arepa*, put it on the table. Told me to eat while it was hot. Asked how the meet was.

I sat, took a bite. Made myself chew before taking the next one. No matter how I felt, I couldn't deny that her *arepa con salchicha* was a whole lot better than the version I sometimes paid for at the corner store. Something she did made the texture of the hot dog snap instead of smoosh. Through a full mouth, I told her the team had done pretty good. "I knew you girls would be great," she said. "Sorry I couldn't make it."

I swallowed. "Why couldn't you?"

She pulled on her gloves, slid the pan into the sink. "I don't expect you to understand," she said. "You're not grieving."

I put down my food, watched her back as she squeezed soap onto the sponge. I thought of all the times she'd patted the arms of a dozen widows, neighbors, and friends as I carried bags of scrap metal out to Sylvia's pickup. All the times I'd pressed my tongue up against my top molar, trying to save my tears for the bathroom to avoid another lecture about hope. A grease smear was thickening and turning yellow on my plate. I felt like I should've wanted to cry. A giant heaviness was all there was.

I went over to Monica's after it got dark that night. There were no lights on, but the kitchen door was unlocked. I let myself in, like I had every day when she used to babysit me. But this time, there was no red-and-white-checked tablecloth to greet me. No table. No chairs. Her pots and pans were gone. I walked through empty room after empty room. Dust outlines of the absent furniture marked the floors. There was still electricity. She hadn't been gone more than a billing cycle. But I thought back to her mug and pot on the shelves of our kitchen. She'd been planning her disappearance for months. I could see the logic in it—with the Gauchos occupying American soil, best not to stay in a town where everyone knew she was a subversive Argentine exile. But all the same I could've used someone that night who wanted to know more about how I was doing than *I'm fine*.

Mom got past her fits and grew into her role as war widow. The belated memorial for Dad was impeccable, with its three rifle volleys and folded flag. Her tears fell with precision during the reading from Ecclesiastes. I spent the whole morning organizing chairs and then reorganizing them as she prepped the house for the reception. My reward was a stiff neck, standing straight through the receiving line of Mom's friends. They each patted my arm and told me some anecdote about how handy Dad was. One of them told me to go ahead and cry, that this was no time to swallow my grief. I figured Mom had told them all about her unfeeling daughter.

That afternoon I took the key to the truck off Mom's ring. Didn't bother asking her, just went outside and pulled the tarp off. Inside, the wooden rosary had cracked from the heat. I could still smell a hint of Old Spice under the musty scent of the unused cab. I brushed dust off the fake wood veneer of the dashboard. In the glove box, the tapes were in the same neat stacks as always. *Live* was written in Dad's cursive on the side of the box I was looking for. The tapes above it clattered down as I pulled it out.

It was empty. The bootleg wasn't in the player. I looked in the cup holders, the pockets in the doors. Under the seats. Dad must have taken it with him, down to the bottom of Cartagena Bay. Why he'd leave the case behind I couldn't figure. I was sore under my shoulder blades. Tired from the long morning. Knew I should've been hungry, but sure didn't feel like eating. Through the kitchen window I could see Mom putting away the leftover sandwiches from the reception. I sat, clicking the clear plastic open and closed for a long while.

Monica's house got eaten by kudzu. Mom and her busybody friend founded the Tampa chapter of the Military Widows Association. The patriotic activities resumed, with my mother now staunchly stoic in the comfort she gave others. As surrender closed in, I carried the piles of newspaper and boxes of scrap metal to and from the house. Helped around the store when I had time. Kept swimming, like Dad had told me to. When it was just the two of us, Mom would occasionally smile wistfully and launch into some anecdote about how she would always find the strangest things in his pockets or how he had snorted milk through his nose trying to teach me to drink from a cup. Her stories were rarely from a time that I could recall, and when they were, the details were wrong.

Sometimes I wondered what he'd remembered as the ship went down. If he'd drowned before the Blue finished wiping his memories. Or if he'd gone into the deep with a clean slate, alone as could be.

I tried not to think about him too much. When I did, it was usually late at night, clicking the cassette case that just said *Live* open and closed. Sometimes I'd bring a tape in from the truck and listen to it while Mom was at the store, but I never did find the song from the bootleg whose lyrics I'd forgotten.

CHAPTER 13

My trip down memory lane lasted me all the way to the southern edge of the pigment's reach. The bungalows of Daly City rolled into view. I felt like a wrung-out dish towel.

"Your neighbor had a point about friends liking to hear what friends have gone through," Doug said. His voice was soft on the radio.

I turned onto San Jose Avenue. "I'll be there in a minute," I said.

Back at the little pink house, Doug and Tommy had two handcuffed crooks sitting on the front lawn. The briefcase of Shamshine was tucked under Doug's arm. He offered to drive so I could take a rest. I was pretty sure as soon as I stopped moving, my brain would start up again. I stayed at the wheel.

We packed everybody into the car and headed out. I recognized the shorter perp as Daisuke Jones, the black sheep son of the owner of Johnny's Garage. My next tune-up was going to be awkward. I'd seen the other's mug shot often enough for him to ring a bell. Tommy sat in the back, shoved between the two men.

We took a detour to the hospital to have the injured pigment dealer's foot looked at. Doug checked in with Meekins, who was getting stitched up down the hall. Came back and gave me a nod. Looked like the man's injury was actually a scratch, and nothing more serious.

At the department, my old friend disappeared into the lab with the brief-case of Shamshine. That stuff, at least, should be straightforward enough to process. I sent Tommy to put the captives in the holding cell while I prepared the interrogation room. Berdie had filled the place with file boxes, and it took some doing to figure out where to stash them.

I ferried cardboard up and down the halls. Here I was. Off the Icarus case. Officially on the Shamshine beat just as backup. But Meekins was busy getting sewn back together. For now, the case was in my hands. I could be the one to get the name of the Pinko members involved in this scheme. The adrenaline from the hurdy-gurdy my emotions had ground through in the last twelve hours had settled into a steady drumbeat of work to be done.

I checked the files for the men we'd captured. Daisuke Jones and Frederick Bentley had played every position on the pigment crime team: over the years, they'd been convicted for small-time dealing, cooking, and buying. No arrests in the last eighteen months, and both had come off parole.

I started out with Daisuke. When he'd come through before, Meekins had been the one in charge of handling him. The harsh light of the overhead lamp brought out the bags under Jones's eyes and made his bald scalp glisten. His faded green T-shirt had LONE STAR NOT SOUTHERN CROSS written over a map of Texas, a protest of Argentina's annexation of the former state.

He wasn't excited to talk, but it only took a little prodding to get him going. They'd bought the Shamshine from "the Pinkos." Taken it to Pimsley, figuring the old man's interest in exotic pigment would make him the ideal client. When he passed on the offer, they'd gone up to Daisuke's place on Shakespeare to plan their next move. Meekins had surprised them there. "We went bang out the back door when he showed up," Daisuke said. "Made it to the car before we realized we'd left the goods inside." Why exactly had they hung around to try to get them back? "We spent a lot of money on that damn briefcase." Told me the guy I'd chased up to San Francisco had been the one who shot my colleague. Took very little to get the man's name.

The choice to go to Pimsley was surprising. Shamshine had gotten rarer since Doug's team up in Boise knocked out the Yellowjackets, sure. But the man's clients prized the outright recherché, not the uncommon. If I'd wanted to unload a briefcase of the fake Yellow I would've gone looking for an unscrupulous pharmacist, not an antique dealer. I pressed Daisuke on the point, but got no better answer than "we knew him."

Finally, I circled back around to the source of the briefcase. Made some noises about cooperation. And just like that, he named the Pinko. Jedediah Perez was a midlevel Hopetroller. Often interfaced with the local media when Ashaji was out of town. He was a bigger fish than I'd expected to net this early on in the game.

So there it was, in half an hour. The smoking gun we'd been tromping around town looking for. I told Tommy to get on the paperwork for an arrest warrant for Mr. Perez and moved on to Frederick Bentley, knowing that Daisuke's info had come out far too easily.

Frederick had a face like warm beer. He was a larger man than his accomplice and the chair looked small underneath him. His injured foot stretched out awkwardly to the side, two inches of hairy ankle showing between his bandage and his sweatpants. I got his story. He talked ponderously, often pausing midsentence to rephrase. Sometimes the pauses lasted a little too long. Like he was remembering something someone had told him, instead of the events he'd lived through in the past couple hours. The details matched very neatly with Daisuke's telling all the way through. A lot neater than I liked.

I let him wind up his tale. The big breakthrough was looking like a dead end. I lined my pencils up on the table between us. Channeled the Chief's poker face. I could leave it be. Ignore the warning ticking against my ribs. And always wonder what I'd missed.

I looked at Frederick. "Daisuke gave me a whole lot of details. He'll be a fine witness on the stand, explaining how you shot Meekins. Now, I just need to know who coached you two in your story. Who put you up to this." He blinked several times, massaged the line on his wrists left by the handcuffs. I got the sense it was news that one of his bullets had found their mark. "You saw the state of my colleague, right?"

His foot twitched. "No."

If he hadn't been there when Meekins walked out of the little pink house on his own two feet, I could use that to my advantage. "He's getting treated. If he doesn't pull through . . . that'll be murder. If I were a prosecutor, I'd have a field day with this. Juries don't like cop killers. We're talking twenty-five to life."

I could see the air going out of him as he realized the full extent of the trouble he was in. He said I had no proof he fired the gun. I told him I knew what I knew. He said he didn't have to tell me anything. Of course not, I agreed. "But if you cooperate, we can try to minimize your exposure. You don't play ball now, they're gonna throw the book at you."

We went around in circles like that for a while. I pulled the old "just giving you a chance to tell your side of the story" line. Told him this was his opportunity to stay out of the defendant's chair. He reached up to wipe the sweat off his forehead and I caught a glimpse of a tattoo on the inside of his upper arm. Face of a baby, *BENJAMIN* inked onto a banner underneath. I asked how old his kid was now. That startled him. "What, you thought we didn't know?" I asked. "How old?"

"Five," he said. Explained why he'd gotten so clean the past couple years.

"You kick a ball around with him, yeah?" He was real still. I put my elbows on the table. "All his soccer games. Prom. High school graduation. You're not going to be there. But soon enough, there'll be another man in his mom's life. And you've gotta know. Your kid will call him Dad."

He covered his eyes with a hand. I pushed a box of tissues at him. The bulb overhead swayed as a truck rumbled down the highway. We sat in the quiet like that for a while. I waited until I could tell he couldn't stand the silence, then waited some more before breaking it. "I need you to help me so I can help you. Who put you two up to this?"

A spot of blood was spreading through the dressing over his toes. He shook his head.

"Whoever they are, they're using you, Frederick." I took his chin in my hand, gently turned his face to look at me. His stubble ran with sweat. "They're using you, and I want to find out why. Just give me a name."

The man licked his lips. "Big Skinny." He pulled back. Crossed his arms, shoulders hunching like a little boy on a time-out. Waiting for worse. "That's all I can say."

CHAPTER 14

I went back to Daisuke to see if the name Big Skinny would shake anything else out of him. Got a whole load of bluster: Frederick was on painkillers, I couldn't take anything he said seriously, it was unethical to question him, et cetera and so forth. Between the lines, I could feel the man's fear. He was terrified that his accomplice had let the name slip.

I was real curious about who this absurdly cognomened crook might be. I'd never heard of him. I doubted that he was local. The whole scheme was significantly more complex than Daly City's usual pigment crime. And significantly more baffling. What, precisely, would be accomplished by handing Pigment Enforcement two petty crooks? And why would our offenders have gone along with it?

Tommy and I took the two miscreants to the county jail for booking. Doug was still mired under his pile of psychospectrometer readouts in the lab. Anybody else would have called a cab hours ago. Plato was probably running his sixth iteration of tests to check his results. We swung back to the department to haul him out before he pulled an all-nighter.

Tommy'd miraculously gotten the warrant for Jedediah Perez, the Pinko provider, so we stopped by his place. There was no sign of the man. Doug and the cadet waited in the Renault as I checked in with a neighbor drinking a late-night beer on the stoop. He'd seen our suspect packing his car earlier in the evening. "Even had the terrarium with the turtles in the back seat!" The man cackled, gap-toothed grin gleaming in the yellow light from the streetlamps. Jedediah had known to skip town.

From there we headed back to the Hotel La Estancia to pick up Tommy's and Doug's cars. The drive was quiet, streets silent and dark. On the radio, *Painted Love* started up. Felt like a lifetime ago we'd listened to the advertisement for it, heading up toward Shakespeare. The soap's mad scientist schemed over a soundtrack of rolling thunder. "*I'll precipitate the emotional fog of their love into pigment,*" Dr. Eldritch said. "*Then run it through my psychospectrometer for analysis to find the recipe*"—the sound of the machine whirring to life—"*and synthesize it, churning out gallons of true love! Then I can make her mine, once and for all!*" The requisite evil laughter played.

It skipped some of the key steps in creating a synthetic emotion from captured miasma, but for the purposes of a soap it was remarkably accurate. Of course, no one had ever managed to capture love in the wild, let alone synthesize it. It was too complicated a feeling.

The gray at Doug's temples caught the moonlight. My mind kept trying to make sense of the night's events and coming up short. It was no use drumming up theories on a pigment-addled brain. The traffic lights blinked yellow as we passed. They'd given up at this late hour. Tommy had called Pimsley from the department and gotten no answer. I could tell that the silence was getting to him.

Back at the charity auction, the caterers were loading out. Tommy's and Doug's cars were among a stalwart few left at Hotel La Estancia. My cadet unfolded from the back seat, heading off to find a pay phone to try Pimsley again. My arms on the wheel were heavy with exhaustion, but I couldn't shake the sense that the events of the past twenty-four hours revealed some sort of pattern. Sleep was going to be a long way off. "*All these years you've loved me—why did you never say so?*" asked the heroine of *Painted Love*.

"*I was afraid you thought me too flighty,*" said the hero.

"These radio soaps are so dumb," I said. Plato sat silent next to me. I turned toward my old friend, wishing my car had headrests. "Any chance I could interest you in a beer? I need to wind down." The leftover Magenta was squeezing the muscles in my sternum. I focused on the image of it as an ugly critter. Probably a hairless rodent. It chanted *Doug* to the rhythm of my heartbeat. I sure didn't need to be left alone with that, pigment-containment mind techniques be damned.

An elderly matron, the last of the hard-core charity partiers, cha-chaed across the parking lot. "A beer sounds good," Doug said. The woman's partner followed at a more stately pace, walker clinking on the pavement.

We crossed the street to La Continental, an all-night pizzeria that moved in with the Argentines. Fake plants decorated the joint. Empanadas sweated under heat lamps on the counter. The red leather booth had crumbs in the cracks and a thin film of grease on the table. The Dead Sentiments' "Hang Myself on the End of Your Rope" came tinnily through blown-out speakers. It wasn't a place you'd want to be when the Hope Count dropped.

We ordered a large pie and a liter of Quilmes. A gaggle of partygoers from La Estancia stood at the counter, their cummerbunds and high heels at odds with the discolored linoleum. The Filipina waitress brought us little dishes of salty snacks with our beer. The imported brew was cold and thin. *Big Skinny*. The bartender at Sharlene's had described a lean and hungry-looking man with Priscilla Kim's party. We drank in silence. Water condensed on the tall bottle's blue-and-white label and ran down onto the table. I thought of the hatchet-faced man who wouldn't let us pass as we drove toward the house on Shakespeare. Daisuke's palpable fear.

When Doug spoke, though, it wasn't about today's developments. "I had no idea your mom took your dad's death so hard. I mean, once she got it. When I visited, she was all sunshine."

"That was years later."

"You're pretty good at keeping everything bottled up, too. You get that from her?"

Mom keeping everything bottled up? If she was a bottle, she was a Coke someone had shaken up in the back of a hot car. If anyone, it had been Dad who kept stuff on lockdown. The waitress setting down our pizza gave me a reason not to answer. Steam tickled my nose, promising roasted red peppers and ham. My stomach rumbled. I grabbed a slice. The dough was gummy, the cheese chewy. It was heaven.

I started talking, running through the list of unusual occurrences from the endless day I'd been through. The bomb's sneaky details. Crooks going into San Francisco. The spooky getaway car. This unknown Big Skinny, a crime boss I'd never heard of when I knew the serious players in the local pigment racket on sight. "It seems like whoever this guy is, he set Frederick and Daisuke up so we could catch them with the Shamshine. What I can't figure out is—why?"

Doug took off his spectacles. Cleaned them on his cuff. "I think I may have part of the answer to that. You know how I said it wasn't really the Shamshine that brought me down here?" He picked an olive off his pizza, lowered his voice. "For the past couple years, a stronger form of Slate Gray Ennui has been showing up across the country. It's high-end—not the sort of thing you can buy on a street corner. Don't know how long it's been around. The difference is only noticeable if you've got an R & D op running samples of everything you're bringing in. I got interested when a colleague of mine passed me some of this stuff she'd taken off a mobster's daughter. The kind of girl where even her pigment is boutique. My colleague Gina brings it to me, and it's in—I kid you not—one of those vials from the early '90s that looks like a perfume bottle."

That had been a short-lived trend. The dealers had realized pretty fast that flashy bottles made it easier to track the source. Getting ahold of the fancy flasks now took some legwork. Doug served me another slice. "Gina's all excited, has even included an attachment on this pigment's particularities in the report she's filed. Next thing I know—she's gone. Transferred out to the boonies near Old Pittsburgh. I start asking around, and she's not the only R & D op who's looked at this special paint and then disappeared. Some of them don't just get transferred to the sticks.

"But the last time we talk before she goes—we don't know it's the last time, she's just bursting with what she's figured out, she has to tell someone—she says that she's run a bunch of tests and she's pinpointed the origin of all of this stuff. And it's coming from Daly City."

The muscle I'd tweaked dragging Nano sent a lance of pain down my spine. A national scourge spreading from Daly City and I'd had no idea. An echo of this morning's Gray whispered *useless*. I took the last swallow of my beer. Managed to keep my voice steady as I asked, "Why doesn't the department down here know about this local special?"

"No R & D ops. Nobody to go to the conventions and hear rumors. Nobody to ask questions. May also be part of why whoever's manufacturing this chose this town as a base." Couldn't tell if it was the whole truth or if he was just letting me down easy. I asked how Shamshine came into it as he topped up my glass. "I'm getting there. What Gina told me had me itching to come down. But I knew I needed a cover story. So when we picked up a Daly City Pinko in Boise carrying fake Sunshine, I figured it was my chance.

"I may have ginned up the report a little. Made it seem like the pigment was more industrial than it was. Normally, we don't go in unless there are signs a manufactory's already up and running, and this stuff . . . Shamshine's not an easy recipe to make. You need a pretty advanced lab, a good hand at mixing. This batch had clearly been put together by an amateur.

"I sent the report off to Old Jim and the Chief. Got the sign-off to come down here. Didn't expect that your whole department would get shifted onto something that I was pretty sure was a wild-goose chase. I was thinking one agent, tops. Hoping it would be you."

The Magenta tried to start up with acrobatics at that statement and got tangled in the damp cobwebs of the fading Slate Gray. "One agent is half our department, Doug. And this is the biggest case we've ever seen."

"Yeah. Coming from Boise, I just didn't realize . . ." Told myself I was too worn out to get mad at his presumption. The fact that he came from a department of hundreds was barely an excuse. He shifted his empty glass like he knew what was going through my head. "I had to make a snap decision. I should've thought it through a little more."

"Well, it wasn't a wild-goose chase. We have a briefcase of Shamshine the Pinkos made."

"That's the thing. They didn't make it." He looked up at the poster of

Maxi del Mundo hanging on the wall, poured the rest of the liter bottle of Quilmes into our cups. "I ran the isotopes while you were talking to the crooks. It's all Boise. Everything in there is straight Yellowjacket, manufactured sometime last year before we busted the cartel. And given what you're saying about Daisuke and Frederick being set up . . . somebody is trying to frame the Pinkos. Keep the department focused on them."

"You're saying the Shamshine is a blind."

"I mean, I don't *know* that it is. But Meekins stomps around asking everybody and their grandmother if they've heard about the Pinkos' new recipe for two weeks, and then someone throws a briefcase of the stuff at us. Sure looks funny."

"But if it's a blind—what's it hiding?"

He spread his hands helplessly. "That's what I don't know. Maybe I triggered something in my search for the source of the Gray. Maybe you were getting too close to something with Icarus. Maybe it's something else entirely. You're the local. You're the field agent. I'm going to need your help to figure this out." Seemed he didn't share the Gray's disdain for my efficacy. He ran his knuckles across the sharp line of his jaw, emphasized by the late-night dusting of his stubble. "Would you think about it? Taking this on with me?"

Wasn't clear exactly what he was asking for. Did I really want to know the details? Him and me, working together. Didn't like the way that made my toes tingle. It had been our teenage dream. My other teenage dreams had gotten me stuck in Daly City.

It seemed like the last twenty years had taught me nothing. "You know the answer to that, Plato," I said. I finished off a scrap of crust. "You're the partner I've always wanted."

Something I'd seen before flitted behind his gaze. "Same here." He held up the remains of his beer. "I've missed you, Ninja. Cheers."

I didn't trust myself to say more than "Cheers" back.

"I've still got some unwinding to do," he said. "You sure you couldn't take something stronger than this watered-down piss? There's bourbon at home."

"I'm recovering from pigment-induced puberty. I unwind any more than this and I'll start telling you about my teenage obsession with that guy." I pointed at the poster of Maxi. "You go find a bar, pick up some nice girl. Get me some stories." I dropped $40,000 on the table to cover my meal.

"How many times do I have to tell you I'm on a break?" He reached out and squeezed my hand, then looked away. "Rest up good, now."

I went home and fell asleep without taking off my boots.

CHAPTER 15

I woke to the phone squealing by the bathtub. My head was twice its normal size. My boots chafed my feet. Every muscle in my body complained in time to the telephone's ring. I'd made it to bed, at least. I stumbled through the kitchen. The clock on the microwave read 7:42. It had been after three a.m. when I got home. The bathroom door squeaked. I turned on the light, winced, turned it off again. Sat on the toilet. Fumbled with the receiver and picked up.

Of course it was my mother. I told her it wasn't even eight yet. "Shoot. I forgot the time difference. The shift to Buenos Aires Standard is so confusing," she said. She'd been using that excuse since the change had been made official five years ago. "I had to call, though—wanted to hear all about Meekins's big night."

I couldn't imagine what she was talking about. "The charity auction?" Had I mentioned that when I left her a message yesterday?

"The Shamshine bust! It's all over the paper. Let me see—'Crazy crooks captured in cuckoo canary con. Five felons fought furiously by fearless enforcement Agent Meekins; four flasked.'"

Jenna Lila Fifi already had the story. Even if she got the number of arrests wrong. I bent down to undo my laces. I had blisters on my toes and a mysterious bruise on my upper arm from yesterday's high jinks. I wished, yet again, that the Pinko Temple in Tampa hadn't enabled delivery of our local rag to my mother's doorstep. The throbbing at my temples told me I needed Sunshine and aspirin stat. I dug through the pile of herbal supplements for something that would have an actual effect and pointed out that "flasked" wasn't in the thesaurus next to "apprehended." Mom told me not to be so negative. "She's a hoot of a writer."

My progenitor went on to read me most of the article. According to Jenna Lila Fifi, the perpetrators had "devastated" the residential neighborhood while defending a dump truck of Shamshine. She'd given Meekins credit for all the arrests, with the only mention of my chase into Magenta territory that a single criminal "cut Curtida's clutches." A separate headline nominated my colleague for the Agent of the Year Award. Mom was thrilled with the news.

She'd been taken with Meekins ever since her first glimpse of his clean-cut headshot and speculated regularly about how his stick-straight hair might combine with my curls for optimal locks on our offspring. I chose not to tell her that the award was something Jenna Lila had invented in the last twenty-four hours.

Even Doug's picture with me in the society pages couldn't knock her off the Meekins horse, although she did comment on how my old friend had gone from "little squirt to tall drink of water." It was probably for the best that she stuck with her usual tune. The leftover Magenta was busy enough flickering *Doug Doug Doug* around my rib cage as it was. Would've expected it to fade by now. Seemed like the idea that he and I would be working together had added fuel to that dumb fire.

I tried to dodge the onslaught of dating advice by asking about Mom's color analysis image consultancy. She gave me a quick anecdote about how the discovery of Pumpkin Solace had all the Autumns coming back in for updates—I thought, yet again, that the people who'd exploited the advent of pigments to add a psych profile to the old "doing your colors" tradition were moneymaking geniuses—but then it was back to questions about *our wounded hero*. It wasn't till I brought up the NFL that I got a topic to stick. News that the league was in talks for the first Super Bowl since the war had her all aflutter. "The Dolphins can't help but win," she said.

Never mind that those same talks happened every spring and fell apart every fall. "The Global Hope Depletion Events still haven't touched you, have they?" I asked.

"A little optimism never hurt anyone," she responded.

Should've seen that response coming. There'd been a while where we didn't talk. She'd sold Dad's store in dollars instead of pesos, ignoring the fact that it was common sense to do real estate transactions in a currency that didn't devalue. I'd spent plenty of my childhood playing with nuts and bolts behind the counter, before Monica showed up and took on babysitting duties. The news that she was selling may have made me madder than necessary. I stopped picking up the phone anytime it might have been her. Took me a couple years to relent, and by that point she was in dire enough straits that she needed money from me to get through each month. After conversations like this, I wondered if I shouldn't have stuck to my guns.

There was no point in trying to get back to sleep. I made a thermos of coffee and took it to the tub. The water was too hot, too cold, the bath had shrunk since yesterday. The one functional light bulb over the mirror burned out with a buzz as I tried to get comfortable. No better way to start the weekend than a call from Mom. After fifteen minutes of trying to convince myself I wasn't bothered by what she'd said, I pulled the plug.

● ● ●

Out on the sidewalk, the sun was shining cheerily. It was the kind of day my mother would tell me to take advantage of. Call a friend. Get some vitamin D. I wondered if getting transferred to Iowa would make her appreciate my dedication to my job more. I squinted my way to the corner store. Grabbed two boxes of mac 'n' cheese. Ashaji's first memoir sat on the magazine rack. I added it to my basket. "Great choice," the cashier said from behind the register. "Just heard a speech of hers on the radio about how the Gauchos have shown that democracy is outdated. Talking about Roman theocracies. Really interesting stuff."

I'd never thought Her Holiness was interested in theories of government. Tucked that tidbit away as I collected the change for my $50,000 bill. Back in my living room, I pulled Pimsley's chair under the bare light bulb and opened the memoir. Had a nice view of my punching bag and the jury-rigged laundry line hanging out of the window of the apartment across the street. Told myself I'd picked up the paperback only to distract myself from mom's nagging comments. Not because I'd overheard Lady Pinko interrogating Trumbull about the victims from Icarus. That I wasn't thinking about the gray area in Doug's request to work together. If the Shamshine were a blind to take our focus away from Icarus, the two of us looking behind the curtain would technically be insubordination. Well, I'd cross that bridge when I got to it. Meanwhile, I could be curious in my free time.

Ashaji had written her first memoir, *Finding Hope, Finding Grace*, during the period of reform following the mysterious demise of the cult's cofounder Pinky. The book covered Her Holiness's spiritual background, awakening, and her version of the group's founding. The whole thing was written in sentences breathless enough to give Jenna Lila Fifi a run for her money.

Daughter of evangelical Christians, Margaret Larsen received divine inspiration at twenty while hospitalized for a nervous breakdown. She emerged from the psych ward to find the only surviving member of her family serving thirty years for running guns for the nascent Knights of Liberty. With nothing tying her to the States, Margareta followed the seraphic call all the way to India. There she met her guru, changed her name, and developed the peculiar blend of self-help, Hinduism, and Christian theology that became the basis for the Pinkos.

Whole chunks of the book were dedicated to Ashaji's argument that the Hope Depletion Events were mass hallucinations. In some ways she was correct; any widespread emotional phenomenon would have been called a "mass hallucination" in the era before the discovery of pigments. But the level of Hope was something you felt in your bones, like the temperature or the humidity. During the Second Global Hope Depletion Event in '91, I'd seen our cowboy professor Tadlock sobbing on the ground between the barns on campus at the academy. I'd been feeling so bad I hadn't even gloated. If it could take down an image-obsessed jerk like him, there was—literally—no hope for the rest of us. Ashaji had never met a logical fallacy she couldn't deploy to counter that obvious fact, though. Seemed her plan was to wear down those unmoved by her rhetoric through sheer repetition.

The only mention of Pinky was in the book's dedication. *Finding Hope, Finding Grace* had been published in 1990. Less than a year after the co-founder's death, Ashaji was rewriting the cult's history. Her hunger for power was already as clear as her sky-colored eyes. And now, she was going around suggesting the States should become a theocracy.

It took me all weekend to get through Ashaji's memoir. The sore muscles from Friday stiffened on Saturday and ached by Sunday. After closing the paperback, I put on my gloves to loosen up with the punching bag. See if I could sweat away the ominous feeling the book had given me.

In the rhythm of kicking and hitting, I thought about Pimsley. He'd told Cynthia he was going underground. I wondered where he'd gone off to. Wasn't the first time he'd taken himself out of play. In '92, he'd been MIA for almost three months. Even Walter'd started to get quiet when his name came up. But he'd reappeared just as suddenly as he'd vanished, sporting a sly grin and the closest thing to a tan I'd ever seen on his alabaster skin.

He'd pulled a similar move on a few occasions in the decade and a half since. Each disappearance coincided with major upheavals in the underworld. The kinds of events that even the papers noticed. The first had been around the time the People's Pigment Movement spiked the confetti at the Dixiecrat National Convention with Bull's Blood Rage and the Knights of Liberty retaliated by assassinating the New Whigs' presidential candidate.

Now that I thought about it, he hadn't pulled one of his Houdini tricks since the lead-up to the PPM going legal and starting their own political party. Things had been real nasty in those months, with clashes between the guerrillas and paramilitary Knights making daily headlines. During the thickest of the fighting, the criminal element in town had gone eerily quiet, and Pimsley had gone on a sudden vacation. The antique dealer's choice to recede from view now made me think something big was afoot, whether or not it had anything to do with Doug's quest for the Daly City Gray.

Plato called that night, asked if I wanted to go catch the Feelies. They were a group of sad sacks who wandered the country, promising displays of emotion untainted by pigment. When they weren't on tour, they lived sheltered lives in rural areas, far from the epicenters of Gaucho hits. In urban environments, they spent most of their time in hazpig gear. For a small fee you could get into the big top; with some palm-greasing you could get a private show. I told him I was surprised that he was into sentimental claptrap like that.

"It's good to remember that some feelings come from inside. Not from pigment," he said. Spoken like an upstanding member of Magenta Addicts Anonymous. I declined. I figured Cynthia must've been busy. It was nice that he'd thought of me, anyway.

● ● ●

Monday morning, Daly City was once again swathed in its lovely blanket of mist. I'd gotten nine and a half hours of sleep. My pot of coffee came out just right, and the tub stayed at the perfect temperature for twenty minutes. I swung by Penelope Crotty's place on the way to my office, dropped off a sack of groceries, and took out the trash. Walking into the Agency, I nodded to Meekins.

"Nice write-up in the *Daily*. How's the wounded hero?"

His hair was parted even more severely than usual, emphasizing his hollow cheeks and pale skin. He didn't turn at my greeting. "I have no idea where Jenna Lila got the story." Quite the welcome. Then again, his ramrod-straight back suggested he had stitches in his side he didn't want to pull. I headed grinning to my office.

We'd rubbed each other wrong since the day he showed up. On the heels of Walter's death, I had no interest in being in charge of someone. Everything about Meekins made me wary: his fixation on rules, his slicked-down hair, his wood-paneled Buick. He could have been the kid brother of the loudest Knight of Liberty in my class at the academy. What I gathered of his family history matched that possibility too closely for comfort. He'd been born into money. In fourth grade, he'd been evacuated to the home of poorer relations out in the boonies. None too soon; the Argentines dropped eighteen tons of Deepest Blue on Denver a week later. It was exactly the profile the Knights of Liberty targeted with their rhetoric about the "good old days."

The Chief had been sharpening her daily supply of pencils when I'd gone to her with my suspicions. I'd tried to explain that the academy was a hot-bed for the right-wing group. How Meekins seemed like the kind of kid they would have recruited before Wednesday of orientation week. "He even drives an American car!" I said. "Who buys domestic? They're too unreliable."

She didn't look up from the shavings on her desk. "Curtida." Her voice was low. "I know all about the Knights of Liberty. I wouldn't have one within a kilometer of this department. Stop inventing stories about your cadet and start training him."

It stung, but I did the best I could to set aside my doubts and teach Meekins what I'd learned from Walter. I was completely unsuccessful in that regard, and now my fellow agent approached fieldwork like a bull carrying a checklist in a china shop. But on days like today, our ribbing felt right. Sure, we'd never see eye to eye. But it gave a certain frisson to the daily grind.

The day ticked by in paperwork. On the way to the department meeting, I got a whiff of old shoe passing the notary's door. The inside of Berdie's cubbyhole was webbed with mushrooms strung on threads, funny-shaped slices and a few that looked like tiny brains. I sped up before he could start espousing the virtues of his haul at me.

The Chief assigned me to "tracking down Big Skinny," which meant I was in some way back on the Shamshine case. I was itching to go look over the little pink house on Shakespeare and Rhine since I hadn't gotten the chance on Friday night. Figured I had an excuse now. I was looking up the details when the phone rang. I picked up.

"This is Agent Cassius, calling from the Pigment Enforcement Agency in Iowa City."

Iowa City. Actually calling. I leaned back in my chair. "Sir. Agent Curtida here."

"We've heard some very good things about you, out here in Iowa." Cassius's voice was a gravelly drawl, like the grandpa who'd sneak you a beer at your sixteenth birthday. "There's a contract in the mail, with a bus ticket out here. We'll be ready for you next week."

"That's . . . very sudden. I'm honored," I added quickly. I should have had more than my egg salad sandwich for lunch. My head felt about to float away.

"There'll be a significant pay raise. We take care of our pack out here in Iowa, not like sweet old Louise. And you get in on our pension action. You do a week here, you can spend the rest of your life drinking mojitos out of coconuts in the Bahamas or tangoing the streets of Buenos Aires."

"Sir." The dig against the Chief stung. Was this a transfer or a timeshare offer? "What's the average retirement age?"

"We've managed to push it lower than any other office in the country. All our agents are off the street by their fortieth birthday."

"With all due respect, I'm thirty-nine. You're saying I'd be in Iowa for about two months."

"We could make it less."

The phone cord was twisted around my wrist. "What if I wanted to work longer?" There was a spider in the corner, spinning away.

"No need to play the Goody Two-shoes with me. You're a hard worker, but you know when to let well enough alone. Certain cases, for example." Icarus. My throat went dry. "Think of this offer as a reward for your good behavior." On the last two words, his voice sank out of grandfather territory and into something darker, redolent of concrete cells and rusty iron.

"Is that a threat?" The words were out of my mouth before I thought them through.

Cassius barked a short, mirthless laugh. "A threat? Why on earth would you think that, Agent Curtida? Just because we know where you live, where you work, your weakness for hot sauce, and that you have no social life?"

"Who are you, my mother?"

"No," Cassius said levelly, "we don't ever forget the time difference."

The line went dead.

CHAPTER 16

All these years, I'd wanted to be up against crooks worth their salt. Well, here they were, with a warrant to wiretap my home line. Bright side was I'd made enough trouble they tried to buy me off. Nice milestone, right before my fortieth.

The stale longing for a cigarette sucked on my lungs. I'd kicked the habit because Walter was trying to. His wife, Linda, had been after him to stop for years, and for her fiftieth birthday he threw out his last pack. Or at least, what was supposed to be the last one. His first couple tries went nowhere. Finally he asked me not to light up around him. "For a bit," he said. "Till I get this under control."

I spent the weekend at the local library reading up on quitting tactics and showed up at the office the next Monday with a jumbo-sized pack of peppermints. The first wave of hyperinflation had slashed the value of my salary in half, so I figured it was as good a time as any to go cold turkey. We finished that bag of candy in a week. We were both grumpy as all get-out, but we managed to avoid any knockdown fights.

At the one-month mark, Walter presented me with a lumpy gift-wrapped package as a thank-you for quitting with him. Inside was a sapphire fanny pack made out of ripstop fabric. "I figured you could use it for all the little things that get lost in your day bag. Linda helped pick it out." His fingers tapped against each other. Until then, I hadn't noticed the thin line of clean white at the base of his nicotine-stained nails. "Do you . . . do you like it?" he asked.

I'd never seen Walter uncertain. My collar felt real tight and my hands were hot. I just nodded, and then he smiled that smile that reminded me so much of Dad. But when I tried to imagine my father asking Mom for help finding a present for one of the cashier girls at the store, I couldn't.

I thought the pack was ugly as sin, but went ahead and loaded it up with my small daily essentials. A miniflashlight, pocketknife, badge, coffee grounds, antacids, tampons. Soon enough I was leaving the day bag at home. I'd worn the thing for more than a decade before the zipper gave out. The woman who'd made the original had left town and never been heard from again. Apparently she'd gone to search for a sister in the dangerous wilds of what used to be San Diego. I couldn't find one I liked. Finally the Chief bought me the replacement I was still using, mostly to shut me up.

My phone's off-hook beep brought me back to the present. The Xerox machine was making the squeak that meant it was about to jam again. Down the hall, Berdie had trapped Cynthia in a retelling of his foraging adventures with his men's group. "During the gratitude ceremony I just— melted—into the earth, the connection was so incredible . . ." Sounded like he may have eaten the wrong kind of mushrooms. The Chief and her office here had its foibles, but no one was outright crooked. Wouldn't be anybody in Iowa City buying me a fanny pack, that much was clear.

I tried to focus on the information about the little pink house as my mind buzzed around in circles. 521 Shakespeare, deed in the name of Sandy Fink Jones. She'd be the wife of Daisuke, the first Shamshiner we'd pulled in on Friday night. She was currently doing time in Nevada. Her mug shot couldn't hold my attention. Sure seemed like the Shamshine was a blind meant to keep me from thinking about the Icarus case.

There was one man who would be able to shed some light on this mess. It was possible the crooks had gone to Pimsley in order to reach me specifically. Our mutually beneficial relationship wasn't the sort of thing either of us advertised, but my car was up by his shop a whole lot more than Meekins's. Normally when Pimsley disappeared I just let him be. Normally I didn't ask him questions. But nothing about this case was normal. This time, I had to try to find him.

I called Tommy over to ask about the message the antique dealer had left him on Friday. Turned out he'd brought the tape to work. Seemed he was antsy about his friend's absence. We commandeered Berdie's answering machine and watched the wheels of the minicassette unspool through the plastic window.

The recording was as strange as Tommy had made it sound. "Hello, dear boy. Just calling to check in about tomorrow. Quite looking forward to—" The bell on the shop's door tinkled faintly in the background. The salesman's voice tightened. "Just calling about that chair—the Louis XIV you were looking for the mate for—well, it'll be in . . ." A pause. A low voice rumbled. "I'll be right with you, gentlemen. Darling, I found a copy of that old Bootsie Poots single you were looking for—you know, la-dum-dee-dee duh-duh-dee-dee—" He sang a tune, static shuddering down the line. "The name escapes me in, mmm, present circumstances, but the one that you said was *very important*. I hope you'll appreciate it . . . Lovely to see you in here the other day, here's *hoping* that you'll swing by soon—I very much *hope* to see you again. Yes, I do *hope* to see you—" With a loud beep, the message came to an end.

Tommy and I stared at each other across the notary's arsenal of stamps. The wrinkled toadstools from Berdie's weekend excursion hung over our heads, swaying gently as they dried. I said, "Let's start with the shop."

In the car, Maxi del Mundo's "*Suspiros de esmeralda*" was playing on KFOG. I'd taped the schmaltzy tune off the radio the summer before heading off to the academy. Listened to it alone in the house while Mom played tennis, or on repeat on my Walkman while organizing the shelves in the store. Keeping them in order had been my job since I'd learned to read. Dad had set me up checking the ones I could see from my seven-year-old height. *Go make yourself useful*, he'd say. That sure rubbed Mom the wrong way. *She can't even keep her dresser tidy and you've got her on duty?*

I never managed to explain the feeling the task gave me. I knew where everything in my dresser was. But stacking the yellow and blue boxes of screws so their corners lined up perfectly, double-checking the labels, taking mislaid inventory back to its rightful spot—knowing Dad would nod at me as he walked by—it all gave me a visceral sense of satisfaction. I took on more shelves as I got taller, until I got too busy with swim team to spend hours puttering around the store after school.

The summer after graduating from Chamberlain High, I was back there every day. When Maxi sang about wanting to listen to my emerald sighs, I'd feel like I couldn't breathe. I'd stop arranging the light bulbs and lean my forehead against the metal supports, imagining something I couldn't really picture. Mom caught me doing that one day and asked if I was sick. I told her I was fine and kept working. Figured I could make myself useful even while mooning over a Gaucho pop star.

And now I had the offer I'd always dreamed of, on the condition of letting sleeping dogs lie. Make myself useless here so I could go make myself useless in Iowa. I imagined filling out paperwork for two months. *While mooning over Doug*, the Magenta whispered. If slapping wrists in Daly City made me itchy, twiddling my thumbs in the Corn Belt would give me hives. A neon sign in the window of a Filipino restaurant flashed on and off. Tommy was quiet in the passenger seat, looking out the window. I wondered what he thought we would find.

Whatever it was, it couldn't have been as bad as the reality. Through the splintered remains of the front door, Pimsley's store was unrecognizable. It had never been an organized spot, but before, the chaos had been consoling— the disarray of opulence, prosperity, the overflow of a treasure chest. Now, it looked like a bombed-out bramble patch. A cracked table leg jutted from a tear in a loveseat's upholstery. Chairs had been lobbed, topsy-turvy, across the space; the shards of broken Tiffany lampshades rubbed up against splinters of fine wood and scattered coins. A rolltop desk tilted forlornly on its two remaining legs. Windows had been smashed, and the musty residue of Friday's rainstorm festered in the fibers of Persian carpets.

I tugged on the strap of my fanny pack and started in. Tommy hung back in the doorway. "We have to look through this," I said. He crossed his arms, shoulders curving over his heart, and stepped inside.

Everything had been ransacked. A close relation of my absurd chair leaned out of a dustbin, frame askew. Tommy had been right to be on edge about the man's silence. The antiques may have been Pimsley's blind, but he'd genuinely loved them. Peering into the wreckage felt like undressing a corpse. Scattered near the middle of the space were a bunch of rationing and home gardening flyers from 1983, *Plant Your Patriotism!* printed in Day-Glo green brush font. A 1982 article assuring the public that President Reagan didn't have Alzheimer's peeked out from under it. Across the room, Tommy made small, pained noises as he went through the wreckage.

A card catalog that could have come out of my high school library hunkered behind the cash register. I didn't recognize it. The drawers lolled out like rectangular tongues. Scraps of fabric were caught in the handles: Pimsley had kept it hidden behind a forest-green velvet curtain. My back knotted up. The time for not looking in dark corners had passed. This had to be the central switchboard of his illicit vintage-pigment business.

The old man organized his wares by age, instead of the standard ROYGBIV setup. Each compartment held a rack covering a yearlong period since the invention of Deepest Blue in '79, leaving two rows at the bottom empty for future use. Inside each one was a tiny rainbow of ancient pigments.

The cabinet was the only place where the vandals had operated with care. We were lucky they had. There were plenty of vials in there capable of turning minds to mashed potatoes if they spilled. Tommy let out a yelp. I looked over. He was holding a porcelain handle, painted with delicate blue flowers. "The Spode tea service," he said huskily. I went back to the cabinet.

As expected, the collection skewed heavily toward vintage pigments. Pimsley had prototypes from as far back as '83, some of which had never seen the market. He had a vial of Magenta from the batch that had taken out San Francisco. Nothing made in the last five years. Doug would drool over this treasure trove. I couldn't just walk away from it now that I'd seen it. I was still Pigment Enforcement, no matter what threats Agent Cassius made. I sent a silent apology out into the ether. Even though I knew that if Pimsley was okay he wouldn't be able to forgive me for taking the cabinet in.

The crooks had been looking for something, but nothing seemed to be missing. Strange. On the street, some of these old colors would go for a hefty sum. I flipped through the years in their neatly organized boxes, trying to work out what the perpetrators were after. Tommy lined up the head of a china figurine, a torn first edition of *Kiss of the Spider Woman*, and a lace gold-rush-era bonnet on top of a footstool with a slashed cushion. After going through the pigment collection a couple times, I figured that if Pimsley kept the key to the record player in a secret compartment, he'd probably hide his most valuable pigments in the same way. It would be just like him to use his restoration skills to incorporate Victorian tricks into an unassuming library castoff.

I ran my fingers along the edges of the case. A subtle indentation on the right side gave under my nail. I pressed until I heard a click. Nineteen ninety-seven, in the middle of the cabinet, sprang open. But this time it showed me more than the experimental vials of Cool Teal and Bull's Blood Rage. The tray of the year's greatest pigment breakthroughs popped up at an angle, revealing the drawer's false bottom. Underneath were three velvet-lined slots. One contained a run-of-the-mill sample of Blackberry Purple. One was empty. The third one contained a sparkling vial labeled *Lavender Hope*.

I pried it gently from its case. If it was what Pimsley's handwriting said it was, it was an incredible find. Could it be synthetic? Almost everything else in the collection came from early experiments at manufacturing the emotions. The ability to manufacture Hope would turn the world upside down. It would probably help with many forms of psychopigment damage, from the holes left by Deepest Blue to the atrophied emotional range of neurotypicals fried by too much Slate Gray or Magenta. Folks would be lining up around the block for their daily pill. Hell, Sunshine was a decent Band-Aid for Depressives, but Lavender Hope might actually alter our way of functioning. Who we were.

But even as I thought it, I had to dismiss the possibility. If someone had been synthesizing Hope, they'd be out crowing about it before the stopper was snug in the first test tube. This had to be captured emotion, like the single vial of Hope kept under lock and key at the Lausanne Laboratory for Official Emotions. Sifted out of the air someplace where people were feeling hopeful. Which meant it would have been caught at some point before the Fourth Global Hope Depletion. But keeping something like this secret for so long would be a big undertaking. How had it ended up in Pimsley's hands?

I held it up to the light. Still wasn't sure I could believe it. I was inclined to trust the antique dealer, though. The pigment was exactly the shade published as Lavender in the Psychopigment Guide, our holy bible at the Agency. To determine if it was authentic, Doug would have to run a comparison with the published formula. I'd never seen anything like it.

The empty niche between the Hope and the Blackberry was baffling. There were no synthesizable pigments classified between those two. But it was the only place where something looked like it had been removed. Pimsley had gotten mixed up in something strange. Something dark. Something big.

I slid the vial back into its slot and called Tommy to show him what I'd found. "Just a second," he said feebly. He was crouched over something in the back of the store, shoulders shaking hard. I headed to him. He held the shattered remains of the Bootsie Poots record Pimsley had been playing the last time we came in. "We should have come earlier." Tommy rubbed fast at his whole face, like he was trying to wake his skin up. When he took his hands away, his cheeks were mottled red and pink. "You should've listened to me."

I didn't know where to look. A wheat penny glinted next to my boot. I fished a tissue out of my fanny pack. He didn't take it. "The carpets under the window are wet. All this happened before Friday's rainstorm," I said as gently as I could.

"If he's not dead, seeing the place like this will kill him. It took—so many years of work, to build this—space—it was . . ." His voice caught. "What he thought the world *could* be. Taking the past—all of it, the best and the worst, and sorting through to find the beautiful. Not forgetting where we came from, but choosing what to take with us into tomorrow. And they just came in and wiped it all away."

More philosophical than I'd ever heard Pimsley be. He'd said Tommy's youth made him feel idealistic. What did I know. I'd found comfort among the baubles and phonographs. In my experience, that sort of feeling was always constructed, whether through pigment or the old-fashioned way. And the antiquarian unfailingly worked all angles.

Walter had first walked me into the shop my third month on the beat. He'd told me I could trust the salesman about anything except the value of his wares. Pimsley had just grinned that mole smile of his. When my mentor passed, Pimsley rustled up an orchid. It was the first time I'd seen one since I'd left Florida. It sat on my desk until the purple flower wilted and fell into my typewriter.

A cold draft blew through the shop's broken doorway. I stood up and pointed at the record. "We'll file that as evidence. You can keep it." Tommy didn't say anything, but he gathered the pieces.

We took a few more pictures to document the disorder. *Quilombo*, the Argentines would call it. Trust them to have the best word for "mess." The cash register was untouched. Whoever'd done this wasn't even pretending it was a normal burglary. I radioed Doug to come pick up Pimsley's catalog of unusual pigments. My cadet's movements were stiff but determined as he systematically packed up our equipment. He wasn't going to be a kid much longer. Probably already wasn't. He straightened, his mouth set in a line. "Where next?"

"I'd say to Pimsley's place, but nobody's ever been able to track that down."

His lips spread. "Nobody except me, then."

● ● ●

Tommy directed me over the Magenta border, on a winding journey into the depths of the ruined city. We squeezed through a blackberry-choked underpass, crossed streets gone to gravel, drove down a half-flooded streetcar tunnel. We emerged on the slope of a rolling hill covered in dilapidated Victorians.

Tommy pointed me to the third house on the right. The tan paint was peeling, revealing layers of ancient colors beneath: pale blue, lilac, dirty yellow. The boards in the windows glowered at the potholes in the street. *SAIGON SALLIES!!!* had been graffitied by a Magenta victim in large letters across the first floor. Someone more lucid had scrawled *GAUCHO GO HOME GOD BLESS AMERICA* underneath, with a rough sketch of the hooded Lady Liberty next to it. A small patch of dirt sprouted weeds between broken bottles.

So Pimsley lived in San Francisco. That explained why no one had ever been able to find his hideout—people just didn't take those kinds of risks. Well, normal people didn't. I thought about the vial of Lavender. Old Pimsley may have been playing a deeper game than I'd wanted to admit.

The disrepair cut off at the threshold of the basement garage. The concrete floor was cleaner than most diner counters in Daly City. Tommy's key ring jingled as he unlocked the door. Their fling had sure flung far. No wonder he'd been so broken up. His back was rigidly straight as he walked into the house.

The place itself was everything one would expect of Pimsley, the walls covered with imported rugs and tapestries, the light fixtures ranging from wagon-wheel chandeliers to stained-glass sconces. Art deco champagne flutes gleamed smugly next to a dour pair of antique muskets. I picked up a tiny glass figurine of a cat. It was the same comforting jumble that his shop had always had.

Tommy'd been over on Saturday night, searching for his beau. Everything had been in its place then. Everything was in its place now. The living room was impeccable, as was the kitchen. Dozens of tailored suits in Pimsley's trademark shade of gray hung sharply in his closet. Just one set of empty hangers. A bottle of blood thinners sat next to his toothbrush. I found my cadet staring at the locks on the front door. Only three deadbolts had been latched. The fourth, a heavy-duty monster that made the others look like toys, wasn't in use. "He only locks that one when he goes on a trip," Tommy said.

Medication left behind, nothing taken out of the closet, and an unswung bolt: the man hadn't come around to pack a bag or shut the house. "You were right," I said. "This doesn't look good."

My concession didn't do much to cheer Tommy up. He wordlessly put on the kettle, then held out a hand for the old-fashioned coffee grounds from my fanny pack. If he wanted a moment to process, I wouldn't hold it against him. I sat at the kitchen table as he pulled out a drip coffee machine from a filigreed cabinet, followed by a pair of green frosted glass cups with matching saucers. I wondered where the salesman was pulling his electricity from.

Once our beverages had cooled enough to drink and Tommy's face had faded back into its usual coloring, I brought up the hidden compartment with its empty slot between Lavender Hope and Blackberry Purple. "Seems like that was what whoever ransacked the shop was after."

He ran his finger over the rim of the saucer. Stood, went out of the room. Returned a moment later carrying a small cut-glass vial filled with a strange mauve pigment. "It was on the table when I was here Saturday," he said. "I put it away in Pimsley's Pigment Containment holder. Figured it was better to have it somewhere safe if I didn't know what it was."

He was all business. None of his usual chipper flair. Well, I didn't feel particularly peppy, either. I picked up the tube. The mauve liquid flickered dully under the light of the hanging Tiffany lamp. If I hadn't just seen the Lavender in the cabinet back at the shop, I would've sworn this was Hope. As it was, I could tell it was a little bit darker. A little bit closer to Blackberry. The perfect fit for the empty slot in the secret drawer.

Tommy had found what the crooks had been looking for.

CHAPTER 17

Tommy tucked the vial into our high-tech hideaway in the crack behind the cushion in the passenger seat then sat, fingers tapping out a sharp beat on the dashboard. I took us out toward the Bay on our way back south. The radio cut in and out as we passed the remains of Union Square and the gap-toothed skyline of the old financial district. "You and Pimsley," I said. "You're pretty close."

His fingers slowed. "He listens to me. Really listens. At first, I thought it was an act . . . you know how it is." The rat-a-tat on the dashboard started up again.

He needed to talk so I said, "I don't."

"With . . . with normal guys, if I have an excess of . . . if I get too maudlin. Or something. I just go off and do a Purge. But the first time I was going to do that—we had a date that night and I called to cancel, said I'd been feeling off, I'm going to go take care of it with a little pigment—and he said no. Come talk. And I did, figuring, well, I could always do the Purge on Sunday. But after we talked . . . I didn't feel like I needed it anymore." Tommy watched the pavement rattle by. The radio crackled into life, announcing that the Daly City Fog had made it to the quarterfinals of the Copa Libertadores. He started up again. "When I started listening to him. Well. It's different. He says things like 'when you're my age' and 'if you want a future, you have to imagine yourself there.' And then one day I realized I *was* imagining myself in my fifties. And I'd never met anyone else like me who'd made it to forty."

Plenty of agents didn't last long past retirement. Plenty of Depressives took an early exit. But it was no secret that the gay ones tended to get swept offstage even sooner. More likely to get hit by AIDS. Less likely to get approved for treatment by the foreign service of a dictatorship that had become ever more focused on "protecting the family." I hadn't paid it much mind. The soccer team's coach rattled off a canned statement about sportsmanship and being the first Americans at this level since the States joined Conmebol. "I'm sorry," I said. "I hadn't thought . . . but it sounds like he's good for you."

"He is." Tommy's voice was rough.

I extricated a packet of tissues from my fanny pack. Handed them over. He blew his nose. This wasn't my wheelhouse. It was one thing to listen to a blubbering witness, say *there there* and other meaningless things. It was different with someone I actually knew. Someone I cared about. I thought about my mother, comforting all her widowed friends. She'd done a whole lot of arm-patting. I tried that, reaching over to lay my hand on Tommy's tricep. That made him cry harder. I left it there, figuring it was better for him to let it out in my car instead of the office. The wool of his navy peacoat was rough on my palm. Kept my eye on the road. If Pimsley didn't turn up soon, my cadet was going to be a good candidate for one of Icarus's Grief Processing Journeys.

It was awkward trying to drive like that. I was glad I'd chosen to go through the flatter part of the ruined city. Fewer gear shifts. His sobs slowly eased. I still couldn't think of what to say. Everything seemed wrong or dumb. The best I could dredge up was, "We'll keep looking, Tommy. We'll keep looking until we find him."

He was quiet for a while. Then "*I thought I'd found happiness,*" he sang as we crossed the Magenta border. "*But all I've got is something like hope.*" I hadn't realized how sad the words were.

Eucalyptus swayed along John Daly Boulevard. I didn't want to take Tommy back to the department like this. Well, we were only a couple blocks from the little pink house where we'd caught the Shamshiners on Shakespeare. It had been part of my plan for the day before Agent Cassius derailed everything with his phone call. Told Tommy I'd let him have some time alone in the car while I looked the place over.

But when we got there, the "Pigment Enforcement Line—Do Not Cross" tape we'd left around the scene had been trampled by workers installing new windows. They were overseen by a lady in a housedress that could've come out of my grandmother's closet. A tinny boom box played old country music. I got out of the car and flashed my badge, asking what they were doing to the crime scene.

The woman turned toward me, jutting out what passed for her chin. "Your so-called crime scene is my so-called *house*!" A broad forehead loomed over remarkably compact features, like her face had been carved in wax and left out in the hot sun. Her hair was dyed bright red. The style was all the rage in Buenos Aires, I'd heard. I told her the house belonged to Daisuke Jones's wife, Sandy, glad I'd done my due diligence before coming out here. "His *wife*? That asshole—" Her eyes went wide, and just like that, the harridan act dropped and she started crying like a little girl.

Just what I needed. An afternoon full of tears. Tommy got out of the car to see what was going on. Looked like his curiosity had overcome his sadness for now. I could tell from his silence that it was only temporary. I got the woman inside with some more arm-patting and the suggestion of tea.

The kitchen was set off from the living room by a bar-high counter. An industrial-sized standing freezer, the kind that had been popular in the late '80s during the meat shortages, overshadowed a turquoise fridge from the '70s. The linoleum was scuffed and dirty. Several of the cabinets had bullet holes.

Tommy put on water. The redhead and I settled ourselves in the living room. Her name was Lucinda Snooker. She'd spent the weekend at her sister's in Gilroy and had come back to find her home taped off and her man in custody. "He'd turned over a new leaf. I'd thought. It was that Pinko support group that got him on the straight and narrow."

Tommy went still in the kitchen. I needed no prompting to follow up on that statement. "What Pinko support group?"

She looked at me over her tissue like I'd just asked if Texas was still part of the Union. "The ones everyone goes to. For folks caring for Magenta victims." The next meeting was about to start over at Ella and Frederick Bentley's place on Bepler Street.

I met Tommy's gaze. Jenny Crotty's calendar had listed a meeting on Bepler for tonight. For the same support group where Priscilla Kim had recruited her and the other guinea pigs from Icarus. And now, according to Lucinda, both Daisuke and Frederick Bentley were affiliated. I wanted to ask more questions but she'd started crying again because apparently the freezer wouldn't open; those worthless jerks had shot up the windows and left the door frozen shut—

Tommy had gone pale. It was a little thing, but I'd overlooked too much in the quest for Pimsley to leave stones unturned. I made my way into the small kitchen and shook the appliance. Nothing rattled inside. I asked if there was a hair dryer in the place. Lucinda bawled her way to the bathroom and back, but she produced the desired tool. I frowned at Tommy. "You want to step out for a minute?"

He shook his head, a small, controlled movement. "I'm fine."

It took some time, but the seal gave before the dryer blew out. We stepped back as the door swung open and Pimsley's frozen corpse tumbled to the floor. Ice crystals rimed his white hair. Rigor mortis had pulled open his eyes and mouth. Purple bruising dusted the bottom of his jaw, the dark blue of his lips a mockery of makeup. His trademark gray suit, with its pale pinstripes and wide lapels, was stained with brown starbursts of frozen blood—bullet wounds, arcing across his torso and landing on his heart. Whoever killed him hadn't taken any chances. His fists clutched empty air, fingernails stark white. He'd been dead for a while before they stuck him into the freezer.

Tommy turned away. I stared at the remains of my friend. A flame of rage inside me kindled. Burned. Burst into a bonfire. They thought they could buy me off with rum drinks in the Bahamas? Scare me with a washed-up trick like tapping my phone? "We're gonna get them for you," I said quietly. "We're gonna get you justice. Vintage style, just the way you'd like it."

Tommy knelt, touching Pimsley's icy hand. Outside, the workers were shooting the breeze, accents from all over our tattered country: New Jersey, Michigan, Arkansas. The Kris Kristofferson version of "For the Good Times" came on the boom box. *I know it's over, but life goes on and this world keeps turning . . .*

I'd heard it often enough in Dad's car. It was time to make ourselves useful. I touched Tommy's shoulder. "Looks like we've got a support group meeting to make on Bepler Street."

CHAPTER 18

As we drove around the corner, I radioed out for someone to stay with Lucinda until the coroner arrived to deal with Pimsley's remains. Doug said he'd swing by when he finished at the antique shop. On KFOG, Indigo Joe reported on a new poll showing 86 percent of Daly City was in favor of changing Magenta Obsession from the "prescription only" pigment category to one that would make it available over the counter. I remembered the riots when Slate Gray was first prescribed to veterans. Then came Sunshine for all Depressives. Then Icarus's Processing Journeys™ and Emotion Purges™, and the TV ads with their smiling actors and *ask your doctor about*'s. Now here we were, in a world where more than half of town was caring for relatives scarred in the '89 Magenta Attack—and given the numbers, some of them supported making the pigment available for anybody who wanted to party.

Heavy clouds hung dark over the hilltops. We turned onto Bepler. City planning didn't reach this close to the Magenta border. Warehouses of odd goods mixed with run-down residential buildings. A shop called Mannequin Market hunched on the corner, windows filled with rows of eerie headless figures. Twilight was drawing in. The lights in a strip joint flickered up.

I rolled to a stop in front of 92 Bepler, an olive drab apartment complex with a layout like a cheap motel. In the center of the parking lot, a pool had been filled in with sand. Someone was trying to grow zucchini in there. The plants' wilted leaves didn't look too promising.

On the far side of the lot, the windows of number twelve cast a warm glow on the pavement. A minivan was parked outside. Through the translucent curtains we could see silhouettes of people sitting.

We slipped under the complex's awning as the skies let loose. As we got closer, we could hear a single thundering voice coming from the support group meeting. It rose and fell, rapping out the cadence of a preacher. I heard *hell to pay* at the top of a crescendo. That was unexpected. I'd thought the Pinkos were more into chanting "om" than screaming fire and brimstone. Then again, given what I'd read in Ashaji's memoir, maybe I'd been mistaken.

From the seam of the door, wisps of pale purple pigment slid out and evaporated into the night. I stopped as soon as what I was seeing registered. Told Tommy to go back to the car to pick up my hazpig vest. And gun. "Bring the Slate Gray slugs," I said. Unlike our usual Cloud Gray Listlessness bullets, the exploding slugs didn't just deliver their colorload to a single target. On impact, they burst, spraying anyone in close quarters with liquid pigment, which then fogged up into the atmosphere. Filled with Slate Gray, they were great for crowd control but terrible for public relations.

It was a risk I was willing to take. The color sliding under the door was exotic. One I'd never seen before. It had to be experimental. I'd bet more than a bottle of hot sauce that Priscilla Kim was in there. This time, I wasn't going to let her waltz out on me.

I watched the fronds drift into the air. Wished I had Doug around to capture the stuff. The fact that it was visible meant it was synthetic. It looked a whole lot like the liquid in the cut-glass vial we'd found at Pimsley's, but it was hard to accurately color-match with vaporizing pigment. What was for sure, though, was that mixed with Deepest Blue it would look just like Blackberry Purple.

Tommy came back, arms full of the equipment I'd asked for. I put on the hazpig vest. If the room was full enough of the pigment that it was coming out through the crack under the door, the loose-fitting covering wouldn't do much. But at least it would keep the Chief from lecturing me.

I swapped the rounds in my revolver for the exploding slugs. Gave the loose ammo back to Tommy. "Go radio for backup," I said. "And wait for me in the car."

He hesitated for a second before walking back across the parking lot, long neck stiff. It wasn't that I thought I wouldn't come out of this. Hell, if I was lucky, I'd walk in, cuff Priscilla, and be out of there. But just in case things went belly-up, it was better for Tommy to hang on to his marbles than risk his mind rushing into the fray. I put on the hazpig mask. Let my gun hang by my side. Knocked on the door. It swung slowly open.

Ten sets of glassy eyes stared at me. The support group members were ranged in a circle around the room. A pair of bottle-blond sisters perched on a love seat that had seen better days, sensible platform shoes crossed demurely. A white middle-aged man with graying temples sat stiffly on a rickety stool. The overstuffed leather sofa held four women with big hair wearing cardigans. They shaded in skin tone from deep brown to ivory. A teenage girl in an oversized coat that matched her chestnut curls huddled on a yellow kitchen chair. A pale boy with glasses hovered next to her. A large man with a handlebar mustache stood frozen, finger in the air—the preacher we'd heard, interrupted midact.

"Psychopigment Enforcement," I said. "What's going on here?"

No one moved. Over the television hung a plaque commemorating the ten-year anniversary of the Magenta Attack. NEVER FORGET. Ananda Ashaji's portrait gazed beatifically out of a rococo gold frame. Next to it hung a cuckoo clock. Battery-powered candles flickered in the corners. Porcelain figurines bent whimsically over cold, shiny sheep on shelves and end tables. Their shadows danced in time to the pulsing light. Tendrils of mauve mist swirled around their clay shepherd's crooks. Time stretched in stillness.

Priscilla Kim had done it again. Fried a bunch of neurotypicals. We could fit three in the back seat. If Meekins came out as backup, he and Cynthia could take another three. Doug would probably be tied up for a while at the little pink house waiting for the coroner. I pulled my radio out and sent word that we'd need an ambulance. Tucked it back in my fanny pack. "Everybody up. Out into the parking lot." They were already pretty cooked.

More time in the pigment-soaked room might not hurt, but it wouldn't help.

Before anyone could move, a muffled voice came from the hallway. "No need, ladies and gentlemen." A tall, gaunt figure in a white hazpig suit emerged from the shadows. The material draped the man from crown to toe, sagging away from a body that was more bone than flesh. "Agent Curtida! I thought you were the cleaning lady. What a surprise."

"I thought you said she was off the case." A diminutive figure appeared behind him. I recognized the voice. Priscilla Kim. From the way the booties stretched on her hazpig suit, I guessed that Tommy's cousin was wearing wedge heels.

I'd never seen the man before. Couldn't see much now, under the hazpig. Through the faceplate, I spotted the top of a nose that listed to the left. That was about all. But he was real thin. I took a wild guess. "Big Skinny."

He laughed, a deep rattle. "That's *Doctor* Big Skinny to you." He'd orchestrated the Shamshine tip-off with Daisuke and Frederick. And here he was, working with Pretty Prissy. Looked like Doug and I had been right. The Shamshine had been a blind. And it had been meant to distract from whatever these two were developing. Using innocents as lab rats.

My rage was taking on a new dimension, anger getting forged into righteousness. I had the urge to push the preacher aside and stick my own finger in the air. The Lord's Prayer started echoing through my head. *Our father who art in heaven.* Put the fear of God into them. *Hallowed be thy name.* Could've used full protective gear like what the crooks were wearing. This pigment had to be powerful stuff to overcome my aversion to public speaking. There was no chance for me to find out what I might say, though, because Big Skinny suddenly had a pigment-dart gun trained on me.

I dove behind the love seat. The blond sisters started praying quietly. *Thy will be done.* The dart exploded onto the clock above me, blue pigment dripping down the face. The last thing these civilians needed was another layer of psychic painting. "Everybody out!" I yelled again.

The cuckoo bounced in and out of its little house, chirping. I tried to get a lock on Big Skinny, but he'd nabbed the curly-haired girl and was holding her like a shield in front of him. *On earth, as it is in heaven.* The whole group was praying, now. One of the cardigans started singing, an eerie gospel wail. Dr. Kim produced a pistol, holding it awkwardly. She let off a shot. Another big-haired woman went down in a burst of Deepest Blue. *Give us this day our daily bread.*

I edged around the room, pushing people toward the door, hoping to get closer to my targets. It was dumb luck that the pigment hadn't turned the support group members against me. My hair tickled my forehead. I pulled my radio out again, holding my revolver one-handed. "For the wrath of God comes upon the sons of disobedience—" That wasn't right. "Tommy, Big Skinny and Kim are here. They've got Deepest—"

Another dart whistled in my direction. I ducked. The pigment boiled into the air. *Forgive us our trespasses, as we forgive those who trespass against us.* Big Skinny had let go of the girl to take the shot. I dropped the radio and steadied my revolver. Deep blue smoke joined the mauve haze. The mix of pigments was doing its work. The guinea pigs were about to start squealing. *Lead us not into temptation.* I hadn't recited the Lord's Prayer since I'd refused to take First Communion when I was eight. My mother, mouth turned down, holding a white cotton-candy poof of a dress. *Your father will be so disappointed—*

Focus. Focus. The room had erupted in chaos, the door slammed shut. The preacher spoke in tongues, mustache wagging. The gospel singer wailed. *"Baruch ata adonai!"* shouted Curls. *Deliver us from evil.* I ought to be worried about them. But I had a holy quest, and it took precedence. The gray-haired man was screaming about demons. I took aim between his stout legs and fired at Big Skinny. My slug found its mark, ripping through his hazpig suit's seam and exploding on his left hip. He dropped to the floor.

A siren wailed in the distance. *In the name of the Father.* Dr. Kim was coming in my direction, pistol braced shakily in her hands. I was in a hot spot about to get hotter. I fired at her. The shot went wide, slamming into the window frame. A puff of Slate Gray spewed into the air. *The Son.* The bespectacled guy got the door open. The blond sisters rushed out, stumbling on their platform shoes. Two of the cardigans and the preacher followed. Kim's small figure ducked and wove through the surge of bodies.

I crawled behind the sofa, staying as far from her as possible, but the woman moved as fast as Tommy mixed cocktails. *The Holy Ghost.* I was face-to-face with her pigment pistol. Crouching at the back of the couch, we found ourselves in a standoff, weapons aimed point-blank at each other. I could hear Tommy trying to corral the crowd outside. I put my finger on the trigger. *Amen.* I squeezed.

My last thought, as a deep blue darkness enfolded me, was, *We must have fired at the same time.*

CHAPTER 19

It took five days for the hospital's stink of floor polish and disinfectant to bring me around. My head felt like rubber stretched across shattered glass when I tried to piece together the events that had put me there. Classic symptom of getting Blued over. Trumbull didn't want to tell me what had happened, just ran a bunch of moral-compass psych tests and then frowned at the results. Stitches itched on my clavicle. Down the hall, Tommy was recovering from a doozy of a Slate Gray hit. The Ennui had left my normally cheerful cadet a despondent lump sprouting IV tubes. He didn't respond to his name, was barely eating, and had been facing the wall the whole week.

The night I came to, Doug gave me the rundown. He'd found me and my cadet stretched out on the carpet of a small apartment on Bepler. Seemed I'd shot up the place, its occupants, Tommy, and myself. "There was some experimental pigment kicking around," Doug said. "The readouts make no sense, but it may be in the fear-inductor class—and you didn't have full hazpig . . ."

I'd been buzzed by something exotic and gone postal. Apparently I'd painted the place with Agency Blue and Gray. I hadn't even heard that Pigment Enforcement had Deepest Blue weapons. The Argentines had taken it off the "verboten" list for the governments of well-behaved allies back in 2005 (a veiled concession to the fact that the recipe had been stolen by several intelligence agencies back in the '90s). I couldn't recall any plans to make it available for domestic enforcement agencies. But Doug had seen a prototype at the last R & D convention, and I'd had both colors of slug in the magazine of my gun. I'd blown up my career well and good. Upside was I could stop worrying about when I'd get retired. I'd be handing in my badge before Trumbull signed off on my release.

The evening breeze cut through the open window. I imagined my finger on the trigger. My cadet's head hitting the floor. My hand, turning the barrel back toward myself. "How's Tommy doing?" I asked quietly.

"He's one of those Depressives that covers it up with compulsive cheeriness. If he's not bothering to put the smiling mask on . . ." Doug pinched at the back of his sagging collar. "I had a friend like that up in Boise. Fun-loving, single guy, a little crazy. Was my wingman whenever I needed one. He got hit with a double dose of Daly City Gray on a routine bust. Recovered fine according to the shrinks, but you could tell his heart had gone out of the work. A couple months later, the Hope Count dropped hard. They found him in his apartment. He'd just about swallowed his revolver."

I sat in the quiet after that. Not sure what to say. There was pizza sauce crusted on his rumpled cardigan. I had the dumb urge to wipe at it. Seemed I was still feeling the effects of my Magenta exposure on the chase up into San Francisco. Would've been nice if the Blue had wiped those memories, too. Let me go back to dealing with Doug like a normal pal. He'd been sleeping on a cot in the hall the whole time I'd been out. Judging by his grubby clothes, he hadn't expected me to wake up. After hearing what I'd done, I wished I'd stayed under. The plastic slats of the blinds swung lethargically. "I made a real hash of things, didn't I?"

He grabbed my hand and squeezed hard, but the Chief coughing gruffly in the doorway cut off whatever he was going to say. He left me to her. The boss came in with the jarring gait of a body running on adrenaline and launched straight into a lecture. "Opening fire on civilians, shooting a fellow officer, shooting yourself . . . just one of those would be enough to take your badge. You're suspended without pay. Mental health break. We'll reevaluate you when all this blows over."

"You aren't giving me the sack?"

"I ought to. Not the first time you haven't waited for backup." Her boot tapped the floor. "You take chances, you improvise. You move fast. Makes you an invaluable part of the team. But sometimes you take a risk too far." She reached into her pocket and pulled out a postcard of the Iowa City Skyline. It was addressed to me, here at the hospital. All it said was *Rest well*.

I turned it over, but there was no indication of who it was from. The skyscrapers gleamed, silver in cold winter sunlight. I didn't know anyone in Iowa. Rest well. Somewhere between *get well* and *rest in peace*. "Weird thing to write," I said.

"There are people who wanted you off the Icarus case, and you crossed them. You don't know what they're capable of. I do. Don't mess around with this, Curtida." There was surprising bile in her voice.

She thought this whole thing had to do with Icarus. Doug hadn't mentioned that case. Although he'd pointed out that the experimental pigment hadn't made sense on readouts. Same as the stuff Priscilla Kim had handed out in the padded room. I just said, "Can't do much from my hospital bed."

"You listen to me. Take care of yourself. You've got too much to lose." The last I saw of her was her hunched back walking out the door.

Alone, I stared at the ceiling, daring sleep to come. The light from the sulfur streetlamps through the window cut a diagonal swath out of the wall. Trumbull'd left my Sunshine drip set to high. Given the circumstances, even that wasn't enough to have me feeling copacetic.

It wasn't my first go-around with Deepest Blue. We'd all been exposed in Tadlock's lab class at the academy so we'd recognize the effects if we got painted in the field. We said things like the Blue "erased" or "wiped out" memories, but the truth was that it repressed them. Marked recent events (or not-so-recent, depending on the dose) as no-go zones. The mind would skirt the area like a member of the Chamber of Commerce passing a homeless encampment.

It took mental contortions for thoughts to skip over the gap, the gymnastics necessary to convince yourself *nothing to see here*. Neurotypical profiles didn't deal well with the effort. Even in Depressives, the strain had repercussions. Especially in those of us pushing middle age. The supple psyches of the young tended to straighten themselves out pretty fast. Not so for folks more set in our ways. Our midtwenties cadets were backup. Tommy could remember things the morning after a hit that would create a permanent block for me. And those blocks built up over time. Enough minor run-ins would result in a head too twisted to keep functioning.

Of course, you could also end up on the receiving end of a weapons-grade blast and forget to breathe. Most folks I knew would choose the one big strike over the suicide-by-a-thousand-cuts that was more common. There was a reason the department had moved up retirement age in the early 2000s. Twenty years in, it was pretty clear that most agents couldn't take more than two decades on the street. If that policy had been in place in the '90s, maybe Walter would still have been around. In spite of the danger, I'd heard plenty of stories of agents using the Blue to forget poor choices.

The wound on my collarbone ached. I'd always figured if I was going to off myself, I'd put the gun to my temple, not on my shoulder. Or charge into battle. If life was meaningless, make my death mean something. The old building creaked around me, settling into night. They said the ghosts of Malvinas veterans walked these halls. The biggest danger to soldiers after the war had been themselves. A touch of the Blue and six days, six months, six years later someone would find them. Swinging. Brains blown out. Bloated in the Bay.

Those were neurotypicals, though. Mostly. A memory pushed its way through the muck: Doug saying *Some feelings come from inside, not from pigment*. When had he said that? Didn't matter. Depressives had always been around. The officer who'd delivered the news of my father's death had emphasized his bravery in his final moments. I always found, on nights like this one, that the word *bravery* sure seemed euphemistic. During the day, stories of suicidal veterans always seemed maudlin. Energy wasted memorializing cowards. In the dark it was another matter. Something rose up and got trapped in my throat. When sleep came, it brought dreams of being chased through the hospital by a tall, skinny doctor as singing patients evaporated into puffs of Deepest Blue.

●●●

The week limped along its sorry way, lousy as a visit from a relative on Ginger Curiousity. To heal the level of Blue knock I'd taken required the kind of work I was worst at. Journaling my dreams, poking at my feelings, letting the detritus that could elude the pigment's repression float back into the light. The process brought up plenty of stuff I preferred to leave buried. Regret that I hadn't seen the signs with Walter. My useless anger at Mom. Chagrin about the times I'd been too impulsive, like charging in to tell the Chief that Meekins was a Knight of Liberty. And all of this, I knew, was just my mind trying to shunt my attention away from whatever had gone down on Bepler.

I had to come at the memories obliquely. Aiming at them head-on sent me down a rabbit hole or spiked me with a migraine. Sometimes I could expand from the fragments I already had access to—Doug spouting Magenta Anonymous talking points about feelings, Mom making my phone ring in the early morning, the dusty smell of the department's filing room. More often than not, it felt like trying to find lost keys in a field of quicksand.

I could read between the lines in Trumbull's instructions: the dose I'd taken had been a doozy. Chances were whatever had gone down at Bepler would be lost to me forever. Doug's retelling of the events had included grounds for firing several times over. The fact that the Chief hadn't shown up with my pink slip in hand made me wonder what details the narrative was missing. But given Trumbull's diagnosis, it was pretty clear I'd never recover enough to piece together exactly what had happened. I still acted like I might, crossing my fingers that sticking to her plan would minimize future psychological repercussions.

With my Sunshine drip for a cane, I'd clomp down the hall every morning to visit Tommy, trying to find words to apologize for what I'd done to him. Mostly I just watched him breathe. Trumbull or Howie the nurse sat with us while I was in there, observing the lack of progress in their two newest patients. During one of my awkward soliloquies, I let slip that my cadet was involved with Pimsley. That got him crying. In the hall after, Trumbull said it was a good sign. Showed that he was starting to process. "Was it a fling with Pimsley or were they more serious?" she asked.

For some reason that question made me think about the texture of a wool peacoat on my palm and eucalyptus trees swaying in the wind. The sound of Tommy sobbing. Then I was mad. Trumbull wasn't a gossip. I'd told her more than I would have under normal circumstances. The two men could do their thing in a freezer for all I cared. Wearing matching gray pin-stripe suits while toasting with art deco champagne flutes. I wasn't going to tell the doctor anything else.

The dull throb of a headache was starting at the base of my neck. I asked if I could have an aspirin. Trumbull wrote something down on her clip-board and told me to make sure I ate all my lunch, dodging my dodge. As I tugged my Sunshine drip back toward my room, I had the slippery sense that I'd just jumped over memories lost to the Blue.

I'd take breaks to wander the ward, feeling about as solid as the fifteen-year-old films flickering on the TV over the desk in the waiting room. I stopped paying attention to the set after the third time I caught the scene from *Nation's Rebirth* where the protagonist was initiated by getting an Oath Tree tattooed on his torso. I'd never understood how a movie about bombing high school history classes had done so well at the box office.

I became a diligent *Daly Daily* reader, getting my updates on the neuro-typical cops' busting of a dogfighting ring and the society pages' portraits of the Library Board members at luncheons. Found out that Meekins's Elvis impression won a karaoke contest benefiting the school lunch program. Jenna Lila had captioned his photo "(Not-so-secret) Agent Man Visits Heartbreak Hotel." Hard to imagine how Meekins had channeled the King with his collar buttoned up to his Adam's apple.

Monday morning, I set myself the task of writing down a list of every time Mom had made some optimistic comment about how my promotion "had to come through *soon*." Six entries in, the sight of the Iowa City Sky-line on the postcard next to my bed toppled the wall blocking the unset-tling call from Cassius. I didn't know anyone else in Iowa City. Seemed the agent hadn't wanted me to forget the offer of the transfer. Or its attending conditions. People who wanted me to leave the Icarus case well enough alone, the Chief had said. I flipped over the postcard. *Rest well.* Read even more sinister now that I knew who had sent it.

As I looked for distraction, the case popped up everywhere. Ananda Ashaji was all over the news, talking about the failures of democracy and the need to find some other form of government. I wasn't a flag-waving Pollyanna about our electoral system, but I'd appreciated the opportunity to vote against Rigby for each of his five terms. Edie came over for a social visit but dropped the news that her boys in the kitchen had heard an "out-of-towner called Big Skinny" was the brain behind the bomb that had taken out Icarus's twelfth-floor security guard. The corporation's steel-eyed R & D boss, Dr. Gruber-Shaw, showed up on Bootsie Poots's afternoon talk show to reiterate his statement from the Magenta Cares event about "bringing back hope for Magenta victims" with "something big" to be announced at Ashaji's book launch. He was the one who'd brought Priscilla Kim on at the Icarus Corporation. More and more I was convinced that whatever he was playing coy about had to do with Pretty Prissy's strange pigment. Less than two weeks till the big day. Knowing that didn't make sitting in the hospital easier.

Doug spent most nights on the cot in the hall. Cynthia came in with him one evening after work, carrying flowers for Tommy and me. She'd even gotten Meekins to sign a card. She laughed hard when my old friend made jokes, and I could see a faint line of surprise under her bleached bangs when he told her he was still spending nights at the hospital. She left shortly after that.

On Thursday, the Hope Count spiked. I could feel it even before Doug woke me up with a paper takeout cup of Edie's coffee. Seemed he'd found the sandwich joint without my help. I carried it down the hall for my daily visit to Tommy's room. My cadet turned his head toward me as I came in. A new development in the patient. Howie checked in on us as he did his rounds, but left us alone with the TV set.

We sat through the news coverage of a middle-aged Knight of Liberty who'd been arrested in Cedar Rapids with a stash of Deepest Blue and blueprints of all the local schools. The emerging pattern of pigment attacks had the experts worried about a shift in power between internal factions in the dissident group. The original Knights had wanted to give the Argentines the boot without relying on the occupier's weapons. The People's Pigment Movement senator, Holly Doyle, came on as a talking head. *The new tactics suggest a more radical wing has taken power in the terrorist organization—*

I flipped to the other news channel. They were running a documentary about the USO entertainers who kept up morale during the signing of the Mumbai accord, the treaty that ended the Malvinas War and established the various Argentine military bases on US soil. Tommy lay still, but his eyes were on the screen. Bootsie Poots showed up, still in her R & B incarnation. Her black hair was shellacked to her head, and her shoulder pads could stop a pigment dart apiece. "This one's from my latest album," she cooed. "*Something Like . . .*" Her lips, garnet red, puckered around the words. The soldiers went wild.

Tommy drew a ragged breath and sat up for the first time in weeks. "Something like hope! It's the song. The message that Pimsley left on my machine—he talked about Bootsie's single—he said he'd found the song that was *very important.*" Lighters flickered over the crowd of soldiers. "*I thought I'd found happiness, but all I've got is something like hope,*" Bootsie crooned. Tommy'd sung it as we crested a hill—as we drove south from—a skeleton key, unlocking a door in a garage. Champagne flutes under ancient muskets. A closet of matching suits. Right before we found—a turquoise fridge, an industrial freezer—

Starbursts of blood on gray pinstripe.

"Pimsley's dead." My voice shook. Maybe this was the Blue trying to redirect me. But the image of purple bruising along the man's pale jaw hung in my mind, urgent and surreal.

"You don't remember—anything from that day?" he asked.

"Bits and pieces." My mouth was dry. Two red spots burned on Tommy's hollow cheeks. He looked like a china doll in need of an exorcism. When his adrenaline dropped, he'd go straight back to the inert melancholy he'd been mired in all week. I told him to keep going, not to worry about me.

His voice was rough after his long silence, but his words tumbled out fast. "He called the station about the Shamshine, but we know happy pills aren't what the Pinkos are making. Doug said that the briefcase was all Yellowjacket vintage. But if they just needed Pims to feed us shoddy information—why kill him?"

Ice crystals scattered across beige linoleum. The smell of chamomile tea. Focus. Focus. "To keep him from talking?"

"Exactly. The tip-off he had wasn't about Shamshine at all. *I thought I'd found happiness*—Shamshine, right? Sunshine Yellow brings happiness—*but all I've got is something like hope.* The Pinkos aren't trying to manufacture Shamshine. They're trying to make synthetic Hope!"

The mauve pigment Tommy'd found—I remembered a vial, sparkling in the light of Tiffany lamps. A color that could've almost been Lavender Hope. Priscilla Kim's willingness to risk it all, drugging the camera room operator and deserting the interview. Gruber-Shaw, sitting on Bootsie Poots's talk-show couch, talking about *bringing back hope*.

There it was. We knew what they were after. We knew why they were doing it.

We'd finally cracked the case.

CHAPTER 20

It took us a week to piece together what had gone down on Bepler. Tommy swung between lucidity and lethargy. The Hope Count spike carried us through the weekend, but he wilted as it dropped. Getting too close to his cousin's betrayal or the specifics of Pimsley's death sent him spiraling into a whirlpool of guilt. We'd lose him for days at a time.

At one point I asked Trumbull if it wouldn't be useful to run him through a Grief Processing Journey. She didn't even look up from her desk. "Pigment can't get him through this. He needs to work it out on his own." I pointed out that maybe it could help. "You stick to solving your cases. I'll stick to the mysteries of the mind." Her voice made clear the conversation was over.

I asked Tommy if he'd be interested anyway. He just looked at me and said, "I don't think painting over my feelings is how I want to live anymore."

Doug came by when he could. He'd handled plenty of Slate Gray cases, and he distracted Tommy like a pro when we approached dangerous territory. His assistance was especially useful because the Blue was continually trying to knock me off target. I'd find myself angry at Tommy when he spoke about the living room at number twelve, or I'd contradict him on things I couldn't remember. Eventually we got through it anyway.

The story wasn't pretty. My shot must have gone wide, because Priscilla Kim was swapping Deepest Blue slugs into my gun when Tommy found her. She'd told him to leave, but when he refused, she had gone ahead and shot him with the Gray. Sounded like her grandmother was right about her being more wolf than poodle.

As we slowly circled Tommy's memory of the attack, pulling him back from the brink of ennui, we decided it was best to call Priscilla's choice of Gray instead of Blue bullets loyalty to family. Doug suspected it was just what she'd had in the cylinder, but he kept his trap shut around Tommy. I'd assumed that without Pimsley's death weighing on him, my cadet would have recovered quickly, but it turned out he had plenty to grapple with in the memory of his cousin sighting him down the barrel of her gun.

After taking her shot, Priscilla made a break with Big Skinny in tow. Tommy recognized the man—he'd seen him walking with Ashaji and Gruber-Shaw toward Her Holiness's bulletproof Rolls-Royce when we went back to the charity auction after our escapades on Shakespeare. Lady Pinko and the Icarus boss had the stink of this mess all over them.

Icarus wasn't allowed to bring in test subjects to develop pigments, so the Pinkos were a golden opportunity to keep the research *sub rosa*. Ashaji brought a king-sized pool of volunteers; Gruber-Shaw turned a blind eye as Priscilla used Icarus's special facilities. The arrangement must've been working real well until the death of Blufftown Tuck tipped off law enforcement that something funny was going on. I figured they'd brought Big Skinny in to run interference after that. From where, I had no idea. The crook's ruthlessness didn't fit with the local scene's bumbling violence. But Gruber-Shaw had brought Priscilla up from Argentina. The man's network spanned the Americas, at the very least.

Doug sat up late with me most of those nights. Sleeping on the cot in the hall left his skin sallow with fatigue, but he looked better than when I'd first come to. His toothbrush and razor had moved into a cubby next to the sink in my bathroom. His deodorant and towel nestled on a small shelf. I pretended to sleep while he did his ablutions in the mornings. It was like being roommates at the academy.

As the case unfolded in its full complexity, I could tell that he was getting nervous. Finally I told him to spit out the nail-biter he'd been chewing over. "PSI. I can't figure out where they fit into the picture. But they've got to be a part of it—why else would they have pulled the case from you?" He'd had colleagues disappear after getting mixed up with the Psychopigment Service Investigators. Suggested that maybe I should use the hit I'd taken as an excuse to lie low, stay out of harm's way. I told him to give it a rest: he'd taken worse during the Yellowjacket case and come through fine.

"I was one of the lucky ones. Other folks . . ." He cleared his throat. "I was seeing this girl, one of the shrinks on the fast-response team. I found her, barely breathing, in my apartment. She's still in the psych ward. I think. She wouldn't remember me, so . . ."

"So you don't bother remembering her."

"That's not . . ." A look that could have rearranged my heart came over his face. It was gone just as fast. "It's . . . I did what you'd do for anyone, you know, CPR, ambulance, ER, but I didn't . . . feel anything. I mean, crisis mode, the usual, but she could've just been a random victim of the cartel. After that, going to the hospital felt . . . like a sham."

Didn't feel anything? I remembered the flashes of Magenta in his eyes during my visit to Boise, all those years ago. "How long . . . how long did the—the Magenta keep you going with her?" I tugged the thin blanket over my knees. I'd turned the lights out in preparation for bed but hadn't gotten as far as lying down. The streetlamp, level with the window, cast a jagged polygon of yellow light across Doug's chair, the Sunshine drip, my bed.

"Are you cold?" he asked. "I'll get you your pullover."

"Plato."

"Curtida—"

"How long?"

His hands smoothed the wrinkles on his striped pajama pants. "Look, a recreational Magenta dose lasts five to eight hours. Always made me—I don't know. Pretty dorky, actually. Like I couldn't breathe because the other person is so perfect. One time I stared at a girl's earlobes for an hour, thinking words like 'nonpareil.' But it's not like it keeps the flame lit between dates—"

Inside me, the remains of my Magenta exposure slammed into my lungs. "What about nonrecreational doses?"

"I wouldn't know. I never took more than a small hit. And I stopped doing it after—after I understood how much I'd hurt you." The sound of the night nurse's footsteps in the hallway echoed softly through the room, then faded. "I'm sorry. I shouldn't have done that with you. I was scared. You were such a good friend, and what if . . ."

I didn't think I wanted to hear the end of that "what if," so I said, "Sure."

"It was a bad decision. If I could do it over. Who knows. You ever wonder what our lives could have been like?"

I told him I was tired. He went back out to his cot. Alone, my eyes wouldn't shut. I'd certainly gotten a lot more than recreational exposure. How many weeks had it been? I watched the spider in the corner. No need to make a fool of myself over a little pigment. No need to be a fool at all.

● ● ●

Doug had already left when I woke up. I drank my Nescafé and ate my hospital toast. Down the hall, I could hear Nurse Howie talking gently to Jenny Crotty, the woman I'd found at Icarus. She still treated everyone like they were a demon, but they'd gotten her Sunshine and Golden Peace drips set to a level where she was no longer prone to violent outbursts.

I could feel the Hope Count dropping, but a cursory look at the paper showed no sign of it. This Magenta thing was getting to be a problem. Of all the people the pigment could have driven me toward, it had to be Doug. We'd been there, done that, and it was terrible. Outside my hospital window, construction was restarting on the long-awaited new wing of the psych ward. The jackhammers sang along to my blues. Doug could sweet-talk me all he wanted about what our life could have been, but a Magenta addict wasn't going to stop dipping into pigment for his old drinking pal. I couldn't go through that again.

Life wasn't willing to let me wallow without making things worse. Nurse Howie stuck his brown curls through the doorway and announced that my mother was on the phone. I went for an extra dose of coffee and dragged my feet to the office. I moved a pile of medical records off Trumbull's cowhide chair and sat. The receiver lay cradled on two crusty espresso cups. I picked it up, the tangled cord bouncing off my wrist. After chewing me out for not listing her as my emergency contact, Susana Curtida got around to lifting my spirits. "I think this is a wonderful opportunity to step back, reevaluate, figure out what's next for you after Pigment Enforcement."

"I'm not leaving the force."

"Oh. From what I read in the *Daly Daily*, I thought . . ." I could hear the ice cream truck tinkling down the street as she switched tactics. "You've really given it your all. I'm so proud of the effort you've made. And you've done some really amazing things, training your first cadet into such a stellar agent and all. But, you know, I think the world is telling you that this isn't the place you'll be able to bloom. That it's time to strike out and find your true passion. Let your buddy Meekins handle things."

"Mom," I started. The word caught in my clenched jaw. I'd been the one who decided to start talking to her again. *Your buddy Meekins*, though. That phrase could frizz hair as straight as Tommy's. At least she hadn't flat out told me I should get around to making my colleague's babies.

I was saved by Trumbull's return from the floor meeting. She ended the call with the ease of long practice, saying things like "for the psychic stability of the patient" and "federal privacy laws." With the phone safely back on the hook, she put two fingers on my wrist to check my pulse. "Huh," she said. "Looks like your mom's as bad as mine."

"She knows where to hit and she doesn't pull her punches." A dump truck rumbled below the window. I felt like I was riding in the back of it. "Apparently it's a positive career development that I'm leaving Pigment Enforcement."

"You're quitting?" She sounded surprised.

"I thought I was getting fired." I looked up at her. She hadn't outright said that she thought the story about me doing all the shooting at the support group meeting was a whopper. But if she'd believed it, she would've been at the front of the line clamoring for the Chief to throw me out on my ear. She wasn't. "Look. This mess I got caught up in . . . I'm going to keep working to sort it out as long as I can. Because if these crooks get what they're going for—whatever it is—the stuff that hits the proverbial fan is going to come back and splatter all of us. Meekins is busy looking into the Shamshine we found, and Doug isn't a field agent or a local. They need my help, even if it's unofficial. But there's nothing I can do from in here."

"Normal recovery time for a serious hit with the Blue is a month. You've only been here two and a half weeks."

I lined a pad of sticky notes up with the plum spine of her DSM-III-Pig. It was time to let her know what we thought we were up against. Even if the case was held together with spit and hunches. "We've got reason to think they're going to be pitching the color they gave Jenny Crotty as Lavender Hope."

That got a snort out of her. "Sure didn't look like it."

"You're finally going to have a wing for the Saigon Sallies Screamers. Do you want to be using it to house the fried neurotypicals that'll be filing in here once that experiment hits the streets?"

Hammers clanged outside. Trumbull dug a patient chart out of her file cabinet. "It's your funeral. I'm going to need you in here nights and mornings. Midnight to noon, on the Sunshine drip. And if a situation even *starts* to get hot, I want you out of there immediately."

"I know how to tell when pigment's messing with me, Doctor."

"Midnight to noon, Curtida. And don't louse this up. It's your own mind you're wagering."

● ● ●

The March day was unseasonably hot, the afternoon breeze recalcitrant. It was official now. I was going directly against orders, digging into the Icarus case. While suspended on mental health leave, no less.

My ultimate destination was the home of Priscilla Kim's father. I didn't have high expectations for the information he'd have regarding her whereabouts, but it was a starting point. My jacket, torn up and stained from the tussle at Bepler, was less than ideal for making first impressions. I'd have to circle past my apartment for a replacement. Tommy'd asked me to grab some clothes for him at his place, too. Felt typical that, as I embarked on my career of insubordination in pursuit of the truth on the biggest case I'd ever handled, two of my first three tasks entailed picking up clean laundry.

Out in the open, the construction noises grated. A fitting soundtrack. I tossed the postcard from Iowa City into the parking lot trash can. I didn't want it in my room, even in the bin. The door handle of my Renault was nice and warm under my fingers. The driver's seat hugged me like it had missed me. It might look like the daughter of a baby shoe and a battered clown car, but my ride was a trusty partner.

The siren and cop radio were nowhere to be found. Someone had collected them when I'd been put on mental health leave. I reached into the crack between the passenger seatback and cushion. There, just where Tommy had left it, was the mauve pigment from Pimsley's. Just like the antique dealer to have stored it in one of the fancy vintage bottles from the '90s. I sent his ghost a silent *Thank you* and put back the vial. Pulled my sunglasses out of the glove box and turned on the radio, heading toward my apartment.

Twenty minutes later, I stood in front of the loosely swinging remains of my door. The lock was broken. Inside the living room, I could see my punching bag hanging limp in the corner, its torn-tire filling spilling out like guts. Pictures of my mother were scattered everywhere. The answering machine was cracked in two.

The entrails of Pimsley's fancy seat were laid out like an offering to a pagan chair god. Its careful butchery gave me a pretty good idea of what the crooks who'd broken in were looking for: the pigment vial we'd found at the salesman's home. Crossing the threshold was out. Trumbull's warning rang in my ears. Didn't want to risk it if the perpetrators had left a nasty present for me. The only thing they hadn't touched was the spiderweb in the corner.

So much for that clean jacket. I needed a telephone. I thought about asking Mrs. Fernandez, but couldn't stomach the idea of being preached to about the Pinkos after seeing what Ashaji was doing with their support groups.

I headed to the pay phone across the street. Dropped in a thousand-dollar coin and dialed the department. Waiting for an answer, I stared at the building that had been my home since I made agent. Through the window, there was no sign of the damage to my apartment. The property was midcentury ugly, four floors of diagonal wooden siding painted puce. It had originally contained eight single-family units, but when even that modest option had proven too high-end for the postwar market, the owner had chopped them up into sixteen pocket-sized one-bedrooms. Most of the residents were retired widows and widowers, scraping by on pensions that bought less every month as inflation chewed away at the dollar.

When Berdie picked up, I pulled out the Florida Latin accent that I'd worked so hard to lose at the academy, reporting the break-in at my apartment as an anonymous citizen. No need for more folks to know that I wasn't still tucked into my hospital bed. He said he'd send someone around to check. I could hear his notary stamp going, a sure sign he was distracted. Wondered if the mushrooms were still drying in his office. I'd get Doug to check in on the apartment just in case.

I still needed something to make myself more presentable. The fact that I'd be showing up and asking questions without a badge was bad enough. I could try to buy a jacket somewhere. Or borrow something of Tommy's. I shuffled my itinerary and set off for my cadet's apartment. In the car, I caught the tail end of an interview with Ananda Ashaji. She signed off with "God Bless America," the Knights of Liberty catchphrase.

I was braced for another wreck at Tommy's, but the goons hadn't found his digs. On a cadet's salary, you tended to pull up stakes every time the rent rose, so his address in the phonebook was probably three moves behind.

His place was in a bleak neighborhood, on the third floor of a building erected on the edge of a ravine. The lock to his studio was finicky, but leaning on the door got it open. Camel-colored carpet sagged where the floorboards had surrendered to the constant Daly City humidity. The stained faux-wood kitchen counter ran along the same wall as the entrance, terminating in the window. Beyond the split panes was a glimpse of the sea, framed by the hills. He'd chosen the place for the view, not the interior design.

The room was messier than I expected. My cadet's desk was always ship-shape, his collars always pressed. Here, the bed was unmade. Dirty laundry lay heaped in the corner. A substantial liquor collection congregated next to the hot plate. Empty bottles were gathered in grocery bags on the floor. A pair of martini glasses sat in the sink, an art deco teacup on the bedside table. I could guess where that had come from. The smell of cigarettes and old booze permeated everything.

I found a cardigan in the closet that didn't look too odd on me as long as I rolled up the sleeves. Pulled out a gym bag to pack for my cadet. The dresser sat by the door at one end of the kitchen counter. Everything in the drawers was neatly folded. On a whim, I tossed a squat bottle of whisky into the bag. It was some Scottish kind I'd never seen before, with too many *g*'s and *h*'s in the name. I listened to the messages—not much there. A couple of saved recordings of Pimsley. I stared at the sink as they played. One of the martini glasses had hot pink lipstick on it.

Tommy didn't strike me as the type to use makeup. He could've had a friend over to chat. I got up to take a closer look. There was an orange rind in the sink. Fresh, still wet. No mold. It had been two and a half weeks since my cadet had been back here. Someone was using the place.

My pulse ticked up a notch. I cast around for a weapon. My fingers closed on a heavy bottle of vodka. Not ideal. But it was something. The intruder might be here, might not. Better safe, I figured. I'd checked the closet, and there were boxes under the bed. Only place left to hide was the bathroom. I kept moving, trying to make it sound like nothing had changed. *Just here gathering clothes for Tommy.* All the while I was searching for something more useful for self-defense.

Small signs of the occupier were all over, now that I was looking. A pile of bobby pins on the windowsill. Lacey underwear peeking out of the bottom of the pile of laundry. I moved the rest of the clothes aside and was rewarded with the sight of a skirt suit and cream-colored stilettoes with INDUSTRIA ARGENTINA printed on the insoles. Next to them lay a pigment gun.

Looked like I could scratch the visit to Tommy's uncle. I'd found Priscilla Kim's hideout.

CHAPTER 21

I hefted the firearm. It was a standard Glock pigment shooter, the kind issued to rookies at the shooting range. I would've expected someone who bought imported shoes to have something more upmarket. Checked the magazine: fully loaded with Deepest Blue. It was a comfort to have an actual weapon. The scientist's choice to hole up in her cousin's digs was certainly utilitarian. I guessed she'd been relying on the Gray shot she'd plugged him with to keep the place unoccupied. It was too bad for her that I'd decided to devote my day to laundry-related tasks.

The coffee in the art deco cup stank of booze. It was still piping hot. Priscilla must have heard me scrabbling at the lock. Slipped into the bathroom before I got the door open. Well, now she was stuck in there. Figured I should check the place better before confronting her. I put the vodka back, went through the kitchen drawers. Nothing more dangerous than a pair of lab notebooks. In the bed, a bottle of Italian liqueur. Her diary was on the bedside table.

I flipped through, reading her entries. Some people with the initials CJA and PGS had decided Kim was a liability. Gruber-Shaw's first name was Patrick, so he'd be PGS. CJA seemed to be Big Skinny. Tommy showing up at Bepler and then surviving his encounter with his cousin had been too much for them. They weren't much for coincidence, apparently. Sure would've been nice for us if she'd been a mole. Gave me a sense of the paranoid sort of operation they were running.

She'd been on the run since the day after shooting the two of us. There was a lot of moaning and griping about her bad luck. The statement *I'm a scientist, not a soldier!* appeared repeatedly. I was pretty sure *soldier* wasn't the right word to describe the role her criminal colleagues had expected her to play. Her attitude did explain the run-of-the-mill firearm, though. She'd probably never held a pistol before getting mixed up in all this. Her handwriting alternated between high-school-valedictorian precision and something a whole lot shakier. The final entry was just the words *WHAT IS THE POINT?* scrawled unsteadily in the center of the page.

Detritus from Icarus's Pigment Journeys mingled with the empty liquor bottles in the bags by the counter, the small tubes of pigment squeezed out and twisted dry. Seemed she'd had a stash beyond the box she'd left under her desk at the corporation. I headed for the bathroom. The door was locked. That confirmed it. She was in there. I was about to say hello when a small voice said, "You found me."

Pretty Prissy came out with her hands up, looking as rumpled as the studio. Her face was flushed. Spider veins lined the outside of her nostrils and reddened her eyelids. Without the layers of makeup, her resemblance to Tommy was much clearer. She was wearing one of her cousin's shirts. It came down to her knees. The wrinkles suggested she'd slept in it. "Oh. It's you," she said, walking past me to the bed. The weapon I had trained on her didn't faze her much. She placed her bare feet very deliberately on the thinning carpet. Sat. Picked up the bottle lying in the sheets and took a swig.

"You're under arrest," I said. Fingers crossed she didn't realize I was on mental health leave.

"Might as well shoot me now, then. You take me in, Cassius will have me out of there and into concrete boots before you could say PSI." Same name as the man who called with the offer from Iowa. My face must've given away my confusion, because she flapped her hand and clarified. "You recognized him at Bepler. Big Skinny? The guy who got us Agency Blue? Oh god, you have no idea what you're up against. I'm so screwed. I should've just finished drinking myself to death."

The liquor smelled strong enough that it might not have been an empty threat. I took it away and told her to get dressed, trying to hide how the information had knocked me off-balance. Cassius and Big Skinny were the same person. And PSI. PSI was running this mess. Suddenly plenty of things made a lot more sense. They'd been the ones that pulled me off the Icarus case. But what was in it for them?

"Listen," she said. "It's my pigment they're using. I dreamed of joining the PPM and ended up in bed with the Knights of Liberty. They've taken my breakthrough and turned it into an abomination."

"You talking about the scam you tried to pull with Silver Lilac Wistfulness?" The topic of the article Trumbull had shown me.

"It wasn't a scam!" Her pickled breath rode her vehemence all the way over to me. She stood. Rocked slightly at the sudden movement. Began putting on her skirt. "There're two ways to develop pigments. The traditional, brute force capture method. And then there's my way. Deduction. Figure out what's nearby. Find the structure based on that. It's revolutionary. It could mean we could actually capture and synthesize *everything we feel.*" She spread her arms, lost for a moment in awe of the vastness of human experience. I caught a glimpse of the ambitious girl Tommy had talked about. The smartest person in any room, ready to change the world.

I also caught a glimpse of the stripe of Cool Teal smeared on her inner wrist. Explained her nonreaction to the gun. Teal made you feel like a star in front of an adoring crowd. Riding the high, you'd never believe your fan would shoot you. She held the showboating pose for a beat, skirt half-zipped over Tommy's oversized shirt. Then her fingers folded sadly in on themselves. "But. A little fluffed-up data, a couple accusations of cherry-picking, and the biggest breakthrough in pigment theory in decades—tossed out with the bathwater. What I get for listening to Gruber-Shaw. 'Publish or perish,' he said. My theory would 'usher in a paradigm shift.' I rushed tests. Cut corners. 'Everyone does it,' he said.

"Well, turns out that it's one thing to cut corners as a WASP with tenure. Another thing when you're just the Korean American postdoc. Nobody even bothered to try to replicate it, they just laughed me out of academia. That had me staring at the bottom of a bottle most days until he came back around. Talking about wanting to use my work for some Gray experiments . . . I was actually *glad*. I was *grateful*. And now . . . here I am. Hiding out in my baby cousin's apartment, thanks to the *quilombo* that man got me into."

She'd clearly never heard *fool me twice, shame on me*. Her pity party was looking like a stalling tactic. I told her it was time to get going. She hesitated. I took her arm and pulled her toward the door. Her voice got higher. "They're going to make Ananda Ashaji into our dictator!"

That was far enough out of left field to stop me. She yanked out of my grasp and stumbled toward the kitchen counter. I drew back to block the exit. She pulled the drawer with the notebooks all the way out and reached behind it. I knew before the gun came out that she'd had a weapon hidden back there. She raised the barrel without bracing herself for the recoil as I threw myself behind the dresser.

The first shot went wide. Not a shock given her grip on the firearm. The only surprising thing was that the kickback didn't knock it straight out of her hand. She'd been serious about the "not a soldier" thing. The second bullet slammed into the dresser. The neighborhood was tough enough that a couple shots would probably be ignored, but if she kept shooting, someone was going to notice. The piece I held was loaded with Deepest Blue, though. Hit her with one of those darts—even just a scratch—and I'd lose all her information. The dresser jumped as the third shot hit the side.

But the next sound that came was the click of the hammer striking the empty chamber. I let out my breath and thanked my lucky stars for her criminal ineptitude. Felt like crabs were crawling through my veins, but I kept myself real steady as I stood, holding her in my gunsight. "Got that out of your system?"

She kept uselessly pulling on the trigger until I twisted her hand to make her drop it. Her shoulders fell. "I had to try. Please. Please don't take me in. I'll tell you everything."

"Finish getting dressed," I said.

"I'm done for. I'm so done for." It wasn't clear if she was talking to me or to herself. Even the Cool Teal couldn't mask the anxiety radiating from her. She picked up her suit jacket, pulled a pack of cigarettes out of the pocket. Argentine Caravanas. Her hand shook as she lit up. Opened the window to blow smoke out into the clear afternoon. Pointed me toward the hidey-hole she'd nabbed the revolver from. "Look in there."

A trick? The trembling tip of the cigarette suggested otherwise. I moved cautiously toward the counter, took a peek. A cut-glass vial of the mauve pigment we'd picked up at Pimsley's was wedged into a crack. She watched me finger the flask, an unreadable expression on her face. "Take it. And the lab notebooks in the drawer. That's the proof."

"Explain," I said, sliding the pigment into my fanny pack. "Concisely."

"You've seen Gruber-Shaw doing the rounds, haven't you? Noticed that he's always saying things like 'We want to bring back Hope'?"

"Concisely," I repeated.

"Whatever. It's not really Hope, but it'll look close enough that folks won't notice at first. It's Hope's bitter cousin—Faith. Mauve Faith. It's going to be touted as a fix for Magenta victims, and an outlook-shifter for the population at large. But we're not talking the quiet, hardworking faith of midwestern Lutherans. This is the potent, book-burning backbone of zealotry. It's the sort of faith that's based in fear of the other. Our early results sure looked like Blackberry Purple, didn't they?" She knocked the tip of ash on the edge of the sill. Watched it drop. I somehow got the sense she was thinking of Blufftown Tuck. "The odd thing is, it does help Magenta victims. It refocuses the deep-seated obsessive impulses on an abstraction: some higher power, some greater good.

"This is where Ashaji comes in. There's one dominant side effect, both in Magenta victims and neurotypicals: what we've called 'imprinting.' When users are exposed to a spiritual figure within a day of dosage, they become dedicated followers. Devotees. If the dose is high enough—for life. Within weeks of the release of Mauve Faith, Her Holiness will have an army of Saigon Sally Screamers fifty thousand strong. Add to that the already dedicated Pinkos, and the grateful families who've been attending support groups . . ." Her lips twisted, like she'd just bitten into something rotten. "If the Faith goes out as the second coming of Hope, *everybody* will be clamoring to take it. This will make Sunshine pills look like small potatoes." She stubbed the butt out and tossed it into the bushes below.

"All that talk about theocracies isn't just talk, then."

"No. It's the plan. A theocracy in the image of the Pinkos. You ever been out to the redemption camp in Turlock?" My neighbor Mrs. Fernandez had described it as a nature retreat for reflection and self-discovery while trying to get me to join the cult. Prissy combed her hair back with her fingers, wound it around into her normal bun. "That's where they'll send me. They say everyone goes voluntarily. But I've never heard of anybody coming out."

If what she was saying were true, we'd stumbled onto a whole lot more than we'd bargained for. "Serious allegations you're making."

"It's God's own truth. Pun intended."

"And you want me to take it—"

"On faith?" She laughed at her own joke. "That's what everything I gave you is for. Hand the notes and the pigment to your R & D guy. Have him use them to prove that we aren't making Hope. You've got the sample, and the antique dealer's collection. He's got Lavender in there. I saw it when I went in after Cassius's goons had decimated the place. To sequence the Mauve Faith, you'll have to alter the code on your spinner. Otherwise the results will be gibberish. You'll need to run the Hope with the same code, or the comparison won't be valid. Do that, prove the differences, publish them, show the world what a fraud this whole thing is. And when you do—" She pulled lipstick out of her pocket. Managed to apply it perfectly without the need for a mirror. "Make sure to cite my work."

And with that, she jumped out the window.

CHAPTER 22

She didn't make a sound going down. I crossed the room just as she crashed into the bushes below. Watched as she tumbled into the ravine, arms and legs limp. Her body stopped at the base of a tangled buckeye. The neck was bent at an angle that made me sick to look at. One of her stilettos had come off and lay heel up in the dirt. A takeout bag had snagged on a stalk of poison oak next to her. It fluttered in the breeze, *THANK YOU THANK YOU THANK YOU THANK YOU.*

I couldn't be seen here. Her death was suicide, but no one was going to believe that with a Pigment Enforcement agent on mental health leave holding a gun on the premises. I opened the diary to *WHAT IS THE POINT?* and left it on the unmade bed. It had my prints on it, but there was no helping that. If it was explanation enough for the neurotypical cops, they wouldn't bother dusting the place anyway. Slid the Glock, notebooks, and pigment into Tommy's gym bag and beat a fast retreat.

In the car, I sat with my hands on the wheel. Trying to catch my breath. My insides were shivering. If what Priscilla had said was true, she'd blown open the case for us. But I couldn't imagine how I was going to tell Tommy she was dead.

I turned on the radio to clear my head. The budget negotiations in Miami dominated the headlines. The chairman of the Fed had gone down to Argentina to ask for yet another loan of billions of pesos. That had sure gotten the New Whigs' knickers in a twist. The senator of the Northeast Territories was on the radio, bellyaching about capital flight and inflation controls. It was the same words every year, with the same end result: less money for government operations, more programs abandoned. The Chief's status as a Twenty-Fiver meant that Meekins's and my jobs were safe, but small departments like ours across the country would be looking to find any fat left to trim. Berdie's job would probably be on the line. I couldn't say I'd miss him or his mushrooms very much. The news didn't take my mind off things the way it normally did. None of it would matter if Ashaji turned us into a theocracy. I doubted those of us investigating her plans would be in her good books, decorated veteran leader or not.

I exited toward the hospital. Every cross street took me closer to the only possible conclusion: there was no way to avoid telling my colleagues what had happened. If I didn't explain that Priscilla was dead, they'd ask why I'd let her go. And I didn't want to leave them thinking that maybe I'd killed her. I could try leaving out the part where Priscilla jumped from Tommy's window. Act like it had happened elsewhere. That wouldn't work. Eventually someone would notice the body and then there would be a police report.

I wished I could let my cadet down easy. This was going to stir up plenty of feelings for him. Especially after she'd shot him full of Ennui. I couldn't get the image of Kim's body wrapped around the tree out of my mind. I'd seen plenty of suicides, from Walter to Blufftown Tuck. But I'd never been there when the person made that choice. I wondered if I could've stopped her. If something in her face had shown what she'd been planning, if I'd known how to look. What the air felt like on the bare skin below her bun as she plummeted.

I arrived without a strategy. I stopped in Trumbull's office on my way in. Made a call to Doug at the lab to thank him for the nice card Aunt Amy had sent me. If this whole thing was a PSI operation, it wouldn't just be my home phone they'd have tapped. Made my way to Tommy's room. Didn't have a chance to keep overthinking what I'd say. The cadet pounced on his bag, thrilled to have his own duds again. The bottle of whisky was on top. "You stopped at a liquor store?"

"It's Priscilla's," I said. "She's dead."

So much for breaking it gently. He asked what happened, and I told him. He slumped into the plastic chair as he listened, looking at his elbows locked together on his knees. "For someone so smart, she was really good at making dumb choices." He stood back up, arms dangling at his sides. Looked around like he'd forgotten what he was going to do. Then he lifted the gym bag and put it on the bed. Stared out the window. Started unpacking. Set the gun, bottle of Mauve, and lab notebooks to one side. "You going to tell me what you got out of her?"

I took his cue to play it cool and forged ahead. He started stowing the clothes I'd brought in the tiny closet, smoothing the wrinkles as best he could out of the button-downs. He was nodding and making noises in the right places, but I wasn't holding his focus. *Cassius-is-Big-Skinny-is-PSI* clearly didn't land. I was laying out the implications of the false Hope's release when Doug showed up and I had to start over.

I pointed him to Priscilla's notes and the Mauve Faith. A quick glance at them was enough for him to confirm that she hadn't been lying about the magnitude of her discovery. "She went back to Munsell." He breathed over the notebook. "She models the known spectrum of pigments in three dimensions. Normally we look at a list or maybe something like a color wheel, right? She's added an axis of luminance—how dark each pigment is. Grayscale, she calls it. Then she places the pigments we know in a sphere. Suddenly you can see—" He pointed to a drawing, shaded carefully with colored pencils. The late lady's teacher's-pet side out in full force. Tommy went back to unpacking. "Blackberry Purple Phobia and Slate Gray Ennui are nestled up next to each other. Which, well. I guess Ennui can be a reaction to more existential fears—the 'freeze' option in the fight, flight, or freeze defense mechanism. But that's not all. Once Priscilla found that relationship she was able to move back up along that grayscale axis to find—oh, this is where her Silver Lilac Wistfulness comes from! This is— If this were public knowledge, it would blow the field wide open. Her breakthrough would allow for the sequencing and creation of a vast array of new pigments."

My cadet was holding an empty hanger, eyes wide and wet. Looked like he needed a good cry. But he wouldn't do it with us around. Or alone, most likely. I could tell Doug was on a roll. No chance he'd notice. I touched Plato's arm, told him to go get Trumbull. The doctor would know how to keep Tommy from shutting down again.

I slipped the gun, Mauve Faith vial, and notebook back into the bag before she arrived. She handed me the whisky without a word and shooed us out to do her work. I wondered if Tommy'd have the sense not to give specifics to her. The fewer folks who knew I'd been in the apartment the day Prissy jumped, the better. I put that out of my mind. There was no point borrowing trouble from tomorrow.

As we walked toward my room, Doug said, "You could've—"

I didn't want to hear it. I was already beating myself up over how I'd broken the news to Tommy. "I could've waited for you to get here before telling him. I know."

"No. You could've called me. From the apartment. What if the clip had been full in her second gun?" I pointed out that it hadn't been, so it didn't matter. He didn't say anything for a bit. Then he hefted the gym bag. "I guess I should get on this."

"Sure," I said and watched him walk away from me. At the end of the hallway, he turned back.

"You don't need to be a lone ranger. I'm on your team, but you've got to use me. Tommy's not the only one I worry about."

Then I was alone with far too much food for thought. Seemed like everyone picked on me for working on my own. *Lone ranger* wasn't necessarily a bad thing. The Chief was a solo operator. Sure. As if I were on her level. She'd become that out of necessity. When Walter had been around, she'd leaned on him plenty. We both had. Of course, I'd been a cadet back then, just learning the ropes. But I hadn't felt like I had on-call backup since he'd passed.

The night I'd found Walter's body I couldn't stay asleep. Kept waking up, heart pounding from nightmares that fled just as fast as they came on. Around six, I had rolled out of bed. Did a workout. My mentor's mantra had always been "sweat it out," no matter what "it" was. Too much to think about? Put on running shoes, hit the track. A cold? Push-ups. Mad, sad, brokenhearted? Tell it to the punching bag.

He'd always been suspicious of Pigment-assisted processing. Icarus's Journeys™ or the more straightforward Purges™ all seemed like newfangled quackery to him. He was more into not having strong feelings in the first place. But that morning, my punches were weak and ungrounded, my focus scattered. Felt like I was coming apart. In the shower, I figured what the hell. It wasn't like he'd know if I used a little paint to glue myself back together.

We always said "grief" as if it were a noun, but it was Pigment 101 that mourning was a process instead. You couldn't just paint yourself with a Melancholy Inductor Class color and call it a day. Luckily, Icarus had me covered. Their Grief Processing Journeys™ promised to let users "work through the five stages of grief in under twelve hours." Only hitch was you needed a prescription to get one, and no psychiatrist was going to see me on a Sunday.

I didn't want to run the risk of ending up with something sketchy. Hadn't skipped Magenta at parties all these decades to pick up a knockoff when it was really important. I got in my car and headed to San Bruno to track down my dead mentor's pharmacist cousin. If anybody would bend the rules for me, I figured it would be him.

He wasn't happy about my lack of an Rx, but I looked nutty enough that he went into the back. I could see him through the open door, flipping through boxes. *Grief Processing Journey™: Wife*, I read on one. *Daughter. Mother.* He was clean-shaven and skinny, nothing like his cousin. I was glad. Didn't know how I would've handled another Lopez with a mustache walking around while the man who'd welcomed me to Daly City lay in a mortuary.

The pharmacist finally found the male options and asked how I would describe my relationship to Walter. I pointed out it was the same damn colors in all of them, and he said the guidance tape was just as important as the active pigments. Then he asked if we'd been lovers.

"I worked with him," I said, my voice going tight. He said most people didn't come around begging for Grief Packets at seven a.m. on a Sunday when their colleagues passed. We went on like that for a while and then he told me he had to make a phone call. When he came back, he handed me a paper bag.

Later I found out he'd rung up Linda. Not sure how I felt about him asking the grieving widow whether I'd had an affair with her husband, but at least she'd convinced him that I wasn't there trying to pull some sort of twisted raid for off-prescription pigment sales. He told me twice to read the directions. Like he thought I'd pull some sort of rookie move and charge in without preparation.

At home, I poured a bowl of cereal and made another pot of coffee. Flipped through the *Daly Daily* like I was reading it. Finally got myself together to pull out the box. It was the same size as the ones Mom's hair dye came in. The cover was a rose superimposed over a photo of a man's silhouette walking into the sunset. The pale blue copy read *Grief Processing Journey*™: *Father.* I guessed that was the closest relationship the pharmacist could find to "mentor." The five stages and their corresponding pigments were denial (Sunshine Yellow), anger (Bull's Blood Rage), bargaining (Cerulean Guilt), depression (Cobalt Sadness), and acceptance (Golden Peace). I wasn't sure how the creators of the pack had decided that guilt was equivalent to bargaining, but I figured that was why I wasn't in the business of treatment.

The pigment came in squeezable hazpig tubes shorter than my thumb, the name of each printed in bold letters across the lime-green material. There were five cassette tapes: pale yellow, dark red, sky blue, navy, and warm gold. The instructions said to place a picture of my "loved one" somewhere prominent before starting. I didn't have a photo of Walter, so I ended up using his department headshot out of the obituary in the *Daily*. Probably the last time the newspaper would run it. Would they throw out the copy they'd kept on file? I taped the cutting to the wall and sat my chair in front of it. The portrait was so small it could've been anyone with a mustache.

I squeezed the dribble of Sunshine out of its packet onto the inside of my wrist. Swabbed it into a stripe and covered it with a smear of Vaseline to keep it from evanescing into the atmosphere faster than it went into my system.

In my childhood comic books, the characters knew immediately when they'd been hit by pigment, even if they couldn't control its effects. Sweat would break out at their temples, the hair on the back of their neck would stand up. In reality, the physiological effects were just the ones caused by the emotion itself. Different for each pigment, different for each person. One kid at the academy had claimed he could always tell when pigment was around, but he was so monstrously even-keeled that I doubted he ever experienced strong feelings without a little color to goose him up.

Sunshine always made my mind and body feel more welcome in the world. Like there was plenty of space for everything. The pigment came on faster through my skin than from the time-release gelcaps I took each morning, a loosening in my joints and more room in my lungs. Suddenly the neighbor's briefs hanging in their window no longer distracted me from the glimpse of the hills peeking past the buildings. The morning fog had burned off and the trees were a rich green in the noonday light. I slid the yellow cassette into the tape player.

"Your father was a very special person," said a man's gruff tenor. It was a good thing I had the picture of Walter to focus on, as the guide kept nattering on about paternal strength and worthiness. Didn't help when I realized I was listening to an actor from a show Dad and I had watched regularly, a sitcom about a group of teens in 1950s Milwaukee. My now-guide had swaggered around in a leather jacket and a pompadour until the whole cast got Blued over in the Hollywood blitz in '83. He'd been the only one who pulled through, resurfacing after a five-year coma to find the States in post-war disarray. Seemed he'd forgotten his experience of stardom, which was probably for the best since America had forgotten about him. He'd landed right in the uncanny valley between fame and amnesia. A voice that was familiar but hard to place. Used it to hustle up anonymous voice-over jobs for pharmaceutical companies, apparently. He droned on somberly about how "denial has a time and a place—but right now is the time and place to let it go."

I stared as hard as I could at Walter's picture, but kept slipping back to memories of sitting on the couch with Dad, fingers greasy with potato chips, the smell of his Old Spice mingling with whatever Mom had going in the pressure cooker. That had been nice. My downstairs neighbors got home from church. The smell of stewing chicken adobo drifted up through the floorboards, tangy and meaty. Under the glow of the Yellow I could feel Walter's loss worrying at me like an unpicked scab. I drifted like that for most of the two hours it took to get through the cassette, listening to the upbeat-but-frenetic banjo picking some genius had chosen to underscore the guide's platitudes. I could measure how much the pigment had worn off by how grating I found the music. I was real ready to move on to the Rage by the time the tape clicked to the end.

The Bull's Blood went about how I expected. The pigment came on with a thunk and then a roar, like a furnace door inside me had dropped open and the banked fire had burst back to life. My jaw went tight, my heart galloped in my chest. Trying to hold myself together around all that had me real twitchy. Couldn't stay in my chair, so I paced around after hitting play.

"Here, we'll face the ways your father let you down," the tape said. Dad's death at the early end of my teenagehood had guaranteed that I'd already run myself ragged up and down that list. Made it a lot easier to stay focused on Walter. When the pacing wasn't enough, I headed to the punching bag. The guide told me to "let your anger flow on through you."

This time, my knuckles struck true. There were plenty of little things to brood about, but I kept coming back to the rotten move of offing himself where I'd been guaranteed to find his body. Spared his wife from that nasty surprise, but Linda had family around. I had no one. Well, the Chief, but she was going through the same mess I was. My hands would be sore tomorrow. Told myself to take it easy. Took a twisted pleasure in ignoring my own advice.

I always found it strange, the double consciousness of the pigment high.

I knew I'd dosed myself. Knew my feelings were induced. The bone-clicking buzz of fury still seemed like it was all mine. I let sweat run into my eyes, spatter across the wall. Felt like it'd been just five minutes before I had to flip the tape, and just another five before the ire began to ebb. My punches became just punches, my kicks just kicks. By the time I moved into my cooldown routine, the usual post-workout blanket of detachment had settled over me.

I took a break and showered again. Made myself four turkey and Swiss sandwiches. Three p.m. was late for lunch and early for dinner, so I decided to get them both out of the way at the same time. For once, I had food in the house. Every few weeks Linda got on Walter's case to make sure I was buying groceries, and this Thursday he'd been particularly insistent about it. Threatened to fill my fridge himself if I didn't carve out time to stop at the supermarket. I hadn't thought anything of it. Now I wondered if he'd had extra reason to make sure my cupboard wasn't bare. I felt nothing at the thought. Seemed the Grief Packet was doing its job. Was real glad I'd convinced the pharmacist to hand it over, instead of suffering another day. High up, thin clouds painted a herringbone pattern on the sky. Dad would've said it would rain tonight. Good sleeping weather. I was looking grimly forward to finishing the task I'd started and getting a solid night's rest.

But the trip on Cerulean Guilt was where things started to get ugly. It came on hard and fast, doubling me over before I even got the tape in. I was instantly hollow, all hat and no cattle, a fake who made life worse for everyone around me. My legs went weak and my palms went sweaty. I tried to breathe through the rush, but there was too much there. With the pigment slashing its way across my mind, Walter's insistence that I get groceries suddenly looked like an indictment. Just one of the many details I'd chosen to ignore. The silences I'd let sit instead of breaking. The signs that something was off.

I hit play to try to get away from my thoughts. No dice. The actor's voice couldn't break past the waves of my regret. At the Magenta Cares charity gala that spring, Linda had asked me how I thought he was doing. It was a strange question but I didn't dwell on it. She'd clearly known what was happening. But I, the person who waited at stoplights, watching him worry at his hangnails, had paid no attention. To that, or the bags growing under his eyes. To the way he'd sit in his car at the end of the day, not leaving the parking lot. So much like Dad sitting in his truck in the driveway, Hank Williams Jr. drifting from the stereo. Staring at the porchlight and not coming in until he caught me watching from my bedroom window.

The cassette reached the end of side A. I got up to flip it over. My thighs were shaking from the trip. The late-afternoon sun crept through the window. Reached my boots, warm on my ankles. The second half of the ride was no better than the first. The pale blue line on my wrist was losing color, but the Guilt still dripped sticky as treacle through my system. If I'd been three years older, I could've enlisted instead of Dad—they were taking sixteen-year-olds by the time he signed up. Told him to stay home, take care of Mom. I would've weathered the Blue hits better than he had.

The thoughts were familiar, many-legged things that had skittered around the edge of my brain for decades. I'd always swept them back into their dark corner as soon as they'd crept out. Now they clung tight to my shoulders, too heavy with pigment to just brush off. The tape ran to static. Clicked to the end, going dead.

I sat there while dusk fell, Walter's picture fading into a dim stain on the shadowed wall. My upstairs neighbor had turned on the evening news. Next door I could hear the theme song of an Argentine telenovela set in the Wild West, and then the familiar cockney patter of the British actors Buenos Aires had hired to dub the cowboys. It was only the thought that giving up after getting this far was a great way for the Guilt to keep me awake all night that got me out of the chair.

I turned on the light. It was way too bright. Not like I had another option. Rolled up my sleeve to make room for the Cobalt Sadness. The three older stripes lingered on my wrist, each more translucent than the next. The bold blue cut a sharp line on the soft inside of my forearm. My back prickled as I swabbed the Vaseline across the stripe. I wasn't looking forward to this one at all.

The waterworks got going before the guide's first sentence about "having a good cry" came off the tape. I'd never understood what people thought a "good cry" would do, other than mark you as easy pickings. "I'm going to ask you to do something that may feel silly," the tape continued, before instructing me to "open my heart center to the sadness" by arching my back over the seat of the chair and letting my arms "drift down toward the floor over your head." I did feel dumb trying to arrange myself in the position, especially with tears running up into my hairline. Stared upside down at the spot where the dun carpet met the dusty white wall.

"Now," the tape said, "breathe in the memories of your father."

And there it was again. Dad on the sofa laughing at the actor letting out an "eeeeeey." Dad switching the radio in his truck. Dad holding the stopwatch at the end of the pool. *Walter*, I thought to myself. Walter pulling a lunch Linda had packed for me from his car under the elm in the department parking lot, but then it was Dad handing me a brown paper bag I knew would hold a PB&J with more jelly than I liked, Dad waiting for me under the one tree in the parking lot at the pool, Dad trimming his beard and mustache in our green-tiled bathroom before we left for my middle-school promotion ceremony. He'd had to shave when he joined up. Only time in my life I'd seen him barefaced. In the living room the day he left it had felt like a stranger hugging me, his smooth cheek alien against mine.

Walter, I thought again, but it was a lost battle. My body was on the carpet. My chest shuddered in and out, an arrhythmic thumping. I was somewhere else. In a bubble up near the bare light bulb. Watching the pigment do its work. The guidance tape murmured truisms about "growing with the pain" and "making your own way through." Noises came out of my mouth, moans that couldn't even choose a vowel. My mouth, or somewhere at the nape of my neck. I couldn't really tell. I'd heard sounds like this, in the dead of the night during those dark days after Mom figured out Dad wasn't coming back. Keening leaking out of her room, out past the roses under the windows, into the dull city glow in the backyard. Felt like her voice coming out of me. Echoing across the years. Felt like puking. Felt like drowning. Felt like gone, and never coming back.

By the time I got to Golden Peace, it was almost eleven thirty. My neighbors' TVs had turned off one by one, leaving the gurgling of the plumbing to keep me company. The struggle to get up the spirit to move once the static hissed out was even harder this time. The last round should be the easiest, I told myself. Ethereal synthesizers came on when I pressed play. The warm color on the inside of my elbow looked like dandelion pollen. "Drink a glass of water and find someplace cozy. You're almost through."

My chair was a good place to take off my boots but wasn't what I'd call comfortable. I got a blanket and lay back down on the floor next to the stereo. The pigment slowly brought me back to myself. Or at least made me feel less far away. Just calm, and sleepy. A worn-out floating sensation. My breath came in, my breath went out. The midnight air was cool in my nostrils. Maybe I'd actually get some rest. "You may feel traces of anger," the tape said. "Like it's still unfair. But remember, death comes for us all." I could skip brushing my teeth. Go straight to bed. *Death comes for us all.* But death didn't come for Walter. Death didn't come for Dad. They went after it. The ceiling was blurry, I noticed, right before my cheeks got all wet again. "More recollections may appear. Let them carry you. Observe them, and let them go."

But it wasn't a memory of Walter or Dad that surfaced. Instead, it was my junior year English teacher leaping around the classroom during his "treasure-hunt" Great Poets unit. None of the pieces he assigned seemed like poems. They felt like they'd fallen off the back of the truck that sold Mom's kind of spiritual mumbo-jumbo: "be more like a goose" and "acknowledge all the people inside you," that sort of thing. Most didn't even rhyme.

When it came time to write a paper, I picked the shortest option. *To fill a gap— / Insert the thing that caused it. / Block it up / With other and 'twill yawn / The more; / You cannot solder an abyss / With air.* I knew about soldering from working at the hardware store so I figured it would be easy going. I got a lot of words out of describing how air was integral to the process of binding metals together, since without oxygen you can't get flame to melt the solder. My teacher's comment was *did not address pain of loss*.

Now, lying on the carpet staring up at the bare bulb, my pigment-soaked unconscious spat the poem back out at me. To fill a gap, insert the thing that caused it. But that thing was gone. Had taken itself away. And here I was, with two big rifts filled to the brim with emptiness. And maybe that emptiness was just what sadness felt like when I wasn't paying attention, but I could spend my life taking Grief Packets and never cry it all out. Or I could try to plug it up with something else. Some other feeling about work, or a hobby, or some other person. But the poet was right. You can't solder an abyss with air. Real dumb but real true.

Blanketed by Golden Peace, the tears running down my face felt fine. I fell asleep on the floor before the pigment wore off. Came to with a stiff neck forty minutes before I had to be at work. At least I was more rested.

Weeks and then months passed and it still hurt to walk by the closed door of Walter's office. But I did sleep better after the Grief Packet. For the most part. Some nights I'd dream I was still lying on the carpet with the knowledge that I'd never feel whole. After I'd wake up, I'd trudge through my routine, knowing what I couldn't unknow.

I was still glad I'd spent that Sunday working all the way through. It had been a kind of hell at times, but better to have gone through it in my living room instead of at the department or the supermarket or the dozen other places that randomly reminded me of my mentor. I'd been completely scattered, with my distracting thoughts about Dad butting in, and it had still helped. I couldn't imagine what it would've been like to walk around my normal life with all those unpurged feelings lying in wait, ready to ambush me at a moment's notice.

● ● ●

It shouldn't have been a surprise that watching Priscilla's suicide would bring up plenty of memories. But I'd been standing in the doorway of my room, unpronounceable whisky in my hand, for a good five minutes. I put the bottle away in the small cubby next to the sink that held Doug's toiletries. A swig would've been nice. But it was still before five and I wasn't as far gone as the late lamented. I wished I'd been able to get clothes from my place. Unpacking would've given me something to do with my hands. I turned on the TV. Nothing shook the image of the dirty stiletto, the broken body.

Somehow it felt inevitable when Howie's curls appeared in the doorway. Doug was calling from the lab, where he was supposed to be running the comparison between Priscilla Kim's sample of the Mauve Faith and the vial of Lavender Hope I'd found at Pimsley's shop. Plato had lugged the salesman's cabinet with its secret drawer back to the department the day after Tommy and I got shot up at Bepler. My stomach twisted as I made my way to Trumbull's office and put the phone to my ear. My old friend sounded far away as he said, "The antique dealer's pigment—it's gone."

CHAPTER 23

With nothing to run through the psychospectrometer, Doug turned around and came right back to the hospital. He brought what little news he had. Pimsley's cabinet of wonders was under quarantine at R & D in Iowa City. There'd been no room for the collection of vintage pigments in the lab, so Doug had stashed it in Evidence. He'd found an empty space when he'd gone to pull the Lavender Hope we needed. The paperwork for cross-departmental requisitioning was tacked to the wall. The form was dated two days ago.

Priscilla must've let slip what was in there, and her collaborators had figured we'd found the vial of Mauve Faith from Pimsley's apartment. When they didn't recover it at my digs, they'd pulled their strings at PSI and sent a lackey over for the other half of the equation. They must've anticipated Pretty Prissy's turning coat. Sans Lavender Hope, there was no way for Doug to run the compare-contrast with the new code, no way to confirm the differences with the Mauve Faith. It would be a mad runaround, trying to prove a negative.

The fall further into the dumps hit us all hard. We talked through the dead woman's revelations, piecing them together with what we'd uncovered of the conspirators' plans. The picture that was forming didn't cheer us up. Priscilla Kim and Gruber-Shaw returning from the Universidad de Comahue with their tails between their legs after overplaying the results for her synthetic Silver Lilac Wistfulness. PSI, seeing an opportunity where others would have seen disgrace, recruiting them to do clandestine pigment development.

Doug looked over everything we had and said he thought the Daly City Slate Gray had probably been the team's first deliverable: the two samples of Mauve Faith were housed in the same cut-glass vials as the flask of boutique Ennui that had put the bug in his ear that brought him down here. Seemed the Psychopigment Service Investigators had decided that a little black-market income boost to their bottom line would be welcome.

No place better to base their hustle than Daly City. It was Priscilla's hometown, offering a cushy job for Gruber-Shaw at Icarus for his cover story, with Cassius coordinating on trips back and forth from Iowa. A backwater borough known for its lack of pigment activity, sitting right under the Argentines' noses. They'd started with the Gray, but Priscilla kept sniffing down the path that had led her to the Silver Lilac Wistfulness. Eventually, her research led to Mauve Faith, and the team realized that what they had could change the country. This time, though, they needed to really test-drive drive it. None of the fudged numbers that got them into trouble at the Universidad de Comahue.

Enter Ashaji, with thousands of devotees who would follow her off a cliff—or volunteer to be dosed with experimental pigment. A spiritual leader for the faith-fried to fixate on. She had what PSI needed. But she wasn't going to give it up without exacting her price: power. She'd been consolidating clout ever since the death of her cofounder Pinky, evangelizing through her memoirs and speech tours of the country, sweeping up the remains of cult after disintegrating cult. Now, she'd take that to the next level as theocrat-in-chief. The group's sudden interest in local real estate made a lot more sense. Investment for an influx of followers in Daly City's future as some sort of mecca.

So here we were. PSI and the Pinkos as uneasy bedfellows, working together on a coup no one would notice until it was too late. Would Cassius be content to pull strings from behind the curtain? Or was he planning to take Ananda out, once they'd used her charisma to abolish the Constitution? Those were questions for the future, but they weren't going to let me rest any easier.

And on top of all that Priscilla had said she'd "ended up in bed with the Knights of Liberty." Shouldn't have come as a surprise. Ashaji's brother had been jailed for arms-dealing for them, after all. Gave a particularly noxious aftertaste to the foul-news cocktail we'd just downed. Doug and I left Tommy staring at the wall.

In my room, I pulled out the dead woman's whisky. The wax of the Dixie cups gave the liquor a Kool-Aid finish. Doug said he'd looked up an old paper he remembered on domestic Deepest Blue exposures, written by one Cassius Jeremiah Abernathy. "From right when the Agency was founded," he said. "Seems he was stationed in Iowa City. Didn't say what his position was."

"Maybe he was an early member of PSI, then."

He nodded. "There was a Twenty-Fiver who went by CJ."

CJ Abernathy. Cassius Jeremiah. I recognized the name now. He'd fought in Charleston alongside our own Louise Knorr. My throat was dry. I wet it with more whisky. "Do you think he's working with the Chief?"

"I don't think she'd have let me stick around down here if she were mixed up in this. But who knows. Maybe they're playing a deep game. Or maybe she had no idea. Or Cassius has dirt on her. Does it matter?" Doug raised his Dixie cup. "To insubordination." Through the blinds, the streetlamp cast striped shadows across the room. A sliver of moon was rising over the building next to Edie's. We drank.

He ended up telling me about the time he and a cousin had pinched two hazpig suits in the '90s and spent the day exploring the remains of New York City. The worst damage was down in Lower Manhattan, so they'd started by driving across the George Washington and Alexander Hamilton bridges into the Bronx. They'd found the family's old street. The structure next door had collapsed, but their apartment building was still standing.

"Everything was in there, covered in dust," Doug said. "All the stuff my parents talk about leaving behind—their wedding album, Grandad's paintings—right where I remembered it. There was no time to pack when we were evacuated. The weirdest sensation, to have it there, on the other side of the hazpig suit, and know I couldn't take any of it to them. The Blue was still way too strong. Any of the mementoes in that room would wipe their memory in no time flat."

The two had driven as far south as they could. The debris from the conventional bombings that had followed the Gauchos' pigment attacks blocked the road at Eightieth. They got out of the car and walked through the subway tunnels, popping up to the surface whenever they found a surviving station. In Times Square, they scared a pack of deer grazing on the Virginia creeper that covered the rubble. "I knew the city would be empty." His glasses flashed sulfur yellow when he tipped his head, catching the streetlight. "But it's one thing to know it, and another thing to see it."

He had a snapshot in his wallet, taken by his cousin. It showed Doug sitting jauntily in his hazpig suit on the old stoop. "My mom almost died when we showed her the photos. Going into the city was the dumbest thing I think I've ever done." Around the edges of the picture, I could see the Blue haze still floating ten years after the attack. He said, "You would've had a blast."

I remembered his parents beaming up at us on graduation day. His mom wore a burgundy church hat and his dad had a matching handkerchief in his breast pocket. They'd held hands through the whole ceremony. I imagined tromping through the wasted metropolis with Doug, framing the shot he'd carry around for the next decade and a half. What our lives could've been like.

I pushed that thought away, off into the shadowed corner of my mind where I was keeping worries about Kim's suicide and the dead end we'd been backed into. I asked for more whisky. Neither of us wanted to face the small hours alone, so he pulled his bedding into the room, dropped it with a clatter. We settled down in the darkness. Just like old times. Just like old friends. His breathing evened out quickly. I lay awake listening. Even after all these years, it felt so familiar. Somewhere at the edge of sleep, I had a blue-tinted dream of him leaning in to kiss me.

●●●

The next morning I opened the window and stood there, feeling the breeze run over my face. The air was damp from a spring shower, full of the smell of sprouting grass. Doug was off at Edie's, getting our morning cups of joe. The pavement below was still wet from the rain. Priscilla's fall had been from twice as high, once I factored in the ravine. I'd slept fitfully, trapped in dreams of trying to save her. In one I'd caught her before she made it over the windowsill. She'd smiled Tommy's smile, grabbed the gun from my hand, and slid it into her mouth. In one I'd fallen with her. The blanket on Doug's cot was still puckered around the outline of his absent body. I was glad I hadn't spent the night by myself.

He came back with the coffee and the *Daly Daily*. The top headline was the one I'd been dreading. "Woman's Body Found in Ravine." A story gruesome enough that it ran without alliteration. Seemed the cops had written it off as suicide. Should have calmed some of my aimless unease, but I could tell that with nothing to fill the day ahead I'd spend plenty of time dwelling on the fact that they'd found her so fast. Wondering if anyone had spotted my Renault. Underneath was an article about the arrests of the leaders of the local dogfighting ring. Jenna Lila Fifi must have been thrilled to have so many options for the front page.

Doug packed up the late scientist's gun. Seemed like he was the best person to dispose of it, with Tommy and me still in the hospital. As he got ready to leave, I asked if there'd been any movement to check on my busted-up apartment. Turned out Berdie hadn't passed the news along to anyone. Well, he wasn't the brightest color on the spectrum. I asked Doug to mention it to the Chief. He said she'd been out with a cold yesterday, but that he'd let her know if she was in.

The woman who'd worked through walking pneumonia was out with a cold? Something frigid ran down my spine. "We need to go check out her place," I said. "Right now."

"You need to stay on that Sunshine drip for at least another three hours. Trumbull told me what her orders are." Apparently no one trusted me to take care of myself. Doug pulled his sweater vest out of the room's closet. "We'll go as soon as you're out this afternoon. I'll come pick you up."

I said "sure" and let him leave. As soon as he was gone, I pulled out the drip and stole down the fire escape to the parking lot.

The drive to the Chief's lasted a century. The light at Hickey and Junipero Serra had gone out, the morning traffic backed up all the way to the hospital. The cop directing the flow of cars seemed like she had a vendetta against my lane. I sure could've used my Pigment Enforcement siren. My knuckles were white on the steering wheel. Clenching my fist pulled on the tender tissue around my shoulder wound. On the radio, a report on a bill to ban Spanish classes in schools. "You don't see Gauchos learning English," said a supporter gathering signatures. The reporter pointed out there were nineteen other Spanish-speaking countries. "Sure, but those people are all in league with Buenos Aires." Those people. On the bus ride from the academy to Daly City, I'd wondered how Chief Louise Knorr felt about having a Hispanic cadet. I'd walked in my first day to find that my mentor's last name was Lopez.

I'd gotten a call from the Chief the Saturday that I'd found Walter. He hadn't been home the night before. The drive to the office that morning had felt a lot like this one. A cramp in my calf, my head a pill bottle stuffed with too much cotton. The hills broke out into a flat stretch, trees replaced with boilerplate split-level condos. A few roofs had caved in near an Envy Green spill, the owners long gone. YOUR FEELINGS ARE NOT YOUR OWN. This time, I was pretty sure they were. If our department's fearless leader wasn't in the office, something or someone was keeping her out of it.

Memories of her in her prime ran on a loop through my head: trademark utility vest and brown hair walking unarmed into an Envy Green manufactory, talking the crooks out of there using a tipped beaker of pigment and sheer willpower; booting the press from the department with a petrifying growl and then turning to Walter and me, beaming like a teenager who'd convinced the Fuller Brush man they were the owner of the house. I couldn't leave her high and dry, even for an extra few hours.

My coffee-only breakfast had burned into an ulcer by the time I turned onto her street. Driving past her pale green house, everything looked in order. The curtains were tied back, the little box hedges undisturbed. I pulled over on the corner. She was probably long gone. Or—if she were there—she might have an unwelcome companion watching over her.

I was in no state to handle a confrontation, especially if it was with someone armed with pigment. I would've traded a lifetime worth of hot sauce to be back on the force, able to just radio Meekins and ask for backup. Never thought I'd see the day that I'd be wishing for him. I got out of the car. Case the joint now, make the call later.

There was no car in the driveway, but the Chief's Russian Lada could be inside the closed garage. I tried the handle, but the door stayed down. Around the back, a gardening trowel lay next to a raised flower bed. Dirt rimmed the spade. Five marigold plants nodded in their little plastic tubs. The sixth languished on its side by a hole. Wasn't like the Chief to leave a task unfinished. My stomach tightened. Around the front, a Welcome sign had fallen onto the steps of the stoop. I took the stairs two at a time. Halfway to the top, a woman's reedy whispering stopped me.

"Who is she? She's someone—I've seen her before. No, I haven't. She's a person. Must be a person. Why is she blue? Blue, blue, blue as the deep blue sea . . ."

I turned slowly. To my right, a tiny old woman crouched behind the hedge under the front window. There were leaves in her thin bouffant. She wore a pink gingham house dress with a ruffled collar. The knees were stained with dirt, but the fabric was new. Her gray eyes slid across mine, wide with carmine rims. I'd seen that lost look on the face of plenty of pigment victims. She was too gone to be a threat. As I reached for the doorknob, though, she let out a high keening noise. "Danger, in there! Dangerous. Dangerous. Bang pffffffff—" Air blew through her lips.

I had a flash of the cuckoo clock at Bepler puffing pigment. Maybe best not to march right in. I leaned to look through the window, cupping my hands to block out the afternoon light. Sure enough, the far wall had the unmistakable bull's-eye mark of a hit from a pigment gun. The bullets had been Deepest Blue.

Who would have done this? I rubbed my neck. Of course I had ideas. But that wasn't the burning question. The burning question was *what to do?* The bull's-eye showed preliminary signs of aging. It had to have been there at least twenty-four hours. The Chief could still be in there—or just her remains. My throat itched for a cigarette. Trumbull'd put the fear of God in me. I'd run straight into enough firestorms in the past few weeks. I needed to pass on this one. I headed to the pay phone on the corner.

This time, I buzzed the police department first. Berdie couldn't ignore the report if the call came in from Daly City's finest. The old woman was a puzzle. The new dress and the coif suggested she wasn't homeless, but there wasn't anyone watching her. She whispered nonsense while I searched her pockets. No ID. I didn't want to leave her there for the police to take in for vagrancy. She knew something about what had happened inside. Chances were she'd been caught in the cross fire.

I couldn't leave a pigment victim sitting on the sidewalk. If anybody in the neighborhood was looking for her, they would have found her by now. Without treatment, victims of the Blue tend to hang around the spot where they got hit. It's spooky going anywhere when you can't remember your own name.

I bundled her into my Renault. The fog burned off. As soon as I heard the sirens approaching we set out for the hospital. The official line was still that I'd painted up Bepler. Better to be nowhere near when the police got to the scene—no need for me to get hauled in for paintballing the Chief's, too. If my boss hadn't made it out of the house, there was nothing I could do for her at this point.

I'd been pacing Walter's office when she got to the department that day. Not looking at the body. The vodka. The pills. The ochre and red flecks of vomit on the teak veneer of his desk. She'd gently led me out of there and brewed me up a cup of coffee, measuring in a strong pour of bourbon from a flask. She'd handed me a Sunshine pill and then sat with her hand on my back. The police clomped back and forth through the hall, barking words at each other; the coroner came. The Chief didn't say anything but she never left my side. If she were gone, who would sit with me? My passenger muttered as I drove. A drizzle started up. My throat itched worse.

Trumbull met me in the waiting room. I was ready for her lecture. I thought. But her first question was, "What are you doing with Marla?" At my blank look, she clarified: "That's the Chief's mom." My erstwhile charge grinned toothlessly, then scampered into my room and occupied the bed. The stories of my boss caring for an ailing mother suddenly made sense. I loosened my fanny pack. Trumbull ran a hand through her short hair. "I guess I should call Louise."

"Somebody shot up her house with Deepest Blue." My skull was heavy. Had this been a warning aimed at Doug, Tommy, and me? Or something caused by our poking around the Mauve Faith? The jackhammers pounded outside. A tremble ran from my jaw down my spine, through my ribs and hips. I folded over my wounded shoulder, suddenly throbbing. My fanny pack had a stain on it, red brown against the navy polyester. Probably Edie's hot sauce. From when? I tried to wipe it away but my fingers were shaking too much.

The doctor caught me. I must've fallen. Her arm held me up, moving me down the hall. My feet got tangled on the way. Howie was on the other side of me, and we were going into a room. Not mine, a different one, but all the same. Gray linoleum, dingy walls with a wide olive band painted across them. I couldn't see if there was a spider. The street-facing window let in the same noises of traffic and construction.

They left me in bed. The drizzle had turned into a full-on rainstorm. Tires sloshed and whined through the puddles below. Thinking the Chief could be gone was a new kind of lonely. Stranger and wider than Walter's absence. I'd learned from her to live in solitude, but never wanted it to be this deep.

About a month after my awful trip to visit Doug in Boise, she had joined Walter and me for our weekly beer. After he went home to his wife, my boss bought me another pint. She mentioned that the two of us were spending a lot of time together. The truth was that my Thursday-night beers with him had also become Tuesday-night beers, and then Monday-night beers as well. I told her I was going through a rough spot. That I'd been lonesome.

She took a long pull of her lager, put down her glass. "Lonesome is what there is in this business," she said. "Someone outside will never understand what it's like to come home after spending a day on a fresh pigment spill. Someone in the department ... well, not just in the department. You like men in any profession in this country, they either died in the war or they're married." Her gray irises reflected the flashing lights of the dive's jukebox, red, gold, red, gold. She held my gaze for a minute, then turned her head. "You like something other than men, better hope the Knights of Liberty don't find out. You've got mentors for a while, but eventually we'll be gone, too."

My friendship with Walter wasn't anything like that, I wanted to tell her, but I got the message and swallowed my emptiness. Even on days when it felt like I was lugging a giant hole around inside me, I'd know she was at the department, wearing her jacket and the frown that could change like lightning to that mischievous grin. I could always count on it, even if the rest of my life felt like an abandoned housing project. But now—I was still shaking. I felt like a drama queen, but hell. Spend twenty years under someone's watchful eye, what do you do when it closes?

● ● ●

They left me alone with Sunshine and apple juice for a couple hours. I slept some. Stared at the ceiling. Around lunchtime I heard Trumbull and Doug talking in hushed voices out in the hall. "I told her I'd come back for her," my old friend said.

"And what? You expected her to do the sensible thing and sit around waiting?"

"She's generally a sensible person."

"Until she's not," Trumbull said. Told him I wasn't up for visitors and sent him away.

The afternoon and then evening ticked away. Tommy and I sat in my new room waiting for news from the department. The rain continued its dreary onslaught. We turned on the television but Ananda Ashaji was on every channel. She was signing off all her interviews with *God Bless America*. Gave me the heebie-jeebies, so we moved on to the paper. Tommy didn't have much to say about the article on Priscilla's body.

I wondered who'd found Tommy's cousin. If they'd identified her yet. How his family would take the news. Wondered exactly what it was she'd worried her colleagues would do to her up in Turlock. The Hope Count was slowly dropping. I felt heavy after my histrionic afternoon.

Doug arrived around nine p.m. He poured himself a Dixie cup of single malt and sat on the bed next to me. The Blue in the living room had been Agency-made, the same batch the crooks had used at Bepler. He, Meekins, and Cynthia had headed over to the Chief's as soon as the call came through from the cops. The neurotypicals had already done a sweep of the place when they arrived, and it seemed the bull's-eye in the living room had been the tip of the iceberg. Blood spray in the kitchen, a trail of gore leading out into the garage. "The forensic med said that amount of blood at the Chief's age . . ." He trailed off.

Doug didn't need to finish the sentence. The Chief was gone. The insides of my head were still two times too big for my skull. Somehow it didn't seem like a surprise. I'd been imagining the worst since he'd mentioned her being out with a cold this morning. My feelings were coming through static. Raindrops pelted the window. The silence in the room was heavy. Tommy had his hands over his mouth, elbows tight together and eyes squeezed shut.

I lay back. I could hear Marla babbling down the hall. Had she watched while they murdered her daughter? Watched, and then forgotten? The stakes were suddenly high enough to give me vertigo. The game wasn't just a nice adrenaline rush for a two-bit player like me. Slate Gray, Magenta,

Deepest Blue—I'd risked my sanity, body, and career on this case, but was I willing to bargain away my mother's mind? Who else would Cassius target? Doug's parents, Tommy's grandmother?

Maybe I should've taken the ticket out when it was offered. This wasn't Curtida as David with a slingshot of Slate Gray against PSI's Goliath with a club dipped in Mauve Faith. It was earthworm versus bulldozer. Pretending I could do anything was just a lie I told myself to keep from facing my uselessness.

Tommy stood abruptly, pushing his plastic chair across the linoleum with a screech. Poured his own Dixie cup of scotch and downed it. "So, what's the next step?"

Out the window, the sapling in front of Edie's whipped in the wind. Doug took off his glasses, rubbed the bridge of his nose. "I'm not sure there is one," he said.

"You know," Tommy said, "the Chief was the only person willing to interview Cynthia and me for fieldwork? Only bites I got were grunt positions in R & D. And Cynthia—I mean, her driving during tactical paintball exercises was *legendary*, and they offered her a secretary position in New Memphis. And then Louise Knorr gets wind of us and the next thing we know we're out here training under a Twenty-Fiver." He was all jitter and angles now, the lassitude that had cloaked him since the news of our boss's disappearance nowhere to be seen. "They killed Pimsley. Drove Priscilla to suicide. Now they got the Chief. I've lost too much to just roll over and play dead. I figure if I do, it'll stop being an act pretty fast. We need to hit back. Or at least try. Aim to take them all the way down.

"Pims had Lavender Hope. That means someone other than the Lausanne Laboratory has managed to capture it in the wild. So why couldn't we?"

"We have no idea when that was from, Tommy," I said. "It was probably bottled before the Third Global Hope Depletion Event. It may've been possible in the nineties, but now . . ."

"Actually," Doug said, "there may be a way."

We both turned to look at him. Outside, lightning flashed, the storm worsening as night drew in. My old friend went to pour himself another round. He loosened his tie, cleared his throat, and launched into a jargon-filled lecture about the theories behind tricky pigment capture.

Apparently, thanks to the Bion feedback loop, everybody assumed the way to capture Hope was to get a group together and harvest from multiple sources. But, just as groups could amplify their emotions and psych each other into feelings, they could psych each other *out* of them.

Plato had long wondered about the possibility of finding a single ideal subject and doing a more focused capture. He cited some paper on the initial harvesting of Scarlet Passion at a soccer match between rival teams River and Boca in Buenos Aires. "The problem is locating someone who still truly hopes. Someone with a strong enough sense of self to not be affected by the low density of Lavender in the wild. Someone stubborn, with immense strength of will. Get them at a life-changing event—childbirth, graduation, a wedding—and I'm pretty sure we'd have a shot at completing the capture. But . . . we'd have to find the perfect subject. And then set up the personal equivalent of a *superclasico* soccer match for them."

Someone who still truly hopes. How many times had my mother told me I just needed to be more optimistic? And how many times had I thought the Hope Depletion Events had somehow passed her over? I couldn't set up the Super Bowl. But she harped on my dating prospects a hell of a lot more than she indulged in her football fantasies.

What could possibly make her more hopeful than me walking down the aisle? Lightning flashed again, thunder rolling close on its heels. I knew who'd have to be waiting at the altar. I looked at Doug, looked at Tommy. The crick in my neck got worse at the thought, but there was no other way.

"I think I'm going to have to marry Meekins," I said.

CHAPTER 24

"**S**o you knew I was barking up the wrong tree—and you didn't tell me?" Meekins fixed Doug with a look like sunlight through a magnifying glass.

The three of us were sitting at Edie's. She'd closed early and headed into the kitchen to give us some privacy, only popping out to refill our cups. The two men had developed some sort of friendship while I'd been recovering from Bepler, so we'd rejiggered the story to ruffle the fewest feathers. I'd still winced hearing my old friend describe everything we'd held back from the department. And Meekins had homed right in on the fact that we'd let him run after the Shamshine blind while keeping the real case to ourselves.

To his credit, he'd eaten his burger. In his shoes I would've walked out before the sodas arrived. As it was, I was rediscovering nuances of his scowl I hadn't seen since he was my cadet.

"We didn't want to split your focus until we were sure something was fishy," Doug said. "We're bringing you on board as soon as we got confirmation."

I was impressed and slightly unnerved by how smoothly he lied. Not even a little fidgeting with his glasses. He'd been real skeptical of the idea of me leading Meekins to the altar, even after I'd explained Mom's romantic fantasies about me and my former cadet. Tommy pointing out that I must be pretty sure about it if I was contemplating nuptials with a man I despised didn't seem to convince Doug, either.

But this morning he'd brought me coffee and sat strategizing. No, Meekins didn't need to know how long we had suspected the Shamshine case was all hot air. No, we wouldn't mention when Priscilla Kim gave us the info. Or where. Or that she gave it to me. Or what she did afterward. "You know it wasn't your fault," Doug had said. I told him it wouldn't be my fault until PSI found my prints on her diary. He shifted on his squeaky cot. "I've known field agents who practically pushed suspects out of windows, so normally I'd say you'd get away with it."

Made me wonder what all went down up in Boise. The Chief would never have covered for an agent who'd murdered a citizen. Wasn't like this was a normal situation, anyway. Now, sitting in Edie's, I was real glad to have Doug in my corner. Even if he didn't seem to want to glance my way.

"I expect this kind of stunt from her," Meekins said. "But you? You didn't think to check in with the department, instead of consulting with an inmate of the psych ward?"

I said, "With the Chief gone, who would he have checked in with?"

"How about the only working agent in the local office?" I could hear the strain as he tried to keep his voice under control. It got higher pitched, anyway.

The whole thing felt awfully like he'd found out we'd left him off the invite list for a high school sleepover. It wasn't his fault he was laced tighter than a soccer star's cleats. In all honesty, I wouldn't have liked anyone who showed up in the dark months after Walter's death. I'd never thought about what that might have been like for Meekins. What it meant to become an agent in the shadow of a man he'd never met and would never resemble. Everything about him was the opposite of my mentor's pragmatism. In a way I'd been leaving him out of the party since the day he arrived.

Edie showed up with water. We sat in silence while she poured. The scar on my shoulder itched. When she left, I said, "You're right. We should've come to you earlier. This mess is too important to go at piecemeal."

"That's true," Doug said before Meekins could get anything past the look of shock on his face. My old friend took a sheaf of papers out of his brief-case and passed them around. They detailed the breakdown of the isotopes from the Blue at Bepler and in the dart at the Chief's. He'd mentioned the night before that they were the same batch. At the bottom of the pile was something new: a multipage fax from Cedar Rapids, detailing the weaponry that had been confiscated from the aspiring school bomber. Doug had highlighted the key markers in the isotope table. They matched the reports he'd run out here in Daly City.

The Knights of Liberty were using Agency Blue to attack kids—the same Agency Blue that had been used to frame me and deal with our boss. Seemed PSI was handing pigment out all over.

Meekins scanned the page with his thumb and forefinger on the bridge of his nose, looking like the onion rings had been a mistake. "What a mess," he said, still sour. "You've put me in a real bind. Normally I'd report you to PSI, but it sounds like they're busy providing Agency weapons to child killers."

I swirled my mug, watched the dregs of my coffee circle the bottom. Across the street, the 398 pulled up to the bus stop, burping an ugly cloud of smoke. Our middle-of-the-night plan was looking like a poor choice in the midday light. But now that we'd told Meekins what we'd been up to, we needed my fellow agent on board. Didn't matter how crabby he was. Or how justified his bad temper. "What we did—it may not have been the right choice. But they offered me a transfer to Iowa if I left the Icarus case alone. If that's what these people want me to do, I figure the opposite is the way to go."

"Right," Meekins said. "Because you always toe the line."

"Look," Doug said. "I know you were suspicious of me at first. With good reason. But this—I'm a whole lot more scared of PSI than I ever was of the Yellowjackets. So when Curtida suggested we come to you"—Meekins dropped the onion ring he was fingering. Doug kept going—"it was the obvious choice. We need you on our team. Because this case is bigger than anything I've ever faced."

He picked up the onion ring again. This time he ate it. "So what are you asking me to do?"

"For starters," I said, "I need you to marry me."

We did almost lose him at that. He didn't punch me, so I figured we were coming out ahead. Doug intervened, explaining about my mom and the Hope. Meekins was skeptical of the idea that we were going to capture Lavender in the wild, but the scheme must've tugged on some adventurous thread buried in his stuffed shirt. Once Doug gave him the rundown of his theory, he came around pretty quick.

Then it was just hammering out the nitty-gritty. Whatever we did wouldn't be legally binding. We'd have a private ceremony, so he wouldn't need to worry about friends or family finding out. "Okay," he said. "But Jenna Lila Fifi can't get wind of this." The scarlet tips of his ears made clear that it wasn't for journalistic reasons that he wanted her kept in the dark. I glanced at Doug, but he was focused on our colleague's face. We'd laugh about Fifi-Meekins later, I figured. I reassured Meekins that nobody needed to know. And just like that, we were planning a wedding.

● ● ●

The to-do list was as long as Tommy's legs. Telling Mom was the next item after roping in the groom. Just the thought was enough to curdle the coffee in my stomach. Probably why I decided I needed to swing by my place to pick up clothes before making that phone call.

I'd asked Edie to recommend a handyman, and she'd sent someone right over. The place wasn't shipshape, but the broken furniture had been towed to the curb and the hole in the wall had been plastered over. The door was back on its hinges.

Would've been nice to call Florida from my home, but the wiretap made that a bad idea. One of Tommy's friends from high school had a "secure line," whatever that meant. The plan was for me to head to his place in San Bruno to break the happy news. We were betting on the crooks not having bothered to tap the phone of the woman who only ever called to make insinuations about my love life.

As I left my apartment building, a small woman in her midthirties stopped me. "Agent Curtida? I'm Karen Fernandez." The prodigal daughter of my evangelical Pinko neighbor. She was dressed in business casual, her gold zebra-print cardigan matching the soles of her platform moccasins. Her black hair was stick straight, pulled back in a high ponytail. She asked if I'd seen her mother.

I thought back. The last time I'd dodged my neighbor had been the Friday of the Magenta Cares gala, after I'd been hit by Slate Gray. I told her so and suggested she check the Pinko Temple on Longview. She fiddled with the hem of her sweater. "I'm a persona non grata, ever since I left the cult. They're not going to tell me anything. I'm worried—" She lowered her voice, in spite of the empty sidewalk. "We were always getting hassled, especially once the Knights of Liberty took over security. Partly because of our last name, but partly because she talked too much for them. Especially to outsiders. I'm worried they've taken her to Turlock."

A little too close to my fears for my own mom. And Ashaji had hired the Knights for Temple security? The crick in my neck tightened up at that. I told her I'd keep an eye out. I wondered how I'd manage on top of everything else I was up to.

I put that thought aside and drove south. The Stanford college station announced that Argentine folk singer Mercedes Sosa had finally been caught by the dictatorship, all the way up in Colombia. She was being held on the Argentine base in Barranquilla, awaiting extradition.

Colombia was one of many countries that had weathered the transition to the new world order better than we had—they were already used to permanently hosting a superpower's military, used to passing along tidbits of intelligence that would keep them on the empire's good side. Used to living with a porous idea of national sovereignty to keep soft power from turning hard.

Sosa wouldn't last long in custody, that was for sure. The blackbird of the Argentine underground would sing no more. I switched away. Found a station playing rock from my high school days and turned it up loud.

Turned out rock was the right soundtrack to prepare me for meeting Tommy's friend. I could hear the Dead Sentiments blasting from the warehouse that served as Juan Rekhi's home as I pulled into the parking lot. A camera peeked out from under the eaves of the gray stucco building. As soon as I killed the engine, the music shut off and a guy with waist-length black hair held back by a lemon bandanna opened the door.

Inside, Juan led me past a three-meter-high pile of gutted domestic appliances and gestured at a phone booth that had clearly been stolen off a sidewalk. "Florida is $70,000 for half an hour," he said. I handed over the cash and shut the door. Through the booth's scratched glass, I saw him settle in front of a screen playing what looked like CCTV footage of a blackjack game. A skinny teen in a black hoodie with *Feelies* printed on the arm was asleep on the couch. I wondered what these kids were mixed up in.

Didn't have long to think about it, though, because Mom picked up after the third ring. When I told her I was dating Meekins, she dropped the phone. I could hear her laughing as it clattered on the end of the cord before she got it under control. "Finally! Oh, your babies will be *so* beautiful—"

I stopped her before she got too far. Didn't want the fact that I wasn't knocked up to bring her down. "I don't know about children just yet, but we are planning to get married."

"You . . ." There was a five-season telenovela in her silence. "You must love him a lot to make such a big decision so soon after your breakdown."

There it was, the old Mom *giddyup-giddyup-giddyup-whoa-boy*. I couldn't win. She'd spout off the most hyperbolic fantasies, but here I was making one real and she suddenly became the picture of caution. I reminded myself that in spite of the difference between "pigment hit" and "psychotic break," Mom could call things whatever she wanted as long as she was excited about my connubial promise. "I just got to thinking after our last conversation. What you said about this being an opportunity to reevaluate what I want, what my next steps might be. And I guess I realized it's time."

"I didn't mean for you to do anything reckless."

I backtracked and told her we'd been discussing it for a while, then leaned against the corner of the phone booth to weather the storm of questions brought on by that tidbit. How long had this been going on? Why hadn't I told her? "I didn't want to get your hopes up," I said, trying not to dwell on the irony of that statement. The interrogation continued: Did his family know? What about our friends? It would've been smart to have had a notepad to write down everything I was making up.

Down the line, I could hear the wrens chirping in the yard. Eventually Mom got chirpier, too. I told her the ceremony was Friday and offered to pay for her ticket out. The compressed schedule was another shock, but there was a tremor in her voice when she said, "I'll bring your grandmother's wedding bands."

I drove back to the hospital through a drizzle like a low-level hangover. Passed a sign reading SLATE GRAY SPILL AT THIS— A sticker of the hooded Lady Liberty covered the rest of the text. The wind rattled last year's anise stalks in the vacant lot behind it.

The wet sputter of the squall matched my jitters. We'd had to move fast, and we had. We'd covered a whole lot of ground in just a few hours. But the windshield wipers were beating out the echo of my mother's voice: *reckless, reckless, reckless.* Last night I'd been real certain about the solidity of her hope. As the afternoon dribbled to a close, I was flashing on times when her silence had been heavier than her words.

A decade and change ago she'd talked a klick per tick when she told me she was selling the store. This was a *good thing*—now she could focus on her colors business—my promotion was bound to come through soon so I could help her weather the transition—but it was the quiet afterward that haunted me.

I'd been back in Tampa for her sixtieth birthday, and I'd ended up the designated driver after she downed a bottle of Malbec at her big bash. She'd glittered the whole night, egging her friend Sylvia on in a flirtation with the bongo player in the band. Mom's laugh as the mismatched couple exited together warmed the whole bar. But alone with me in the car after the party, she'd seemed hollowed out. Her shoulders folded in around her oversized handbag as the turn signal ticked all through the long light at Gandy Boulevard. I heard despair in her hushed breathing.

Which, then, had been real? Her optimism about what was to come? Or her anguish over what she'd lost? I was betting the fate of the nation on the former. Her initial reaction to the news that I was fulfilling her dream by marrying Meekins made me think that I might have bet wrong.

I passed a slow-moving Argentine transport, grunts in pale blue uniforms sitting in rows under the canvas-covered back. I'd played my chips. I just had to keep going and assume Mom had the quality of hope that we needed. *The quality of hope that we need.* Like she was a cow. My fanny pack lay heavy on my gut. It was too late to turn back now. Either Cassius's theocratic conspiracy got outed or I'd have plenty of time in a musty cell to regret my gamble.

That thought wanted to drag me down a dark rabbit hole. Edie's blinking neon sign convinced me I needed more coffee. The proprietress took one look at me and reached for the pot.

The tables had been rearranged in their normal configuration, ready for the dinner crowd's arrival. I followed her over to the window. Once the mug of steaming black ambrosia was in my hands, I asked her to be my maid of honor. After a series of snorts that escalated into guffaws, she wiped her hands on her apron and sat down across from me. "I thought the Gauchos abolished that godawful bridesmaid tradition."

"I'm bringing it back. Just in time for me to contract holy matrimony with Meekins."

"Meekins." Her voice could have dried puddles all the way up to the Magenta border. "You better throw a good party."

"Maid of honor duties include lots of quality time with my mom. The wedding's not going to be all fun and games. But if it works out, the Pinkos may suddenly find themselves too tied up elsewhere to buy this place from your landlord."

"Not sure what you're up to, but it's matron of honor when the lady in question is married. I'll bring Pablo and Jason and throw in a bottle of my hot sauce as a wedding present."

Something tight between my shoulder blades unknit itself. Edie had my back. I cleared my throat. "We may need a safe house after. For my mother."

"And where are you gonna go?"

"I can take care of myself."

"Sure thing," she said. "The way you've been doing these past few weeks?"

"I'm still here, aren't I?"

She shook her head. "You look after you, I'll drum something up for Mama Curtida."

● ● ●

Back at the hospital parking lot, I ran into Tommy and Doug. My old friend needed a bunch of fancy equipment for the pigment capture at the wedding and didn't want to request it from Boise. Tommy'd offered to let him raid Pimsley's home lab.

My cadet's hair was clean and his street clothes hid the worst of his raw-boned angles from weeks in a hospital bed. He was fresh for his first outing since rolling into the pigment ward on a gurney. They were taking Doug's Peugeot station wagon since they'd need the full trunk.

The question of how Pimsley had gotten ahold of the Mauve Faith had been bothering me. The antique dealer had been interested in dusty relics from the early days of pigment, not new breakthroughs. He stayed abreast of the goings-on in color development, but his cabinet had mostly been loaded with vials that were pushing thirty years old. What network would have connected him to Priscilla Kim? And been close enough to both to fence the vials to the salesman? I joined my colleagues on their field trip. I figured it was the best chance I'd get to answer those questions. Even if I didn't find anything useful, they'd need an extra pair of hands to carry their boxes.

We went under the freeway on the same road we'd taken after the charity auction, racing to back up Meekins. The anti-Argentine graffiti was now surrounded by blowfish. Tommy chattered about wedding venues. A cut through the intersection at Bepler jarred some nastily Blue memories. I closed my eyes against the brewing headache that went with them, shunted my attention to another time. Walter Lopez, driving me up and down these small streets, getting me used to the city's ombré shading from tree-lined to seedy. Once I made agent and bought the Renault, Walter'd race me on slow days: who could cut off whom, who got caught behind stoplights. Sometimes, the Chief would join in her fancy Lada and beat us both. The memories played in my mind like old film reels projected behind glass in a museum. Like things that had happened to someone else.

When I opened my eyes, we were well inside Magenta territory. Tommy had gone from his thoughts on church ceremonies to the pros and cons of begonias versus peonies as he guided us toward the salesman's home. I remembered what Doug had said about Depressives with a cheery front.

The Peugeot was too big to fit in the garage, so we parked on the street. The facade was unchanged from our earlier visit, no marks on the door—nobody else had found the antique dealer's lair. Tommy's stream of prattle dribbled away. Doug met my gaze as we got out of the car. The two of us crossed the street to give our young friend some space. We stopped by a pile of debris, rotting clapboard siding and broken bricks. I checked my watch and waited for Tommy to get himself under control. Still didn't understand why Trumbull didn't just give him something to get through his feelings faster.

When the cadet waved us to follow, his nose was red. He took Doug toward the back to the at-home laboratory. I wandered the place while they worked, picking up and putting back tchotchkes, running my fingers down the spines of the books. Photos sat on the mantel: a twentysomething Pimsley and another man, dressed in matching seventies plaid, holding hands under a sign on Castro Street that said CLONE CROSSING. Another of my friend, looking fresh out of high school, sitting on a ratty couch with a laughing curly-haired girl. On the back, *FOR WHAT A HEIGHT MY SPIRIT IS CONTENDING! 'TIS NOT CONTENT SO SOON TO BE ALONE. LOVE ALWAYS HOLLY* written in faded brown ink. In the bedside table drawer, I found the man's calendar.

Pimsley had recorded his daily comings and goings with painstaking detail, appointments neatly laid out in his slanting cursive. Tailoring appointments, antiquing meetups, lunches and dinners. Looking closer, though, many of the meetings had specific color descriptors. An entry on January 11 read *Call Patsy Atchity re: Magenta Cable-Car model*, with a phone number scrawled below. Ronnie Atchity had been one of the hippie perpetrators of the Magenta Attack. Patsy must be a wife or daughter. It barely counted as a cipher. This was the record of his underworld contacts. The old man must have been counting on his home's covert location to keep his secrets.

My fingers moved faster, flipping forward to the week of his fateful call. That Monday, he'd listed *Minnie Cucci. Bespoke Mauve two-piece. Fitting at Ticky-Tacky Tuxy, 2:30.* I looked at the closet hung wall to wall with gray suits. No way was that Mauve the color of a jacket. I'd found it. This had to be the fence who'd sold him the crooks' new pigment. And then turned around and sold him out.

I made my way back to Pimsley's lab. Stopped in the doorway as the smog of stale feelings left over from pigment samples turned my stomach. Wire racks of equipment lined the eggshell-white walls. Many of the pieces were decorated with a pale blue band, a sign that they'd fallen off a truck aimed at the Argentine base in Palo Alto. Doug and Tommy stood behind a high steel table complete with psychospectrometer and built-in Bunsen burner. Doug was expounding on the foibles of a vintage separator, a tube-lined bowl that looked like a chandelier crossed with a bidet. I interrupted the lecture to ask my cadet if he'd ever heard of Minnie Cucci.

"She's got a low-end clothing rental 'business,'" Tommy said. "Gives her a reason to keep a big warehouse. She was part of that dogfighting ring the neurotypicals have been going after. Pimsley said something about kennels in the back."

I pulled open the calendar. "She was one of his last appointments. A fitting for a two-piece *Mauve* bespoke suit at Ticky-Tacky Tuxy." I looked up at them. "Worth checking out. I do need a wedding dress, after all."

CHAPTER 25

In the car, Doug radioed Meekins that we were picking up donuts for Aunt Amy—code to let my colleague know we were following a lead and to ask if we should wait for him to tag along. The response was a stiff no. "I like the guy, but he's a terrible actor," Doug said. "You really had to pick him as your groom?"

I was tired of defending my mother's regrettable taste. And tired of not talking about the other reasons Doug might be touchy about me tying the knot with another man. *What our lives could've been.* We'd mostly managed to banish the shadows of our late-night heart-to-heart in the light of day, but apparently my state of incipient matrimony was a bridge too far. Told myself not to dwell on it.

Spent the ride down to Minnie Cucci's turning over what Tommy had said about kennels instead. I knew the Chief was gone. But the fact that she'd called in sick wouldn't make sense if she were dead. Then again, she could have actually had been sick. Or maybe it'd been a note the crooks had left somewhere, and Doug had been confused when telling me the story. If only Mom could see me now. She'd be so proud of my speciously optimistic train of thought.

Ticky-Tacky Tuxy was in a neighborhood kept on edge by the lingering effects of a decade-old Envy Green explosion. The establishment itself was a dilapidated storefront built into a rickety warehouse. A neon sign in the window advertised "Elegance for Every Occasio," the "*n*" in "occasion" having burnt out sometime last century. Across the street, a burrito joint pumped the smell of fried meat and tortillas over a vacant, dandelion-filled lot. We circled the building. There was no back exit.

Inside, the place smelled of mothballs. The costume jewelry was dusty, several pieces featuring obvious containers for psychopigment—a nasty classic. I'd imagined the proprietor would be all cleavage and leopard print, but Cucci's skeletal body was encased in an Easter-egg bedazzled sweat suit. I quickly picked my wedding dress—the best option was a taffeta two-piece gown with puffy sleeves, hung between a cream all-lace jumpsuit and an eggshell flounce that felt like it'd been made from recycled plastic bottles. Paid up. My name on the deposit form gave away that we were Pigment Enforcement, but she took my $100K anyway.

Doug stepped in with a few questions, and the woman was as forthcoming as could be expected for a two-faced fence. She kept her hand on the ruff of an obese Akita's neck the whole time. The dog wore sequined bunny ears that swayed as his owner played dumb.

She bolted when Doug pointed out the pigment paraphernalia in the costume jewelry case. The Akita started barking. Tommy trapped it behind a crate of clothes. Doug nabbed Minnie before she made it out of the parking lot and handcuffed her. Tossing me her heavy key ring, he told me to case the joint.

I headed behind the counter. The room I let myself into was dim, lit by a dirty skylight and a single bare bulb. Heaps of faded prom dresses crowded the space, leaving a narrow passage to Minnie's real business area.

Through another padlocked door was a dank void. Sawdust in the air made me cough. It stank of dog. There sure as hell weren't clothes in here. My pocket flashlight illuminated a row of tall, rusty kennels to my right. Empty, with grimy floors. In the final cage, a dark lump started singing. A high, thin sound. *"Devil will come, come what may, take your home and make you stay away—"*

I hadn't heard that song before, but I knew the voice. It had been crooning along to the Saigon Sallies the last time I'd heard it. Penelope Crotty, Jenny Crotty's Magenta-struck sister. In the havoc of the aftermath of Bepler, she'd slipped my mind. And now she was trapped in the dark behind Minnie Cucci's.

The Magenta victim sat twitching in the same house robe she'd been in when we met, the pink fabric hanging loose on her hollowed frame. Her hands rhythmically clasped and unclasped, the same tic I'd seen in her pigment-fried sister when I interviewed her in the hospital. Penelope had been sad the last time I saw her, but now her emotions were dominated by something new: a fear that made her look behind her regularly. I undid the lock. Got her up, got her out. She was unsteady on her feet. She asked if I could take her to the hospital. "The demon doctor with the pretty shoes said she'd fix me, but it didn't work . . ."

Kim had said the cover story for the rollout of Mauve Faith was *something that could help Magenta victims*, that test results had been promising. Jenny Crotty and Leonard Gobble were out of their mind on the experimental paint Pretty Prissy had given them, and Tommy and I had been recovering from our own hits. Penelope had been ripe for the picking, with nobody around to notice her disappearance.

In the Peugeot, I found an old ration bar for her to chew on. Cucci sat stone-faced between Tommy and Penelope. She was in trouble and she knew it. A little pigment in jewelry would get her a slap on the wrist. Detaining a pigment victim was another story entirely. We could charge her straightaway, keep her for questioning as long as we needed.

She had to have known we'd look in the back. But clearly something was keeping her from talking. Fear of the people she was protecting? Or the expectation they'd get the charges dropped? Doug radioed Meekins that he was coming in with a potentially useful suspect and drove the rest of us to the hospital.

Trumbull was ensconced among her towers of paper in her office, filling out charts on top of a pile of books on her desk. She sat back in her cowhide chair when I walked in with Penelope. We must've looked a sight. I was covered in sawdust from Minnie's warehouse. Penelope clutched at her filthy robe, crooning her ditty under her breath. At least she'd calmed down some after getting food in her stomach.

I introduced her to the doctor. When Penelope said her problem was the devil, Trumbull told her it sounded familiar. She sent the new patient off with Nurse Howie to bunk down with the Chief's mother, then made me come around the desk so she could check my vitals. "You sure are filling up my wing fast," she said, pushing up my shirtsleeve to check my pulse. "And on top of that Edie tells me you're getting hitched."

"Sure am," I said.

"To Meekins? You couldn't think of anyone else?"

"I don't know anyone else." The Magenta creature squeaked *Liar*, but it could go suck on a golf ball.

Satisfied with my blood pressure, she turned back to her work. "You let me know when the ceremony is. And whether I should be prepping for new patients."

"The way things have been going lately," I said, "you definitely should."

● ● ●

I didn't feel like eating by myself that night, so I bought Spitfire burgers for the Chief's mom, Penelope, and Tommy. There was plenty in my head I didn't need to be alone with. We were a dopey group and I ended up back in my room sooner than I wanted.

I tried to distract myself with an old chestnut on TV about a group of refugees trying to make it from pigment-strafed Chicago to the promised land of Boise. It had all the usual tropes: the implausible recovery of an elderly Deepest Blue victim just in time to orient the group at a crossroads; attacks by rogue Argentine soldiers; a crotchety Twenty-Fiver with a heart of gold rolling up in a pickup truck just as the minivan broke down. Her crew cut put me in mind of the Chief's. After the emotional reunion between the protagonist and his dog, I turned in early.

Doug crashed into the room around midnight. Apparently he, Meekins, and Cynthia had gone out for more than a few Fernet and Cokes. He rattled around the room looking for either whisky or toothpaste, telling me that Meekins wasn't that bad. "You two just keep having pissing contests. The trick . . . the trick is to lose them." I asked after Cynthia. He took a while to respond, then just said, "She's nice." I was glad to go back to sleep.

In my nightmare, I had a gun in my hand, and my mother was chattering away about how happy she was for me. I knew that as soon as she mentioned Meekins, I would pull the trigger and shoot her. She kept talking about the wedding bands she was bringing. I was waiting, and waiting. I couldn't help it. A small part of me hoped she wouldn't say the groom's name, that I could get away without gunning her down, but the rest of me knew that I was about to kill my mother. *I'm about to shoot my mother.* My stomach twisted and she said "Meekins" and my finger, my finger was squeezing the trigger and she went down, down in a cloud of Blue—

"Hey." Doug's hand on my shoulder pulled me out of sleep. "Hey. Bad dream?"

The sickly gray yellow of predawn was creeping through the window. "Yeah." I could still feel the weapon's cool metal in my palm.

"Do you . . . do you want me to hold you?"

A car drove past outside, engine puttering the ragged tune of a Citroen 2CV. I nodded. He climbed up onto the hospital bed. His shoulder got tangled in my Sunshine drip. The needle jerked in my arm, but the tape kept it in place. I shifted to make room for him. He draped an arm across my throat. I moved it down so I could breathe. He moved his other arm up and his elbow jutted into my head. I rolled over. My pajama shirt hitched up a little. He moved his hand down gingerly, like he was trying not to spook a feral cat. Felt like I could've poured my whole self through the spot where his skin touched mine.

I closed my eyes. My lungs weren't working right. Fourteen years wasn't long enough to forget the taste of tuna salad on a lonely, angry bus ride down from Boise. I'd known when we were fresh out of the academy that I didn't want to get mixed up with him. Why couldn't I have kept that straight at twenty-five—or now?

Walter Lopez had picked me up at the bus station that day. My mentor took one look at me and drove straight through the drizzle to the old high school training field. I threw up after the three hundredth push-up but completed the ten K. I felt like I'd been running ever since. Straight back into Doug's arms. I shifted as far from him as the twin mattress would allow. "You can go back to your cot," I said.

"You're still shaking."

I pulled the scratchy hospital blanket tight. "I'm *fine*."

He sat up and scrubbed at his hair. Ran his hands over his forehead and temples. Put his palms over his face. My digital watch flipped over a minute, and then another. "I think I should go home," he said.

"Plato," I said. "You and me—it's just a bad idea."

"Won't you try?" he asked. "Don't you even want to try?"

"It's not about what I want. It's about what I know." About every time I'd seen him walk out of a party with a Magenta glint in his eye and a new girl on his arm, and every time I'd heard that girl crying in the dorm bathroom two weeks later.

"What you know," he said, like he was trying the words on for size and finding them too tight. "What you know." He swung his legs off the bed and pushed himself up to standing. The first rays of the sun were peeking through the window. He walked over to his cot and started pulling on his pants. "You know we slept together at the reunion three years ago?"

I'd woken up that Sunday morning in my motel room with a splitting headache, an empty minibar, and an embarrassing number of condom wrappers in the trash can. I'd often wondered what knucklehead I'd chosen to scratch that itch. Whoever it was had paid the bill for our fun-sized boozefest on his way out. Somewhere I must've already realized. Nobody else from the academy would've done that. "Makes sense. I'm sorry. I was really drunk."

"No," he said, "you weren't. We had one pint at the bar. Then you asked if I wanted to go somewhere more private. You held my hand in the stairwell, but not when we were out in the open." He picked his sweater up off the chair and shrugged it on. "I woke up about four. You were in the bathroom with a syringe of Deepest Blue. I begged you to put it down, but you told me you'd been curious but couldn't stand thinking of yourself as just another fling. I didn't get a chance to say anything before the needle was in your arm." He was standing with his back toward me, hands in his armpits like the room had gone chilly all of a sudden. "I stayed long enough to make sure you'd be all right. Cleared out the minibar so you wouldn't wonder why you'd blacked out.

"At first I hoped it would wear off and you'd remember eventually. The dose had been small. Maybe you'd wonder about your headache and follow that path . . . but the Blue's more effective when the person wants to forget. Finally I figured you'd really meant it. So I got mad. Tried to forget you. You know how that went." The girl he'd been seeing during the Yellowjacket case. Who *could've been just anyone*. And how many others just like her. "I've kept your secret for you, all these years. This past month, I thought—maybe if I show that I'm doing things differently, show that I'm sticking around, that this is something real, not some fantasy I need Magenta to hold on to—maybe then you'd . . . you know." He let his arms fall. "Like the fool I am."

It felt like an earthquake. Like it couldn't be true. He'd been thinking about this for years? No. Worse. I'd painted over that evening. I'd done what? I groped for some splinter of memory from that weekend, anything to contradict him. It was like trying to wake up from a dream. Like wading through quicksand. I recognized it then. My mind had been more than happy to hold up the mnemonic fence the pigment had built. I swallowed but my mouth was dry. "How did I have Deepest Blue?"

"You bought it off Tracy. She was hawking some stuff at lunch she'd skimmed off a bust in Boulder. So yeah, you planned it." He bent down and grabbed his shoes. Crossed the linoleum in his socks. A Blue flash: the moldy grout of a public bathroom's beige-tiled floor. Tracy's blond bangs, gray roots showing at the top. *Guess the "square" finally got "hip,"* schoolyard slang coming stale out of the cracked rouge of her lips as she handed over a vial. One of my monitors beeped angrily. Doug stopped in the doorway. "Seems like we both use pigment to handle our relationship fears," he said.

The back of my throat was wide open, but I didn't know what I wanted to say, so he left and I stayed. That was it. Twenty-odd years of this fragile balancing act. All over. I could blame the Magenta for knocking us off-kilter.

Or the stress of the case. Or Doug's—whatever it was he thought he was doing. But we'd been heading toward this since our first day as lab partners. I'd seen the parade of girls he went for, and they were everything I wasn't: charming, tender. Soft where I was hard. Runners with long legs, not swimmers with broad shoulders. We'd laughed about his escapades when they were over. I'd never wanted to wonder who he'd laugh with about me.

I ran through my usual litany of justifications. Counted them off like rosary beads. Just reminded me why I'd stopped praying. That same hollow feeling. I'd spent a whole lot of energy telling myself I regretted the choice I'd made fifteen years ago in Boise. When I'd gone and done it again in a heartbeat soon as I got my hands on some Blue.

If we were right where I'd always known we'd end up, what had I been fighting this whole time? Here I was, empty-handed. Empty-headed, in the cold dawn. Without even the memory of his embrace to warm me back to sleep. I sat in bed and watched the stripes of sunlight slide brighter and brighter across the wall, thinking about every dumb choice I'd ever made.

CHAPTER 26

The next few days slammed past like an 18-wheeler riding the Pampas highway. The hour for the ceremony was set (the earliest opening at the cheapest chapel in town was Friday at noon), the makeup lady booked, the flowers ordered. Doug remembered that the room he'd rented at the extended-stay hotel was useful for more than storing clothes. Stopped spending nights at the hospital. It was better that way. Gruber-Shaw's announcement was due at Ashaji's book launch the following Monday. I couldn't afford to be distracted from my five-kilometer-long to-do list.

Thursday afternoon, I drove out to Diego Armando Maradona Airport to pick up my mother. Before the war, there were three international airports in the Bay Area. Oakland and San Francisco were bombed in '82. San Jose got painted with Bull's Blood Rage in a pigment spill that taught the powers that be ground shipping was safer. Now, domestic travelers had to rely on the extra flight slots on the Argentine-constructed runways down near Palo Alto.

On the sidewalk outside the tiny arrivals lounge, my mother was finishing a bag of pretzels. Her exuberant curls sported an auburn dye job. A pink wool sweater encased her ample bosom. She was wearing a matching knit scarf and an ancient peacoat. There were probably long johns under her jeans. She was every inch the Floridian preparing for the Pacific fog.

This far south on the peninsula, though, the skies were always blue. She'd stripped three layers before the crew finished unloading her two bags from the sixteen-passenger plane. Fifty kilos of luggage for a weekend jaunt. I bit my tongue as I started the car. Asked instead how the flight had gone. She responded by yanking my ponytail out and attacking my hair with her homemade "curl revival" spray. I ducked but there was no stopping the on-slaught of grooming. "I suppose he loves you just the way you are, anyway," she said eventually.

I went with yes as a response, wondering if I'd ever get the stink of sage and chamomile out of the upholstery. Told her she looked exactly the same as her last visit, two years ago. It was true, aside from the hair color. Same clothes, even. Although that was probably because she used them only on visits to chilly California. Judging by the snapshots on my fridge, she kept her Florida wardrobe up to date.

We made our way to the freeway, heading toward lunch with her future son-in-law. The Argentine money in the Palo Alto area kept it from suffer-ing Daly City's blighted fate. Bamboo fronds crested over freshly painted fences. Potted marigolds sat in front of mid-twentieth-century ranch houses with long sloping roofs and high windows. The flowers put me in mind of the wilted plants at the Chief's.

As we headed north, Mom gave me the list of the Tampa Bay Military Widows Association personnel who sent their well-wishes for my upcom-ing nuptials. At the Oregon Expressway exit on 101, signs for the Julio Ar-gentino Roca Military Base had been tagged with the inevitable *GAUCHO GO HOME.* Underneath, someone angrier had added a cartoon blowfish and *God Bless America.* I tried not to wonder what my mother would think of Meekins in person. She'd had years to build up a fantasy based entirely on his headshot. Would it be worse if the stale wonderbread that passed for his personality was a letdown, or if that was what she thought I needed?

My ostensible fiancé was waiting for us at the Fog City Grill. The counter was real wood and the booths were leather instead of vinyl. Every-thing about the place made me feel underdressed. My colleague had put on a tie, which didn't help.

I went to sit by my mother. Caught myself when Meekins scooted toward the wall to make room for me. Mom produced a bottle of cham-pagne from her handbag and paid the corkage fee. We made small talk over our glasses of tepid bubbly. Meekins was stiff but proficient on the weather.

He managed to discuss the Shamshine case without grimacing. Mom chattered away, barreling over any potential awkwardness. She was so happy to finally meet him—she'd been pestering me about him for years, surprised he hadn't been snapped up already—oh, look how I was blushing, but that was a mother's job, wasn't it, to embarrass her children.

A waitress in a clementine uniform that matched the booth came and took our orders. Mom really couldn't believe he'd been single this long, his headshot practically had "eligible bachelor" written across it. She'd thought that even before the news about Agent of the Year. Neither of us told her that was an invented award. Neither of us mentioned the other reason Jenna Lila might think he deserved it. Our food arrived. I bit into my soggy burger and wished we were at Edie's. Meekins picked at his club sandwich. Mom served more champagne. "So tell me," she said, "when did you know she was the one?" My colleague choked on a french fry.

● ● ●

In the car afterward, Mom said, "I didn't imagine him quite like that."

"He was nervous," I said. We passed the 398 bus, making its slow way down the peninsula to Palo Alto. "He takes a while to warm up to people."

"Hmm," she said. Then she was quiet. We wound south under the gray sky. I kept my hand on my knee to keep it from bouncing.

She needed a nap after the trip and the heavy lunch, so I dropped her at my apartment. We'd considered putting her up at a hotel or sending her straight to Edie's hideaway in case things got heavy, but we'd decided that would make her suspicious. Didn't want any extra questions interfering with her hopefulness. Not that it would matter if she wasn't convinced by Meekins.

I helped get her suitcases up the stairs. The one I ended up carrying was heavier than a bookcase. My workout for the day. Told her I had errands to run. Made a beeline to the department, nerves buzzing. If the bubbly had provided any lubrication, it had dribbled away in the face of Mom's lethargy. Now I just had an ache at the top of my neck.

Meekins was nowhere to be found. Doug was out, too. Probably having a decent burger at Edie's. Tommy was on the phone in the cadets' office, haggling over last-minute details with the florist. Cynthia sat at her desk doing paperwork and occasionally making suggestions of flowers I'd never heard of.

I told them lunch had been a disaster, Meekins as charming as a damp sock. From Mom's reaction, we'd be getting no hope out of her in the morning. Tommy handed me an aspirin and traded looks with Cynthia. "Sounds like you'll be needing a bachelorette."

They sent me home. Told me someone would be by at six. Seemed I was the only one caught off guard that Meekins's debut performance as my one and only had fallen flat. I drove back slowly, wondering what to do with Mom until nightfall. Back at my place, her kitchen gloves were drying on the border of the sink. I couldn't figure out what she'd found to wash, but something hadn't been up to her standards.

The door to my bedroom had swung open a crack. The crooks had ruined the latch, but I didn't have time or money to track down a new handle. She was a dark lump on my patched-up bed, outlined by the light from my window. As usual, she hadn't pulled the blinds. Her clothes were already hanging neatly in what was left of my closet. On the floor, she'd placed a copy of *Still Hoping: Reasons for Optimism in an Age of Despair* facedown. Ashaji's third tome on spirituality. Definitely the book for this weekend. I didn't want to wonder why Mom had felt the need to pick up that particular title just now.

She slept the next few hours and was peeved when I woke her up to get ready for the bachelorette. She took a bath and grumbled about how she hadn't brought any extra party clothes. "What are you wearing?" she asked me. I had no good answer for that. I ended up in my black dress yet again, and this time I had to wear my heels.

Finally Cynthia buzzed. Mom made me drag the heavy suitcase back down the stairs. I didn't ask, figuring it would just annoy her more. "I'm sorry," Mom said to Cynthia as we loaded the bag into my trunk. "Kay didn't warn me there was an event planned this evening." Her voice was treacly enough to ice a cyanide cake.

"She didn't know!" Cynthia's teeth were a flash of bright white in her crimson smile. "It's a surprise some of us girls threw together at the last minute. Couldn't let Curtida tie the knot without a good bash. I'm here to lead you to the secret location."

We followed her black station wagon north. I figured out pretty quick that the "secret location" was going to be Edie's. Mom spent the ride doing her makeup. Even with my Renault's faulty suspension, she was dead accurate with her lip liner. I wondered who the hell *some of us girls* could be.

Turned out it was Trumbull and Edie. We pulled up at the sandwich shop as the sun was setting. Jason had pasted a piece of paper in the front window reading *Closed for private party*. Inside, the two women were stringing up paper letters, CONGRATULATIONS spelled out in dusty blue and faded vermilion. The windows were golden squares of electric light under the pink-bellied clouds. Down the hill, I caught a glimpse of the steel line of the sea.

Just for a moment I imagined that all this was for real. Of course, it wouldn't be Meekins I'd be marrying. Mom would fly out. My friends would set up this party. The Chief would be in there, directing Trumbull as she stood on the counter pushing thumbtacks into the ceiling. My lungs were tight. No trail of corpses: Blufftown Tuck, Pimsley. Priscilla Kim's broken body. No looming national cataclysm. Would've, could've, might've beens. I got out of the car and plastered a smile on my face.

The suitcase contained eighteen bottles of champagne, cushioned in long johns. No idea how Mom had gotten it on the plane. She and Edie hit it off immediately, discussing hair care regimens for curls like theirs. They got up a friendly competition trying to keep our glasses full.

A bottle went back to the kitchen, and soon enough Jason and Pablo had come out and were sitting around the table, with a tray of cheeseburgers to sop up the alcohol. Everyone was working to pep Mom up, saying all sorts of nice things about Meekins. Many of them were even accurate. But I could tell that "hardworking," "thorough," and "solid" weren't the swoon-worthy adjectives she'd dreamed up with her morning *arepa* and the *Daly Daily* over the years.

Halfway through the night, Tommy and Doug crashed the party with a boom box and a load of what looked like old coffee cans. They plugged the stereo in by the door and started playing schmaltzy music. Doug came over to greet my mother and give me a hug. It was the first time we'd touched since our fraught conversation. My stomach squeezed up at the smell of his aftershave. He launched into what I assumed would be singing Meekins's praise, but started off with, "When we met, I asked myself—*really?* This is the man for Kay?" Didn't help my collywobbles.

Once he got going, though, he did a decent job spinning tales about good times with my starchy colleague. For all I knew they were the truth. Tommy was futzing in the corners of the restaurant. I had no idea what they were up to, and it was getting on my nerves.

Edie pulled me aside and told me that one of her boys had been offered a gig putting the kibosh on a wedding. "His cousin's in the Knights," she said. "Seems they're trying to take care of a 'distraction' for the higher-ups. Bet they figure tomorrow's as good a chance to catch all of you together as they're going to get."

Tommy and I had stayed based in the hospital, trying to look like we were still too weak to be up to anything. Now that Doug had remembered his hotel room, we were rarely all three in the same place. The Knights probably didn't know exactly what we were working on, but our flurry of activity had caught their attention. If they were referring to us as a distraction, they'd decided that anything out of the ordinary was worrisome. And apparently they were willing to come after us preemptively. In a church. Never mind the risk to innocent bystanders.

I shouldn't have been surprised at the lack of ethics. These people were planning to brainwash a significant portion of the US to get themselves into power. I asked her to discreetly suggest to the other guests that we arrive early at the chapel.

Mom was chuckling at Doug and Cynthia's description of the night they and Meekins got drunk together. The night of our discussion. I didn't know what to think about how calm my old friend seemed talking about it. My jaw was on edge. Mom's laugh got louder and louder. I didn't know what that meant, either.

There was no time to dwell on any of those questions, because the overheads suddenly shut off and the door to the restaurant flew open. Tommy's coffee cans turned out to be some sort of jury-rigged theatrical lighting instruments. They spotlighted Meekins, posing with a microphone in the doorway. He had on a tight white collared shirt, sleeves rolled up to the elbows. He'd lost the tie and the pomade. His hair was, apparently, naturally wavy. Without the wax to hold it in its normal helmet, it curved down into his eyes. His top four buttons were undone, showing off the edge of a furry chest. I realized that his prepubescent uptightness had made me assume he was bare as a seal. He'd never struck me as adult enough to have developed body hair.

In the corner, Tommy hit play on the stereo. A synthetic organ rumbled, followed by the tinny notes of a harpsichord. Meekins took a breath and looked up at me. His cheeks colored. Cynthia whooped and Edie followed suit. Even I had to admit the effect was sweet.

Then he opened his mouth and launched into Maxi del Mundo's "*Suspiros de esmeralda*," and I was the one blushing. "*Solo quiero escucharte,*" he sang, "*tus palabras de diamante, tus silencios perlas negras—*" His voice was a breathy baritone, a well-done imitation of the sound of my teenage obsession. He pulled a rose from his back pocket and tossed it at Mom. She snagged it out of the air and let out a hoot.

Next to her, Doug met my gaze. I'd off-handedly mentioned my thing for Maxi at La Continental after the chase through Magenta territory. He'd remembered. And put the memory to good use, picking out Meekins's selection for this absurd spectacle. He winked at me. My face got hotter. Something inside of me, too.

Meekins was prowling across the floor toward our table. "*Mujer mujer, suspiros, suspiros de esmeralda, mujer!*" As the inane chorus drew to a close, he suddenly pulled out a pirouette, and then a jump that landed him on his knees in front of me. He'd gotten another rose from somewhere. I didn't dare make eye contact with anyone as he extended his hand toward me and launched into the verse, this time in English. "I just want to hear you, your words made out of diamonds—"

I took his proffered fingers, and he was tangoing me around the restaurant. Tommy did something with one of the coffee cans and suddenly the light went a sultry red. It was worse than peeing onstage at the seventh-grade assembly. Then a spin as the chorus repeated, one final vibrato-studded *mujer!* and a dip that ended in a kiss.

His lips were stiff, cold, and moist, like mollusks with rigor mortis. Everyone applauded. I hadn't experienced that shade of shame in nearly thirty years. "Sorry," he mumbled into my mouth. "Tommy's idea." Mom was crying and laughing at the same time. Doug was clapping along with the crowd, but he was looking at the floor. The fact that he wasn't watching made me feel a little better.

After we stood up, Mom grabbed Meekins and planted a loud smack on his forehead. "She must really love you. The number of times I came into the house only for her to turn that song off—I thought she'd take that secret to her grave!"

I'd thought I would, too. But if it convinced Mom, it was worth a little humiliation. We had a nice time after that. My ersatz groom didn't have to do much other than smile and nod after his performance. Once he'd downed a mug of bubbly (now chilled to an appropriate temperature, thanks to the kitchen deep freeze) he even started laughing along to the jokes Edie and Mom were cracking.

The two women switched lipsticks, and then had the brilliant idea to try the colors on everyone else. Edie chased Tommy into the kitchen. Jason locked himself into the bathroom, giggling hysterically. Pablo happily submitted to Mom decorating his face. The caper let me momentarily set aside the news about the Knights planning to hit us tomorrow. There was nothing I could do about it now anyway. I'd seen Mom be the life of the party with her friends, but this was the first time I'd seen her doing it for me. Might as well try to enjoy it.

Trumbull got a call on the phone by the register and came by for one last round of well-wishes. "Penelope needs some pepping up. Enjoy tomorrow," she told me. She wouldn't be making it to the ceremony. Better, if the Knights of Liberty were planning a paint party for all of us. She turned to my mother. "Your daughter saves minds and lives in this job every day. Daly City is lucky to have her."

"Boise would be lucky to have her," said Doug. It may have been the champagne but it sounded like he meant it. My feet hurt in my shoes, but I found myself smiling at everyone. I drank more than I meant to. I got tipsy enough that it barely hurt when I wondered what the Chief would've said about our absurd plan.

Trumbull had let me off the requirement that I stay in the hospital overnight before my wedding. I packed Mom and her still-heavy bag of booze into the Renault around midnight and took us home. She spent most of the drive stumbling off-key through some salsa song about plastic people. Her scarf was wrapped around her head like a turban, with a few curls peeking out of the top. Edie's red was smeared down her chin.

I waited for the inevitable collapse into mean drunk, but it didn't come. As the bungalows of my neighborhood popped up around us, she started digging in her handbag. She pulled out a bundle of ivory lace and deposited it on my lap. Underpants and a garter. "For the wedding night. The panties have a little pocket you can slip a vial of perfume into." She sighed and leaned back, then remembered my car didn't have headrests. Her scarf turban wobbled as she snapped upright. "I had my doubts about Meekins, after meeting him today. Really did. I always thought Doug would be your big romance. But tonight—I've never seen you so happy."

The dark streets were quiet and calm, motorcycles sleeping in driveways under cobalt tarps. The clouds at sunset had given way to a cool, clear night. Stars flickered overhead. I thought of the moment before we'd gone into Edie's, the warm glow of the windows outlining the *could've beens*.

I'd assumed Mom had the idea of Meekins firmly fixed in her head. Hadn't even occurred to me that she'd had earlier fantasies involving a pack of Nambi-Curtida brats. No chance of straight hair with the two of us as parents, though. Would've, might've. No point in thinking too much about it. A little pocket could be useful for storing the captured Hope. I said, "Thanks."

"The stories were very impressive. What the doctor was saying about the people you've saved—and Jason would've gotten fifteen years if it hadn't been for you—they weren't just being nice to your mom. You're really good at your job." She yawned. "Why didn't I ever know?"

Because you never listened to me, I almost said. But I had too much on my mind to get into it with her. A trio of raccoons watched us from the open dumpster as we pulled into the parking lot. Upstairs, I tucked her back into my bed. She muttered something and fell into a deep sleep. Between the time change, the travel, and the champagne, anybody would've been laid out. My mother was no spring chicken. I popped two Sunshine pills (Trumbull's orders) and pulled bedding out for myself.

As I left the room, I took a peek back at her. She looked happy, wrapped in my covers. Figured that was a good sign. I wondered what my relationship with her would be like after tomorrow.

CHAPTER 27

The day dawned bright and sunny. Mom did, too. Long before I was ready to crack a lid, she'd thrown off the champagne mantle of slumber and was banging around in the kitchen. At least she made the coffee. She wore a dark brown skirt suit and a long rope of turquoise beads, saying "I would've bought something more festive, but there just wasn't time. Edie promised to lend me a hat."

I assured her she looked great, scrutinizing her back over the sink. I wondered if her brisk movements meant the doubts Meekins's performance had buried were resurfacing. *Still Hoping* had moved to a new spot in the bedroom, suggesting she'd been reading up on reasons for optimism. Couldn't tell if it was the hangover or that thought that had my head throbbing. Or it could've been the word about the Knights of Liberty. I had plenty of reasons for pessimism to choose from.

It wasn't yet ten a.m. when we pulled up in front of the Hallowed Sacrosanct Chapel. Doug, Meekins, Cynthia, and Tommy had all left their cars near the exit of the parking lot. My groom's wood-paneled Buick had been done up with crepe paper streamers and had *Just Married* written across the back window in soap. In the case of any infelicitous incursions on the ceremony, Meekins and Cynthia would drive away in his car while Tommy and I escaped with the Hope in Cynthia's station wagon. At least, that was the plan. So far no crooks. I had my fingers crossed. For all the good that would do.

The faithful had done their best to erase the building's past as a video-rental shop, but there was a reason it was cheap and available all morning. The false steeple on the roof was a bold move, but the outline of the phrase "No late fees" could still be read on the front window. The foyer was about as deep as a grave is long. The industrial gray carpet didn't do much to perk things up. A crucifix hung on fake-wood laminate between large mirrors. A noticeboard listed babysitters' numbers and the schedule for choir practice. My mother swept inside like it was the Cathedral of Buenos Aires.

The chapel itself was nice enough. The carpet had been replaced with hardwood floors, and the pews passed muster. Heavy velvet curtains hung behind the altar, giving the place an ecclesiastical hush. Fake stained-glass windows blocked off the corners, lit from behind to give the illusion of the sun's beams. A single bathroom sat next to the altar, its window the only source of natural light in the room.

Meekins had hung a checklist of everything that needed to be done by the door. He'd brought the full force of his nitpickery to bear on the process of convincing my mother the wedding was for real. For once I was appreciative. Tommy and Cynthia were working on item #3—*Tie bows on pews (42 cm ribbon/bow)*. Tommy was in a gray suit and wearing a bow tie. Pimsley's, I'd bet. Cynthia had on a high-necked embroidered kaftan. Looked like she'd raided a community theater's costume bank. I heard the faint crinkling of hazpig gear under their formalwear as I greeted them. Edie's warning had made the team go all out on precautions.

My putative husband-to-be and Doug were tackling item #1—*Baby's breath/daisy/fern bouquet near altar (12 stems each, 40 cm from Mother of Bride seating)*. I went over to check in with them. Meekins managed a wooden peck on my cheek before Mom descended, saying it was bad luck for him to see me before the ceremony.

As she marched my future ball and chain out to the foyer, Doug began surreptitiously planting the pigment capture equipment into the flower stand. I told him about my secret pocket and he agreed to hand off the vial once the Hope had liquefied. Didn't much want to discuss my lacy underthings with him, but he was mercifully stone-faced about it. I thanked him for suggesting Maxi del Mundo for Meekins's song. Asked how he'd known to pick "*Suspiros de esmeralda*."

"You sang it to me." He was very intent on the gadget he was fiddling with. "In your motel room at the reunion."

Luckily Edie walked in then, so I had a reason to leave him. She didn't say anything about the heat in my cheeks when I walked up. Her navy skirt suit was surprisingly conservative, but her lips were the same red as ever. Jason towered over his petite mother and stepfather in a brown velour blazer and khakis, loaded down with two hatboxes, a cake, and jugs of orange juice and coffee. Pablo wore a cerulean shirt with a cream-colored tie and held the all-important paper cups.

"I've got a few of the boys watching the door," Edie said as she handed me a steaming dose of caffeine. I told her I'd make it worth their time. She said not to worry about it. We settled on settling up once all this was over. It was the only option, really, since it wasn't like I had the cash on hand. Or in my bank account. I'd pay the piper later.

I sent her family to recruit Mom for #4—*Refreshments table,* which had six subitems including *plastic forks laid out in curve.* Everything felt unreal. Fraudulent, of course. That was the plan. But normally while waiting for an ambush I wouldn't be concerned about the placement of begonias. Pretty soon I'd need an itemized checklist for my worries. At least we were on track for an early start.

I headed off to part one of *Curtida bridal prep,* which the groom had left mercifully vague. I hurried the makeup lady along with the promise of a $50,000 tip. Edie came in afterward to help squeeze me into the getup from Ticky-Tacky Tuxy. First thing she did was open the little window to air out the hairspray fumes. She stood, hands on her hips, watching me wrestle the taffeta monstrosity from its dress bag. "Wouldn't it have been easier to do this with Doug? Get some use out of that chemistry?" she asked. I dug around in the skirt, trying to find the sash. She took the bodice from me and turned it right side up.

Here I'd had the notion I'd kept my feelings under wraps. I thought about Mom saying she'd expected Doug to be my big romance. About my old friend's fingers deftly positioning the intake needles and pigment capture cube in the flower arrangement. About his gaze locked on his task when I asked about the karaoke song selection. "It would've been too risky," I said.

"Curtida worrying about risk," she said. "Never thought I'd see the day."

She'd fastened the top half of the two-piece gown onto my torso when Tommy stuck his head into the room and suggested I check out the situation in the parking lot. I didn't like the vague way he was talking. The coffee was skittering through my veins, the corset's stays pressing down the waistband of my jeans. I told Edie I'd be back to put on the skirt in a minute.

Outside, Meekins was standing behind his Buick, holding placating hands up to Jenna Lila Fifi. The journalist was clutching her camera like a Maxi del Mundo fan with a ticket to a canceled concert.

I wondered how the hell she had known. Then wondered how I'd thought Berdie could keep his nose out of this. The notary might not be capable of keeping Pigment Enforcement business straight, but he'd know where to go with a juicy piece of gossip. As I got closer, I heard my colleague saying "cannot comment on any investigation that's underway—" I picked up my pace. The man was trying to avoid a breakup using the department's press-handling strategy.

"This whole thing is fake." I cut straight to the chase. The time for caution was long gone. Meekins pressed down his hair as I explained about the conspiracy to overthrow the government using false Hope. He didn't want me talking, but he didn't stop me.

I told Fifi that Ashaji had designs on the presidency, that the Knights of Liberty were involved, that I had no romantic interest in my colleague and vice versa. Even her perm looked skeptical. "Believe me or not, but either I've given you the scoop of the century or you can give Meekins an Asshole of the Year award."

Meekins said it was unethical to talk to the press, and I told him I was the one breaking the rules. I promised to spill the whole story after the ceremony and told her not to say anything to my mother. Color was coming back into her knuckles on the camera.

Meekins pulled open the door of his car and took out a gift-wrapped package. He handed it to Jenna Lila. "I'm sorry I didn't tell you. This is the 'wedding present' I was taking to Curtida." The journalist opened the box. Inside was my department-issued pigment gun. He tugged on his shirt cuffs, doing everything but slapping his own wrist. "Do you want a photo?"

She took a snap, then straightened the ruffles of her black off-the-shoulder dress. "We'll discuss this after." Her tone suggested that was meant for Meekins. We watched her walk away, hips stiff in the tight satin skirt. Meekins looked like a toffee that had fallen under the driver's seat, staring into the abyss of a dusty, lonely eternity. If his face kept sagging like that, even Mom wouldn't be picturing a rosy future for the two of us. Assuming she was picturing one now. My skin itched under the beauty products. Not much we could do other than keep moving. I thanked him for the gun and told him to blame everything on me.

"You can bet I will," he said.

He went inside. When this was over, Jenna Lila would forgive and forget and come up with another set of imaginary laurels to hang on him. And I'd do—what? Mom was going to be furious once she found out the wedding was a sham. It would be her turn to stop taking my calls. The Chief was gone. Tommy'd be in the hospital for a while, but Trumbull'd be sending me home soon. And then I'd be alone in my empty apartment, working my tiddly-wink Daly City cases, just a little lonelier than before.

Doug was leaning against the wall by the dumpster, hunched around a cigarette. He'd be driving his Peugeot back up to Boise on Monday, if this worked out. He'd probably already packed his bags. My feet took me toward him. I stood a couple meters away, watching as he tapped ash onto the pavement. Camels. Just like the packs he'd smuggled onto campus at the academy. Hadn't seen him with one since finals week, our last year. He looked at me, took another drag. I wasn't sure whether to go closer or turn on my heel and run. "This," I said. "What we're doing. It's crazy, right?"

He went nearly motionless. Just the thumb of his free hand running back and forth across his knuckles. Put me in mind of his stillness in Tadlock's lab at the academy, Bull's Blood Rage coursing through his system. He was quiet for so long I thought he wouldn't answer. Then he blew smoke out through his nose, shook his head. "You just realized?"

I wanted to say something clever but all that came out was "yeah." I went to the wall. Nudged him over to make room for me. The taffeta of my sleeve scritched against the concrete. He stubbed out his cigarette, let the butt drop to the ground. His fingers were next to mine. I could feel it in my bones, suddenly. We could be dead within the hour. I grabbed his hand.

His palm was rough, with calluses on the pads. No idea from what. Even with everything I knew about him, there was still so much I had no idea of. I squeezed. After a while, he squeezed back. There was a thought somewhere in my head, behind the buzzing nerves and tightness at my temples. Something about how he'd said Magenta made him feel like he couldn't breathe because the other person was so perfect. But the feeling he gave me was the opposite. Like there were parts of my lungs I'd never been able to open up, and air was hitting them for the first time. That hadn't come from a joyride through Dolores Park. Even I knew that. *Some feelings come from inside,* he'd said when he invited me to the Feelies.

"There you are!" Edie's voice broke the moment. I jumped away from Doug like a shoplifter caught red-handed. I could feel my skin heating up all the way down to the rhinestone-studded neckline. "Curtida, your groom is lurking by the bathroom looking like half-and-half at the end of the night shift. I think we'd better get a move on before he decides his antacids aren't strong enough and makes a break for it." I kept my eyes on her headpiece as I followed her inside. It looked like a stuffed pigeon. Must've been what she'd brought in the hatboxes.

I caught a glimpse of Meekins through the doors leading into the chapel as we crossed the foyer. He looked just as sour as Edie'd said. My stomach twisted. Doug went straight to his flower stand up by the altar. I hadn't asked if he'd finished setting up his equipment. No time to worry about that now.

By the refreshments table, Mom was fluttering over Jenna Lila's presence

("I've read *all* your stories!"). She was wearing a fascinator that looked like a plate of spaghetti had come alive. Edie'd outdone herself with their hats. My matron of honor hustled me toward the changing room and stuffed me into the massive white skirt, then gave me a quick peck on the cheek. "Good luck with whatever this is." She pushed a bouquet of cheap flowers into my hand and was off to take her place.

Cynthia brought in the gift box with my gun and a package Trumbull had sent from the hospital. It contained a bottle of Sunshine and an envelope addressed to me in all caps. *This was at reception*, the doctor had scrawled on the outside. Inside was a photo of Priscilla Kim's diary. PSI had connected me to her death and wanted me to know it.

Another thing I didn't have time to worry about. My fanny pack had to stay in the dressing room, so I swallowed an antacid of my own and threw the pills and my sunglasses into the tiny purse that had come with the gown. Didn't want to leave the picture lying around, so I stuffed it and the envelope in, too. Nothing else fit.

The gun was preloaded with department Slate Gray Ennui. I double-checked the safety and slid it into my garter. An elastic bandage from the church's surprisingly well-stocked first aid kit completed the makeshift holster.

Music began playing in the other room. I checked my watch. We were starting forty-five minutes early. With luck, we'd have the Lavender Hope captured and be out of there before anyone untoward showed up. If Meekins got his face in order. If Mom's hopefulness wasn't a facade. If Doug had everything ready. If his theory worked. And then we'd get Ashaji and Gruber-Shaw in the clink, and they'd testify against Cassius, and everyone would live happily ever after. It would've been nice to be able to take a few deep breaths, but my dress stays got in the way.

In the foyer mirror, I looked like the casino version of a doll bride. The puffy sleeves of the gown reached nearly to my ears. The rhinestone-bedazzled bodice made hay of what cleavage I had. The only upside to the tumescent skirt was that I could wear my usual boots. Nobody would see my toes. My hair was plastered in whorls, towering fifteen centimeters above my skull. A fake white rose poked up under my veil like a drowning man trying to break the surface.

The overall effect was like glitter poured over a cupcake. The makeup lady hadn't been able to hide the deep circles under my eyes. The ludicrousness of what we were doing was almost overwhelming. Well. Too late to back out now. "Here's looking at you, kid," I whispered to my reflection, and hesitation-stepped out into the aisle.

The priest, a gray-haired Filipino with a nose that testified to an earlier career as a boxer, smiled beneficently at me. Meekins was on his left, Edie on his right. In the front row, my mother held a tissue in one hand and a bottle of champagne in the other. Seemed she hadn't had time to return it to the refreshments table before she was ushered into place. She dabbed at her eyes.

If our haste had lowered her spirits— I shut that thought down. Along with doubts about whether we should've chosen a chapel with more exits. My pulse thudded in my shoulder wound. Doug had his hand in the flower vase. Calm. I was calm. I wasn't thinking about capturing Hope, about Priscilla Kim, about Cassius. About the Chief. I was exhilarated. Blissful.

I took my place at the cleric's right hand. Meekins was standing at attention. Seemed that was the best he could do. I might've wished for something a little more limber. Excited, even. From the pews, Jenna Lila's camera was trained on the groom like a threat. Looked like the kiss he'd be planting on me would be even stiffer than last night's. The priest said some truisms about love and sacred institutions and then launched into the ceremony.

I glanced at Mom. She gave me the kind of smile I hadn't seen since I was a kid. It made her wrinkles look like laugh lines instead of furrows. Something untangled itself in my chest. Maybe it was true. Maybe all that hopefulness was rooted deep enough in her that nothing—not the war, not the Global Hope Depletions, not the wear and tear of everyday life—had managed to rip it out.

We got to "to have and to hold," and my voice was firm and clear as I said "I do." Doug's tongue was just visible between his teeth. The vase rocked slightly. Mom pulled her tissue back up to her face. Would anything I actually did ever make her this happy?

A sudden scream outside interrupted the priest's litany. A yell, and the wet thud of something hitting the ground. Cynthia slipped from her seat and went to stand by the door. Our curate went calmly back to the beginning of his question for Meekins. I didn't like his lack of surprise. Another howl from beyond the foyer. Still no reaction from him, just *in sickness and in health.*

Well. He would've been the one who'd sold us out. It'd been bound to happen. With all the vendors involved in wedding prep, keeping the ceremony fully under wraps would've been impossible. If it hadn't been him, it would've been the florist or the caterer. Easy enough for our enemies to offer a reward for any info about when and where we were planning to do it. For a cash-strapped operation like this one, it had clearly been one temptation too many.

All of us from the Agency had shifted, hands drifting toward our concealed firearms. Mom's tissue was still at her eyes, but she'd stopped moving it. There was a creak as the front door opened. Then silence. Then a pigment grenade rolled into the room.

They'd been banned from Agency use in the '90s, but the Pigment Enforcement logo on this one hadn't faded. Meekins hissed. Doug stopped what he was doing. I could hear the blood rushing in my ears.

Tommy clearly couldn't tell what the thing was. They hadn't been passing prohibited explosives around the classroom by the time he got to the academy. Didn't matter. We had four seconds to deal with the little smoking ball. None of us at the altar could reach it before it blew.

Cynthia didn't seem to recognize the weapon, either, but it didn't stop her from throwing herself on top of it. I sent a *thank you* to the Chief's ghost for seeing the girl as field agent material. There was a thump and the cadet's body jolted like she'd been punched in the chest.

Mom dashed out of her pew, heading for my fallen comrade. I scrambled after her. Cynthia would be fine. The bomb would've winded her, maybe left some internal bruising. But my mother would be first in the line of fire if a thug followed that opening salvo.

I no sooner had the thought than a keg of a man crashed through the door. "Mom!" I yelled, as the interloper lifted a paint gun in her direction. She looked up from where Cynthia was slowly pulling herself to her knees. Saw the barrel coming her way. Whipped the champagne bottle straight into the man's head.

After that, everything started happening real fast or real slow, adrenaline unspooling time in rushes and hitches. Edie and her family hustling Mom out the door, switching hats on the way; someone holding me back as she went—Doug—his hand up under my veil, pulling on my bobby pins. The flower stand toppling. The room, suddenly full of people. Must've been about seven. Felt like dozens. Edie's boys, Knights of Liberty, punches and pigment shots. A spray of Envy Green showering down from the ceiling, a bullet gone wild. Jenna Lila's flash, going off again and again. The brawl blocking the door.

Cynthia, pulling off her Gray-soaked kaftan to reveal the full hazpig suit beneath. Throwing the pigment-stained garment over a bruiser, who abruptly went slack. Brass knuckles crunching into my ribs. My fist, slamming into someone's jugular. Meekins, shooing us out of the melee toward the bathroom, the only other exit. The endless dash away from the cover of the pews.

The moment when the crooks realized where we were going, reoriented to come after us. A Knight of Liberty grabbing Doug around the neck, my old friend yelling something about Aunt Amy and then *go go GO!* The short fall from the bathroom window onto the bushes, the outer layer of my skirt tearing.

In the parking lot, Tommy and I stood under the midday sun. Not a cloud in the sky. From inside the building, shouts and groans. Doug was still in there. Tommy tugged me toward the cars. I pulled back. "If they can't take care of themselves, us getting painted over isn't going to help," he said.

"The Hope," I said, but he didn't respond, just pulled me over to Cynthia's station wagon and handed me the keys. Through the windshield I saw a page taped to the dashboard: directions, with a map. *The cadets had it under control*, some part of me thought, while another part of my brain was going *Doug, the Hope, Mom, all for nothing—*

I got in the car and drove. Our goal was a motel in San Bruno, the Red-wood Inn. We'd hit the freeway before we noticed our tail: a Peugeot 106, hot-rodded to the gills. I stepped on the gas. "Cynthia would love this," Tommy said grimly.

I cut off onto neighborhood streets, pulling tricks from long-forgotten sessions with the Chief and Walter. I followed tracks I'd traced twenty years before, drilling for a moment I'd thought would never come. In all that training, we'd figured I'd be the one doing the chasing.

I reached around and undid the clasp holding together the top of my dress, trying to get more room to breathe. The expansive feeling I'd had leaning against the wall with Doug was long gone. In the rearview mirror, sunlight flashed off the barrel of a gun poking from our pursuer's window. More evasive maneuvers. More sharp turns. The scar on my shoulder joined the chorus with my aching ribs.

Tommy had his weapon out and was trying to get in a shot. The bumps and jerks of my driving were throwing him off his game. He wasn't decisive enough to take advantage of the few smooth seconds when they came.

The passenger in the car behind us canted his body out, squeezed the trigger. I jerked the wheel, skidding us toward the middle of the road as the rear window fractured. A dart exploded in the center of the roof. A Deep Blue cherry on top of the ruinous sundae that was this morning. No Hope, our comrades stuck in a pigment-soaked chapel, and now imminent memory loss.

I told Tommy to take the wheel, leaned out the window, and let off three Slate Gray bullets at the front grill and the windshield. Cracks spider-webbed across the glass.

I couldn't tell whether I'd hit flesh, but the Ennui took effect fast enough. The supermini slowed to a crawl and finally stopped. I put my seat belt back on and took over the steering from my cadet. I could already feel the Blue beginning to fuzz my brain. I turned the car back toward 82 and handed Tommy the clutch purse. He extricated some of Trumbull's Sunshine and we dry-swallowed two pills apiece. Some of the fog lifted.

My cadet read the directions to me on repeat, but the dart in the ceiling continually puffed pigment into the atmosphere. We were in a neighborhood filled with brightly painted clapboard bungalows. Tulips swayed in the April breeze. My heart was pounding. South on 82, Chinese restaurant, Mexican grocery store, body shop, abandoned train station. Where were we headed?

The sky was bright, with a few wispy clouds. We were out of the hills, on the plain that rolled down to the wetlands and the Bay. A sign said Euclid. It was one of the street names Tommy kept saying as he rocked in the passenger seat. I turned, then took a right on Hensley. The instructions ended at a fawn two-story building with a mural of a conifer painted on the side.

After a moment sitting and staring at the place, some small adrenaline-packed part of me screamed *Go!* "In?" I asked the person next to me. Who was he?

"Uh," he said, but he opened the car door.

We stumbled into reception. A bald man behind the counter was saying words. I pointed at the car. His mouth turned down, and then it dropped open. He took the keys from my hand. A small girl with black curls and a violet headband came out and shrieked, pointing at my other hand. I looked down. There was something in it. A gun.

The man pushed the little girl into another room and carefully led us down a hallway. There was a door, and then a bed. I was on the bed. The man said something else. He was holding other keys. He left. Then I was asleep.

● ● ●

The next morning, I woke with a lead ball of defeat in the pit of my stomach. I didn't know what had happened, but I knew we didn't have the Hope. The only memory I could access was the feeling of Doug's palm, rough in my hand. How that had occurred I couldn't fathom. Thinking about it made me want to cry. Even I could tell that wasn't an effect of the Blue.

Through a crack in the blinds, I saw one of PSI's trademark obsidian Ford Falcons lurking across the street. Looked like it was official. Cassius was going all in, no longer delegating the dirty work to the local hoodlums.

Tommy and I threw together what outfits we could from our gore-smeared finery and slipped out the back alley to a diner that stank of old frying oil. I was wearing the wedding dress's underskirt and Tommy's suit jacket. He was in his ratty undershirt and wrinkled gray pants. He'd refused to leave the bow tie behind. It hung absurdly around his bare neck. He had a shiner and I had a bruise on my jaw. He could've been doing the walk of shame after prom night gone wrong, and I could've been Bootsie Poots's strung-out cousin.

I dropped a thousand dollars into the pay phone by the counter and dialed Edie. She told me my mother was somewhere safe. I asked her to pass along that I was fine, too. For all the good that did us. My memory of the wedding was foggier than my water glass at the greasy spoon. I remembered Mom holding a champagne bottle, Doug's fingers moving under baby's breath.

I didn't recall when I'd gotten the picture of Kim's diary, but its message was plenty clear. I'd be fighting off charges for her death soon enough. Tommy filled me in on the broad strokes of the rest. My smarting rib had clued me in to the brawl, but the fact that we'd left our colleagues in the chapel gave me a cramp in my leg. "As we left," Tommy said, wrapping up his tale, "Doug yelled something—about Aunt Amy and your hair?"

Aunt Amy. The Blue veil parted, and I saw Doug's anxious face, a meaty hand wrapping around his neck. *Aunt Amy loves your hair.* I reached up to the rumpled silk rose I hadn't managed to disentangle from the shellacked helmet the makeup artist had constructed from my curls. Underneath, my fingers bumped the shatterproof glass of a pigment vial. I pulled it out. The Lavender sparkled gemlike in the morning sun, filling the whole container. We'd done the impossible. We'd captured the Hope.

CHAPTER 28

We cadged a ride from a Mohawked sixteen-year-old who managed to seem like she was playing hooky even on a Saturday. The department was quiet when we got in. We found Meekins and Cynthia in the meeting room, staring at a postcard of the Iowa State Penitentiary. The kettle was steaming. The edges of the pigment poster on the wall fluttered in the smoggy breeze from the window. *Bull's Blood Rage, Ginger Curiosity, Apricot Awe*.

"I've got the Lavender," I said. Cynthia's eyes were rimmed with red. Meekins's shoulders hunched around his ears. I swallowed, trying to wet my throat. "Where's Doug?"

Cynthia pushed the card across to me. *Have your R & D op*, the note read. *Happy to exchange him for the Hope. Offer lasts till 9 a.m. Monday. Otherwise—Nambi'd look good painted Mauve. P.S. Sure he'll appreciate it if you get in contact sooner rather than later.* Cassius had known he wouldn't need to sign it. It was 11:30. We had less than two days until the deadline. My scalp ached.

"It was waiting here when we got in this morning," Meekins said.

They'd just returned from checking the obvious places Plato could have been held. We had the two samples of the Mauve Faith: the one Priscilla had given us and the vial Tommy'd found at Pimsley's. Now we had the Lavender Hope, too. But without Doug, we had no one to run the comparison. And without the comparison, we'd have no proof that Gruber-Shaw was lying when he announced that his team had synthesized Hope.

We were back to the same checkmate we'd been in two weeks ago. Except now, Doug was being held by folks who thought nothing of dyeing a mind funny colors. My old friend's worst fear, losing himself to psycho-pigment.

Meekins suggested heading up to Boise. There were other Agency outposts with R & D departments: Boulder, Carson City. But the closest place that would have all the equipment and the expertise necessary was up in Idaho.

The idea gave me the heebie-jeebies. It meant losing twelve hours to the drive, plus however long it would take to get the big-city agents to listen to us nobodies. And who was to say if we published the results that Cassius and his crew wouldn't just paint Doug Mauve anyway?

We argued. Berdie popped in, made himself a cup of tea, and stepped out again. I wanted to ask what he was doing in the department on a weekend, but Meekins was busy laying out the pros and cons for the sixth time. At about round eight, I had a terrible idea. By round fifteen it felt like the best of the awful options. "What about the Argentines?" I said.

There was a long silence.

"What about them?" Meekins asked.

"Preventing illegal pigment development is pretty much why their base is here," Tommy said, catching on.

We could set up a rendezvous to turn over the Hope, and use the Gauchos as manpower to trap Cassius. It was a wild scheme, but I was more in the mood to break things than take a twelve-hour road trip. This way, we'd get Doug back. Cynthia was skeptical, but she looked ready to change her tune when I pointed out this was the only sure way to keep my old friend's brain from getting fried with experimental pigment.

Meekins stood abruptly and crossed to the window, habitual scowl settling back onto his features. He jammed his hands into his pockets. "I lost my dad to those blow—Gauchos."

We'd worked side by side for sixteen years, and I'd never known. "They got my dad, too," I said. "Battle of Cartagena. '84."

Meekins didn't turn. "Shanghai. '83." He was outlined by the spring sunlight, a dark silhouette against the new green leaves of the Valley Oaks leaning over the freeway. "You kids can't remember. But, Curtida, you know how it was. Different. We were our own country. And now they're here, on our soil. And they interfere, and we get so used to it that we end up going to them. Against other Americans."

"This is what it was like for the rest of the world, most of the twentieth century," I said. "The folks we're up against want a country with no place for most of us. Ashaji's started using the Knights of Liberty sign-off."

Meekins turned back toward us. I saw him take in the fact that he was the only person in the room the Knights would want doing his job. He pressed on his slicked-down hair, opened and closed his fist. But it was Cynthia who made the objection. "I don't think the Argentines are a much better option than the Knights of Liberty."

Stories of the disappeared hung in the air between us. *Dead for thinking women should be able to work*, my exiled neighbor Monica had said about her daughter, left behind in Buenos Aires more than thirty years ago. Nothing I'd heard made it sound like things had gotten better.

"It would be treason," Meekins said.

"Don't exaggerate," I said, but I knew I had lost. Even Tommy voted to go to Boise. I was still on leave, after all. There was no reason they should listen to me. I chose to stick around Daly City. I couldn't stand the thought of sitting in the back seat of the wood-paneled Buick, putting miles between us and Doug.

Meekins took Pretty Prissy's Mauve sample but insisted we split the vial of Hope. "It was your mom who made it possible, and we only need half of it to run the comparison," he said. Some consolation prize.

I turned in the gun that I'd used at the wedding. Cynthia had brought me a change of clothes from the hospital, so I put those on. I didn't mind tossing the lacy panties. Fresh jeans couldn't change the fact that I felt all hollowed out on the inside. Like I might just float off into nowhere. My cadet gave me his keys to the office, just in case. They were cold comfort in my hand as I walked away from the department.

●●●

There was nothing left to do but face the wreck I'd made of my relationship with my mother. I headed to Edie's to ask where she'd squirreled her away. She gave me the address of Pablo's cousin in Fremont. I felt around to see whether she'd mentioned that the wedding was a sham. She just crossed her arms and went "Hmph," so it seemed that would be my coffee to grind. She'd brought my car up from the chapel, but insisted I take the bus as a precaution. There'd been no news tying me to Priscilla Kim's body, so I thought it unlikely anyone was tailing a soon-to-be canned Pigment Enforcement agent, but I did it for Edie.

I found a strap to hang on to on the 47, shoved in with families heading across the bay for Saturday lunches and afternoon outings. Snatches of Spanish and Tagalog floated above the roar of the diesel motor. A drooling, dark-haired baby sitting on his mother's thighs took one look at my face and started screaming. *You and me both, soldier.*

The Dumbarton Bridge soared into view, a pearl concrete arc reaching up toward the azure sky. The smell of rotten eggs from the old salt flats provided an appropriate counterpoint to the decades-old relic of an imagined, glorious future. I felt like I was back playing cloak-and-dagger games with Doug at the academy. Right now, though, there was no one to play with. A pothole sent pain spiking through my ribs.

Pablo's relatives lived in a subdivision that had seen more than half a century. The graying clapboard needed a few liters of paint, but someone kept the topiary lining the sidewalk in tight trim. The doorbell made no discernible noise, so I knocked and waited. Voices drifted from the backyard, a roar of laughter, the shrieks of kids in play. I could smell something spicy, meaty, and smoky. I should have been hungry. I knocked again.

The sunlight, painfully bright on this side of the Bay, warmed my back. If they were making good time, my fellow agent and the cadets were probably past the Oakland hills out into the Central Valley. I rolled my head, trying to loosen some of the knots in my neck. It hurt and I could hear my tendons creak.

I told myself to focus on what the hell I was going to say to Mom. *I never had any interest in Meekins, but if you want to eat peaches you're going to swallow fuzz.* A woman yelled a child's name in a tone that suggested the kid had been climbing the wrong tree. *The whole wedding was fake, we just needed to milk you for some Hope.* That would go down smooth.

Maybe Mom'd already guessed that something was up, had had a few hours to stew, and would be ready to talk. The fact that Edie'd had a hideout prepared might have tipped her off. And maybe my colleagues' Idaho trip would go off without a hitch and Doug would be totally fine and Mom would say "*Colorín colorado, este cuento se ha acabado*" like at the end of the picture books she'd read to me as a kid.

A slim pigeon of a woman opened the door, wearing jeans and a spattered gingham apron. She had on tennis shoes instead of the ridiculous platforms everyone seemed to be wearing these days. Her scowl suited her delicate bone structure. "You must be Susana's daughter," she said, leading me into a carpeted hallway.

It had been a while since anybody called me that. Family photos lined the walls, stacked five or six high. The smell of chili peppers intensified as we moved into the living room. The wall behind the television was painted teal. It was complemented by a rainbow glare of crocheted blankets, tablecloths, and rugs. Even the phone's handset had a little sweater. Sliding glass doors opened onto a dusty yard, showing the end of a table covered in orange-and-hyacinth-striped oilcloth.

In the kitchen, a radio played the traffic report. Mom was at the sink in a burgundy tank top. Apparently the weather here was more acceptable than on the fogbound peninsula. She dropped a handful of forks with a clatter at the sight of me. I started saying, "I need to—" but she interrupted my confession with a massive hug.

"Oh, sweetie, I'm so sorry! Your poor face—poor you—having your wedding day ruined like that—" Her curls smelled of her homemade rosemary shampoo. Same scent as always. The vitamin supplements changed once a month, but her hippie hair wash stuck around. "—I'll go with you two to the courthouse—where is Meekins, anyway?"

"He's—working—"

"Going after those goons? What a guy you picked out."

"Well, yes, that's," I said, and then she was loading up a plate of rice and chicken in a glistening brown sauce and sweeping me outside. Two dozen adults and half a dozen teenagers ranged along four folding tables covered in Quilmes bottles and cans of a dark Mexican brew. A toothless grandmother in a wheelchair sat under an awning, wielding a crochet hook on a pile of yarn. A blow-up pool held a handful of diapered toddlers and a dachshund. Preteens swung from the branches of a redwood standing against the back fence.

Mom launched into a round of introductions and a wildly exaggerated account of the ambush at the wedding. She didn't get too far before someone made her switch to Spanish for the benefit of the grandmother. I sure didn't want to tell her the truth and then face the scene she'd make with all these people around, so I ate as she talked. Would they be pushing a heel of hard bread at Doug right now? Or just letting him go weak with hunger? Forty-three hours and seventeen minutes until Cassius's deadline. Nobody searching for him. Nobody worried except an idiot like me.

Somebody passed me another portion. At least I'd have my strength. Fat chance I'd need it. I'd probably just be sitting on my rear until nine a.m. Monday. After that, I'd sit on my rear in a cell. The chicken was hot and spicy and disappointingly good. I'd been aiming to do penance while chewing. A teenage girl with bad acne tried to strike up a conversation with me. I grunted a couple times. The minutes rattled past.

Mom reached the climax of her story. "*Casi me muero cuando aparece la granada, pero mi yerno se tira encima—*" She had the table spellbound. Never mind that it had been Cynthia who jumped on the grenade, not Meekins. Mom spent a long time describing our virtuosity in martial arts. "*Edie me mandó acá, y bueno. Me han hecho sentir verdaderamente en casa.*"

The silver-haired patriarch stood and proposed a toast to my bravery, and to Meekins's success "at work." I raised my glass of tepid water. One of the toddlers fell down and scraped his knee. His wails drowned out all conversation while his mother put a Band-Aid over the wound and offered a shoulder to cry on. Now or never. "Mom," I said. "I need to talk to you."

"And we need to do something about that hair." Mom's response got a giggle out of the pimple-faced teen. "What did that makeup lady use on you?"

I found myself whisked into a lobster-colored bathroom and seated at the sink. She ran her homemade shampoo through the layers of encrusted gel and hair spray, and then slathered my curls in aloe vera. It was the best chance I'd have to get her alone.

The only response I could imagine once I'd told her I'd lied would be fireworks. Outrage. Cutting me out of her life. Figuring the best offense was a good defense, I started from the beginning. Maybe if she knew why we'd done it, she wouldn't take it that bad. As she worked the tangles out of the remains of yesterday's updo, I talked about Icarus, the Mauve, the Knights of Liberty. Cassius and Priscilla Kim. She put down the comb when I explained Ashaji's involvement, but she didn't interrupt. I'd just gotten to the disappearance of Pimsley's cabinet when Pimples stuck her head in. "There's tres leches cake if you two want."

"Oh, I couldn't miss that!" Mom said, rinsing her hands.

"There's more—" I said, but then we were back in the fracas out in the yard, eating creamy-sweet cake and drinking instant coffee. I kept attempting to pull Mom aside, get a few more moments alone. She kept brushing me off. Finally she hissed at me that these people had accepted her into their *house*, she wasn't going to insult their hospitality by ignoring them, that my story was fascinating but it could *wait* for a *minute*. We'd leave after lunch, head back to my place, talk in the car.

There were so many things wrong in that statement I didn't know where to start. She was right, though, about having time. Even though my mind kept repeating *they've got Doug and there's only forty-one hours left*, there was nothing I needed to do. Nothing I *could* do. My buddy Meekins was handling it, just like Mom had suggested. Agent Curtida was no longer a player. Now I was just Kay. Just Doug's friend, watching from the sidelines. Mom's daughter, who'd lied to her and used her. Might as well wait for the right time to tell her. The Nescafé tasted like dirt.

I watched the shadow of the redwood creep across the lawn as the day escaped. Mom did get out of her chair, eventually. I gathered an armload of dishes and followed her back into the kitchen. She had her latex gloves on, the ones she carried everywhere in her purse in case she needed to clean. The muscles on her upper arms, wiry from tennis, tightened and relaxed under her loosening skin as she scrubbed. The radio played a nostalgic bolero. Her curls were pulled back up in a loose bun instead of spilling over her shoulders.

I caught a glimpse of the constellation of tiny stars she had tattooed behind her ear, running down to a thin line of gray she'd missed at the nape of her neck. She'd gotten shorter. I had a flash of who she must have been forty years ago: tomboy turned flower child turned housewife, married to a solid guy whose family had emigrated from Colombia two generations before hers. They would've just purchased the house where I was born. Her biggest problem would have been a hectoring mother-in-law pushing Tide and Bisquick on her.

She'd been raised in the time between the wars. A time when single-digit inflation was considered a problem instead of a goal. A time of space races and civil rights. A time when the US had been a real contender. She hadn't been raised to deal with a husband who'd enlist in the navy in a fit of midlife patriotism. With young widowhood and a sullen teenage daughter. With a landscape pockmarked with lacunae of forgetfulness.

And still she stood, pushing seventy, back straight as she washed dishes in a strange house in a strange state. A woman who relied on the optimism of an earlier age to make her way through the world she'd been dealt. With a daughter who'd taken advantage of that optimism. The bolero wrapped up, a ranchera came on. My black eye throbbed. My confession was stuck in my craw. Felt like undermicrowaved mac 'n' cheese. Might as well tell the truth, take the hit while I was down. "Mom, I never meant to marry Meekins."

She reached for the soap. "Love is so strange, isn't it? I never thought I'd end up as a wife, either."

"That's not—we needed Hope. Pimsley's cabinet was gone, and we needed Hope, and we came up with a plan to capture some in the wild." In for a Benjamin, in for a Monroe. "A plan that meant I had to lie to you. About a lot of things." I told her how we'd set up the Lavender Hope capture. How it had hinged on her ignorance. How we'd thought it was impossible, but we'd been wrong.

Mom listened, pulling her gloves off finger by finger. Dried her hands on a towel. Folded it up, wiped down the stove. The news came on the radio. The Knights of Liberty had Blued over a school in Wisconsin. Finally she asked, "Who else knew? The doctor lady?"

My silence was enough of an answer.

"Edie?" She put down the towel, rubbed her head. "You offered me up— what, to feel important?"

"We were trying to save the country from—"

"'We' who? You're off the force. This wasn't your case."

"I was moving things forward—"

"Oh, of course. You were the special one, the only one who could possibly handle things." She pulled her gloves back on with a snap. Plunged her hands into the soapy water. "You're not the only competent person in the world, Kay. Sometimes you're even incompetent. Sometimes, you need to get out of the way of the people who are actually getting things done."

I thought I'd been ready to take what she'd throw at me but that blow landed. I told her sure, she was right. Even though I didn't believe it. I didn't, I told myself. My mouth tasted like rust. I said I was sorry. I couldn't tell if saying the words helped or just showed how far from enough they were.

While I talked she scoured a cup with steel wool. "I can't believe I maxed out my credit card for this."

"I'll pay for it," I said.

"With what money?"

I didn't want to think about that so I picked up the towel and started drying the dishes. My ears were burning. I wet a finger in the water in the tray under the rack and ran it over my earlobes, trying to cool off. It helped my skin but didn't do much for the nerves that were fueling the heat.

The traffic report started up again on the radio. Two cars abandoned after a fender bender on I-80 in Sacramento. An eyewitness talked about a high-speed chase and then a cloud of what he swore was Slate Gray. "Couldn't it have been smoke?" asked the announcer. My hands on the china slowed.

"No," said the caller, "the Buick was smoking, but this was a nastier kind of Gray. Somebody in the black car had some kind of a gun, and—"

The Buick was smoking. In spite of the big lunch, I felt light-headed. I leaned on the counter. Took a breath, closed my eyes. I could feel Mom watching me. "Meekins's car. They were trying to get to Idaho," I said. My colleagues had been caught. Were now on the run. Or worse. In any case, the Boise gambit had failed. "I told them we should've gone to the Argentines."

"Oh, of course, you were right. What did I just say?"

I said sure. The voice on the radio talked about someone stumbling out of the Buick and falling over. Which of them would it be? Tommy had pulled on reserves he didn't have, yesterday during the fight. He was still weak from his time in the hospital. I tried to get my tongue up behind my molar but a heavy tiredness swamped me and I didn't get there fast enough. My vision blurred.

"*Ay, por dios.*" Mom handed me a paper towel. "Don't take it like that."

I found myself saying, "It's just that they've got Doug already." My voice was real thick. Then I was telling her about Cassius's threat and his deadline and the fact that now there really wasn't anybody doing anything to find my old friend. I wiped my face and blew my nose. I was careful, but it still came away bloody.

She was looking at me like I'd seen her looking at clients in Dad's store who wanted to buy a fancy faucet she knew wouldn't fit their sink. Weighing the hassle of processing the return against the bottom line if they failed to bring it back. Her lipstick had faded. The dark liner made her mouth look pinched. After a while my breathing evened out.

She took my makeshift tissue. Threw it in the trash. "Did you get the Hope?"

I nodded.

"Let's get you to the Gauchos, then. Don't you dare have put me through all this for nothing."

●●●

Before I'd realized what was happening, the head of the Newark chapter of the Military Widows was drinking tea in the living room with us. Elvira Bravo was a retired librarian and sister of the American liaison on the base in Palo Alto. She had giant glasses and a perm that outdid even Mom's curls. She wore polyester pants and a knitted sweater vest that fit right in with the room's décor.

Mom laid out an edited version of the situation with the efficiency and delicacy of a veteran of decades of committee meetings. Elvira's daughter, it turned out, was the notary up in Boise, so she knew Doug. I tried not to wonder how well. The news that he'd been captured got a very serious "Oh, my" out of our visitor, as did the radio's confirmation that the Buick belonged to Meekins, of the Daly City Psychopigment Enforcement Agency.

Elvira had clearly been expecting the emergency to be something closer to a canceled party venue, but she shared Mom's ability to handle curveballs. Seemed to be a widow thing. "Yes. Yes," she said, voice barely above a whisper. "I'll get you onto the base. You'll need a typed report, preferably in triplicate. But who . . . which of them should you see?"

The radio announced five o'clock. A whole day gone. Only thing accomplished was handing my colleagues and half the Lavender Hope over to the bad guys. My earlier light-headedness had settled into a palpitating ache at my temples. "I need to move fast," I said.

"There's something you both should know," Mom said. "Kay, your father was a perceptive man. You know that. You've read his letters."

"What does Dad have to do with—"

Mom stopped me with an irritated flick of her fingers. "In his unit, there was a guy he never quite trusted. Something a little off about Tony. Supposedly Italian American from Boston, but his vowels shifted when he got drunk. Your dad saved him in some skirmish, coming around a corner under fire—said he pulled him back when he could've saved one of his men that he was closer to . . ."

My impatience had my leg jittering like I was impersonating Tommy. *Don't think about Tommy.* "I remember Tony. He was always bugging Dad about my swim times."

"Well, he was the only survivor. Captured right before the attack that took down the ship, prisoner of war, then he disappeared." Mom leaned forward on the sofa. "Tony Moretti."

The hundred-dollar coin dropped. Antonio Moretti, medals jingling, up on stage at the Magenta Cares event. "Tony" Moretti had been the spy in Dad's unit. *Frst thing he did when we got into port was find the nearest bar,* Dad had written. "Dad knew the general at the base in Palo Alto?"

"Your father saved his life. Try to get her to him," Mom said to Elvira. "He'll listen."

"I'll do my best," Elvira promised in her solemn librarian voice. Then it was time to go.

Mom saw us out. At the door, we hugged. I remembered her packing me onto the bus to the academy with my duffel bag right after my eighteenth birthday. "Please don't go back to Florida. Not just yet. Let the dust from all this settle," I said. "Please."

She made the sign of the cross over me and then walked back down the hallway. The afternoon sunlight outlined her silhouette, turning her hair to a red-tinted halo. I wondered when I'd see her again.

CHAPTER 29

Elvira dropped me off in a back office at the Newark Library with broken beige venetian blinds and an ancient IBM Selectric typewriter. "It's best if I talk to my brother without you," she said and left me alone with my doubts.

The farther we got from Fremont, the less sense the plan made. I was going to type up a report for the head honcho on the base. He'd read it, the scales would fall from his eyes, and he'd immediately commit troops to stopping Cassius and tracking down Doug and the rest of my colleagues. Just like that.

The big picture felt like a drawing scrawled by a child, and the nitty-gritty didn't look much better. Would the American liaison have the heft to get me in to see the general on a Saturday night? Or at all? ALs were generally figured to be on-call yes-men to the Gaucho brass, not power brokers. Hell, did I even believe that the general was that guy Dad saved? Why would an Argentine spy have used his real name when enlisting in the American navy? The headache sent a preliminary pang down my neck. The page was still blank. I set myself to writing out the information about the case.

Every sentence was marked by Tommy or Doug. Meekins and Cynthia popped up, and the Chief's loss loomed in the margins. *Where is she, where is he, where is she, where is he* . . . Doug's fear of losing his mind to pigment loomed over me as I typed up the unethical testing practices of Cassius's crew. I couldn't help but picture Plato getting hotboxed with experimental colors. Penelope singing *devil go away*, Jenny Crotty crouched on a chair ready to spring.

Cassius had promised to hand Doug over whole if we came through with the ransom—but we weren't going to come through with the ransom—and what did "whole" mean to a man like Big Skinny, anyway? A clock on the wall ticked. The carriage return dinged softly. Panic crawled spiderlike up and down my spine.

The warm sunlight through the blinds had shifted to the cold blue of streetlamps before Elvira got back. I'd finished the report, proofread it, typed up an extra set of copies, and had plenty of time to dig my mind into a dark place. She brought sandwiches, which helped. "We'll meet my brother at nine p.m." Her hushed voice matched the worn carpet and card catalogs. "Robert will take you directly to the general."

I chewed my ham and cheese. "Good news," I said, since it seemed like she was waiting for a response. I'd be meeting Moretti thirty-six hours before Cassius's deadline.

We found the American liaison sitting on a rocking chair on his front porch. Robert Bravo had thrown a blazer over his sweat suit. His wavy, graying hair was cut into a matinee-idol shag. Either Elvira's curls weren't entirely salon based or vanity was a family trait. Reticence certainly was. Robert tuned into the classical music station and drove us north without a word.

Four blocks from the entrance to the base, he turned onto a dark street and told me to get in the trunk. Sixty-meter-tall Hangar One soared against the starry sky behind him. He pushed the cuff of his sweatshirt up under his blazer sleeve. "I'm doing my sister a favor, but nobody can know I'm the one who got you in there. If you get caught—if I hear even a whisper that they suspect me, I'll make sure you never work for the government again."

So I was contraband. Seemed about right. "Sure," I said and went around to the back of the car. Impossible to get comfortable in the cramped space. My injured rib hurt no matter how I shifted. A Germanic symphony came on, muffled by the seats in front of me. The thundering drums were appropriate.

The Roca Base was massive, four kilometers square, stretching from the 101 all the way to the Bay. Felt even bigger, rammed into a trunk. My stomach joined in with my rib's griping. After two Wagnerian movements, we slowed to a halt. The lock popped and I could see the moon.

I climbed out, wishing there was time to stretch, but my guide was already taking the back way into the blocky, five-story building. He led me up and down stairs, through a maze of corridors. We arrived at a set of glass-paneled double doors. The gold plate inscription read *General Moretti*. It was locked, but Robert let us in. "You have a key to the general's office?" I asked as we entered.

"Only the waiting room," Robert said. The chamber lived up to its description: pale teal and pink upholstered seats, a desk for a receptionist, a bookcase breaking up the space. Two smaller rooms opened up to the side, with a grandfather clock ticking between them. A carved mahogany portal behind the desk led to Moretti's sanctum sanctorum.

Robert went into a side room and emerged with a folder and a Vulgate Latin bible. "The general comes by around ten p.m. every night. I'm leaving you here. Anybody else shows, I had nothing to do with this. Sit tight and be quiet, understood?" At my nod, he repeated, "And I had nothing to do with all this," flipped off the lights, and exited. I'd been real lucky that Mom had known to call Elvira. I crossed my fingers that my fortune would hold for the next forty-five minutes until the general showed.

There was nothing to do but wait. I tried sitting on the upholstered seats, but the stomachache I'd developed in the car had transformed into a buzzing infestation of dread in my chest. Lucky break or not, my body needed to move.

I poked around the unlocked areas: the conference room the AL had gone into; another small space with a second desk, two chairs, and bare walls. In the main area, the low bookcase divided an overstuffed armchair from a sectional couch. My knuckles hankered for my ruined punching bag.

I flipped the two envelopes containing my report through my fingers. I'd labeled both of them *ATTN: GENERAL MORETTI*, and put my name in the upper left-hand corner with "Daughter Lt. Curtida" in parentheses underneath. Now I was leaving sweat stains from clutching them too hard.

I put them on a coffee table and did some push-ups, listening to my breathing and welcoming the twinge of my shoulder wound. Anything to distract me from the line my subconscious kept serving up, a rhythmic ditty of names: *Doug. The Chief. Tommy. Pimsley. Meekins. Cynthia. Doug. The Chief. Tommy. Pimsley. Meekins, Cynthia, Doug . . .*

The clock chimed out ten p.m., and then ten thirty. The fluorescent light from the hall cut through the frosted glass, leaving the shadow of Moretti's name outlined backward on the mint-colored carpet. Aside from the timepiece's occasional interjections, the room was silent.

I touched the Hope in its shatterproof vial, nestled in my front pocket. Adrenaline was giving way to exhaustion, with despair sneaking in close behind. Robert Bravo had been wrong. There was no way the general was coming in on a Saturday night. I'd failed to protect the country. Failed to protect my friends. I was even failing at treason.

I started pacing to keep sleep at bay. On the receptionist's desk, I found a box marked *Bandeja de entrada.* I left one of the envelopes on it and slid the other under the mahogany door. Soon as it'd disappeared, I realized how dumb that had been. The general wasn't going to read a letter slipped onto his office floor like an anonymous love note in an academy dorm.

I picked up the copy I'd left in the in-box. In the dim light, I could make out the photocopy of a journal article lying under it. *"Anhelo melancólico lila de plata: entre el ennui y la esperanza."* The paper on Silver Lilac Wistfulness that Trumbull had shown me.

A note, paper-clipped to the first page, said something about Priscilla Kim. Stapled to the back were several articles in Spanish. One in English about the faked data scandal that had cost Priscilla her academic career. The note on the front had the word *fraude* underlined.

Had Tommy's cousin brought her tale to the Gauchos before she went into hiding? If so, it didn't look like they'd believed her. What were the chances they'd believe me? I tucked the second copy of my report into the waistband of my jeans, knocking my keys out of my pocket. They fell with a jingle to the floor. I bent to pick them up, wishing I had my fanny pack.

A shoe scuffed in the hall. My gut clenched. I stood slowly. Was it the general? Or was it someone else? The frosted panels were the same empty rectangles as before. Didn't suggest that Moretti was on his way in. Didn't mean there wasn't somebody out there.

If it were a routine sweep, I could squirrel myself away in one of the smaller rooms or under the desk. But guards doing their regular rounds would have walked past the doors already. I moved carefully, hugging the back wall as I scanned the blurry view of the hallway for the blue of a Gaucho uniform.

There was nothing. My heart rate wouldn't drop, though. Somebody had been out there. If they were hiding, it didn't bode well. If it were Moretti, I didn't want to be concealed when he came in—acting like the fugitive that I was would make him less likely to listen. If it wasn't him, I didn't want to be an easy target.

What would Walter do, in this situation? Thinking about Walter made me think about the Chief. That kicked off the damn litany of names again. *Doug, Tommy, Meekins, Cynthia...* I made myself breathe deep, then darted into the armchair next to the bookcase. I could duck down out of sight if the figure in the doorway didn't match the general's profile.

When they came, they weren't the general. A squad of four soldiers, guns out, burst into the room. The light from the hall rippled on the jointed black plates of their hazpig suits, a far cry from the baggy green affairs of Pigment Enforcement. I jumped out of the chair. They'd surrounded me before I landed. Nobody moved. The only sound was the breath hissing through the filters on their masks.

They were close enough I could see the upraised fist embroidered on their ridged epaulettes. The *Manos de Dios*—the Hands of God squadron. My rib and shoulder ached in time with the throbbing in my head. The *Manos* were the special ops force, the ones who did the dirty work. I kept my palms visible as I inched them toward the ceiling. *"No armas,"* I said. I wasn't sure whether I'd just said I was weaponless or had no arms.

"Shut up, *yanqui de mierda,"* said the tallest of the soldiers, voice muffled by his mask.

"I'm here to deliver a report to the general. That's all," I said.

"Uh-huh. Soon we'll see why you're here," another of the soldiers said. He had the nasal, plummy accent of a *porteño* schooled in annexed Britain. He gestured with his gun, and the tall one pulled my hands down roughly behind my back. Handcuffs fastened around my wrists with a click.

They marched me into the hall. "I'm Pigment Enforcement," I said. That got me a slap across the face. I kept talking. "There's a conspiracy to develop an illegal pigment, with a network that stretches from here to Iowa City . . ." Every few words, I got another slap. I pushed through the story, anyway.

I didn't want to think where we were going. I remembered Monica, my next-door neighbor, talking about the mass graves her daughter had disappeared into. I remembered a professor at the academy saying it was better to have the Argentine *militares* kill you fast than take you prisoner. There were places in Buenos Aires where passersby could hear the screams from two floors belowground.

My cheeks burned from the repeated blows, but I kept talking. The Mauve, Priscilla Kim, Cassius. Slap. The kidnappings, the ransom request. Slap. Ananda Ashaji's plan to take over the government. Slap, slap, slap.

As I spoke, I watched the unfamiliar corridors pass, searching for an exit. The wall decorations were themed: this hall was hung with photographs of pigment bombs through the years, the next one over had airbrushed posters of fighter jets. Portraits of the dictators popped up with regularity. The way out stayed hidden around corners. *Doug, the Chief, Tommy.* One slap hit the bruise on my jaw, and I tasted blood in my mouth.

The Hands pulled me into a stairwell. It smelled of disinfectant and rust. We started going down. Terror seized my throat. Our feet clanged on the metal stairs. We emerged into a passageway with a cement floor and bare bulbs hanging from the ceiling. But there—just to our left—was a door with a window, facing out into the night.

I faked a stumble, pulling down one of the soldiers holding me. He slammed into the wall. I swept out with my right foot, tripping the other guy, then spun around to grab the door handle with my cuffed hands. It wouldn't turn. I felt for a lock with my fingers, but there was none.

The two I'd knocked over were standing up, the other pair heading back toward me. I threw my shoulder against the glass of the door, pain lancing through my old wound. The window cracked but didn't give. The tall soldier reached out and spun a lazy roundhouse punch. I ducked. The dodge took me right into his uppercut. My vision swam and my knees buckled. Next thing I knew they had me pinned to the floor. Hadn't been my ticket out. At least antagonizing them might get them to kill me faster.

"*¿Y esto?*" The voice was deep, unmuffled by a pigment mask.

"*¡Mi general!*" The knee on my back pressed down more heavily as its owner snapped to attention. I craned my neck. Moretti was walking down the hall toward us. I could see my face and the soldiers' boots in the distorted reflection of his patent leather oxfords. My captors burst into a volley of salutes, one of them pattering out an explanation. The machine-gun speed of the *porteño* accent kept me from catching all the details, but I heard the words for *office* and *yankee* and something that sounded like *we'll make her talk*.

"I'm Agent Curtida of Pigment Enforcement," I said. "I have a report—" A gloved hand covered my mouth.

"Pigment Enforcement?" asked the general. Another barrage of words flew over my head. More than one soldier was talking. The man holding me down took his hand off my mouth to accentuate a point.

"I'm Lieutenant Curtida's daughter!" I said through the noise. "Please—for what my father did for you, *listen*—"

The hubbub continued. The general shifted, giving no sign that he'd heard me. Finally, at a word from Moretti, the noise cut off. "*No necesitamos problemas con los locales. Tomá su reporte y sacala de acá.*"

"*Mi general, ella estaba en su oficina—*"

But the shiny black shoes were walking away. My captors hauled me to my feet, and back we went up the stairs and through the winding corridors. I didn't dare wonder what was happening. There had been something about problems with the locals. The interior design at this level included sconces. That had to be a good thing. We passed the office where they'd found me. The carpet gave way to tiles, then linoleum, then back to carpet.

We emerged into a high-ceilinged lobby. A giant Argentine flag hung in the middle of the space, its light blue stripes encasing a leering sun. The marble floors were threaded with lapis and gold inlays, reflecting the flag in their polished gleam. Even the metal detector had been painted azure. Through the glassed revolving door, sulfur streetlights glowed. My captors uncuffed me. "The report. Give it to me." The tallest soldier took off his pigment mask, revealing deep-set brown eyes.

I fished the envelope out of my waistband. "It's just everything I told you earlier."

"General's orders. We are to receive the report," he said. I passed it over. "Now get out."

I didn't know how to feel. I wasn't going to be carried out of the Argentine base feetfirst. At least that was something. *Doug, Tommy, Meekins, Cynthia.* I swallowed the lump in my chest and pushed my way through the door. The moon had set, and clouds blocked the stars. I looked back in. The tall soldier was talking to the security guard, waving the envelope I'd gone to so much trouble to get to him. The guard pulled out a wastebasket, and the Hand of God soldier dropped my report into it. My jaw, shoulder, and rib were all tender. I trudged west toward El Camino Real, wondering if the night bus to Daly City was still running.

CHAPTER 30

The bus was not running.

I walked an hour and then jogged north on El Camino, trying not to feel the night's chill. About five kilometers up the road, I found an intersection with a twenty-four-hour grocery store on one side and a scuzzy motel on the other. The Glass Slipper Inn looked like the kind of place Cinderella might have hocked her fancy footwear to pay for when things didn't work out with the prince. To one side, a lightbox advertised H T WATER. They'd run out of letters or amenities or both. My rib started whispering about falling asleep in a steaming tub.

I ducked into the All American Market and pulled the last two hundred grand out of my account. Blew half of it for a roach-filled room. As advertised, the water was hot. Through the door of the bathroom, the bedside clock taunted me as it flicked from 12:59 to 1:00. Thirty-two hours to Cassius's deadline.

I shifted against the edge of the bath and was hit with a wave of longing for my tub at home. My tub, my car, the life I'd had till the day before yesterday. My colleagues, rotting away god knew where. Doug's calloused palm in my hand. Maybe it would have been better if the Argentines had snuffed me out. At least that way I'd know I'd done all I could.

I pulled a tangle of long blond hairs off the pillowcase. With the lights out, the cool sheets felt fine against my skin. I was likely the only one in the department sleeping in a bed tonight. It would've been nice to have someone to pray to. I remembered Mom droning mantras to Ganesh and San Gregorio Hernandez in her bedroom before the news came about Dad. She'd probably lit a candle to whatever saint Pablo's relatives had handy as soon as I'd left with Elvira. I sent a thought of safety to my friends, out there in the darkness. The only person it helped was me.

The half vial of Hope on the bedside table gleamed in the glow from the clock. My nose was all stuffed up. I had no Sunshine pills with me. Tomorrow was another day. I'd deal with it when it arrived. I was asleep before I finished rolling over.

I dreamt that the Chief was alive, held by PSI in a decaying hospital in Turlock. Through a glass-paned door, I saw my boss slumped in a chair, hands tied. They had Doug manacled to the wall behind her. I turned the handle. My old friend's mouth opened as if to shout a warning. The latch clicked. A massive explosion thundered over us all. The back wall fell into the room, knocking Plato over and burying the Chief. The ceiling crumbled, raining iron beams and bricks. I watched, helpless, as Doug was crushed. A dark pool seeped from under the rubble. Behind me, stanchions groaned. The doorway's lintel cracked, showering me with dust.

I lay down to wait for my death.

I woke and fell asleep several times, stalking halls through variations on the dream. It always ended the same way. With the first thin rays of dawn, my eyes wouldn't close. 6:01, said the clock. Just shy of twenty-seven hours to Cassius's deadline. My mind shuffled through the facts of the situation like a blackjack dealer killing time between hands. The thud of footfalls through the ceiling. The radio.

Then my brain dealt me a trump card: Berdie. Berdie, the keeper of all the files. Berdie, who could be anywhere in the office without raising eyebrows. Berdie, who was too peabrained to take seriously as a threat. Berdie, who'd told no one about my totaled apartment.

Berdie, who was the only person from the department sleeping in his own bed.

He'd come in for tea while we argued over going to the Argentines. If anyone had tipped off the crooks about Meekins's itinerary, it would have been him. Of course, PSI had been on Tommy's and my tail from the Redwood Inn, so they could've been watching the department and followed the wood-paneled Buick—but then again, how had they figured out what motel we were at? Berdie could've overheard the cadets' plans.

The adrenaline from the nightmare droned through my veins. I got out of bed and stuck my head under the faucet. My nose started running. What came out was tinged with blood. The bridge was all swollen. A souvenir from last night's shenanigans. The water on my scalp was cold enough to freeze my thoughts for a minute. As soon as I came out of the bathroom, though, my mind was at it again.

I pulled on my clothes. I hadn't noticed the bloodstains on my shirt last night. It was what it was. I considered phoning Mom, but didn't know the number of the place in Fremont. I pocketed the vial of Hope. I needed to get moving. Didn't really matter where to.

By the time the bus showed up, Cassius's deadline was twenty-four hours away. The slow ride from Palo Alto sunshine to Daly City murk gave me plenty of time to wear grooves in my gray matter. No matter where I started, I always ended up back at Berdie. If Tommy'd come to me insisting the notary was a mole, I would've told him where to put his hunch. Even through the fug of my anxiety, I knew that. But I needed to do something. We passed an Argentine military transport. I didn't want to look at it. The bus bumped along, pulling in at every single stop.

I was too impatient to let public transit eat up my time. I'd need my car. Using it would be risky—I'd be easier to spot. But it was a sure thing I'd accomplish nothing if I spent all day waiting to get where I was going. Edie's, first, then. Probably the department after. I'd need Berdie's address. Go to his home—and then what? Wasn't sure I wanted to know my answer to that.

In the sandwich shop, the smell of caramelizing onions punched its way through my congestion. Pablo and the boys in the kitchen were in prep mode for the lunch crush. Edie's fussy relief made me feel like a real turkey for not keeping her posted.

When I requested my car keys, her manicure went motionless on the countertop. Five pink almonds against cracked red Formica, like Easter candy snuck into a belated Valentine. She asked what I was planning. I didn't know what to say to her. I left pretty fast.

I parked on the frontage road by the freeway and walked the four blocks to the department's back entrance. Through the window in the door, I could see the glow of lights. Those shouldn't be lit on a Sunday morning. Especially with most of the department kidnapped by the crooks. I tried the handle. It turned.

I could understand Tommy or Cynthia forgetting to flip a switch before heading out, but locking up was the kind of thing Meekins would triple-check. I moved into the hallway, wishing I'd scoped out the parking lot for black Ford Falcons. Wishing I had my gun. The fluorescents at the front end of the hall were off. Whoever was in here was in this half of the building.

The cadets' office was bolted. The file room was closed. My search for Berdie's address could wait. The linoleum kept mum under my feet. Next came the lab. Light shone through the crack under the door. I nudged it open.

The wave of stale pigments washed over me, mixing with the nerves capering through my veins. I held on to the frame until my vision cleared. And there, leaning over the desk like a psychedelic vision of a casino joker, was a cyan-and-yellow houndstooth suit. Berdie, back to the door, was reading Doug's notes.

I had to find a weapon. My eyes skipped over the bins of equipment lining the walls, the file boxes and technical library. The emergency exit at the far end. Across from the notary's back, a steel-topped table jutted out from the wall. The psychospectrometer's sable cylinder rose above a built-in Bunsen burner, a frame of test tubes, and a cluster of jars. Within the jumble, an amber flask. Exactly what I needed: the lab's emergency chloroform.

Far as I knew, Berdie hadn't been exposed to any unstable pigment mixes, but bending that rule was the least of the transgressions I was about to make. I padded across the floor, grabbing the bottle and swiping a stack of muslin wipes from a shelf.

The notary flipped over a page and bowed closer to the desk. I got right behind him before I unscrewed the cap. The sickly sweet smell spun up around me, bringing back memories of leaning on Doug's arm in Tadlock's barn at the academy. I slapped the chemical across one of the cloths, wrapped an arm around Berdie's shoulders, and covered his nose and mouth.

He was about my height and had twenty kilos on me, but between the chloroform and my regular workouts he didn't stand much of a chance. After a three-minute struggle I had him on the floor. Two minutes later, he'd gone from dopey to lights-out. I left the muslin over his face, just in case. Working fast, I tied two of the extra rags together and secured his hands behind his back.

I dragged him out of the lab, chewing over where to take him. His two-tone shoes left scuff marks on the checkered tiles. Keeping Berdie in the department was a no go. All the information he'd been trying to pilfer was right here, if he managed to get out from under me. He may have told his coconspirators about his plans for the day. I needed a place I could keep him contained. A place no one would expect us to be.

We were nearing Evidence. I left him in the hall and went into the room to get Minnie Cucci's key ring. The kennel-filled back of the warehouse where I'd found Penelope Crotty would do well enough.

A dusty pigment gun sat on a shelf next to the keys. I nabbed that, too. It had a squib jammed in the barrel. I didn't have any cartridges, anyway. I was banking on Berdie's field sense being on par with his self-defense.

The notary's car, a crimson-and-ivory Volkswagen Bug buffed like it had just rolled in from the '60s, sat alone in the parking lot. The fog was gone, and the midmorning sun blazed down on the asphalt. I strapped my unconscious companion into the passenger seat, then arranged myself on the driver's side. I let the pigment gun rest against his belly and pulled the rag off his face.

We were halfway to Ticky-Tacky Tuxy before Berdie emerged from his chemical haze. He moaned. Blinked. Started, realizing his hands were tied. He took in the dashboard, the seat belt, the gun. He sat very still. "I'm just taking you somewhere safe to ask a few questions," I said. "I'm trying to locate our colleagues. You know—Meekins, Tommy, Cynthia . . . the folks that would take a bullet for you?"

"I don't—" His voice was rough.

I hushed him, prodding his soft flesh with the dart gun's muzzle. "We haven't started yet." Exhaustion tugged at my temples, dragging at the adrenaline still thrumming in my gut. The vengeful fantasies I'd had on the bus were losing color in the face of Berdie's vulnerability and ridiculous sartorial choices. But I'd started down this path, and damned if there was another one I could think of. No need to be harsh with him. No need, unless he didn't want to talk.

Indigo Joe came on KFOG. *Daly City police have put out a warrant for the arrest of Kay Curtida of Psychopigment Enforcement, suspected of murdering Priscilla*— I snapped off the radio. Berdie looked like he wished I'd kept him chloroformed. The rest of the drive went by in silence.

Cucci's warehouse welcomed us with the smell of mildew and aging dog piss. The sun poked unsuccessfully at the moldy skylights before giving up and heading to greener pastures. I led Berdie to the cell where I'd found Penelope. He quailed at the grime-covered floor. I tied him to the bars and went to get him a chair. Somehow I didn't want to see him stain his tailcoat.

I regretted my generosity as the hours ticked by. Berdie was a pompous idiot, but the same qualities that made him so silly made him a tough nut to crack. His train of thought was missing a few connectors between carriages. He wanted our missing colleagues located as much as anyone, but he knew nothing about it—and chloroform certainly wasn't the way to move my search forward. The Notary Guild would hear about this. Yes, I'd better believe he'd report me. He offered me a handkerchief to wipe my nose, which was bleeding again. It was right there, in his breast pocket— why would I find it suspicious that he was in the lab? He should be asking *me* what I was doing in the department. I was, after all, the one on leave due to insanity.

Around and around we went, from ruffled feathers to long-suffering superiority to concern for my mental state. I would've thought getting kidnapped by a woman wanted for murder might have concerned him more. Seemed like that hadn't quite sunk in. Then again, this was a man who regularly ate strange mushrooms he'd picked in the woods.

The afternoon marched relentlessly on. The warehouse got stuffy. I went out to Cucci's office to mix up some Nescafé, leaving him alone in the dark. The woman had a selection of espresso cups and a single old-school mug with "Aunt Minnie" written on it in glittery puff paint. The name was surrounded by hearts and stars.

My eyes itched from three restless nights. My injuries kept reaching for my attention. I couldn't find the swagger I normally put on for interrogations. The quick thinking that had gotten Big Skinny's name out of Frederick Bentley seemed pulled out of some other life.

How much of my confidence through the years had come from knowing I had backup, knowing I was part of a team? Meekins and I had different ways of getting things done, but I'd learned to trust that he'd come through. Now he was god knew where, and I was failing to come through for him. Mom's words kept intruding on my thoughts. *Sometimes you're even incompetent.* I dumped half the jar of instant coffee into the puff-painted mug. What if Berdie wasn't even working for Cassius? What if I was barking up a tree sewn whole cloth from my desperation?

That was ridiculous. Why else would the notary have been in the lab on a Sunday morning, leafing through Doug's notes? I just needed a pick-me-up and I'd get back on track. The electric kettle hissed doubtfully at that thought. I stirred the gunk in my cup with a pen until it settled into a grainy ooze. I headed back to the cell.

Berdie started talking as soon as I turned on my flashlight and kept right on going as I came toward him. "I'd heard the stories—Meekins confided in me early on. I suppose the poor boy saw me as a sort of father figure, a level head from outside all of the chaos. I let him talk, but I wasn't sure what to believe. I mean, you seemed so even-keeled. And would the department keep working with a suicidal agent who'd run into a Slate Gray manufactory without protective gear? I did think about that when I heard the story about what you'd done at Bepler. This is clearly a woman who can't function unless she's got someone there to keep her under control. Honestly, the fanny pack made me wonder early on—"

By the time he stopped, I was close enough to smell the sweat beading on his scalp. He blinked up at me. Shifted in his seat, waiting for me to say something. I stayed quiet. Outside, a truck rumbled past. The wind rustled around the walls. Holding still was making my bruised rib complain, but I wasn't going to make the first move. Finally, he pointed his chin at the coffee. "Is that for me?"

"Yes," I said and began dribbling the sludge across the lapels of his beloved suit. He hunched back, so I dumped the rest of it on his crotch. I crouched down to his eye level. Steam rose from his pants. "I don't think you've been taking this seriously. We both know who you're working for. We're going to start over, now, taking that as a given, and you're going to tell me what they wanted you to look for in Doug's notes."

"The Argentines aren't the enemy—"

My palm lit out across his cheek. The rage had dropped from nowhere, an electric bolt burning away the numb haze clouding my brain. Hard to believe that he would try to convince me he was a spy for the Argentines. Of all the cock-and-bull lines to come up with. If our department merited a spy, they would have chosen someone more useful.

He started crying. I started my questions again. I rode my wrath through his excuses. He swore his bosses didn't have our colleagues. If they did, they'd lied to him, but I didn't know them like he did. They weren't like that, no matter what people said.

I thought about Pimsley's frozen body. Slapped him again. We went round and round the denial carousel. At least he'd admitted he was passing on info. Some part of me knew that I was going about this ham-handedly, that I would've had plenty to say to Meekins if he'd been the one cuffing a suspect. But without my fury, I knew I'd go back to the wet piece of cardboard I'd been through the first hours of questioning.

After admitting that the arrangement had been going on for "several years," he started hyperventilating. I didn't let up, and eventually the hysteria got the best of him. His eyes rolled up into darkness and his head lolled forward.

With his hands still tied to the bar, he looked like a Velcro-pawed toy monkey. I slapped his scalp lightly. No response. I was sweating and breathing hard. I took off my jacket and went outside for some air.

The bright sun stung after so many hours in the dark. The dandelions in the vacant lot next door bent under a sudden gust. My body ached with the memory of cigarettes. I knew the exact hunch of my shoulders to light up in the wind. The sudden clarity of that first rush of nicotine.

My breath slowed as I cooled down. Seemed I could feel Berdie's limp form sagging in the back of the warehouse behind me. A delivery boy wheeled a beat-up bike out of the Mexican place across the way and headed off down the hill. I was hungry and queasy at the same time. I could've used some clarity.

I went back into Ticky-Tacky for a disguise: a blond bouffant wig off a dusty mannequin, a purple velour blazer, and a frilly black shirt. Heart-shape sunglasses covered my shiner and completed my costume. The outfit was as absurd as I felt, playing dress-up between bouts of interrogation. I could pass for one of the misfits who had migrated down from Haight-Ashbury after the Magenta Attack. Better than looking like a wanted murderer.

I got a burrito for $12,000 of my remaining cash and took the foil-wrapped tube back to Minnie's front step. The cashier had watched me cagily when I walked in, but she'd taken my money. I touched my nose. Dried blood flaked off on my finger. The sun was sinking toward its five p.m. glare, the last flash of the afternoon doldrums. I'd always hated the butt end of the day at work. Too late for coffee, too early for a beer. Nothing but traffic jams and an empty apartment on the calendar. And today, what did I have to look forward to? An evening of backhanding Berdie?

Last night I'd been spooked about what the Argentines might do to me. Now I'd gone and replicated their tactics, with nothing to show for it but a sore palm. Who was I kidding? Berdie had no training to resist interrogation. If he hadn't cracked and let what I was looking for slip, it meant he didn't know where my colleagues were. His sobs still sounded in my head. I was a full-on idiot who'd traded a fog of numbness for one of anger. A tight heaviness spread across my back.

A page of yesterday's *Daly Daily* blew past, featuring a picture of Meekins pointing a gun past my veiled curls. Forty-eight hours of ups and downs. The bumpiest part of the ride had been my mood this afternoon. If I kept up like this, I could join the Feelies and tour the country showing off my pigment-free emotions.

I'd done everything I could think of. Some unthinkable things, too. Tomorrow, Gruber-Shaw would make his announcement. Tomorrow, Ashaji's new book would come out. Within months—weeks?—this country would be transformed into a theocracy. Camps like Turlock scattered across the map for dissidents. A puppet of the Knights of Liberty at its head.

Sixteen hours to Cassius's deadline. I felt the lump of the half vial of Hope in my pocket. I couldn't save the country. I probably couldn't save myself. But I could still try to save Doug.

CHAPTER 31

I let myself back into the shop. The bedazzled formalwear glittered in the afternoon sunlight. One last chance to salvage something from this mess. I'd go home and make a call to get PSI's attention. Grab the gun I had hidden there, just in case. I'd hand over the Lavender and watch Doug walk free. I straightened up, wiped the crusted blood off my nose with my burrito-smeared paper napkin. The heaviness was still there, a guilty weight on my shoulders, but at least I had a plan.

My personal pep rally was interrupted by the sound of Berdie's voice. It wasn't coming from the back of the warehouse. It was coming from inside Minnie's office. "Yes," he was saying, "it does back up the story—they needed Hope, though . . ."

I threaded quietly and quickly through the clothing racks. He kept talking, giving no sign he'd heard me enter the building. "Well, how could I have—yes, of course, sooner would've been—mea culpa, mea culpa, man—"

I opened the door. My captive started, dropping the phone. Tattered muslin hung in ghoulish bracelets from his wrists. He must've come to and managed to shred my makeshift cuffs against the rough iron bar. I should've locked up behind me. I sure hadn't been thinking clearly.

Then again, having a direct line to the crooks worked fine with my plan. I strode over to him and picked the receiver off the floor. "Tell Cassius I know where the other half vial of Hope is, and I want to ransom Doug." An intake of breath, and then silence on the other end. "I'll be home in an hour. Tell him to call and we'll discuss. To call. If he shows up, the deal is off." I hung up.

"Who's Cassius?" Berdie's tongue darted into view, then hid itself.

I told him to turn around so I could tie him up again. "I'll tell them to send someone for you."

I expected a comment on my getup, but instead he said, "Take me with you. Let me be your backup." He shifted, trying to look tough. He achieved constipated. It would have been funny if I'd had time for it. He gave up that tactic and started pleading. He wanted our colleagues back to safety—never would have done this if he'd known what these people were capable of—he promised he'd behave—

A deep knot was forming under my shoulder blades. If I took Berdie home, I'd be able to keep an eye on him. I could decide what to do with him there. Worst-case scenario, he was easy to overwhelm. I told him to shut up and get in the car.

His silence lasted almost to downtown. As we passed the first of the restaurants advertising a special meal in honor of the Daly City Fog's big match in the Copa Libertadores, he asked if it was okay if he smoked. I gave him the go-ahead and he pulled a crumpled pack of off-brand domestics out of the glove box. Offered one to me and lit up when I turned it down. Inhaled deep.

"I'm trying to quit." He looked out the window as the red awning of La Continental rolled by. "I know my job's going to disappear this budget cycle. And then . . . I have no idea what I'll do." There was none of his usual bombast. "I figured it would just be a year playing this spy game, but then the Chief got my contract renewed, and renewed again . . . I sock it all away, because pretty soon I'll be living on my pension."

"Sock it away in bow ties?"

"Most of my wardrobe was my grandfather's," he said stiffly. "The newer stuff I usually swap for. Pimsley was always interested in what I offered."

I didn't have much to say to that. I turned on the radio. Got on the free-way, then got off early to put distance between us and a neurotypical patrol car. The wig itched. Didn't think they'd pay much attention to the blonde driving a Bug, but figured it was better to be safe.

Another Argentine military transport showed up as we rolled into my neighborhood, taking the same streets as I was as it headed for whatever training exercise the southerners had come up with to occupy their time. Just my lot. A day I could do without seeing a Gaucho, and they were everywhere.

A neurotypical officer was loitering in jeans and a varsity jacket across the street from my apartment. I'd worked with the guy on a case down in San Carlos, and he always wore the same outfit for plainclothes work. I'd cursed their incompetence for decades, but now I was glad Daly City's finest were performing at their usual standards.

We went up the back way. I sent Berdie ahead of me. I reasoned it was acceptable to use a double agent as a guinea pig. Nobody had been there to set up any booby traps, though. My sleeping pad was still in the living room, the crumpled comforter right where I'd left it. One of Edie's boys had come by for Mom's suitcase. They'd missed her periwinkle bra hanging in the shower.

I got out a kitchen knife and set to work tearing up the living-room carpet. Berdie watched me from over by the bookcase, keeping very still. I got annoyed with the scrutiny and sent him to the kitchen to make us coffee.

It had been one of Walter's rules: always have a backup weapon. He'd had caches scattered across town, in homes of friends or buried in vacant lots. A few months after he passed, the landlord had replaced the foul linoleum in my living room with an equally ugly dun-colored shag. While the workers were out, I hid one of my mentor's guns and a clip of department Gray cartridges under a floorboard in the center of the room.

The day had finally come. With some yanking and hacking, I got a couple square meters pulled away, then lifted the board that had protected the revolver all these years. The gun was dusty but otherwise in good condition. I took it into the kitchen to clean it anyway.

Berdie shrank against the drip coffee maker. I handed him a mug and told him to go sit on my bed. I could smell the solvent and gun oil through my congestion, but the repetitive movements of brushing out the barrel weren't enough to soothe me. I couldn't forget Mom's bra in the bathroom.

I had no way to contact her without making the trek out to Fremont—and the last thing I wanted was to give the crooks a bead on where she was hiding out. Russet droplets of oil spattered on the floor and my jeans. The stains joined the crusted blood on my pants. I couldn't head out to face Cassius without leaving word for her. It was five forty. I had a few minutes before he got in touch. I put the revolver back together, washed my hands, and called Edie.

I told her I was going to cut a deal with the folks who had Doug. "I figure if I've got something to trade—at least I can try to get him back." She breathed in with a hiss. She knew what that meant, and what the risks were.

She didn't bother telling me to be careful. I wanted to say I was sorry it was going to end this way. I wanted to say call Mom. I wanted to say thank you for being a great friend. What I said was, "Sorry I wasn't able to break the arrangement between the Pinkos and your landlord."

"We'll make do. We always find a way."

"Things might get hot for you."

"That was bound to happen after Friday."

"Well," I said. "I just wanted to call and let you know. You let folks know I was thinking of them." I hung up after that. I didn't like to hear her cry. Was tucking the gun into my shoulder holster when the phone rang. "You're calling early," I said.

"Early for what?" Cassius's voice was the same deep growl. "You think you have something we want. I'd like to know what that is."

I told him that we'd captured more than the half vial of Hope I was sure he'd found on Meekins. That I had access to the other half and a sample of the Mauve Faith. That I was willing and ready to take them to the Argentines if he didn't agree to my terms. Berdie started whimpering in the other room. I tossed him a roll of paper towels. "I want the whole team back," I said.

He told me I had some nerve, but said he wouldn't mind handing off "the cadets and the altar boy."

"And Doug," I said, maybe too fast.

He let out his grandfatherly chuckle. It rubbed like sandpaper on the sore parts of my brain. "Fine. I'll set up a romantic reunion for the two of you. You ever seen the Golden Gate at sunset?"

●●●

I told Berdie I was off to meet his coconspirators, then jammed a bent spoon through the broken latch of the bedroom door to lock him in. As I climbed into his car, he threw the window open and started yelling down at me about how it was insanity to go to the Golden Gate. The Argentine patrol passing by enjoyed the show. As did the plainclothes officer, watching the front. In the rearview mirror, I saw the moment he realized that Berdie was leaning out of the window of my apartment.

The wig and unknown car were enough to keep him from noticing me, but I could bet he was calling for backup as I swung onto Rockridge Avenue. Well, that was one way for the notary to get himself out of there. The door into my place would be off its hinges again after the cops broke in. My landlord would be spending my deposit and then some.

I dodged a couple patrol cars on my way north. Saw yet another Argentine transport near the department when I stopped by for a hazpig suit. Passing my office, Walter's paper and ink smile caught me for one last look. *One last look.* I was getting maudlin. I could hear the traffic on the freeway, the machine-gun rattle of a helicopter somewhere south. Felt like I should say some words. Leave a note. But I just stood there a minute. Touched his old gun, nestled in my shoulder holster. The Hope and the vial of Mauve clinked in the suit's breast pocket. I headed back to the Bug and took off for Magenta territory.

I skirted the edge of the ruined city, just on the wrong side of the border. I figured the cops wouldn't cross the city line, but I didn't want to venture closer to the epicenter where I'd have to put on the hazpig mask. My route wound out to the coast. A fogbank was rising over the Pacific. Berdie's crumpled pack of smokes eyed me from the ashtray. Cassius had told me to meet him at 7:30. My watch read 6:45. I pulled up to the rubble of an old concrete barrier meant to keep the sand off the road. Took the wig off. Rolled down the window and lit up.

The burst of clarity as the nicotine hit was every bit as good as I remembered. I watched the waves slide up and down the beach. The orange sun, the steel-gray water, the milk-white foam. The tang of the Pacific, colder and lighter than the smell of the Gulf back home.

Here I was again, in the ruins of San Francisco. Back for the final round of treatment for my terminal infatuation with Doug. After tonight, he'd know that I was the one who saved him. It wasn't like I could find words better than this action to let him know how I felt. It was a more fitting end to our decades-long dance around each other than him walking out of the hospital room in the thin light of dawn. Or a furtive hand clasp against a concrete wall. As the Chief had said, *Lonesome is what there is in this business.* I took a last pull. Dropped the butt of the cigarette onto the sandy pavement. Set out to see what Cassius had waiting for me.

Under the Golden Gate's rust-colored struts, a phalanx of goons stood at attention. Had to be twenty of them, all wearing the forest-green hazpig of PSI. Cassius stood a head taller than his minions, wearing the skintight, armored pigment protection of the Twenty-Fivers. Instead of the military-issued waders, though, he sported black combat boots. Probably felt the galoshes didn't fit the slick look. Next to him, the PSI suits seemed as ill-fitting as my department-issued lime-green kit. He was still too thin to loom.

My colleagues knelt on the ground in front of them, hands tied and hoods over their faces. The martial picture was somewhat spoiled by the two fourteen-passenger vans parked to the side, looking like they'd made a wrong turn on their way to a high school athletics tournament.

I stopped the Bug ten meters away. Adrenaline was making my calves shake. Well, it would be over soon. Got out but left the engine running. The show of force had me wary. Didn't want him thinking about strong-arming the vials from me.

I held up the Lavender Hope and the Mauve Faith for Cassius to see, then put the Lavender on the ground and rested my heel on it. The shatterproof glass wouldn't last long if I stomped down with my full weight. Threw the Mauve to Big Skinny. Told him he could have the Hope once my comrades were in the car.

He waved a long-fingered hand at the men standing guard. One by one, the hostages were unbound and shoved my way. Cynthia was first. She stumbled as she reached me. I caught her. Pulled off her hood, taking advantage of the opening to lean close. "You take the driver's seat. Make sure everyone's belted in. When I go to hand over the Hope—if there's even a hint of something funny, you get them out of here."

She nodded imperceptibly, bleached bangs falling over her eyes. Walked unsteadily to the car and settled herself in. Then came Tommy, then Meekins. Then Doug.

My old friend was favoring his left leg. Still wearing his suit from the wedding, a big rip in one shoulder. I didn't like to look at the wilted carnation in his buttonhole. I gave him a hug. *To fill a gap— / Insert the thing that caused it*—told myself the hole opening inside of me would be gone soon enough. Along with everything else. Told myself it was no time to be remembering poetry. Watched him climb gingerly into the back seat. The light of the sunset picked out warm highlights in his black curls. I pulled the pigment out from under my boot and turned back to face our enemies.

"That one's too valuable to throw," Cassius said, strolling toward me. "Hand it over and let's shake, like civilized people."

His henchmen followed, still in formation. I glanced back at the car. They were all buckled in. Cynthia was watching. I moved forward to meet Big Skinny. He took the vial, rolled it across his palm. The Lavender Hope sparkled like a dream fulfilled. As he slid it into his breast pocket, the first tough moved on me.

I'd figured it was coming, so I ducked the first few punches pretty easily. I knew too much. Had been too much of a bother. Cassius had no plans to let me go. Or my colleagues, for that matter. The lackeys not focused on taking me down had their weapons aimed at the Bug.

None of them had bet on Cynthia's driving skills. She peeled out in reverse, zigzagging across the broken concrete. Puffs of Mauve Faith rose from the pavement around the car, but none of the slugs came close to brushing its bumper. I tossed a man over my hip, right into the face of one of his associates. Through the tangle of opponents' limbs, I watched the Beetle do a one-eighty and vanish into the encroaching fog.

I got enough space to draw my weapon. For a split second caught a glimpse of Cassius, standing outside of the fray. Pigment would slide right off his armored uniform. At best my shot might dent it. But his *boots*—his feet were unprotected. I had time to wish for a quip about Achilles's heels before the men in front of me closed in again.

I dodged a kick, frustration like tinfoil between my teeth. I'd missed my chance. But I was a beggar here, not a chooser. I had six bullets. I made them count. This one for the Chief. This one for Pimsley. Point-blank, the lead tore right through PSI's hazpig fabric. The men fell at my feet.

My opponents couldn't shoot back for fear of hitting each other, but I had a wall of targets at arm's length. This one for Penelope. This one for Priscilla, and how her death affected Tommy. A rhythmic *chop chop chop* sounded. Could've been a helicopter or my pulse. This one for Jenny Crotty and Leonard Gobble. This one for Freddy Bentley and Daisuke Jones, trying to get clean. For all the folks who'd been pulled in and warped by Big Skinny and Ashaji's ambition.

The chamber was empty. I dropped Walter's gun, ducked to pull another from one of the bodies. Got a kick to the head along with it. Fingers clenched around the weapon, I tumbled onto the ground. Tried to roll away from my attackers, seeing stars.

One of them tackled me and pinned me to the pavement. Another kick, this one to my side. And another. And another. My faceplate was cracked, cold air flowing into my mask. It was over now, I knew. I'd be dead soon. Or worse, fried with the Mauve Faith. A brainwashed automaton, following the orders of the Knights of Liberty.

"Gentlemen," Cassius drawled. "Allow me."

The feet surrounding me moved away. The pressure from the crook pinning me down let up. The butt of the gun I'd snatched dug into my abdomen. My vision was clearing. And there, walking toward me, were Cassius's obsidian boots.

Play dead. I inched the weapon under me into position. I'd be torn apart as soon as I plugged him, so I had only one shot. He pulled out his own piece, a Remington from the war adapted for psychopigment bullets.

Now. I lifted my battered rib cage, raised the gun, and blasted his leather-clad ankle. Got the gratification of watching him fold like a rag doll. My breath and blood thundered in my ears, louder and louder. Wind was rising, whipping up tendrils of fog. I shut my eyes. The plan had never been for me to get out of this. Gave thanks I'd gotten to go out with a bang, not a whimper. Ready for the end.

One of the thugs suddenly dropped on top of me. Another sat down, put his head between his knees. A strange silver rain was falling through the thickening mist. The drops bounced, tinkling, off the concrete.

Needles. Weighted needles of Slate Gray, designed to penetrate hazpig gear. A sophisticated weapon, created for full-out combat in a war zone. I craned my neck around to look up. Above us, the source of the drop hovered: a sky-blue chopper, emblazoned with the emblem of the Argentine air force.

The Gauchos had come after all.

CHAPTER 32

I t was like we'd been shooting a B movie in Chowchilla and a Buenos Aires blockbuster had shown up on set. A stream of black-suited *Manos de Dios* jumped out of the helicopter to clean up the PSI goons who were still standing. I crawled out from under the Ennui-stricken tough who'd incidentally protected me from the hail of Slate Gray needles. Took a break after getting that far.

I put my arms over my head, but the Argentines took one look at my lime-green hazpig and left me alone. Cassius twitched next to me. A seizure, most likely, his brain frying as the pigment coursed through his bloodstream. Mauve rose from his foot wound, evanescing through his running blood.

I pulled myself away from the amethyst steam. Didn't want any of the stuff seeping through the hole in my mask. He shuddered once, twice. If I was lucky, he'd be sane enough to testify against Ashaji. I ran my fingers over my ribs. Didn't seem like anything was broken. My breath evened out, my heartbeat slowed. I was still here.

Sound came back. The thud of falling punches and the occasional shot as the *Manos* tracked down the renegade agents. The helicopter, circling above. The densest fog had blown past, heading over the Bay. Sunset had turned to dusk. My shoulders rose. Fell. Rose. My back was tight. I was still here.

Around me, cries of "I surrender—*me rindo!*" PSI agents had their hands in the air. *Me rindo*, the words our parents had shouted to the Argentines on battlefields the world over. The words Dad had never said.

I was still here.

Cassius had gone slack on the ground, whatever fit the Mauve Faith had caused now passed. My belly felt all gnarled up. I pulled the two vials I'd given him from his breast pocket. Unzipped his hazpig suit, checking for hidden weapons. There was a small lump at his waistband. Opened his shirt to investigate.

A tattoo stared back at me: the Knights of Liberty oath tree. It was a massive oak, gnarled, with dozens of roots and what must have been a hundred branches. The Hooded Lady Liberty stood by the trunk, torch aloft. Looked like PSI wasn't the only organization where Cassius wielded influence.

I'd seen the tree depicted in movies, read about it in the paper. One root for every step up the hierarchy, one branch for every violent mission. This one was huge, wrapping from the man's solar plexus all the way around his sides. Over each shoulder, indigo lightning struck the leafy crown. From the bottom of the tree, one root—the same color as the lightning—plunged downward. The golden ink was fresher, the colors brighter and edges sharper. It could be only a few months old.

I wasn't an expert on the Knights' use of pseudo-Masonic imagery, but I could guess at the meaning. Cassius had gotten so high in the organization that he'd had to switch root colors right around the time that the Knights had started using Agency Blue to bomb schools. The experts had been worried that the switch from Molotov cocktails to pigment-based explosives indicated a change in leadership in the organization. Looked like I'd found the man responsible.

Priscilla had said he was the one who provided the crooks with the Blue bullets she'd used on me. And he'd clearly handed the stuff out willy-nilly to his terrorist underlings. Seemed he saw no problem using the tools PSI gave him access to for his own twisted ends.

We'd known the paramilitary organization was involved in this boondoggle. But I'd been imagining that they'd come in with Ashaji's brother, or some flunky at PSI who liked to don a hood now and then. Not that the mastermind of the entire Mauve scheme was also giving orders to the terrorists.

Raised scars across his abdomen spelled out *The tree of liberty must be watered, from time to time, with the blood of patriots and tyrants.* Wasn't sure whether the junior high kids the Knights had Blued over counted as patriots or as tyrants. Had a feeling his plan for Theocrat Ashaji involved her martyrdom in the not-so-distant future. I would've been angry if I hadn't been so tired.

I felt around the lump on his belt that had led me to pull his shirt up. It was a hidden pocket, with the other half vial of Hope inside. Seemed it had been too valuable to trust any of his underlings with. I tucked our hard-won pigment into my suit. Doug had made it out. I'd find my way south, rendezvous with him and the others at the department. He'd run the tests. We'd expose the scheme. Stop Gruber-Shaw and Ashaji in their tracks.

Exhaustion, thick as nausea, poured over me. I took off my mask, touched my pounding temple. My fingers came away wet and red. The wind tugged on my hair. The Argentine squad had moved on to laying out the dead around me. The corpses were all my countrymen. Edie's words when I'd been weighing my options about the transfer to Iowa came back. *Tends to be that when the devil offers you a bargain, he catches you in the fine print.*

I was still here.

The chopper thundered onto a cleared space on the deck. Three more men in the black uniform of the *Manos* got out. One of them came over and looked me up and down. I recognized the brute with the British accent from the base as I put my hands back up. "Seems we're on the same side, this evening," I said. He made an unpleasant noise and muttered something in Spanish, then went back to the helicopter. My knees ached from kneeling. I didn't want to risk moving.

After a moment, General Moretti climbed down. Today his shoes weren't shiny. He was dressed in battle hazpig. His second-in-command, El Gordo, followed close behind. They walked among the *Manos de Dios*, conferring with one, giving orders to another. Catching sight of me, Moretti came over. "Agent Curtida. Seems like you're always on the ground when I encounter you." He had a broad smile and a broader Boston accent. Dad had written about that in his letters. I didn't trust myself to say anything. I gave him a nod. "You were going to take all these guys by yourself?"

"I didn't have much choice, sir."

"You sure are Lieutenant Curtida's daughter. You got his crazy—but I can't complain about that." He patted me on the back. My stomach was too heavy for me to react. "You've been very helpful this weekend. I'm glad you slipped that report under my door. Sent Berdie around to check it out soon as I read it this morning. He was, you know, a bit delayed corroborating the details, but he did get them to us—" He chuckled. My face must've looked real dumb. Berdie was a double agent *for the Argentines*. Tommy was right: the department had a Gaucho spy, and it was the notary.

The pieces tumbled into order. Berdie, on the phone in Minnie Cucci's office, telling someone we'd needed the Hope. The silence down the line when I'd taken over. Cassius asking me *Early for what?* when he called after I'd rung Edie. Berdie, leaning out the window of my apartment, yelling to the Gaucho patrol below about me going to the Golden Gate. The patrols I'd been passing all day, on the bus, in my car, in the notary's Bug.

The man's small eyes peering up at me above his coffee-spattered collar, saying *The Argentines aren't the enemy.* He'd told me and I'd ignored him. Had the Chief known Berdie was working for them? Meekins? It hurt to breathe.

Moretti watched the hundred-dollar coin drop in my head, scratched at the hook of his nose, and told me he'd be recommending I receive a commendation. That he'd be real interested in seeing the Mauve, if we had any extra lying around. I was sure he would be. Then he offered me a lift back to the department, "since it looks like you missed your ride earlier."

● ● ●

The lab door was open and spilling stale pigment residue into the hall when I arrived. Inside, Doug was pacing back and forth, an elastic bandage bracing his left knee. His undershirt was sweat-stained. "You should keep your weight off that leg until you've seen a doctor," I said, digging the vials out of my hazpig suit's pocket.

He turned at the sound of my voice. Another time, I might've killed for him to look at me that way. He hurried over, hands out. The aging colors in the air mixed with the smell of Spitfire burger and unwashed flesh. None of it helped the queasy feeling leftover from the bumpy chopper ride down with Moretti. Plato eagerly grabbed the three vials but didn't let go of my fingers. His skin was warm and dry. "I . . . I didn't think you'd make it . . . In the car, I just kept—"

I cut him off, telling him we needed the results as soon as possible. Didn't want to say that I hadn't planned to make it. That I had no idea how to deal with the fact that I had. He'd be gone by the end of the week anyway, back to the bright lights and big-city life up in Idaho. A wave of heat swept over my body, then a chill, settling on my sweaty palms. I just about got to the bathroom before losing what was left of the burrito I'd eaten at Minnie Cucci's, four hours and a thousand years ago. I sat shuddering over the toilet bowl and told myself there was no reason to feel like crying.

I called Edie, asked for the number to reach Mom. The phone in Fremont rang and rang, but no one picked up. I showered and let Tommy clean and bandage my head wound. Doug had the full report ready by midnight. We got on the phone with Old Jim, chief of the Boise Department. He confirmed that Cassius was the head of PSI. The news of the man's Tree of Liberty tattoo provoked a long pause from Doug's boss. He told us to take the whole thing to the press. They sure did things differently up in the Big Potato.

Meekins wasn't happy about going to the newshounds, but we eventually convinced him it was the quickest way to nip the conspiracy in the bud. If I'd been the one dating Jenna Lila Fifi, I would've been glad to see the department policy change. Then again, Meekins always needed something to scowl about.

Once we'd agreed, Old Jim told us he'd be down on the first plane in the morning and signed off pretty quick. He had a long night of negotiating with the Argentines ahead of him—we wanted Cassius in our custody to get testimony against his coconspirators. Assuming he was still capable of it. I was pretty sure Big Skinny's brain was fried, but hurting all over was making me pessimistic.

Tommy drove off in Berdie's Bug to see if the notary was still locked in my apartment. Meekins went to help the neurotypical cops track down Ashaji and Gruber-Shaw. Cynthia took Doug to the hospital, wrapping her arm around his waist to hold him up. His leg had stiffened during the phone call. At least that was what they said.

I headed off to leak the proof of everything we'd been doing to the *Daly Daily*. Jenna Lila was surprised to find me on her doorstep at two a.m., but perfectly happy to take the thick envelope I handed her. After she left to go watch the leader of the Pinkos do her perp walk, I sat in my Renault 4 and tried to decide where I was going.

I could make my way to Fremont. The thought of the drive made my bones ache. Showing up in the wee hours of the morning wouldn't endear me to Mom's hosts. Reached to turn on the radio and remembered there was still a warrant out for my arrest. Took the backstreets to the hospital.

Across the way, the lights were still on at Edie's. I gave in to temptation and went in through the kitchen. A raucous party was in full swing, burgers flying off the grill. Bottles of Cerveza Sol passed hand to hand, as well as one or two of champagne. Seemed Cynthia had brought the news of the Pinkos' downfall when she dropped Doug at the hospital. Edie welcomed me with a giant hug.

Then a second set of arms pulled me firmly into an embrace: my mother. "*Ay, mija,*" was all she said. Promise of a talking-to to come.

Susana Curtida had succumbed to her perennial inability to sit on her hands around the time that Moretti had dropped me off in the department parking lot. She'd convinced the pimple-faced teen to bring her across the bay. Her driver was in the corner with Jason.

It was hot and close. I'd ditched the hazpig suit at the department, but was still in the ridiculous clothes I'd lifted from Minnie Cucci's. The synthetic lace of the shirt was sticky with my sweat. I watched the wash of booze and congratulations and happy faces as the restaurant staff celebrated.

Mom decided that I looked pale, packed me up a doggy bag, and walked me over to the hospital. The cool air and quiet let me breathe a little easier. She put her arm around me. The sulfur streetlamps washed the color out of her hair and lipstick, leaving her looking like a sepia print. "I was hard on you yesterday. But I'm very proud of what you've done."

"You're the reason it all worked," I said. She asked how I was feeling. When I said tired, her arm tightened. "I made it back. That's good, I guess." Wasn't my best attempt at buoyancy, but it was all I had in me.

She laughed. "So dramatic! There was never a risk of you not making it back."

The night security didn't even blink as we walked past. Seemed Trumbull had left instructions to let me through. My room was waiting for me. The cops weren't. Small blessings. Mom settled onto the cot that Doug had used, insisting I take the bed. Marla's snores echoed down the hall. I wondered what would happen tomorrow. Didn't think about Doug's fingers in mine. At the wedding, or in the department lab. I lay awake for a long time, listening to Mom breathe.

● ● ●

I was up with the blue jays, guzzling Nescafé and fretting uselessly over our next move. Trumbull came by with her battery of psych tests and the *Daly Daily*. The story had broken like a tsunami, making headlines from Albuquerque to Zanesville. Gruber-Shaw's announcement was canceled, Ashaji's book release "delayed indefinitely."

The president was calling for investigations into PSI's involvement in terrorism and other treasonous activities. Old Jim sure had friends in high places. I'd always assumed our Dixiecrat in chief was a Knight himself. Could be he was part of the faction that preferred to bomb schools with Molotov cocktails instead of pigment. That set had surely been waiting for a way to take back power in the group.

On my fifth thimble of coffee, Trumbull asked me to go see Penelope. "She's been frantic ever since you didn't come back after the bachelorette. Thinks the devil kidnapped you."

I thought about my deal with the Argentines, the dead Americans lined up on the bridge. Moretti's smirk as he patted my back. Wondered if Penelope wasn't on to something. Trudged down the hallway, dragging my Sunshine drip. Would've preferred to be checking in on Doug, but he was still asleep.

Penelope ran to the door at the sight of me. She grabbed me hard. Apparently the head bandage made me look embraceable. It took a while to make sense of the story she'd come up with. Eventually I pieced together that she believed the devil had been keeping me in the apartment she'd shared with Jenny and Leonard. I asked why I would've been there instead of behind Ticky-Tacky Tuxy. "That's where they left the bloody lady," she said.

The crooks had left Penelope alone in the Crottys' apartment until a few days before we'd found her at Minnie Cucci's, only to replace her with a short-haired woman bleeding copiously from a head wound. All that coffee I'd drunk suddenly felt like a bad idea. Was it possible that they'd taken the Chief there for medical treatment? That they'd been keeping her alive, for whatever reason?

The Crotty place had bars over all the windows, a reinforced front door, and a chain ending in a manacle. An anonymous apartment built to keep someone in, with neighbors used to strange noises at all hours. Exactly what you'd need to hold someone like Louise Knorr. I could've kissed Penelope, but settled for giving her another hug on the way out.

Trumbull caught me near reception. When I explained where I was going, she marched me right back to my room. Apparently she'd already headed off two requests that I be released into the neurotypicals' custody, acting like I was under sedation. Cowed, I asked her to let Meekins know while I cooled my heels in bed.

So in the end, Meekins and Cynthia found our boss. They took their usual tack of stomping around Penelope's building asking questions, but this time they struck gold in the form of a gossipy widow on the first floor. She was thrilled to tell the Agent of the Year all about the suspicious happenings upstairs, including a pair of thugs loitering round the clock on the landing.

Once they'd confirmed the Chief's presence, Meekins and Cynthia took advantage of the construction going on in the apartment below to saw a hole into the Crottys' kitchen. The crew's foreman had lost a cousin to Big Skinny's illicit pigment tests, and he'd been happy to help. After that, it was a simple matter of cutting our resident Twenty-Fiver's chain, getting her down the ladder to the second-floor apartment, and carrying her out in a carpet Cleopatra-style. The goons guarding Penelope's door didn't even notice. It was a typical ham-handed Meekins move, but surprisingly effective.

I made my way to the Chief's hospital room once she'd settled in. Tommy'd told me she'd had her drivers swing past the department to pick up a pile of forms and her typewriter on the way. I laughed when I heard that, on a high from her miraculous resurrection. He stayed solemn.

He'd taken dictation for several of the forms already, and they lay in a pile on the bedside table. I sat in the creaky plastic chair and waited for her to speak. Above her bandage, her pink scalp was showing through her hair's thinning roots. Eventually, she tapped the papers on the table.

I lifted the first one. It reinstituted me fully as an agent, complete with back pay and a raise. First salary increase in a decade that beat the rate of inflation. I could afford to fix the carpet in my apartment. I thanked her, saying it meant a lot. She tapped again. Her nails were chipped and her knuckles bulged. I picked up the second form. It was a promotion. She wanted me to be the Chief.

"But you're—"

"Tired," she said. Her voice was mostly breath.

"You'll feel better once you're healed."

"I've been tired a long time. Locked in that apartment . . . had a lot of space to think." She raised herself up with difficulty. I helped her adjust the pillow behind her back. Offered her water. She waved away my attentions, got back to the matter at hand. "I've kept myself real busy all these years. It's been a good way to keep from paying attention to what I might want." Her IV drip sighed, clicked. "And then I come to with that chain on my leg. The decades have passed and a whole lot has become what I *wanted*, past tense. Figure I'd better get going on the little that's left. So it's time for me to move on."

What she wanted? She'd always seemed so sure of herself. It wasn't like I'd ever thought she was unhappy. Or happy. Just that those questions had never seemed to apply to her. My busted ribs throbbed. I thought about all the things I'd wished I could've asked her the past few days. My deal with the devil. The choices I'd made because I'd felt alone. All I could think to say was, "What'll you do . . . ?"

She shrugged, tubes rustling against the sheets. "I've always wanted to learn how to sing." A flicker of her lips, like she knew how hard it was to imagine that hoarse whisper turning into a croon. "You'll be fine." And with that, my interview was over. I looked down at the forms as I walked out. Consoled myself that none of it counted until it was notarized.

Doug was leaning on a crutch in the hallway, waiting with updates. Cassius had been released into our custody. "He had keys to every office in the department and the Chief's desk on him. Old Jim's organized a press conference at four p.m. and wants you to make a statement."

The thought of our adversary going through the Chief's drawers made my teeth ache. I pointed out that there was an active warrant for my arrest and suggested Meekins might be a better department spokesperson. Doug said I should take it up with the Boise boss, and that Edie had sent over sandwiches for the whole team and a full thermos of real coffee for me.

Socializing during lunch made even Spitfire burgers sound unappealing. "The Chief doesn't want to be chief anymore," I said. If she ever had.

I had to say something to someone. Wouldn't stay bottled up. I could see *Who can blame her?* crossing through Doug's head. "She wants me to take the job."

"Oh." His voice was quiet. "I thought—maybe—Old Jim said he wanted you up in Boise with us."

My big-city dream. Right there, on a plate. And the curveball the Chief had tossed in my hand. *I kept myself real busy,* she'd said. Quite a way to describe a career like hers. Would she have felt better in a bigger town? Plato's hand played up and down the metal beam of his crutch. His camel sweater vest matched the ersatz leather of the crosspiece. I wondered when he'd had time to go home and get clean clothes. Wondered if Cynthia had gone for him. The ghost of yesterday's nausea hovered at my temples. "He hasn't mentioned anything to me," I said and headed back to my room to see if I had an unstained jacket to face the day.

CHAPTER 33

I made my way to the department to draft a statement for the press conference I'd been mustered into. I could've stayed and used the Chief's Remington to type it up, but that felt too much like accepting her proposal. I had to borrow $25,000 from Doug to put a half tank into my Renault 4. The whole drive, I couldn't get the idea of Boise out of my head. Up there, they had real uniforms. Actual patrol cars. Challenging cases as a norm, not an outlier. I'd heard you could even get beer other than Quilmes in most restaurants.

The stoplight on Eastmoor and St. Francis was busted again. I waited behind a silver Topolino, watching a rookie traffic cop panic as he tried to control the six-way intersection. Boise could be the chance of a lifetime. No more getting news second- or thirdhand when a big-timer came to visit. Hell, maybe I'd even make my own friends in PSI who would let me in on state secrets after a few too many pints. My apartment was a mess anyway. I could write off the deposit and leave it for the landlord to fix. I turned into the parking lot and told myself to focus on the task at hand.

But sitting in my office, the task at hand didn't want my focus. Every time I started a sentence, my eyes slid off the page: to the stacks of unfinished paperwork, to the framed profile of Walter, to the spiderweb in the corner. I should be worrying about the Chief. I should find Old Jim, ask him what Doug was talking about. My ribs complained.

I wrote *We have arrested several members of a conspiracy to overthrow the government.* The Chief's skin, thin and pale as paper. Her cracked lips.

Notably, Dr. Gruber-Shaw of Icarus Corporation and—her knuckles, thick lumps standing out from her bony fingers. Her wheezing voice.

Was it just hunger and captivity that had left her like that? Going without Sunshine for a week? She was a Depressive, I told myself. But it had been months since I'd seen her mischievous grin. The way the fight had gone out of her the minute she'd spotted Cassius's involvement wasn't like her. I told myself to stop procrastinating. Pushed my broken-down chair away from my typewriter anyway, and headed over to Evidence for Cassius's keys.

A thin layer of dust lay over everything in the Chief's office. I'd never seen that before. We'd taken that long to track her down. On the tabletop, a clean rectangle marked the space where her Remington had been.

Just as Doug had said, the key labeled "Knorr drawer" on the crook's ring turned like butter in the lock. There was a leather box containing the department seal. Several folders marked *CONFIDENTIAL*. A bottle of Sunshine rattled in the back. I set it in the dustless area. Propped up a vial I'd swiped from the lab and broke a gelcap into it.

The Yellow that spilled out didn't look right. Dark currents swirled through the golden liquid. The steam that puffed at the surface was the wrong color. I broke one of my own Sunshine caps into a second vial, and it lolled in the bottom like a baby in a kiddie pool.

Hard to be sure without a psychospectrometer, but the vapor in the first tube sure seemed like Slate Gray. I capped both containers. My head wound itched. PSI had been spiking the Chief's pills.

Footsteps padded down the hallway. Turned out I wasn't the only person in the department. I slipped my science experiment into my pocket, put away the bottle of Sunshine. A tall, stooped man in a tweed jacket appeared in the doorway. His salt-and-pepper hair fell in a curl over his pale forehead. He carried two espresso cups.

"Agent Curtida," he said. "Coffee?" I'd heard him on the phone last night and seen his face in the papers plenty of times: Old Jim Broadback. He looked more like a middle-school math teacher than a department head. I bet he got a lot of mileage out of that.

I accepted the steaming Nescafé, tried to figure out if I ought to offer him a seat. It wasn't my office. Not unless I took the Chief up on her offer. Eventually he took the initiative and folded himself into the oak visitor's chair. I leaned back against the desk. No way I was sitting in her place.

He didn't ask what I was doing in there. I didn't ask what he was doing making coffee for me, but he cleared that up pretty quick by himself. "This sure has been impressive. A lot of us in the Agency have been worried for a couple years that PSI was gunning for a coup, but there's never been anything conclusive. You're wasted down here in the middle of nowhere. I want you on my team up north. Imagine what you could do from the center of the action."

"I'm honored, sir." I'd said the same thing to Cassius a month ago. This time I meant it. But something made me add, "Thing is, looks like the Chief is going to be stepping down and—she asked for my help with the transition."

"You know, Cassius was keeping her alive as insurance. Figured he could turn her on you if this thing went to trial. Terrible business, all of it." He shook his head, a movement that seemed to involve his whole body. My impression of an enthusiastic math teacher got stronger. "Doug said you were loyal. That's good. That's very good. I don't need an answer just yet. But a little advice—I hope you don't mind. Don't let yourself get buried out here like Louise did."

I said something about needing to finish my statement. He had to go finalize details for the press conference. He mentioned that he'd gotten the warrant for my arrest dropped. We shook hands and he headed out. He had the firm grip of a man used to getting his way.

Seemed he'd wanted to make sure I knew who to thank for no longer being a murder suspect. Ruffled my feathers. Of course I was grateful the cops had dropped the warrant. But what if I'd actually pushed Dr. Kim? Doug had said he knew agents who had gotten away with murder.

On the wall, the Chief smiled down from the photo with President Rigby. I wondered where Old Jim had gotten the intel on why she hadn't been left to bleed out. She hadn't *let* herself get stuck out here. She'd been ostracized by the people who had been her comrades, blackmailed, her family devastated.

It may or may not have been what she wanted. But there'd been nothing passive about the way that she'd handled her exile. I'd say my boss had done pretty well. Until Cassius had showed up, spiking her pills so he could get away with his schemes.

Sure, this case had been extraordinary, and sure, everybody knew Daly City was the middle of nowhere. But that was why nobody paid attention to what was going on here. Why had Doug been the first R & D op to get detailed to our office, if folks across the country had been asking for years about the strength of the Gray peddled by our crooks? The chiefs in Boise and Iowa City were like our spring spiders—they sat at the center of their webs, thinking they were the middle of it all. Waiting for everything to come to them. But really they just covered their little corner. Out here in Daly City, at least I knew I was crouched on the edge.

I moved to the Chief's chair. Pulled it out. Sat down. It was hard, the padding just for show. No wonder the woman had always been so straight-backed. It was not an ideal accommodation for my torso the day after getting kicked silly by PSI's goons. I could bring over my broken-down roller seat. Turn the place into a disaster zone like Trumbull's office.

I imagined an art deco throne stolen from Pimsley's, the wastebasket full of wrappers from Edie's. Maybe the budget would go up now that we'd blown the Mauve case open. Maybe we could get uniforms. Patrol cars. All the things I'd fantasized about having in Boise. Well, maybe not all of them. But down here, at least, I could start the process of forgetting Doug.

It was too much to think about on three nights of too little sleep. I went to the lab to leave the vial of contaminated Sunshine for Plato to run through the spinner when he had time, then back to my own office. The department was coming alive. Meekins was getting a head start on his paperwork. Tommy and Cynthia gathered things for the press conference. Footsteps and the sound of the photocopier drifted down the hallway.

The statement wasn't any easier to write after my unexpected encounter. My back was cramping up again, a burning knot where I'd been kicked between my shoulder blades. Doug stopped by half an hour later with a printout of the results: Slate Gray at about twenty-five percent. I told him I hadn't expected it so soon.

"Old Jim wants me to give a report in Boise tomorrow, so I'm heading out this afternoon," he said.

Not even time for a goodbye beer. I rubbed my neck. "He came by. Offered me the job up there."

He watched me finger the printout. "I thought you'd jump at the chance."

"It's definitely interesting—but with the Chief the way she is . . ."

"Right," he said. He stayed for a second in the doorway, leaning on his crutch. Then he left. Sure, I owed the Chief, but staying could be the second-biggest mistake I'd ever make. Right on the list after joining the Daly City department in the first place.

Walter smiled down from the wall. The pain in my back had been joined by a hollow spot under my breastbone. The plan had been for me to go out with a bang. Not hang around, picking up the pieces to build a new life. I popped a Sunshine and another Tylenol and went to find Tommy.

● ● ●

My cadet's enthusiasm kept me focused enough to write up a passable summary. As I put the final period on the page, he said, "We did good, didn't we?"

All I could see were the things we'd glossed over. My mother's anger. The Chief, locked up and starved. Doug's hollow cheeks. Our leaving Penelope Crotty ripe for the picking. All our injuries. Tommy's depression after Bepler. But here he was, bouncing with excitement. At least he'd been able to spring back from our mistakes.

The price had been high, and we'd keep paying it, but we'd managed to do something. *All of this has been very impressive.* Old Jim's words. "Sure," I said. I could feel the corner of my mouth twitching up. "We did real good."

Even Meekins approved of the statement. I offered to let him read it to the press. He scratched at his scruffy face and shook his head. I wasn't the only one with an aversion to public speaking. He'd shaped his stubble instead of shaving it all off, leaving the outline of a future beard along the sides of his face and under his chin. Made him look like Abraham Lincoln with a bad case of heartburn, but I was in no position to comment on his personal grooming.

And then it was time to go face the newshounds. Meekins took Tommy and Cynthia. Doug had slipped away before any of us. I stayed to close the department. It was nice to have my own set of keys back. On my way to return Cassius's ring to Evidence, I stopped by the Chief's office. Didn't want to leave her drawer open, even if the head of PSI was safely locked up.

Some emotion washed over me as I walked down the hall. Like the green linoleum was giving me the indigestion of preemptive nostalgia. I looked over the Chief's bookshelves: *Dead Ends '98–'99. Mid-Year Report '06.* Wiped a fingerful of dust from the tops of the binders. A copy of form P-17, *PERSONNEL REQUESTING DEPARTMENT CHANGE,* was sitting on her desk. I picked it up. How many other folks had Old Jim offered to take with him up to Boise? Maybe Meekins had opted for a change of scenery to match his new facial topiary.

But the form wasn't asking for a transfer out of Daly City. It was an application to join our down-at-heel department. It had been filled out quickly, the block capitals running into one another. The signature at the bottom read *Doug Nambi.*

CHAPTER 34

In the overheated dressing room at Hotel La Estancia, I washed a cold Spitfire burger down with colder coffee. My looming public appearance had sapped my appetite, but the jitters meant eating wasn't optional.

The crush of interest from national press and concerned citizens had forced us to schedule the conference in the ballroom where the Magenta Cares Gala had taken place. I'd be announcing Gruber-Shaw and Ashaji's downfall on the stage where they'd first talked about "bringing back hope." Poetic justice. Or just the constraints of small-town life.

I'd sent Tommy away after he'd suggested he could lead me in some vocal warm-ups. Being alone wasn't ideal, but it was better than getting nattered at about releasing my pelvic floor. Mom had packed a "curl-emergency kit" in with the sandwich Edie'd prepped for me. The silver-wrapped package glared under the lights outlining the mirror.

I listened to the hum of the crowd, building out in the ballroom. My watch's display flickered from 3:49 to 3:50. I'd be out there soon enough. For now, though, it was just me and the jumble of my thoughts. The Chief, Doug. Daly City, Boise. Things had been nicely separate until Plato's transfer form showed up. He was out on the stage, setting up folding chairs. His Peugeot was in the parking lot, suitcase in the trunk.

We hadn't said much of anything to each other when I walked in. Especially about the page still sitting on the Chief's desk. I'd beat a path to the dressing room, trying not to think about the sharp clarity of the lonely cigarette I'd indulged in before facing down Big Skinny and his henchmen. The quiet certainty of watching the surf roll up and down the beach in the ruins of San Francisco. Smoke in my lungs. Knowing my feelings about Doug had nothing to do with pigment. It had sure been easy to know what I wanted when I'd figured I was hours from my death. Now, thinking about it made my sinuses hurt.

I swallowed the last bite of burger. Finished off the coffee. Boise, Daly City. Doug, the Chief. Who found leading the department to be—just something to keep her occupied, day by day. Something to keep her from dreaming of singing. *I come to with that chain on my leg. The decades have passed and a whole lot has become what I wanted, past tense*, she'd said.

I tore open the hair-care package. Laid out the wide-toothed comb and the toothier hair clip, the small pot of coconut oil and rosemary extract. Started fighting my curls into something Mom wouldn't hate. Despite the fireworks of pain the movement sent across my back and ribs, it was more pleasant than dancing around desires that might be better left to wither.

My attempt at styling was interrupted by a brusque tap at the door. Tommy wouldn't knock—he knew I was decent. Neither would Mom. Told myself I didn't want it to be Doug before calling out, "Come in."

The woman who entered was petite and plump, with a mile-high pile of graying frizz on her head. The olive skirt suit she wore made the drab room feel even stuffier. Took me a minute to recognize her from the papers. Senator Holly Doyle, of the People's Pigment Movement.

She'd been one of the founding scientists of the guerrilla group, and her expertise on the development of new colors had won her a spot on the Psychopigment Regulation Committee that would take over the case now that PSI was implicated. It made sense she'd come down. Hadn't expected her to show up before the official announcement, though.

I offered her the room's single seat. She refused, told me to go ahead and finish what I was doing. "It's nice to finally meet you." At my confused look, she clarified. "Pimsley used to talk about you. So I'm not at all surprised at the good work you've done here."

"Right," I said, as if that statement made sense. She used to talk to Pimsley? "He was something special."

"He really was. Lord. We had rooms in the same co-op when we were at Cal. He already had a knack for knowing things he had no reason to—whenever it was my turn to kill the rats, he'd show up at the neuroscience lab dressed in black and recite funeral elegies for the critters. Byron and Wordsworth and Keats—I could've written a thesis on English Romantic poets by the time we graduated." She shook her head. In the mirror, I watched emotions flash across her face: frustration, regret, remorse. "The last time we talked, he said something was afoot out here. I always told him. Whenever you need help, you have my number. I guess he didn't have the chance to call this time."

Wrangling my curls into a twist felt even fiddlier with someone watching, but it gave me an excuse not to respond immediately. The former leader of the PPM had been an old friend of Pimsley's. The tender spot where I'd been kicked between my shoulder blades twinged. I remembered the photo of the curly-haired girl at the salesman's hideaway, with poetry and *LOVE ALWAYS HOLLY* scrawled on the back. Middle age had grayed her hair and padded her out, but it was the same woman.

Pimsley had been PPM all along. Not one of the ones who made the papers, but one of the ones who made things happen. The guerrillas' larger-than-life showmanship fit the late salesman's matinee-idol flair. Explained his disappearances at the height of the tumult between them and the Knights in the '90s and early 2000s.

I picked up the shark-toothed clip. Managed to get it open one-handed. Must've held on to my poker face as the realization shocked its way through my system. That, or the woman was real good at being polite.

Either way, she didn't comment on my befuddlement. Just slid a hand in and out of her suit pocket and shook her head. "I keep seeing things that just—make me think, oh, I should call Pimsley, I need to ask him . . . It's so hard to remember that he's gone."

Need to ask him. I suddenly felt his absence, too, an ache in my throat to go with all my other tired pains. It was plenty easy to picture a teenage Pimsley ostentatiously soliloquizing at rat cages in a college psych lab. There were so many questions I'd put aside while he was alive, telling myself to let sleeping dogs lie. Wasn't like we'd been close. But I'd always imagined that maybe someday, when we were both old and retired, we'd get past the banter. Settle in with something stronger than coffee and tell each other all the things we'd kept from each other for our work. Wasn't that the rub. So much we didn't know about each other, and then one day all of it vanished. Pimsley wasn't the only old friend I'd regret not asking all the questions I had.

If I kept going down that path, I might as well head back to my apartment and draw the curtains. Turn on the Dead Sentiments and crawl into bed with a bottle of whiskey. But something about the wrinkles around Holly Doyle's eyes kept me from brushing off my sappy fit. "I miss him, too," I found myself saying.

She smiled, a small and sad expression. "I was glad he wasn't around to read that obituary, though. I think he would've died all over again."

"He survived a decade of Jenna Lila's alliteration. He knew what to expect if he stuck around out here long enough for her to be the author."

"Well, I've always said the most important thing is to have good people everywhere. Never know when you're going to need them. So I'm happy that you're here." She pulled a business card from her pocket. Crossed out the printed phone line and scrawled a different number underneath. "That reaches me direct. You ever see anything that you think could use my attention—you give me a call. Even if it's just a hunch or a suspicion. Ring me up. I'll know to listen to you."

After she left, I fingered the card. It was good stock, thick but not ostentatious. "Auld Lang Syne"–ing about Pimsley aside, I was pretty sure she'd just tried to recruit me as the Daly City informant to replace the antique dealer. Then again, I would've been real grateful to have had the direct line of a senator a couple weeks ago.

There was no harm in hanging on to her digits. Chances I'd want to use them were slim to none. She was interested in my thoughts on the goings-on in our foggy underworld, not any novice observations I might have if I went up to Boise. And this was the biggest case I was likely to see down here, as

Old Jim had none too subtly pointed out. If I stuck around, I'd be back to my daily grind of wrist-slapping.

To many ifs. At least my hair was done. My nose had started bleeding again, to make up for it. I plugged it with a tissue and leaned my head back as I made my way out to the wings.

The commotion of the packed reception hall had moved from hum to roar. I hadn't addressed this many people since the assembly in middle school when I'd peed myself. Leonard Gobble, Penelope, and Jenny Crotty had arrived, accompanied by Nurse Howie. Tommy led them to their places on the stage. Having victims of the illegal pigment tests up there with us had been Old Jim's idea. The man sure knew how to sell a story.

I tossed the bloody tissue and stepped out onto the stage. The audience quieted down. The lights were hot. Penelope, Jenny, and Leonard sat in wheelchairs on the side, watched over by Howie. Meekins, ramrod straight, came next, then Cynthia, Tommy, and finally Doug. Old Jim stood by the podium.

Down below in the audience sat a smattering of muckety-mucks who'd come for the photo op: the head of California's Bureau of Security, the executive assistant director of the FBI's Psychopigment Technology branch. I gave them a nod, smoothed out my statement, and began.

"Senator Doyle, directors, Chief Broadback, members of the press. Citizens. As many of you know, over the past two days we've arrested several members of a conspiracy to overthrow the government using an illegally developed psychopigment. Most notably Dr. Patrick Gruber-Shaw of Icarus Pharmaceuticals; Ananda Ashaji, née Margaret Larsen, of the Pinkos; and CJ Abernathy, head of Psychopigment Service Investigators.

"These three have been arrested on suspicion of creating a Mauve psychopigment that causes users to experience false hope through a paranoid form of faith, allowing them to be easily manipulated. We have reason to believe that the same faction of the Knights of Liberty that has been attacking schools with Deepest Blue is ultimately behind this conspiracy."

I read through the compiled information, two dry pages summarizing the roller-coaster month that had upended my life. I pointed out Penelope and Jenny, mentioned the late Tucker Cutts. Reinforcements from Boise had raided the "redemption camp" up at Turlock, where they'd found dozens of people babbling about the devil in louse-infested cages. The other prisoners, including my neighbor Mrs. Fernandez, had been sent home.

Given the volume of missing persons reports that had been filed in Daly City in the last few months, we'd found only a fraction of the Mauve Faith victims. We were working on tracking down the rest. Seemed Minnie Cucci's place had been the holding station before the operation moved pigment-fried Pinkos out of town. It had been pure luck that it was Penelope we'd found there.

I said that anyone affected should get in touch with the hospital. Dr. Trumbull, sitting in the first row, nodded. She had plenty of work ahead of her. They'd better get that new wing finished soon. Announced that the Chief had been injured in the line of duty.

I thanked Boise, Doug, and everyone who'd helped and wrapped up with the news that Tommy and Cynthia were being promoted to full agents. It would be an uphill battle to get that budget increase approved, but it would be easier if the politicians were wary of demoting heroes.

As soon as I'd said, "Thank you for your time," a clamor of shouted questions broke out. I handed out a dozen "No comments" and thirteen variations on "We'll update you as the situation develops."

Four weeks ago, I'd been resigned to my role as a small-town cop fighting small-town crooks. It had been a wild ride. Would've been nice to settle back into the humdrum routine of the past twenty years for a while, but that wasn't an option. If I stayed, I'd be stuck staring at the Chief's empty chair at department meetings. If I left—Old Jim towered behind me. The man was one of the best. Had to be, to have made it as head of Boise. I had a hunch that, under that affable surface, I'd never really know where I stood with him.

The place was full of media and TV crews who'd flown in overnight, from Iowa City, Boise, Miami. There was even a correspondent from the *Buenos Aires Herald*. And, of course, Senator Doyle's gray halo of frizz. This was the big time. But there were plenty of familiar faces, too. The police officer who'd greeted us at Icarus leaned against the wall in the back. The bartender from Sharlene's sat in the middle of the audience. Lucinda Snooker's shock of red hair seemed out of place this far from the little pink house on Shakespeare. Even the Mohawked teen who'd brought Tommy and me up from San Bruno was there. My friends, too: Edie and Trumbull frowning solemnly up front. And next to them, my mother, beaming fit to beat the band.

"I'll take one final question," I said. The room erupted again. I pointed at Jenna Lila.

"Rumor has it you've been offered a transfer to Boise, with a promotion involved. Will you be taking it, or staying with us?" the journalist asked. My mother's hand clasped her turquoise necklace. When I waffled, Jenna Lila interrupted me. "Now, don't tell me that you have 'no comment while the investigation is underway.'" Everyone laughed.

I could feel my ears changing color. Old Jim shifted behind me. I glanced over at Tommy. The set of my cadet's shoulders made clear that the question had blindsided him. My former cadet. Now my fellow agent. Doug's face was frozen in a half smile. If I accepted his transfer request—I tried to imagine showing him where the toner for the Xerox machine was kept. Filing his reports, passing each other in the halls, collegial happy hours. No indecent heart-to-hearts, just office scuttlebutt.

Would that be enough, after everything we'd been through? The light gleamed off his glasses. He met my gaze. We'd made this mess together. With a little help and a lot of hindrance from Magenta and Deepest Blue. Maybe without them, we could figure something out.

I turned back to the audience, all the usual and strange faces there because of the work that our team had done—Tommy, Meekins, Cynthia. Doug. I knew the answer to Jenna Lila's question. I'd known it for a while, now. "No," I said. "I'm honored by Chief Broadback's offer, but I will not be taking the promotion in Idaho. I will be staying here, in Daly City."

It was, after all, my home.

ACKNOWLEDGMENTS

An incomplete list of thanks:

To my agent, Julie Barer, for reading an early draft and saying there's work to be done—and then doing the work with me. To my editor, Peter Borland, whose uncanny ability to not only put his finger on the problem but point the way to the solution made this book the best it could be. To Sean Delone at Atria, for always asking the big questions and being excited to jump into Curtida's Renault 4 with me. To Nicole Cunningham at the Book Group, for deep notes and quick responses alike.

To the whole team at Atria, especially Libby McGuire, for her early and ongoing support, and to Jason Chappell, for keeping the book moving smoothly at every step of the way. To Laurie McGee, for her meticulous copyedits; to Will Staehle, for a paint-by-numbers cover that's smarter than anything I could've dreamed; and to Yvonne Taylor, for an interior design that brought that cover inside the book.

To the folks at the Michener Center, who helped nudge *Shamshine* from a shaggy manuscript toward a book. Jim Crace, thank you for lending me your cruel pen. Elizabeth McCracken, thanks for telling me to let this be a novel of ideas. Michael Adams, for marking every vague turn of phrase. Kirk Lynn, for the reminder that novels are longer than plays. Bret Anthony Johnston, for telling me to stop writing like I was getting away with something. To my fellow students in Elizabeth McCracken's Fall 2016 workshop, who cheered the book on without letting me off the hook. To Marla Akin, who always made sure I had room in my course load for revisions.

To the friends who asked for drafts I didn't send and buoyed me up along the way, especially Anna Christina Büchmann and Elizabeth Caudill. To the Djerassi Foundation for the gifts of time, space, and every snack a pregnant body could want. To the Latinx Theatre Commons for getting me to Djerassi at just the right time. To Kalu Uribe, Belen Gonzalez Gallo, Sandi Borger, and Gabriela Beatriz Ojeda Catalán, for the childcare that let me keep writing.

To my father, who pulled *Cyteen* and *Neuromancer* off the shelf at Know Knew Books for me. To my sister, who had the idea for the Hope Count. To my mother, purveyor of champagne and hair critique, and tireless champion of Curtida through every single draft.

To Elías: may you always make up words when the ones you know don't fit the story you want to tell.

To my husband and life dramaturg, Enrique Lozano. Reading to you by the fireplace is the real reward. Our words our bricks to build our home: here are a few more.